New Interpretations of Beckett in the Twenty-First Century

Series Editor
Jennifer M. Jeffers
Department of English
Cleveland State University
Cleveland, OH, USA

As the leading literary figure to emerge from post-World War II Europe, Samuel Beckett's texts and his literary and intellectual legacy have yet to be fully appreciated by critics and scholars. The goal of New Interpretations of Beckett in the Twenty-First Century is to stimulate new approaches and develop fresh perspectives on Beckett, his texts, and his legacy. The series will provide a forum for original and interdisciplinary interpretations concerning any aspect of Beckett's work or his influence upon subsequent writers, artists, and thinkers.

More information about this series at
http://www.palgrave.com/gp/series/14737

Cristina Ionica

The Affects, Cognition, and Politics of Samuel Beckett's Postwar Drama and Fiction

Revolutionary and Evolutionary Paradoxes

Cristina Ionica
Fanshawe College
London, ON, Canada

New Interpretations of Beckett in the Twenty-First Century
ISBN 978-3-030-34904-2   ISBN 978-3-030-34902-8   (eBook)
https://doi.org/10.1007/978-3-030-34902-8

This Palgrave Macmillan imprint is published by the registered company Springer Nature Switzerland AG.
The registered company address is: Gewerbestrasse 11, 6330 Cham, Switzerland

Acknowledgements

First, I would like to thank my former Western University professors Thomas Carmichael, Martin Kreiswirth, Allan Pero, and Peter Schwenger, whose support of my ideas has been unwavering over the years. Tom, thank you for your generous feedback on so many academic article drafts, including the article (published in *Angelaki*) in which my ideas on Beckett's paradox-based discourse first started to crystallize. Marty, thank you for introducing me to cognitive narrative theory and for supporting my academic progress and my work on this project throughout the years, even after you left Western to take on a new position at McGill. Allan and Peter, thank you for seeing something of value in my perspective on Beckett's work with "the absurd" and for encouraging me to pursue this project on many occasions when I feared I had reached a dead end. Your trust in my academic abilities has meant more to me than you could ever know.

I am grateful to the Palgrave peer reviewer for pointing out several ways to strengthen my argumentation in Part I, and to the editorial team (the series editor, Jennifer M. Jeffers, and the editor and editorial assistant, Allie Troyanos and Rachel Jacobe) for their investment in my project and support in bringing my ideas to their final form. I would also like to thank the design and production team – Friedhelm Steinen-Broo (eStudioCalamar), Tikoji Rao and Brian Halm (Springer Nature), and Divya Anish and Sylvia Anand (SPi Technologies) – for their careful and patient management of the design and production process.

Some of the arguments developed in the Introduction and in Part I of this book are based on ideas originally presented in my article "Halting the Production of Repression: Deleuze, Guattari, Beckett, and the Schizo's

Stick," which appeared in *Angelaki: Journal of the Theoretical Humanities*, vol. 21, issue 2, 2016, pp. 99–118. I would like to thank the general issue editor, Salah el Moncef bin Khalifa, and the journal's anonymous reviewer for their feedback and encouragement.

My partner Claudiu and my closest friends Gianina, Duru, and Amanda—thank you for your emotional and intellectual presence in my life during the writing of this book. Our conversations always gave me new ideas and propelled my work forward.

My Fanshawe College and Western University colleagues' friendship and encouragement has taken me through many difficult moments during the last few years. Thank you, Amy, Aaron, Jeff W., Jeff D., Brian, Mel, Curtis, and Lindsay.

The love of my parents, cousins, aunts and uncles, and nieces has been a constant source of energy for me during the writing of this book. Thank you for always being the warmest, loveliest people.

CONTENTS

ABBREVIATIONS

Referenced Work	Abbreviation
Beckett, Samuel. *The Complete Dramatic Works*. Faber and Faber, 1986.	*CDW*
———. *The Complete Short Prose, 1929–1989*. Edited by S.E. Gontarski. Grove, 1995.	*CSP*
———. *How It Is*. John Calder, 1996.	*HII*
———. *The Letters of Samuel Beckett*. Edited by George Craig, Martha Dow Fehsenfeld, Daniel Gunn, and Lois More Overbeck. Cambridge UP, 2009–16. 4 vols.	*L1; L2; L3; L4*
———. *Malone Dies*. Edited by Peter Boxall. London: Faber and Faber, 2010.	*MD*
———. *Molloy*. Edited by Shane Weller. London: Faber and Faber, 2009.	*M*
———. *Nohow On: Company. Ill Seen Ill Said. Wostward Ho*. John Calder, 1989.	*NO*
———. *Watt*. John Calder, 1963.	*W*
———. *The Unnamable*. Edited by Steven Connor. London: Faber and Faber, 2010.	*U*
Deleuze, Gilles. *The Logic of Sense*. Translated by Mark Lester with Charles Stivale, edited by Constantin V. Boundas. The Athlone Press, 1990.	*LS*
Deleuze, Gilles and Félix Guattari. *Anti-Oedipus: Capitalism and Schizophrenia*. Translated by Robert Hurley, Mark Seem, and Helen R. Lane. U of Minnesota P, 1983.	*AO*
———. *Kafka: Toward a Minor Literature*. Translated by Dana Polan, U of Minnesota P, 1986.	*K*
———. *A Thousand Plateaux: Capitalism and Schizophrenia*. Translated by Brian Massumi, U of Minnesota P, 1987.	*TP*

CHAPTER 1

Introduction to Beckett's "Absurdist" Excess

1.1 ABSURDIST EXCESS AND POLITICAL VALUE

On 19 November 1957, the San Francisco Actors' Workshop presented Beckett's *Waiting for Godot* to an audience of 1400 convicts at the San Quentin State Prison in San Rafael, California. As Herbert Blau and other members of the cast and production team state in interviews included in a documentary by Adams, the prisoners' laughter and applause frequently interrupted the performance. Apparently, the fragment that elicited the most intense audience reaction was Lucky's speech—certainly not the most straightforward part of the play. Armed robbery convict Rick Cluchey, perceived as a security liability and required to remain in his cell during the representation, heard the play on the prison's loudspeakers and gathered the visual details from other inmates. Deeply impressed, he worked with other convicts to create the San Quentin Drama Workshop (still active today). Released on parole in 1966 due to his involvement in that project and support of other inmates' commitment to change, Cluchey met Beckett in 1975, played Krapp in a 1977 production of *Krapp's Last Tape* directed by Beckett himself, and—as an actor, director, and playwright—dedicated the rest of his life to the theatre. In his 1961 *The Theatre of the Absurd*, Esslin mentions, based on press reports, that "Godot himself, alongside turns of phrase and characters from the play, have become a permanent part of the private language, the institutional mythology of San Quentin" (21). The major impact of the play on the San

© The Author(s) 2020

C. Ionica, *The Affects, Cognition, and Politics of Samuel Beckett's Postwar Drama and Fiction*, New Interpretations of Beckett in the Twenty-First Century, https://doi.org/10.1007/978-3-030-34902-8_1

Quentin inmates is confirmed by several members of Blau's group and by several former convicts interviewed by Adams for his documentary, including Cluchey and jazz artist Ed Reed, a member of the San Quentin jazz band at the time.

A common critical claim is that Vladimir and Estragon's endless waiting in a hopeless wasteland resonated strongly with the convicts' bleak life experiences and general dispiritedness. However, this does not fully explain the intensity of this peculiar audience group's first reactions or their lasting commitment to transform their lives. *Waiting for Godot* has, by now, a long history of successful representations in prisons and areas marked by natural disasters and various forms of social upheaval. The earliest known instance is the Lüttringhausen Prison staging in Germany, which premiered on 29 November 1953 under the direction of convict Karl-Franz Lembke, who had translated the play from French into German earlier that year. Beckett became aware of this representation through his publisher Jérôme Lindon (Éditions de Minuit), who sent him two cuttings from German newspapers, a letter from Lembke, and one from the prison chaplain, Ludwig Manker, on 12 October 1954. Lembke writes, "Your Godot was a triumph, something wild!—Your Godot was 'our' Godot, ours, our very own!"; Manker identifies in the play "the real truth about the real situation of humanity today" and adds, "Our men accepted it as their play, and I am keeping the tree that was used on the stage, now in my room in the sacristy, for it has become for me the tree of life" (see footnote 1 to Beckett's 14 October 1954 letter to Lindon, *L2* 504). The editors of the second volume of Beckett's letters also quote from Pastor Peter Schippel's recollections of a 1954 performance: "During the performance the walls became transparent. In the end, the whole prison was a 'Waiting for Godot.' In a sense, so was the whole world to which we returned" (Schippel, qtd. in footnote 1, *L2* 505).

For Lembke, Manker, and Schippel, as for the other spectators whose experiences they convey, the play seemingly functioned not as a symbolic but a raw, unmediated materialization of their conditions of existence, in prison and in the world. All three quote positive reactions—joy ("something wild"), solidarity (Godot became "ours"), renewed hope ("tree of life"), and enhanced (self-)awareness ("the walls became transparent"). The significance of this experience of the play as a *positive and transformative event* and the political import of its success in a technically unpropitious cognitive environment did not escape Beckett, who wrote to Lembke, on/ immediately after 14 October 1954, "In all my life as a man and writer, nothing like this has ever happened to me. ... I am no longer the same, and will never again be able to be the same, after what you have done, all of you. In the place where I have always found myself, turning round and round, falling over, getting up again, it is no longer wholly dark or wholly silent" (*L2* 506). Such relatively unqualified expressions of elation are *rare* in Beckett's letters.

Within days of his response to Lembke, on 18 October 1954, Beckett reports to his Grove Press editor Barney Rosset the following conversation with well-known British actor Ralph Richardson:

> [He] *wanted the low-down on Pozzo, his home address and curriculum vitae, and seemed to make the forthcoming of this and similar information the condition of his condescending* to illustrate the part of Vladimir. *Too tired to give satisfaction* I told him that all I knew about Pozzo was in the text, that if I had known more I would have put it in the text, and that this was true also of the other characters. ... I also told Richardson that if by Godot I meant God I would [have] said God, and not Godot. *This seemed to disappoint him greatly.* (*L2* 507, my emphasis)

The emphasized passages express sarcasm and barely veiled disgust, as do the emphatic and repetitive formulations in the sentences on Pozzo and Godot—including the phrase "if I had known more I would have put it in the text" (variations of which appear in a number of Beckett's letters and interviews), whose semantic and pragmatic context indicate that it was primarily meant to deride the obtuse character of the clarification request rather than express ignorance. Beckett shows more patience in a letter dated 25 June 1953 to Carlheinz Caspari, director of a German production of *Waiting for Godot*, who had asked for staging guidance in light of what he perceived as the presence of expressionist, symbolist, and other attempts at "abstractization" in the play. Beckett rejects those assumptions:

> First and foremost, it is a question of something that happens, almost a routine, and it is this dailiness and this materiality, in my view, that need to be brought out. That at any moment Symbols, Ideas, Forms might show up, this is for me secondary—is there anything they do not show up behind? In any event, there is nothing to be gained by giving them clear form. The characters are living creatures, only just living perhaps, they are not emblems. ... I would urge you to see in them less the result of an attempt at abstraction ... than a refusal to tone down all that is at one and the same time complex and amorphous in them. ... If his [Godot's] name suggests the heavens, it is only to the extent that a product for promoting hair growth can seem heavenly. ... Others, more fortunate, will see in him Thanatos. (*L2* 391)

Beckett seems strongly resistant if not hostile to alignments between his brand of immediacy, "dailiness," and "materiality" and the realist or naturalist tradition, as his response to Richardson's approach reveals, as well as to symbolic, "abstracted" readings of his barely living "creatures," as seen in his response to Caspari. His characters are neither real people with a street address nor "emblems" of the human condition in some "metaphysical simplification" (*L2* 391) schema. Most importantly, they must not be reduced to univocal meanings ("clear form"). Beckett's elation at the Lüttringhausen convicts' experience of the play arguably derives from the apparent consequences of their adoption of this premise. They did not *interpret* the play as a sophisticated abstraction, nor did they see it as a realistic scenario. Instead, they seem to have *experienced* it as an immediate, material "outing" of their conditions of existence, complete with an intimate and transformative call to disengage from stagnant or destructive societal arrangements and seek more positive and beneficial means to connect and to act.

Representations of Beckett's *Waiting for Godot* in areas marked by natural disasters, political repression, or war appear to have yielded similar results. In a 2009 article prefacing a new British production, Smith, Carter, and Carnwath present statements from several artists who pursued such dramatic projects: Cluchey, who played Vladimir in two San Quentin Prison productions; Benjy Francis, the director of the first South African production allowed by Beckett (with an all-black cast)[1]; Haris Pašović, the producer of Susan Sontag's 1993 representation in the besieged Sarajevo; and Wendell Pierce, who played Vladimir in a Hurricane Katrina-inspired Classical Theatre of Harlem production eventually performed in the ninth ward of New Orleans, in the middle of "square miles of destroyed homes." These contributors report positive and empowered reactions both from their collaborators on those projects and from their audiences.

Citing Saiu, Bradby, and others, Morin notes that Beckett's "early plays were commonly perceived as having a stark, yet somewhat imprecise, political dimension" (8) in Eastern and Central-European countries during and immediately after the communist rule. Indeed, as Saiu notes, *Waiting for Godot* was translated and published late (during or after the late sixties) in most Eastern-European countries, and performances were often delayed, crippled, or banned by state censorship institutions, mostly

---

[1] Beckett had systematically rejected requests to allow his plays to be staged there, in protestation against apartheid.

for fear that the play's "waiting" would resonate with citizens' hope in an American overthrow of communism (260–65). Bradby stresses another aspect of the play consistently perceived as subversive: its ostentatious incongruities, which seemed to speak to "the absurdities and frustration of life under a totalitarian regime" (165). More recently, news coverage of the conflict in Syria offers additional evidence of the perceived positive, action-oriented, *political* content of Beckett's works. Morin quotes news reports filed between 2012 and 2014 by Ian Pannell for *BBC News*, Matilde Gattoni and Matteo Fagotto for *Newsweek*, and Emily Jane O'Dell for *Salon*, mentioning a refugee who perceived "the absurd wait" of Beckett's "dispossessed characters" as a reflection of his country's political situation and found consolation in "memories of Beckett's humour"; another refugee's idea to use a performance of *What Where* to explain torture to those around him; and a game devised by two homeless Syrian children living in Beirut, consisting of an endless repetition of "I am Samuel Beckett!"—"No, I am Samuel Beckett!" (Morin 251–52). The solidarity-based, action-oriented, empowering dimensions of these reactions could hardly be contested.

Waiting for Godot undoubtedly strikes a raw nerve for anyone who has experienced states of confinement, from constraining socio-economic conditions and various forms of discrimination to actual imprisonment or life in a war zone/ under totalitarian rule. Still, it appears to consistently elicit (and to be consistently suspected that it might elicit) action-oriented feelings of revolt and hope in audience members rather than a passive state of "wise" acceptance. Furthermore, Beckett's destabilizing, "difficult" linguistic operations appear not to hinder and perhaps even to enhance these effects—the "absurdities" and "abstractions" involved are eerily substantive, clear, and moving. A brief discussion of the play's subversive rendering of suicide might begin to clarify what activates these effects. In Act I, Vladimir and Estragon, seemingly overwhelmed with boredom and despair, decide to attempt suicide by hanging, excitedly anticipating an erection in the process, but give up because they have no rope and the tree branches seem frail. The idea re-emerges in Act II, and they test the cord holding up Estragon's pants, but it breaks—so they decide to find a sturdier rope by "tomorrow" (*CDW* 86). This hopelessly botched and eerily cheerful iterative suicide act has been universally read as a tragicomic existentialist depiction of the human condition (devoid of hope and substance, the characters are still pursuing "empty" sexual gratification), but this reading fails to account for the odd joy and productivity of this apparent exercise in futility. We might come closer to an explanation if we read the episode, instead, as a paradox-based, slapstick-style, *mocking* response to existentialist philosophy—especially to existentialist notions of freedom.

In his 1942 essay *The Myth of Sisyphus*, Camus describes the absurdity of existence as a given and proclaims the need for a heroic response to the question "whether life is or is not worth living" (3): *revolt* rather than suicidal despair. However, his notion of revolt has little in common with Beckett's paradox-based mayhem, especially since it involves an ethically questionable aggrandizement of the (male) subject. First, his category of "absurd heroes" strangely encompasses Sisyphus and stage actors alongside notoriously exploitative/ genocidal male figures like Don Juan and colonial conquistadors. Second, even his discussion of his title character is problematic, as he insists that Sisyphus must have experienced inner freedom and happiness in the exertion of his torturous tasks—arguably a return to the logic of (self)-sacrifice, mind over matter, use and abuse aligning the Christian martyr and the romanticist megalomaniacal genius. Adorno posits this aggrandizement of the subject as a problem with existentialism in general, in his seminal 1961 text "Trying to Understand Endgame"—and, on these grounds, caustically rejects associating Beckett with existentialism:

> The catastrophes that inspire[d] *Endgame* have shattered the individual whose substantiality and absoluteness was the common thread in Kierkegaard, Jaspers, and Sartre's version of existentialism. Sartre even affirmed the freedom of victims of the concentration camps to inwardly accept or reject the tortures inflicted on them. *Endgame* destroys such illusions. The individual is revealed to be a historical category, both the outcome of the capitalist process of alienation and a defiant protest against it, something transient himself. (*Notes* 1: 249)

Vladimir and Estragon's grotesque dabbling in suicide ostentatiously lacks the dignified philosophical stature of Camus or Sartre's reflections on meaninglessness, responsibility, and freedom. The corresponding scenes do not articulate an ironic comment on Vladimir and Estragon's failings or on human failings in general but an attack on the social order and on language as its main enforcement tool, since the culturally common proscription of suicide invariably supports established hierarchies and the discourses that sanction them. More specifically, Vladimir and Estragon's iterative attempt to "solve" their "existential" problem denounces the ferocious nature of the suicide interdiction. The problem, in Beckett's enactment, is not whether or not one *should* commit suicide but whether or not one *can*. While posing as the deepest, most authentic expressions of social concern for the individual's well-being, suicide interdictions are but falsely benevolent guises for mechanisms of exploitation and repression meant to discourage engagement in destabilizing actions within the social assemblage. Vladimir and Estragon's iterative pursuit of suicide *and/or* erections implicitly denounces existentialist musings on freedom, choice, and the meaning of life as sanctimonious and profoundly disconnected from the horrors of confinement, repression, and pain. This denunciation of supposedly beneficial social constraints continues during Vladimir and Estragon's interactions with Lucky and Pozzo—the latter, proud owner of a much better-quality "cord."

Pozzo and Lucky first enter the stage in the following manner: "Pozzo drives Lucky by means of a rope passed around his neck, so that Lucky is the first to enter, followed by the rope, which is long enough to let him reach the middle of the stage before Pozzo appears. Lucky carries a heavy bag, a folding stool, a picnic basket and a greatcoat, Pozzo a whip" (Beckett, *CDW* 21). Pozzo frequently "jerks the rope" while barking his commands, and Lucky remains standing, with his chin in his chest, holding the bags, even after Pozzo sits on a chair to have lunch. Vladimir and Estragon disgustedly notice deep rope marks on Lucky's neck:

> V: A running sore!
> E: It's the rope.
> V: It's the rubbing.
> E: It's inevitable.
> V: It's the knot.
> E: It's the chafing. (*CDW* 25)

Besides being rendered revoltingly grotesque, Lucky's state of enslavement is equated with *death*—specifically, death by hanging: adding to the effect of the rope marks, his eyes are "[g]oggling out of his head" (25), he "[l]ooks at his last gasp" (25), and, throughout most of the scene, he is limp, silent, and upright. This ostentatiously burlesque enactment denounces the "social contract" and any hierarchy-based notion of social responsibility or connectivity as barely disguised means of capture, exploitation, and consumption. In Act II, when Pozzo and Lucky reappear on stage and interact with Vladimir and Estragon again, Pozzo's rope is much shorter. This change—seemingly felicitous, since Pozzo, now blind, can thus still "drive" Lucky—in fact causes Pozzo to fall and deprives him of any sense of direction whenever his jerking of the rope causes wobbling

Lucky to fall. Like Vladimir and Estragon's botched suicide attempts, this slapstick-style reiteration-with-a-difference *gives body* to traditional notions of social cohesion and sabotages their mechanisms of subjection. During the 1957 San Quentin performance, the disciplining nature of supposedly benign and necessary social "ties" found an additional, serendipitous way to make itself obvious. Eugene Roche (Pozzo in Blau's production) recalls that, between scenes, he had to give the rope—for safekeeping—to the prison guards placed around the stage (see Adams).

The 1957 San Quentin convicts, as many readers or spectators exposed to this play since, likely could not unpack its sophisticated language operations and knew nothing about existentialism. Still, as discussed so far, significant anecdotal evidence indicates that the play can "move" readers/spectators in radical ways *regardless of their socio-cultural background and level of knowledge.* This book uses such evidence as a starting point for an analysis of the affective and cognitive work of Beckett's paradox-based language operations, aiming to theorize the *revolutionary* and *evolutionary* import of Beckett's drama and fiction in a global context defined by increasingly ubiquitous and insidious mechanisms of (corporate) capture, exploitation, and repression, alongside unprecedented demands for high-volume information processing and connectivity. I argue that Beckett's paradox-based literary discourse articulates an accessible and contagious attack on socio-political mechanisms of repression, generating powerful liberatory effects under the harshest conditions and in the most unexpected of places—and that it has this power because its attack on the socio-linguistic "organism" is more basal, radical, and definitive than one might assume. In addition, I show that Beckett's works can weaken the cognitive dominance of constrictive "frames" in readers/spectators, so that parasitic ideological formations such as the association of safety and comfort with simplicity and "sameness" are rejected and more complex cognitive operations are welcomed instead—a process that bolsters the mind's ability to operate at ease with increasingly complex, malleable, extensible, and inclusive frames, as well as with increasing volumes of information.

"The absurd" as a lack of sense, in strict correlation with existentialist philosophy, is an unproductive interpretive category largely abandoned in Beckett studies following Esslin's years of critical prominence.[2] However,

---

[2] Interpretations of Beckett's works such as Esslin's or Blocker's are typical of earlier critical assumptions that the Theatre of the Absurd gives artistic expression to existentialist philosophy, and that Beckett is an existentialist writer. For some recent contributions to the discus-

the word has consistently been used as an umbrella term for radically divergent aesthetic and philosophical approaches to the unknown and the assumed misery of the human condition. Some of these do bemoan a constitutive meaninglessness marring human existence and explore notions of freedom, responsibility, and guilt mostly at the individual level—as one presumably should as laws and secular institutions progressively supplant transcendent determinations. Others, however, depict humanity as perpetually force-fed institutionally generated meanings to exploitative and repressive ends and use seemingly illogical and "excessive" linguistic constructions to denounce and neutralize any totalitarian dangers lurking within purportedly "natural," "organic," and innocuous processes of meaning formation. I associate existentialism with the former category, and early twentieth-century avant-garde and "theatre of the absurd" authors such as Tzara, Artaud, Genet, Ionesco, or Beckett with the latter—and I define Beckett's black humour and paradox-based ("absurdist") linguistic excess within a theoretical framework mainly (though not exclusively) based in Deleuze's *The Logic of Sense* (1969) and collaborative works with Guattari.

Camus defines the modern "feeling of absurdity" as "the divorce between man and his life, the actor and his setting" (*Sisyphus* 6)—a disillusioned but engaged rapport with reality lucid individuals should entertain. He attempts to distance himself from "religious philosophers" (47) like Kierkegaard, who seek to *escape* the feeling of the absurd rather than engaging with it fully. However, as previously discussed, his selection of "absurd heroes" and extended analysis of Sisyphus reintegrate his argument into a transcendentalist framework. Sartre's approach to the "absurdity of existence" belongs to the same category. He defines the human "situation," in *Being and Nothingness,* as an indeterminate mixture of facticity ("givens" like our language, socio-historical environment, prior choices, and nonconscious selves—our being "in-itself") and transcendence of that facticity through consciousness (our being "for-itself"). As we cannot be reduced to the "givens" of "facticity," we are "condemned" to freedom and to an increasingly alienating feeling of absurdity within modernity (a function of the clash between the human need for meaning and the indifference of the environment in which we exist and act). Given his privileging of intentionality and individual moral responsibility over

sion of potential connections between Beckett's works and the thinking of Camus and Sartre, see Bennett and Connor (*Beckett, Modernism*).

structural causation, Sartre appears to define the absurdity of existence as a convenient, morally weak psychological projection born at the mind's contact with surrounding objects. As early as Adorno's aesthetic interventions in the early sixties, however, a number of theorists have argued that this conceptualization does not define the works of writers such as Kafka, Beckett, Genet, Ionesco, and other "absurdists" too easily placed under the banner of existentialism.

Adorno's insistence to detach Beckett's engagement with socio-historical "catastrophe" from existentialist confrontations with the absurdity of existence is not a mere matter of aesthetic taste or preoccupation for taxonomies or filiations. For Adorno, Beckett's work articulates an ideal mode of engaging reality devoid of the risks of "officially committed" art yet capable to instil in readers/ spectators a propensity towards ethical attitudes and actions. Adorno relates Beckett to "the Anglo-Saxon avant-garde," mentioning specifically Joyce and Eliot, and further explains, "For Beckett, culture swarms and crawls, the way the intestinal convolutions of *Jugendstil* ornamentation swarmed and crawled for the avant-garde before him" ("Trying to Understand Endgame," *Notes* 1: 241). The implications of Adorno's claims are far-reaching. Existentialism maintains "straight" philosophical filiations and an attachment to traditional modalities of meaning-making (differences in attitude and ideation aside, Sartre and Camus both write "philosophical" novels and plays in which narrative progression and character development derive from and remain subordinate to core theoretical debates). Conversely, Beckett, Kafka, or Artaud squeeze and bind the history of culture into residues and "quoted discourse"—the limitations of philosophical discourse are as much an object of mockery as, say, the pretense at objectivity and psychological plausibility characterizing realism and naturalism. Nothing is taken at face value or treated in an entirely "serious," subject-inflating fashion. In addition, perhaps insufficiently emphasized in Adorno's analysis as in other discussions of Beckett's relation to existentialism is the *lack* of humour in existentialist texts and its *explosive presence* in works by Beckett, Ionesco, Genet, or early avant-garde writers such as Jarry, Apollinaire, Artaud, or Tzara. Indeed, the Dadaist-surrealist tradition appears to be much closer to Beckett than Sartre and Camus in terms of language operations, narrative instability, character (de)construction, use of dark shades of humour, self-mockery, iconoclastic attitude towards tradition and culture, and (explicit or implicit) commitment to a "direct" form of reader/ audience engagement.

Weller points out that Beckett expressed appreciation for Sartre and Camus and was published in *Les Temps Modernes*, the influential review initiated by Sartre and de Beauvoir, but "resisted the labels 'existentialist' and 'absurdist'" ("Post-World War" 163). However, Beckett may have rejected both of these labels precisely because, for some time, in France and elsewhere, they were used in tandem. The same abusive cultural conflation might have determined Ionesco (another "absurdist" who resented being associated with existentialism) to end his play *The Killer* with a scene during which the gun-carrying protagonist is confronted with a physically frail serial killer in possession of a knife, loses himself in a lengthy existentialist blabber, and ends up dead. The scene (or, rather, the entire play) communicates as much appreciation for existentialist ideas as Vladimir and Estragon's loosely suicidal search for elusive erections.

The anti-representational linguistic operations and ideological positions equally defining avant-garde art and the work of "theatre of the absurd" authors such as Beckett, Ionesco, or Genet in fact greatly diverge from existentialist ethical and aesthetic allegiances. Perhaps Deleuze captures this difference most astutely in *The Logic of Sense*: existentialist absurdism bemoans a *lack* of meaning, while the brand of "absurdism" or "nonsense" practiced by Carroll, Jarry, Artaud, Kafka, or Beckett (frequently quoted in Deleuze's individual works and collaborative works with Guattari) constitutes an *excess*. For Deleuze, existentialists understand nonsense as an *absence* of sense, and their "feeling of the absurd" is a perception of meaning as lacking and inaccessible *because it has been lost* (*LS* 71). Deleuze dismisses this implicit positing of meaning as formerly present as neo-transcendentalist. He provides both a curt, tagline-style verdict on the "philosophy of the absurd"—"Carroll, yes; Camus, no"—and a more elaborate but equally venomous one: "New theologians of a misty sky (the sky of Koenigsberg), and new humanists of the caverns, sprang upon the stage in the name of the God-man or the Man-god as the secret of sense. Sometimes it was difficult to distinguish between them" (71). In contrast, the writers he appreciates understand "nonsense" as an *excess* of meaning. In the most basic terms, in isolation from their contexts of enunciation, words carry a plurality of undifferentiated, disorganized potential meanings, so they can neither transmit information nor demand a response—and sense is a *product* generated, within various acts of enunciation, through processes of exclusion/ actualization. The production of sense thus depends on contextual conditions that integrate it into *structures* recognizable by a community of speakers. What some explorations of "nonsense" or "the absurd" attempt, then, is to explicate the process whereby enunciations acquire single, univocal meanings, including its risks and consequences. Insofar as it draws attention to the man-made and reductive/ disjunctive character of meaning-making operations usually perceived as givens of experience, this "excess of sense" is deeply subversive.

In an interview with Juliet, Beckett objects to "the idea of the theatre of the absurd," as "that implies value judgements" (Juliet 148–49). This may apply to Esslin's attempt to grasp the specificity of Beckett's work, but what Deleuze defines as "nonsense" is something different: a falsely chaotic—in fact, *systematic*—application of corrosive language operations meant to restore meanings lost in the process of actualization, conse-quently displacing univocal or fixed meanings (blocking them from domi-nating the text and returning it to a comforting, numbing, stultifying state of actualization). Beckett's hostility to attempts at "clarifying" his *Godot* comes to mind. This form of sense play is subversive because, in its attack on univocal meanings, it equally corrodes the structures—habits and memories—words stamp in the flesh. As Deleuze explains in "The Exhausted," it is for this reason that corporeality becomes so obsessive— and so obsessively displaced—in Beckett's late works.

In "The Exhausted," Deleuze implicitly situates Beckett's language operations in between Carroll's and Artaud's, as defined in *The Logic of Sense*. For Deleuze, the fundamental difference between an artistic genius like Carroll and a thinker whose aesthetic and philosophical views have been transformed by repeated encounters with the limits of sanity like Artaud is that, for the former, the tension between nonsense and sense remains a game of surface structures, while for the latter, insofar as *there is no structure anymore*, that tension becomes a painful experience located in the depth of the body. Deleuze is referring here to what he defines as the schizophrenic's perception of the body as "a sort of body sieve" (*LS* 87) no longer separated from the outside by a protective "skin," no longer a spatially anchored, socially and medically (that is, institutionally) func-tional "organism." But if there is no surface, there can be no inside and outside, no whole and parts, no freedom or enclosure *as separate states*; rather, all become possible positions in a network, ranges of movement and fluctuant identifications, or—in a horrific-comic depiction introduced in *Anti-Oedipus* to further clarify the specificity and disruptive potential of Artaud's perception—such former oppositions should be reconfigured as "the two ends of a stick in a non-decomposable space" (*AO* 76).

Indeed, it is the treatment of the end point as a supposedly reachable and definable location that is, nevertheless, never to be reached that makes the evolution of Beckett's characters irresistibly comic even in later works, where the minimalist narrative details might rather invoke fear or horror—but earlier works are already explicitly set up within this corrosive, destabilizing conceptual framework. *Endgame* starts with the word "finished," craftily reinforced by parroting Christ's dying words only to then allow doubt to syntactically and semantically emerge and expand: "Finished, it's finished, nearly finished, it must be nearly finished" (Beckett, *CDW* 93). *Waiting for Godot* begins with "Nothing to be done" (10), and then countless things of seemingly little socio-economic import happen—which is perfectly understandable, *or* justifiably disquieting, *or* tremendously funny if instead of chronology and hierarchy we have a *range* with no sense of direction. These are not reversals but corrosive enactments of the processes whereby reversals (and their attendant anxieties) are produced. While their content may be horrific, their mimicry of the mechanics involved in defining limits and reinforcing them is disdainfully comical and empowering.

The paradoxically productive quality of Beckett's engagement with presumably negative categories has been an object of fascination for other influential philosophers, as well. Against a vast critical tradition of reading at least Beckett's late works as unbridled expressions of nihilism—of the "paralysis" of the modern subject, the infinite obscurity of language, and the failure of reason and civilization—Badiou claims that, even at its most extreme minimalism and condensation, Beckett's work does not express "nihilistic destitution" or "a radical opacity of significations" ("Tireless Desire," *On Beckett* 55). For Badiou, to read Beckett's disenfranchised characters as mere embodiments of a disaster-stricken humanity is to adopt "the point of view of an owner"—Beckett's "vagabond" is equally "one who has succeeded—*volens nolens*—in losing, amidst the vicissitudes of experience, all the disastrous ornamentations of circumstance" ("The Writing of the Generic," *On Beckett* 3). Badiou insists that to neglect the humour, warmth, and "bizarre energy" ("Tireless Desire," *On Beckett* 38) of even the most nihilistically sounding sentences in Beckett's works is to abuse the text. What Beckett offers is "a lesson in measure, exactitude and courage" (40), and his narratives generate the conditions of emergence for the "event" (Badiou's concept of a rupture in the laws that govern being and appearance that makes truth momentarily discernible)—hence the positivity of Beckett's textual enterprise.

According to Gibson, what attracts Badiou to Beckett's works is their "fierce resistance to *doxa*" and ability to "[open up] a space for a different construction of the world through an axiomatic procedure founded on hypothesis" (132–33). Gibson contrasts Badiou's ethics-based reading to "the postmodern or poststructuralist Beckett" (119) of the eighties and nineties—an interpretive trend privileging "the logic of reversal; the general economy; repetition; the instability of the name; the dissolution of the subject" (118) so as to "rethink the Beckettian project as determined less by mood (the angst or despair of the existentialist, for example) than by ... the diagnostic attitude" (119). Gibson identifies in studies by Hill, Trezise, Connor, Katz, and Locatelli, despite differences in approach, a common conviction that Beckett's work explicates and denounces a fundamental "indifference" (Hill 10), "instability" (Locatelli 229), or "emptiness and exhaustion" (Connor, *Repetition* 23) of language in relation to the referent, the "illusory priority of consciousness" (Trezise 32) in relation to language and alterity, and ultimately, the dissolution of the metaphysical subject (Katz, *Saying "I"* 182). Conversely, Badiou's reading foregrounds the "historicity" and "antagonism" of Beckett's work: Badiou sees Beckett not as a deconstructionist but an active opponent of the real-world oppressive effects of *doxa* (Gibson 120–21)—one who, fully aware of the illusory character of "ends" of all kinds, "tentatively, contradictorily, fitfully, and by a variety of different means ... edges towards a faith in possibility" and in the "transformation of language itself" (133). Gibson's phrase "pathos of intermittency" (also used in the title of his book) aptly approximates the energetic preparedness and lucid anticipation of the "event" accomplished in Beckett's works through an obstinate engagement in subtraction—a process of infinitesimal progression of seemingly little import in an idealist or positivist perspective, but which painstakingly and audaciously creates the conditions for change.

Working within a different theoretical framework, Critchley, too, hails Beckett's ability to destabilize consecrated modes of thought and expression through repetition and excess. Critchley sees in Beckett's "sardonic laughter" a "site of uncolonizable resistance to the alleged total administration of society" (*Very Little* 187), and in Beckett's "come and go," a powerful destabilization strategy (194). Used in several works by Beckett, this phrase defines a permanent state of unrest at the level of character identity and language—both "wheel about as if with one foot nailed to the floor" (*Very Little* 196). For Critchley, these "endlessly proliferating and self-undoing" patterns of language and behaviour articulate a "syntax of weakness" (Beckett's phrase in a 1962 conversation with Harvey, Harvey 249) that operates as follows: "a coherent and perhaps even formalizable technique of repetition is employed to give the appearance of randomness and chaos" (*Very Little* 196). After a detour through Cavell's interpretation of Beckett's work with meaning—"The discovery of *Endgame*, both in topic and technique is not the failure of meaning (if that means the lack of meaning), but its total, even totalitarian success—our inability not to mean what we are given to mean" (Cavell 116)—Critchley offers his own approximation of Beckett's excess: depicting the world as "overfull with meaning," so that "we suffocate under the combined weight of various narratives of redemption—whether they are religious, socio-economic, political, aesthetic or philosophical" (*Very Little* 211). Beckett's "radical de-creation of these salvific narratives" in fact "saves us from salvation" (or redemption)—it liberates us from patterns that otherwise transfix us and prevent us from enjoying "the very extraordinariness of the ordinary" (211).

What Critchley seems to propose, despite the lyrical tone of some of his pronouncements, is a reading of Beckett's work as a celebration of lucidity. In an endnote, he adds to his claims, "The cruel power of Beckett's humour exhibits a *joyous* relation to finitude, a celebration of human limitedness that is replete with sardonic, side-splittingly anti-depressant comedy" (note 85, *Very Little* 265). Whether or not we accept Critchley's assessment of Beckett's work as a celebration of the "very little... almost nothing" of human existence, his analysis of Beckett's humour aptly emphasizes its *anti-depressant* quality and *formalizable* appearance—aspects that challenge Beckett's relegation to the "nihilistic" front. In a subsequent study, Critchley further defines Beckett's humour as apt to encourage the formation of an ethical subject whose "experience of conscience is that of an essentially divided self, an originally inauthentic humorous self that can never attain the autarchy of self-mastery" (*Infinitely Demanding* 11)—a subject apt to find "an alternative, positive function for the super-ego" (82). In other words, there is a large margin of positivity in Beckett's articulation of the split subject, as the split creates the conditions of possibility for a state of lucidity conducive to a less antagonistic and more ethical existence: "Humour is a more minimal, less heroic form of sublimation that allows the subject to bear the excessive, indeed hyperbolic, burden of the ethical demand without that demand turning into obsessive self-hatred and cruelty" (78–79). Implicitly, this form of sublimation constitutes "an actually existing and thoroughly everyday practice, where ethical experience is both staged and assuaged" (85).

Despite obvious differences in theoretical approach, Adorno, Deleuze and Guattari, Badiou, Gibson, and Critchley all identify in Beckett's work not just a radically new vision or critique of language, the subject, and reality, but also a radical *practice*. All conclude that, through perhaps formalizable modalities of repetition and excess, Beckett's works enact an ethical experience that may radically reshape the subject's self-perception and social articulations. Several critical readings of Beckett published since 2000 share this position, arguing for a deep political dimension in Beckett's texts. Thus, for Prigent, Beckett's violent linguistic displacements prevent the coagulation of language into the kind of *doxa* liable to endorse totalitarian socio-political norms. For Federman, Beckett's destabilizing treatment of the self implicitly denounces the self-centred, self-important model of the romantic/ realist/ existentialist hero as partly responsible for our adherence to discourses of discrimination throughout history. Erickson sees a concern for justice vs. totalitarian practices as central to Beckett's writing, offering evidence of Beckett's denunciation of both fascist and communist attempts to "solve" the problems of communal living. Diamond outlines, in *Waiting for Godot*, a critique of identificatory politics:

> Within the discourse of rights and reason, the foundation of Western politics, Beckett finds and abhors the worst aspects of the identificatory relation: the enraged (because unachievable) assumption of a regulatory ideal and the concomitant misrecognition of the other—my demand that the other be me, be captured in my image, and if not, be cast from me, expelled, annihilated. ("Blau, Butler, Beckett" 40)

Diamond stresses the political potential of Vladimir and Estragon's theatrical rehearsals of social interactions in describing them as "exercises in negotiating power relations without coercive identifications" (41). McNaughton sees political import in Beckett's critical relation to language, explaining that it denounces the process whereby "language, by its increased abstraction and move to facile conceptualization, bleaches memory" ("German Fascism" 114). Johnson notes a "fundamental resilience, tenacity and paradox at the heart of the modernist subject" as envisioned by Beckett, which translates into a "non-escapist and anti-nihilistic aesthetic" (47). All these commentators credit Beckett's destabilizing linguistic operations with energizing, action-prompting effects. Part of my contribution to Beckett studies is to advance this line of investigation by explicating how these linguistic mechanisms operate, how they may produce empowering effects, and what new model of power/ empowerment they may propagate socially.

1.2   Revolution, or, The Paradox and Affect

As Gaensbauer notes, Sartre, distrusting the incommunicable as "the source of all violence," states, in *What is Literature*, "If words are sick, it is up to us to cure them" (qtd. in Gaensbauer xix), whereas Beckett and Ionesco, like the Dadaists and the surrealists before them, manifest a radical distrust in language and labour to denounce its faults and trickery (xix). While Gaensbauer does not explicitly privilege either perspective, her observation correlates with Adorno's warning that, insofar as Sartre's "thesis-art" is an appeal from a subject who perceives himself as cohesive and capable of ethical choices to subjects who belabour under the same false assumption, it does not articulate a viable model of resistance.[3] This recurrent notion that there is something about Beckett's (and a limited number of other "absurdist" writers') unruly literary form and corrosive linguistic operations that strikes at the heart of exploitation and repression carries significant implications: first, that these texts employ formalizable means to create that effect; second, that the effect can be perceived by enough readers/ spectators to gain socio-cultural relevance; and third, that this perception can influence attitudes and behaviours to the point of constituting a "social practice." Deleuze and Guattari's theorization of the paradox and the abstract machine offers an effective modality to explicate this process. Recent advancements in cognitive narrative theory also provide suitable theoretical tools.

Deleuze and Guattari connect this liberatory textual effect to the presence of the paradox[4]—which, in opposing *doxa* through a mockery of

[3] In Adorno's view, "Art is not a matter of pointing up alternatives but rather of resisting, solely through artistic form, the course of the world, which continues to hold a pistol to the heads of human beings. When, however, committed works of art present decisions to be made and make those decisions their criteria, the choices become interchangeable" ("Commitment," *Notes* 2: 79)—that is, the same discourse and methods can be used by otherwise mortal enemies in pursuit of their (supposedly opposing) goals: "Many of [Sartre's] phrases could be echoed by his mortal enemies. The idea that it is a matter of choice in and of itself would even coincide with the Nazi slogan, 'Only sacrifice makes us free'; in Fascist Italy, absolute dynamism made similar philosophical pronouncements" (81). One example provided by Adorno is the persecution of anti-representational artists both in Nazi Germany, where their work was condemned as "cultural bolshevism," and in Stalinist Russia, where it was deemed "reactionary" or "decadent" (78).

[4] For a discussion of the paradox and the abstract machine more focused on the specificity and more faithful to the vocabulary of Deleuze and Guattari's works, see Ionica, "Halting the Production of Repression: Paradox-Based Humour, or, Deleuze, Guattari, Beckett, and the Schizo's Stick."

basic logical operations, allows us "to be present at the genesis of the contradiction" (*LS* 74) and exposes the machinic and hierarchical nature of the distinctions and oppositions we live by (*AO*). In other words, paradox-based textual constructs force us to acknowledge how functional distinctions (such as white vs. black, male vs. female, mind vs. body, good vs. evil, etc.), once accepted and used as organizational principles, acquire a definitiveness they do not objectively possess, form paradigms through associations that are not inherently logical (such as white/ male/ mind/ good vs. black/ female/ body/ evil), and become "naturalized." Implicitly, the organizational principles they were meant to serve evolve into hierarchies that, in turn, acquire the appearance of "natural," "organic" social growths. Paradox-based textual constructs render this "naturalization" process uncomfortably obvious and utterly grotesque—a horrific-comic display too excessive and unsettling to remain unnoticed, irrespective of readers/ spectators' *comprehension* of all aspects of the process. Moreover, insofar as they forcefully denounce the primarily coercive and punitive character of countless social assemblages that pretend to foster safety and social cohesion, such constructs are apt to mobilize powerful affects.

In *Anti-Oedipus*, Deleuze and Guattari propose, as the most compelling means to generate paradox-based constructs, the schizophrenic's transformation of the disjunctive "either/or"—the most basic principle of machinic functioning, as well as of hierarchical and institutional organization—into an "either... or... or..." (*"soit... soit... soit..."*). They designate this paradoxical formation as "disjunctive synthesis" (76), "free disjunction," or "inclusive disjunction" (77) and explain it with the help of Beckett's character construction, as follows:

> He is man or woman, but he belongs precisely to both sides, man on the side of men, woman on the side of women. ... [He] is dead *or* alive, not both at once, but each of the two as the terminal point of a distance over which he glides. He is child *or* parent, not both at once, but the one at the end of the other, like the two ends of a stick in a nondecomposable space. This is the meaning of the disjunctions where Beckett records his characters and the events that befall them: *everything divides, but into itself.* ... The disjunction ... will liberate a space where Molloy and Moran no longer designate persons, but singularities flocking from all sides, evanescent agents of production ... all inhabited by a faceless and transpositional subject. (76–77)

This disjunctive synthesis does not equate to a Hegelian "synthesis of contradictory elements" (76). The schizophrenic dismisses all means of *containing* contradiction, thus disturbing even the most covert operations of the "disjunctive switch" and sabotaging the work of the linguistic-based socio-political machine (which is a disjunction-based working machine, just like technical machines, even though its products—subordination and repression, alongside the illusion that such products are givens of experience—seemingly lack physicality). Most importantly, this act of sabotage concomitantly *repurposes* linguistic-based socio-political machines so that they may become what Deleuze and Guattari designate as "desiring machines," carrying a potential for change.

This is, Deleuze and Guattari explain, also the essential operation of black humour and of avant-garde art—black humour "does not attempt to resolve contradictions, but to make it so that there are none, and there never were any" (*AO* 11), surrealist artworks like Dali's "ensure the explosion of a desiring-machine within an object of social production" (31–32), and writers like Artaud, Kafka, or Beckett are quintessential users of schizo-procedures of tremendous affective power. In the Notes to his translation of *A Thousand Plateaus*, Massumi defines Deleuze and Guattari's conceptualization of "affect" and "affection" in the following terms:

> AFFECT/ AFFECTION. Neither word denotes a personal feeling (*sentiment* in Deleuze and Guattari). *L'affect* (Spinoza's *affectus*) is an ability to affect and be affected. It is a prepersonal intensity corresponding to the passage from one experiential state of the body to another and implying an augmentation or diminution in that body's capacity to act. *L'affection* (Spinoza's *affectio*) is each such state considered as an encounter between the affected body and a second, affecting, body (with body taken in its broadest possible sense to include "mental" or ideal bodies). (*TP* xvi)

This aspect of Deleuze and Guattari's approach makes their theorization of socio-linguistic "machines" particularly apt to explain the oddly universal appeal of Beckett's "abstracted" works. "Machines" is a felicitous word choice that emphasizes the man-made, mechanical rather than organic or "natural," scripted, and ultimately *avertible* character of socio-linguistic processes, despite powerful resistances derived from their typical ossification into norms. What Beckett's works seemingly mobilize is a *perception* of these "machines" *as machines* (rather than as immutable *data* of experience)—a perception whose immediate correlate appears to be an urge to *act*, both physically and mentally, to achieve positive change. (This process is discussed at length in Chap. 2).

Chapter 2 ("Repetition, Deliberation, and an *Other* Power: The Paradox as Practice") connects Beckett's syntactic and semantic forcing, paradoxes, and psychological and narrative entropy to Deleuze's notion of the absurd or nonsense as an *excess* (not a *lack*) of meaning, suggesting that the *accessibility* of Beckett's works rests on subtle structural repetitions and reverberations and consistently (often recursively) applied destabilizing techniques apt to generate a sustained flow of angry laughter—a solidarity-building, action-oriented affect rather than a momentary and individualistic form of release. I rely on key elements of Montague's linguistic theories in my analysis in this chapter as a means to evince the *systematic* character of Beckett's manipulations of natural language and to explicate their uncanny effectiveness in prompting readers to re-examine the constitutive logic of socio-historical arrangements in a manner maximally liberated from ideological clutches. My main claim is that Beckett's paradox-based discourse sabotages coercive couplings of the subject to the social machine by translating subordination and repression into *processes* rather than *data* of experience—processes that can be sustained or, conversely, suspended. As my discussion shows, this suspension generates powerful affects rather than mere feelings of liberation, as it is not a momentary release but a *diagrammatic* manifestation of a *reproducible* process meant to secure a more permanent collective state of alleviation of repression—not as an unattainable "ideal" but an immediately accessible vicinity. Beckett's structural repetitions and consistent sabotage of the principles that govern linguistic and socio-cultural equivalencies, similarities, and differences continually project, strengthen, and illuminate this pathway in ways that may allow readers/ spectators, whether or not they are trained in textual analysis, to perceive and begin to pursue it.

The last subsection of Chap. 2 explicates the role of Beckett's systemic and rhythmic repetitions in establishing the *attractiveness* and eerie *positivity* of his works. As discussed, although in their immediate narrative details Beckett's works ceaselessly excavate disease, monstrosity, and death, readers/ spectators tend to perceive exposure to them as liberating and inspiring. In my view, this happens because Beckett's paradoxical linguistic formulations and grotesque representations of human interactions de-naturalize the assumption that the possibility of change/ pleasure rests on the subordination/ humiliation/ pain of others, as they denounce the subjection of others to unwanted treatment as a *conservative* systemic practice. Thus, while

Beckett's texts destabilize readers/ spectators' perception of socio-cultural "belonging" and denounce countless mechanisms of injustice, they also project a *formalizable* and, therefore, *reproducible* modality to achieve and manifest a form of individual power that can grow not at the expense but to the advantage of others. This figuration of forms of power and empowerment that do not derive from traditional religious, socio-economic, or militarist models—whereby power is a finite value in a relatively closed system (a finite amount is available, so that one individual's accumulation of power reduces its availability for others)—bears immediate import in today's global context of ascension of *corporate* capitalism. More specifically, Beckett's grotesque social assemblages—from the master-slave couplings of *Watt*, *Waiting for Godot*, or *Endgame* to the nightmarish "searches" from "The Lost Ones"— resonate at uncanny intensity with contemporary corporate capitalist attempts to capture and consume all available human energy and potential while callously reducing compensations to dehumanizing levels.

In Chaps. 2, 3, and 4, I bring significant contributions to the interpretation of several major texts by Beckett in stressing gender and class aspects that have received little critical attention so far. These original interpretive elements reinforce my claim that an action-oriented mood underlies even some of Beckett's reputedly darkest texts, like the story "The Lost Ones" or the drama "*Play.*" In my reading, what makes the models of empowerment and solidarity offered by Beckett's texts insidiously apt at articulating strategies of resistance and circumventing total capture is their rejection of linear and rule-based (hierarchical/ organizational/ institutional) functioning modes and adoption of contagion as their functioning principle.

Chapters 3 and 4 ("The Liberating Laughter of 'Nearly There': Beckett's Solidarity-Building Dramas" and "Under-the-Radar Derision and Anger: Becoming Revolutionary in/ through Beckett's Fiction") explore the implications of Beckett's corrosive staging of consecrated socio-economic means of capture and exploitation, as well as of the new mode of empowerment his texts generate, by relating his sophisticated use of repetitions and reiterations-with-a-difference to his paradox-based humour. Unsurprisingly, paradox-based humour has a deeply horrific dimension, as it grotesquely enacts the subject's internalization and perpetuation of countless patterns of abuse defining repressive social assemblages (Oedipal, capitalist, fascistic, etc.). However, as I show, there are major positive effects even to this negative dimension, as paradox-based attacks on the subject always target the machinic switches governing the production of confinement and pain. Thus, Beckett does not articulate a univocal "comedy of misery" by extracting comedic moments out of some "tragedy of being human." He articulates, instead, an aggregate, versatile, multipronged attack on ossified, exploitative social structures and the language and "habits" that sustain them.

The self-perpetuating and self-serving character of any *logic of repression* (religious, economic, Oedipal, or socio-political) is put on display and ridiculed in Beckett's texts to the effect of producing, in readers/ spectators, an action-oriented, collective, and connective angry laughter. I derive the positivity of reader/ spectator reactions to Beckett's works from these texts' facilitation of the intuition that change comes from sustained anger and a refusal to comply—not from "coping" states of "inner peace" and acceptance. Laughing angrily at mechanisms of exploitation and repression usually shaped as expressions of care and concern for individuals and communities is likely to translate into a readiness to act, immediately and in solidarity with any perceived victims, for the correction of social injustice. Beckett's humour of structures elicits this type of response by emphasizing the grotesquely excessive and redundant redoubling of mechanisms of repression on multiple machinic levels (Oedipal, communitarian, cultural, economic, etc.) all broadcasting the same old lure: that the binds that cut into our flesh merely aim to prevent us from falling into some consuming, terrible abyss.

In contrast to previous readings of Beckett's humour, I argue in these chapters that anger, and not despair, remains the dominant mode even in Beckett's late texts, and that it prevents both the humour from dissipating entirely in the presence of horror and the mood from becoming passive or acceptant. I conclude by proposing Beckett's paradox-based humour, in Deleuze and Guattari's terms and in correlation to Nail's recent theory of revolution, as a *becoming revolutionary* that avoids the dangers of corporate, authoritarian, or fascistic containment by galvanizing a new form of solidarity based in a state of mutability facilitating immediate and continual transformation at the contact with others' struggle and pain.

1.3   Evolution, or, Beckett's "Script Multiplication and Enrichment"

Cognitive narrative theory offers another framework apt to approximate the profound effects of repeated exposure to Beckett's paradox-based texts. Drawing on studies in artificial intelligence and cognitive science alongside structuralist narratology upgrades and "possible worlds" theories by Gerald Prince, Lubomir Doležel, Monika Fudernik, Thomas Pavel, Marie-Laure Ryan, and others, Herman proposes that, through "*contextual anchoring,* or the process by which cues in narrative discourse trigger recipients to establish a ... direct or oblique relationship between the stories they are interpreting and the contexts in which they are interpreting them" (*Story Logic* 8), stories engage interpreters in intense processes of drawing connections, assessing possibilities and probabilities, and making judgements and predictions. Herman employs P. N. Johnson-Laird's notion of "mental models" to explain that these mental processes mobilize information not explicitly present in the narrative *text* as such (17). Interpreters' engagement with texts is mediated by "frames," "scripts," and "schemata" (85)—concepts Herman borrowed from cognitive theory and artificial intelligence studies by Jean Matter Mandler, Marvin Minsky, Roger C. Schank, Robert P. Abelson, Teun A. van Dijk, and Walter Kintsch, where they designate stereotyped states and sequences of events formed through lived experience. Herman's interpretive model stresses *reciprocal* changes in scripts and stories—changing social conditions change readers' interpretations of stories but also modify narrative conventions (structures perceived as artificial storytelling stereotypes are discarded), ultimately prompting processes of "script multiplication and enrichment" (108). Herman uses Diderot, Flaubert, and Sartre as examples, citing their "reconsideration of linear, deterministic models of human behaviour," denunciation of the "cognitive inadequacy ... [and] destructive power of Romantic paradigms," and problematization of the ability of the narrative model to capture consciousness, respectively (108–9).

In combining linguistic, discourse analysis, cognitive theory, and artificial intelligence concepts, Herman's cognitive narrative interpretive model offers the technical vocabulary needed to unpack the complex cognitive processes mobilized by Beckett's paradox-based texts. As I elaborate in Chaps. 5 and 6 ("Beckett's 'Script Multiplication and Enrichment': Rejecting Toxic Disjunctions and Seeking Inclusivity" and "Evaluation, Expulsion, Expansion, and Reframing: Building Processing Speed and Tolerance to Cognitive Strain"), Beckett's systematic use of several types of repetition (structural echoes, recurrent destabilizing techniques, reiterations with a difference, etc.) compels interpreters' engagement with increasingly complex aggregates of divergent frames and scripts, "training" them to operate at increasing levels of connectivity and speed while becoming increasingly comfortable with such complex operations.

One aspect that makes Herman's approach particularly useful to my analysis is his application of this interpretive model not just to more traditional narratives but also avant-garde or experimental works like Kafka's *Metamorphosis*. Herman derives the "shock effect" of this text from "the way it subverts expected coding strategies"—specifically, from its reconfiguration of "a predicate that normally operates in binary fashion (human/inhuman or ±human)" within frameworks like realism or naturalism (45). Readers expect a transformation if the initial entity disappears/ is replaced by another, but "Gregor" inexplicably remains unchanged as a discursive entity although his fictional body presumably suffers a "radical change of state" (45). Herman later connects such "scrambling of the codes" (a "schizo procedure" in Deleuze and Guattari's terms) with an actualization of power/ ideology issues in their connections to language. In a discussion of stylistic shifts, he notes that "fictional styles invite reflection on how discourse is an instrument that can either work against or reinforce patterns of conflict—more or less unquestioned hierarchies and antagonisms—operative in society at large"—which renders style a "jointly formal and social phenomenon" (207). According to Lecercle, Deleuzian theory treats matters of style in much the same way—as "political" (246).

Beckett's texts operate with shock and anchoring effects of various orders, and Kreiswirth's metatextual engagement with his own essay's introductory section in "Trusting the Tale: The Narrativist Turn in the Human Sciences" offers an insight worth extrapolating here. After a four-page discussion of relevant studies on the topic, Kreiswirth abruptly stops to ask if his "diachronic construct" of theoretical developments is itself a "story," and how a story composed of "ideas, concepts, or intellectual categories" might differ from one dealing with "representations of people" (633–34). This question may illuminate one of the most transfixing qualities of Beckett's texts—namely, their ability to dramatize and narrativize not just "stories of people" but also literary, art, or conceptual histories, exposing them to the same compulsive scrutiny. Indeed, some of the shock and anchoring effects achieved in Beckett's texts derive from the dramatization and narrativization of anything from the "anxiety of influence" (Bloom's phrase designating the pressure of earlier models on emerging artists) to mathematics—and the horror of the discovery of the narrative foundation of all "origins" and "fixed" categories is constantly derailed by the comedy of the mind's ability to use categories against themselves while still processing, ordering, and storing information.

As my cognitive narrative reading of Beckett's texts in Chaps. 5 and 6 shows, Beckett's root articulation of shock and anchoring effects consistently generates an uncanny concentrate of anxiety and weightlessness. Abbott's proposition of the "garden path" model in reading the cognitive effects of Beckett's texts aptly approximates the processes involved: while these texts unremittingly solicit adaptive moves, the expected stress and strain of the process continually dissolves into laughter ("Garden Paths"). The "infinite" productivity of the procedure is itself exhilarating—and, repeatedly applied, it can loosen various preformed structures that govern our understanding, prompting interpreters to question their assumptions and welcome cognitive frame renewal.

My analysis of Beckett's humour in Chap. 5 shows how all aspects of Beckett's texts—from representations of bodily functions and psychological states to allusions to other artworks, philosophical, and religious texts—work to expand the horizon of meaning(s) in ways that *provoke* anxiety while also supplying strategies of *reframing* it. While I subscribe to Deleuze and Guattari's claim that Beckett often creates a "schizophrenic discourse" for his characters (*AO* 2–3), what I find more compelling from a cognitive perspective is that this schizophrenic discourse always appears in *dramatized* form, as quoted and framed discourse, even when it seemingly takes over the text—so that a margin of safety and sanity always remains in effect. This violent juxtaposition allows interpreters to experience, within a controlled framework, the threat of dissolution alongside the hope of connectivity.

In Chap. 6, I propose that repeated exposure to Beckett's violent linguistic operations and multifold textual excess might foster interpreters' increased tolerance to prolonged states of cognitive-emotive flux and information/ connectivity surcharge. As also discussed earlier, Beckett's texts do not appease interpreters' anxieties—they discourage basic, univocal readings, and as Critchley notes, never provide reassurance through "redeeming" narratives (*Very Little* 211–12). On the contrary, they use all available means (narrative, stylistic, performative, referential, metatextual, etc.) to produce multiple layers of anxiety to the point of displaying (and denouncing) both the social *mechanisms* of *producing* anxiety and its *systemic function* (its role in maintaining the status quo). Thus, the liberatory procedures offered in Beckett's texts bypass traditional (patriarchal, parochial, patronizing) forms of reassurance, operating instead through a kind of forced exposure whereby any repression mechanisms embedded in the frames and scripts interpreters process mentally and live by become grotesquely, unbearably present. As they start to perceive these frames and scripts' modes of articulation and parasitic nature, interpreters are prompted to expunge them and generate more satisfying frames and scripts. Beckett's incessant use of literary and cultural allusions offers interpreters, from this perspective, countless occasions to exercise and develop their cognitive functions of evaluation, expulsion, enrichment or expansion, and reframing. In a global context requiring continually increasing abilities to incorporate, process, evaluate, and connect information, as well as increasing agility and adaptability in connecting with others and operating in complex socio-cultural environments, exposure to Beckett's paradox-based works may foster interpreters' development of higher cognitive-emotive function and thus prove to have evolutionary utility.

My conclusion ("Textual Excess: Revolutionary Potential and Evolutionary Utility") emphasizes the political value of Beckett's texts today by making connections to a series of contemporary media products whose progressive political potential has been universally acknowledged in recent years and which seem to use paradox-based discursive techniques similar to Beckett's in their assault on inequality, discrimination, and exploitation. Some such media products are the discontinued *The Daily Show with Jon Stewart*, *The Colbert Report*, and *Key and Peele*, alongside more recent productions such as *Full Frontal with Samantha Bee* or *Last Week Tonight with John Oliver*. Like Beckett's plays, these shows have baffled audiences and critics trough an uncanny combination of sophistication and accessibility, and while some received massive critical attention in the last decade, few commentators have acknowledged their recurrent— indeed, ostentatious and obsessive—use of paradox-based humour and of other destabilizing techniques reminiscent of the historical avant-gardes (particularly Dada and surrealism). What I see as a consistent, though perhaps not always explicitly articulated conceptual framework connecting avant-garde art, Beckett's works, and such contemporary media products is their framing of mutability and flux as positive and productive categories and of security and stability as repressive/ exploitative/ exclusionary lures. In my view, these texts work to unsettle the role and functioning of *anxiety* (alongside other mechanisms of containment) within the social machine. As they encode traditional disjunctions such as threat and safety not as objective, "natural" oppositions but as values controlled by socio-historical (machinic) switches, such texts sabotage social constructs based on oppositional or hierarchical logic, forcing interpreters to acknowledge the artifice and the imposition of power that form the basis of the oppositions they live by and of the anxiety that consumes them, ultimately prompting them to develop a more empathetic view of the other and to act to achieve social justice. Placing Beckett's works in dialogue with contemporary media forms that appear to relate to audiences through similar means and to prompt similar affective and cognitive responses allows for the articulation of an even stronger case for Beckett's continued relevance today.

1.4   Scope, Approach, and Main Contributions

This book analyses prominent plays (starting with *Waiting for Godot*) and prose works (starting with *Watt*) by Beckett in an attempt to theorize the *revolutionary* and *evolutionary* relevance of Beckett's works in today's global context. My selection of texts is determined by my main thematic concerns. Since I am interested in Beckett's articulation of a paradox-based discourse apt to corrode inherited forms of affect, cognitive processing, and action and to generate models of empowerment and solidarity that can circumvent attempts at interruption and capture, Beckett's pre-war prose, which generally follows less complex and disruptive, usually opposition-based, "ironic" (rather than humorous or horrific-comic) discursive patterns is of little interest for my project. Of Beckett's paradox-based texts, I focus mostly on those where Oedipal, gender, and/or class components feature prominently, given my interest in exploring how Beckett's model of empowerment may corrode systemic attempts at reducing power to hierarchical allocation models based in discrimination, exclusion, and exploitation. Furthermore, since my theorization of the socially corrosive and restructuring function of these texts connects this feature to a recognizably Beckettian brand of black humour, my selection of texts privileges those where Beckett's humour is at its darkest and, in my view, also its angriest.

These thematic concerns limit my choice of texts far less than readers might assume based on previous assessments of Beckett's works. Plays like *Not I*, short stories like "Enough", and novellas like *Ill Seen Ill Said* or *Worstward Ho* are examples of texts generally read as maximally distanced from humour and an action-oriented mood—a view I challenge in my analysis in the following chapters. The plays I discuss at length are *Waiting for Godot* (originally written in French, 1948–49; first performed in Paris,

1953), *Endgame* (originally written in French and first performed, in a French-language production, in London, 1957), *Happy Days* (originally written in English, 1960–61; first performed in New York, 1961), *Play* (originally written in English, 1962–63; first performed in German, Ulm-Donau, 1963), *Not I* (originally written in English, 1972; first performed in New York, 1972), and *What Where* (originally written in French, 1983; first performed in English, New York, 1983). The novels, novellas, and short stories I discuss in detail are *Watt* (written in English during the war; first published in English, 1953); *Molloy, Malone Dies,* and *The Unnamable* (originally written in French, 1947–50; first published in French in 1951, 1951, and 1953, respectively); *Texts for Nothing* (written in French, 1950–52; first published in volume format in French, 1955); *How It Is* (originally written and published in French, 1961), "Enough" (originally written in French, 1965; first published in French, 1966); "The Lost Ones" (originally written in French, 1969; first published in French, 1970); *Company* (originally written in English, 1979; first published in English, 1980); *Ill Seen Ill Said* (originally written and published in French, 1981); and *Worstward Ho* (originally written and published in English, 1983; the only major work by Beckett published during his life-time which he did not translate from English to French or from French to English himself[5]).

My main concern is to offer a comprehensive theorization of the affective and cognitive processes arguably activated, even under unpropitious psycho-social conditions, by Beckett's drama and fiction. Although I acknowledge Beckett's bilingualism and self-translation as defining features of his work, for practical reasons—to maintain my thematic focus while keeping my close readings at a reasonable length—my analysis is based almost exclusively on the English versions of Beckett's texts. For the same reasons, I refer to details from earlier drafts of published works only if they contribute significantly to my argument while not taking the text in a direction unsanctioned by the published version. The same applies to biobibliographical material such as Beckett's theatrical notebooks or let-

---

[5] Beckett also did not translate into French his early works *Dream of Fair to Middling Women* (originally written in English in 1932 but first published posthumously) and *More Pricks Than Kicks* (1934). Of his works originally written in French that he did not translate into English himself, the most substantial is the play *Eleutheria*, completed in 1947 but never published or performed during his lifetime.

ters, easily available now in print. For instance, I engage with Beckett's letters and notebooks, within the context of my analyses of individual works, as a means to offer additional insight into Beckett's creative process and ideological allegiances—and, at times, I use recurrent elements of his works to propose new interpretations of some of his best-known claims in interviews and letters (such as his reference to a "syntax of weakness" or his desire to "drill holes into language").

In Chap. 2, I discuss a small number of Beckett's works as I explicate the affect-based interpretive framework used throughout Part I. In Chaps. 3 and 4, I discuss Beckett's plays and fiction, respectively, emphasizing both important differentiating factors and aspects that connect the two types of texts in ways that reinforce my claims concerning the *accessible* and *contagious* character of Beckett's liberatory procedures. Rather than deriving my organizational pattern from major thematic concerns such as Oedipal conditioning and class-based exploitation, I generally discuss each work at length, in chronological order, exploring its corrosive attack on socio-cultural mechanisms of subjection on multiple levels. While seemingly less sophisticated, this analytical pattern allows the validity and relevance of my core arguments to emerge fully. As my analyses of individual works show, the affective and cognitive power of Beckett's texts derives precisely from the *aggregate*, multipronged character of their attack on socio-cultural mechanisms of exploitation and repression—from their ability to corrode machinic mechanisms of interruption and capture and provide a glimpse of *accessible and reproducible* liberatory practices *on multiple levels* and *in one move*. It is this trait of Beckett's works that accounts for their action-oriented character and distances them from passive forms of critique. In Part II, I follow the same pattern, though my analyses of individual works will generally be shorter, given the contextualization work previously done and the general applicability of some theoretical concepts and critical observations introduced in earlier chapters.

Several recent critical and philosophical assessments of Beckett's writing intersect with my thematic concerns or with elements of my theoretical approach. While I engage productively with such assessments in this study, my core argument concerning the revolutionary and evolutionary value of Beckett's works is entirely original, as are my component arguments concerning the affective and cognitive work of the paradox, the action-oriented character of Beckett's black humour and "absurdist excess," the presence of this type of humour even in Beckett's latest texts, and the role of anger in Beckett's attack on class and gender-based forms of exploitation and repression. In the following paragraphs, I briefly discuss six recent studies whose core arguments resonate with some of my main points of focus (humour, ethics, Deleuze and Guattari's notion of "abstract machines," the representation of the body in Beckett's works, and Beckett's political allegiances), and I engage with many more article- and book-length studies with which I share such common ground throughout the book.

Similarly to my project, Salisbury's 2012 study *Samuel Beckett: Laughing Matters, Comic Timing* attempts both an original interpretation of a fundamental dimension of Beckett's works (comedy in Salisbury's case and paradox-based discourse in mine) and a theorization of the ethical import of this dimension. Both Salisbury's study and mine explore the ways in which Beckett's use of language and theatricality may forge connections between the self and the other (such as new forms of solidarity). However, Salibury's analysis does not entirely break with the logic of role reversals and disjunctive values characterizing most theorizations of comedy, though her positing of a relation to language that partly evades repression by mimicking the "gag reflex" and her acknowledgement of a consistent wave of anger in the *Trilogy* at times place her analysis in close proximity to my discussion of the procedures of ejection of machinic switches omnipresent in Beckett's texts. In contrast, I explain Beckett's ability to dislocate repressive and oppressive structures within the logic of the paradox—as an affect-based, action-oriented attack on the disjunctions, conjunctions, reversals, and juxtapositions that structure communal living. In this reading, Beckett's depiction of acts of resistance has a *diagrammatic quality*— it approximates accessible and reproducible practices rather than merely offering a glimpse of how things "ought to be" (*Laughing Matters* 94; formulation attributed to Peter Boxall).

In Salisbury's view, "the temporal, peculiarly passing, experience of the comic that Beckett's work elicits can be related to a historically specific hope for an ethics of the aesthetic" (*Laughing Matters* 14). She offers a sophisticated analysis of both the more explosive humour of Beckett's earlier works and the "atrophied comedy" (183) of his late works, but her assessment of the ethical impetus of Beckett's humour does not identify, as my reading does, an active and empowering dimension in Beckett's late texts. My discussion of the positive and connective dimensions of Beckett's paradox-based humour—including in his late texts, where the categories of the tragic and the horrific may seem dominant at all levels—advances significantly previous analyses of Beckett's humour alongside previous articulations of the political dimensions of Beckett's works. Additionally, my Part II discussion of the potential *cognitive* effects of exposure to Beckett's texts offers original insights into a largely unexplored aspect of Beckett's humour, and of Beckett's works in general.

Weller's 2006 *Beckett, Literature, and the Ethics of Alterity* and Fifield's 2013 *Late Modernist Style in Samuel Beckett and Emanuel Levinas* engage, as I do, with the ethical dimension of Beckett's work, but in different ways. At the end of a critique of earlier interpretive attempts to argue for an ethical dimension of Beckett's works (by Critchley, Gibson, Badiou, Adorno, etc.), Weller concludes that Beckett's impetus is "anethical"—a category he defines as "neither an ethics nor an alternative to ethics, but rather ... a failure either to establish or negate the difference between the ethical and the unethical, nihilism and anti-nihilism, philosophy and literature, thought and action, the terminal and the interminable" (194–95). For Weller, Beckett's works consistently emphasize an *inability* to express ethical judgements, generating a literary form that remains, ostentatiously, neither ethical nor unethical, and is defined by this proclaimed inability. Beckett's "indecision" generates "ways in which the experience of the disintegration of both art and ethics might be rendered visible—or audible—on a page or a stage" (194)—a gesture Weller derives from Beckett's deep suspicion that any ethical judgement would carry the potential of a return to totalitarian destruction ("an appeal to values that will always negate the very things they are there to save," 195). Fifield allows for an ethical dimension of Beckett's works but connects it to the ethics of Levinas, claiming that Beckett's works both emphasize and attempt to avoid the pitfalls of literary production discussed by Levinas in his dismissal of literature as a superficial and deceitful form of engagement with alterity.

Both critics have points of focus different from mine, and our investigative modes and conclusions diverge. Weller engages less than I do in close readings of Beckett's texts and does not see, in Beckett's humour, an action-oriented dimension or a large enough margin of positivity. While he relates his exploration of the notions of truth and alterity in Beckett's works to humour and acknowledges Beckett's corrosive articulations of language and institutional power, his analysis operates under a definition of humour grounded in opposition and disjunction-based theorizations such as those of Bergson and Freud—which are less likely to render visible the action-oriented effects based in solidarity and directed at machinic repression that my paradox-based reading allows me to theorize. Fifield, on the other hand, engages minimally with Beckett's humour because, as he notes in the Introduction, "comedy plays … a small part in Levinas's ethics, and the ludic quality of literature, which might be seen as germane to laughter, is actively frowned upon" (9). Taking distance from Weller, he sees positivity and a constructive dimension in Beckett's "indecision," relating it to Levinasian ethics: "this 'shuffling to and fro' is precisely the manner in which Levinas describes the other's appearance in his formulations of the 'trace' of the other" (72). However, again in keeping with Levinasian theory, Fifield proclaims that even literary discourses that come "closest to emulating this form" are *unethical* (72). In fact, for him, Beckett's ethical gesture consists in obsessively staging this ethical failure—making it utterly visible, in all its subterfuges and effects. Still, ultimately, Fifield sees in this gesture merely a form of *resigned witnessing* rather than an active denunciation (163). Furthermore, within the same theoretical framework, he claims that, when humour is present, Beckett's writing can acquire "a more actively destructive quality" that makes this form of witnessing "indistinguishable from participation" (163–64)— although he does acknowledge that Levinas may not be the ideal choice in analysing Beckett's representation of relationships and solitude (164–65). What allows my approach to Beckett's texts to evince an action-oriented dimension and a larger margin of positivity than generally acknowledged in criticism is precisely my engagement with the ways in which Beckett's humour, insofar as it derives from the paradox rather than from disjunction-based structures, facilitates action-oriented forms of solidarity anchored in intratextual and extratextual relationships (between characters, as well as between characters and interpreters). I subscribe to Fifield's assessment that Beckett's ethics is anti-identificatory, but as my project shows, perhaps the more important point is that it is *relational* in a *revolutionary* and *evolutionary* fashion.

Dowd's 2007 study *Abstract Machines: Samuel Beckett and Philosophy after Deleuze and Guattari* examines the impact of Deleuze and Guattari's engagement with Beckett's works (as constitutive of their philosophical thought) on subsequent critical assessments of the relation between Beckett and philosophy in particular, and between literature and philosophy more generally. While Deleuze and Guattari also feature prominently in my study, Dowd's interpretations of Beckett's texts have a primarily philosophical focus, whereas in my reading, the focus is primarily sociopolitical. Dowd uses an interpretive framework derived from the works of Deleuze and Guattari, in the chapters that engage directly with texts by Beckett, to assess Beckett's philosophical positioning (his peculiar modes of engagement with philosophical concepts) within the context of other philosophically focused readings of Beckett's works. My analysis of Beckett's texts within a Deleuzean framework is more focused on these texts' ability to generate action-oriented affects in readers/ spectators, including the articulation of revolutionary practices that move away from traditional revolutionary forms such as the capture of the state or the centrality of the proletariat.

Connor's reading of Beckett, in his 2014 volume *Beckett, Modernism, and the Material Imagination* (a collection of previously published independent essays), as a writer profoundly concerned with material existence (the body, human connections, the natural world) resonates, in part, with my analysis of the obsessively corporeal articulation of Beckett's "abstractions" in my discussion of humour. However, my thesis and main supporting arguments take a different direction. Connor reads Beckett's concern for the flesh mainly as a rejection of metaphysical impositions and does not explore other potential political implications of that obsessive textual presence. For example, his extensive discussion of Beckett's preoccupation with ingestion, digestion, and excretion in Chap. 3 draws similarities and differences between Beckett's figuration of the body and Sartre's (in *Being and Nothingness*), focusing mostly on Beckett's "nauseous" descriptions of the bodily mechanics involved in these processes, largely removed from what I define as their machinic context. Beckett's figuration of the forces (machinic strata that form the plane of immanence, in Deleuze and Guattari's terms) whose concerted acting on the body makes the most grotesque forms of resistance necessary thus falls outside of Connor's main concerns—and, as a result, Beckett's diagrammatic figuration of procedures of resistance to capture registers only in the form of an almost entirely abstract revulsion towards "self-coincidence" (46). Similarly, Connor's discussion of machinic patterns of behaviour and "switches" in Chap. 5 does not explore potential political implications in *What Where*, although several elements in the play point to political repression. In contrast, my project foregrounds the political nature of Beckett's textual engagement with corporeality.

Finally, my focus on the political dimension of Beckett's works deeply resonates with Emilie Morin's exploration of Beckett's political allegiances in her 2017 book *Beckett's Political Imaginary*, although our methodological approaches and analytical goals differ, and some of our conclusions diverge. Morin examines an impressive corpus of biobibliographical material—letters, petitions, acts of donation, interviews, conversations documented by friends, the contents of Beckett's library, the newspapers and magazines he read, his translations, some manuscript drafts, and so on—to demonstrate the untenable character of the long-lived critical fiction of a deeply apolitical or even "anti-political" Beckett. Contrary to his prevailing image as uninterested in everyday political practice, Beckett signed dozens of petitions in support of human rights issues and free speech, as Morin documents (in between the 1931 Scottsboro petition initiated by Nancy Cunard and the 1989 condemnation of the fatwa against Salman Rushdie, he endorsed petitions condemning anti-democratic practices in postwar France, Algeria, South America, and Eastern Europe). Morin also carefully analyses Beckett's politically engaged translation of the essays included in Cunard's 1934 anthology *Negro*, showing that he consistently gave more compelling expression to political points "dealing with suffering, poverty, distress and the work of colonial administrations" (97). She stresses Beckett's personal and financial support for his editor Jérôme Lindon, who published several books exposing the atrocities committed by the French military in Algeria at great personal and financial risk—and she traces, in Beckett's letters from the Algerian War period and in manuscript drafts, indications that his knowledge of those atrocities shaped major elements of *Rough for Radio II*, *Rough for Theatre II*, and *How It Is* (185 *ff.*, 220 *ff.*). She also points out disjunctions and tensions between some elements that define Beckett's "political imaginary." For instance, she notes that Beckett's lifelong alignment with the political left—from his connections to leftist Irish circles in his youth (31–34) to his preference for leftist publications after the war (25)—did not also translate into open support of labour movements through petitions (74). She also notes that, although Beckett had many female friends and collaborators and his love interests were intellectually and ideologically engaged women, "feminism and women's rights were not among his political priorities," and his public gestures of support "remained in keeping with the conventions and dynamics of the professional networks in which he operated, and almost exclusively benefited male artists and intellectuals with credentials that matched his own" (74). Morin concludes that, while Beckett avoided the more visible forms of political engagement typical of, say, Sartre, both his literary works and his social and intellectual interactions offer "abundant evidence of the energy and integrity with which Beckett expressed his concerns for justice, solidarity and the conditions in which freedom is lost and regained" (249). Moreover, his consistent focus on "raw power and domination" (250) and on power structures' tremendous ability for self-preservation makes of his works an ideal reflective medium in areas marked by natural disasters, conflict, or political repression, as a number of news reports and academic studies referenced by Morin (8, 25–52) show.

I consider Morin's work crucial in dispelling the image of Beckett as "the high priest of failure, resignation and acceptance" (250) that remains dominant in both academic and popular culture contexts to date—and my analysis begins, in a way, where Morin's ends. I engage with some archival, biobibliographical, and/or historical approaches to Beckett's works in my project, as I see Beckett's works and overall socio-aesthetic vision as deeply resonant with the violent historical realities he experienced or witnessed. However, I identify, in these texts, a political dimension that extends, in peculiar ways, beyond the limits of a critique of a given socio-historical context. As Morin and others note, and as I discussed earlier, interpreters as distinct as the maximum-security convicts at San Quentin, the survivors of Hurricane Katrina, citizens of Eastern Europe living under communist rule, or, most recently, Syrian refugees consistently claim to hear, in Beckett's *Waiting for Godot*, echoes of their own experiences of dispossession and pain. However, they do not identify there some overarching, "universal" rendering of the experience of waiting, or a majestic meditation on failure and doom. On the contrary, each group sees the play as an intense enactment of their individual, deeply socio-historically contextualized and intimately experienced distress, and each discovers in it an incentive to reclaim life (to "go on"). The play does not, then, offer soothing but momentary feelings of release—it powerfully mobilizes affect. It does not offer an uplifting but ultimately tranquilizing meditation—it entices readers and spectators to internalize the diagram of an action-oriented practice. My focus, in analysing Beckett's works, is on tracing this diagram, which appears to systematically make itself conspicuous to audience members irrespective of their knowledge or understanding of the socio-historical determinants that may have shaped Beckett's writing, of the philosophical and aesthetic notions he may have recycled/ displaced/ mocked in his works, or of his intellectual exchanges with friends and collaborators throughout his career and life.

PART I

Contagion and Accessibility: Revolutionary Beckett

CHAPTER 2

Repetition, Deliberation, and an *Other* Power: The Paradox as Practice

2.1 Textual Entropy and Machinic Disruption

One of the unsettling voices heard in Eliot's *The Waste Land* (a more sarcastic than generally acknowledged foray into the relation between modernity and the literary and cultural tradition) denounces the repressive work of the "roots that clutch," growing inexplicably "out of … stony rubbish" (lines 19–20). As early modernist and avant-garde writers were fully aware, uprooting parasitic socio-cultural constraints from communal structures they had almost dried out would not restore vitality unless these constraints were prevented from propagating through language. However, these writers' most remarkable contribution to a stronger, politically apt formulation of this intuition is their constant enactment of the aggregate or machinic character of this relation, which accounts for its immediacy and unavoidability but also offers efficacious ways of countering at least some of its damaging effects. The telephones in Kafka's *The Castle* and the writing/ torture/ execution machine from *In the Penal Colony* are obvious examples, but an obsessive mimicking of machinic functions only in order to denounce, suspend, or subvert them dominates, for instance, dadaist and surrealist poetry, drama, and visual art—as Deleuze and Guattari put it, surrealist machines busily produce "anti-production" (*AO* 31). This chapter discusses Beckett's intuitions concerning the machinic articulation of language to social interactions, imaginary investments, and theoretical models, using as main investigative tools Deleuze's notion of

© The Author(s) 2020
C. Ionica, *The Affects, Cognition, and Politics of Samuel Beckett's Postwar Drama and Fiction*, New Interpretations of Beckett in the Twenty-First Century, https://doi.org/10.1007/978-3-030-34902-8_2

absurdist language operations ("nonsense") as a form of "excess" and Deleuze and Guattari's conceptualization of the schizophrenic's language, the paradox, and the abstract machine as constructs apt to sabotage socio-historical structures of capture, exploitation, and repression.

A few linguistic concepts borrowed from Montague's treatment of natural language as a formal language may add analytical precision to my discussion of the import of Deleuze's notion of *excess* in evincing the deliberate, systematic, and purposeful nature of Beckett's destabilizing language. Montague's most influential works were published in the early 1970s, around the same time as Deleuze's *The Logic of Sense* (1969) and Deleuze and Guattari's *Anti-Oedipus* (1972). While there seems to be no direct relation between these theorists' works, they share a common preoccupation, in their approach to language, for the articulation of what Montague called the "syntax-semantics-pragmatics interface"—a marked shift from Chomsky's formalist grammar. A mathematical logician specializing in set theory and modal logic, Montague retained Chomsky's notion of recursion as a basic commonality of natural languages but rejected his positing of linguistics as a branch of psychology (more on Deleuze and Guattari's reservations towards Chomsky's theory shortly). Recursion—the process of reapplying compositional rules to their output to obtain longer/ more complex sentences from more basic structures, as in the example "Ann claims that Mary said that John came yesterday"—is a trait shared by formal languages based in logic and mathematics, where it is used for calculations and demonstrations involving repeatedly applied operations under predefined conditions. To enable his analytic model to cover pragmatic aspects of language, Montague added to it elements of logic and linguistics introduced by Charles Sanders Peirce, Rudolf Carnap, Gottlob Frege, and Alfred Tarski, as well as elements of set theory. Thus, his notions of *intension* and *extension* relate to Carnap and Frege's search for ways to distinguish between *denotative* components of an expression (all the potential referents of an expression—real/ fictitious, present/ past/ future, common/ uncommon situations it might reference) and the *actualization* of *one* specific sense through contextual constraints. His focus, however, was on connecting the two levels through formally expressed rules (see "English as a Formal Language," *Formal Philosophy* 217–18). Furthermore, he integrated into his model set theory concepts such as logical consequence, logical truth, and logical equivalence ("Pragmatics and Intensional Logic," *Formal Philosophy* 127). Finally, he adopted Peirce's notion of "indexes" (elements pointing to events unspecified as such—for example, a bullet hole as a sign that a gun has been fired) but extended it to cover various elements of an expression providing contextual clues concerning the "possible world" associated with each utterance—facts about the world, time and place of utterance, surrounding discourse, and other relevant variables. (Such information is often expressed through deictics—words like "here," "now," or "I," whose semantic content is clear but whose reference varies with the context.) He thus came to define the *intension* of an expression as a *function* that generates *extensions* (the term designates the *thing/ person/ set of objects* named, but also its *truth value*) from series of *inputs* (*indexes*).

While Montague does not address the specificity of literary discourse and illustrates his descriptive model through relatively simple sentences, his mathematical approach to natural languages confirms early twentieth-century avant-garde and modernist writers' intuitions concerning the aggregate, machinic character of language. If the meaning of an expression is a *function* of its syntactic arrangement and (contextual) indexes, then language is neither an organic emanation of transcendent origin nor a more or less neutral or clear communication medium—it is a *meaning-making machine* always regulated by conservative systemic forces in the absence of forceful interventions at the syntactic or pragmatic level. Deleuze's claim that absurdist language operations create an "excess" (not an absence) of sense then translates, in Montague's terms, into a claim that absurdists manipulate the syntax and the pragmatic context of each utterance to sabotage the operations of the function that produces unambiguous, unproblematic extensions as single-member sets. Absurdist language operations consistently deliver, instead, extensions consisting of multi-element sets (multiple sense assignations corresponding to multiple possible referents). In so doing, they sabotage traditional communication modes and expose the mechanics of the communication process—the "wiring" of the syntax/ semantic/ pragmatic interface. Insofar as they frustrate interpreters' expectations of a one-on-one correspondence and make sense perplexingly manifold, such operations produce disorientation and anxiety. There is, however, also joy in this process—that of suddenly discerning a world of infinite combinations and implicitly pausing, for a time, our consuming immersion into production-oriented language. In any case, in exposing the mechanics of sense-making (the "function"), these operations render suspicious data of experience formerly perceived as incontrovertible and intractable and codified as such at the level of language. This effect is strident and shocking enough to be perceived even by interpreters unaware of the operations behind it.

Before elaborating on the forms of "absurdist excess" privileged by Deleuze and Guattari and explicating their political import, let me illustrate this destabilizing effect through an example from Beckett's 1938 novel *Murphy*—the much-quoted opening sentence "The sun shone, having no alternative, on the nothing new" (1). "Having no alternative"—technically, a misplaced modifier—makes it mockingly ambiguous whether the sun is hopelessly bound to shine or has nothing of value to shine on, thus foregrounding a peculiarly cynical narrative voice of unknown origin, whose presence is additionally emphasized through the creative noun phrase "the nothing new." The indexes of the sentence are puzzling. Space/ time references are vague (somewhere under the sun, maybe in the early morning, probably in the past—though the past tense simple might merely be a jab at narrative conventions). The placement of the sentence at the start of the text elicits a comparison to incipit techniques in various historically consecrated prose forms—and its content derides, specifically, claims to objectivity, authenticity, and plausible contextualization typical of realism and naturalism.[1] Arguably, then, the primary purpose of this sentence is not to depict anything real or imagined but to "shine on the nothing new" of meaning-making—to expose what Deleuze and Guattari designate as the *diagram* of the relation between language and reality by revealing that the work of the meaning-making machine rests on predefined hierarchies, divisions, disjunctions, and allocations of power. In allowing a disorderly accumulation of meanings to emerge while barring it from acquiring a familiar, less disconcerting structure, the sentence exposes meaning-making as a process of organization of non-hierarchic, nonstructured material into stable semiotic formations under the pressure of socio-historical forces. Most readers would likely react to the comedic entropy[2] unleashed by such a sentence and *experience* its liberatory energy even if they lack the expertise needed to "understand Beckett." Deleuze and Guattari describe the work of writers like Beckett or Kafka as having "a double function: to translate everything into assemblages and to dis-

[1] The "context" here is not, say, Balzac's Paris with its stratified social system encoded in the reputation of an arrondissement, the smoothness of a building façade, or the worn-out fabric of a sofa, but the solar system. Indeed, what could be more irrelevant from a practical perspective—and what could be a more complex and destructive attack on the relevance of the (bourgeois) practical vision? For Cavaliero, the first sentence and, in fact, the entire novel "parodies the ideal of fictive naturalism" (204).

[2] O'Neill defines black humour such as that practiced by Beckett as "the comedy of entropy"—"the humour of lost norms, lost confidence, the humour of disorientation" (89).

mantle the assemblages" (*K* 47). Such writing can "tear a minor literature away from its own language," barring impositions from a "literature of masters" (19), and can "kill metaphors," ensuring that there will be "no longer any proper sense or figurative sense, but only a distribution of states that is part of the range of the word" (22). "Anti-realistic," "abstracted," "absurdist" writing like Kafka's or Beckett's consequently interferes with the pragmatic level of discourse (implicitly sabotaging its hierarchical foundations and systemic maintenance effects) by denouncing it as a *conservative* meaning-making machine. In foregrounding the *collective* character and effects of discourse ("The most individual enunciation is a particular case of a collective enunciation," *K* 84), such writing implicitly translates "the subject" (individual, localizable, stable) into a fuzzy psychosomatic formation shifting about at the intersection of multiple collective linguistic and power structures (81). As Deleuze and Guattari put it, "everything in [minor literatures] is political" (17).

2.2 Abstraction and Accessibility (Trees vs. Diagrams)

As previously stated, Beckett's destabilizing linguistic operations seemingly enhance readers/ spectators' engagement with his texts rather than hindering it through their "difficulty." As I show in this and the following chapters, what renders Beckett's texts accessible is their relentless horrific-comic sabotage of the (disjunctive) switches that regulate the production of meaning alongside the production of structures of exploitation and repression within the socio-linguistic machine. This *diagrammatic quality* arises from Beckett's extensive use of paradox-based language and imagery. Paradoxes ensure accessibility but also generate empowering effects that are contagious and collective rather than strictly individual and/or momentary. That is, paradox-based discourses can generate affects—they can mobilize massive amounts of psychosomatic energy, enabling affected bodies to *act* (experience and cause inner and environmental transformation). This quality distances paradox-based constructs from traditional modes of understanding and representation, recommending them as forms of collective *practice*.

Deleuze and Guattari applaud Beckett's diagrammatic textual mayhem but reject Chomsky's linguistic formalizations because, in failing to connect language to the social field, they are (at the risk of shocking everyone exposed to "trees" in Syntax courses) "not abstract enough" (*TP* 7). That is, they "do not reach the abstract machine that connects a language to the semantic and pragmatic contents of statements, to collective assemblages of enunciation, to a whole micropolitics of the social field" (*TP* 7), so they cannot produce a "diagram" of the socio-linguistic machine apt to destabilize socio-linguistic impositions and foster positive change (91). From this perspective, Deleuze and Guattari operate under the same premise as Montague, who aimed to enhance generativists' abstract models by offering a comprehensive formalization that no longer favoured syntactic over semantic and pragmatic concerns. However, while Montague's focus was strictly theoretical (increasing the reach of the formalizations offered), Deleuze and Guattari's is socio-political (searching for means of producing viable *diagrams* that can be broadcast through flows of affect).

Deleuze and Guattari consider the reach of generativists' linguistic approach limited because their analytical model presupposes a disjunction between expression and content, while abstract machines cover "the entire plane of consistency" (*TP* 11), denouncing all disjunctive operations as machinic interruptions of socio-historical affect-based flows. Rather than examining content and expression through Saussure's surface distinction between the signified and the signifier, we should, then, consider them in terms of their *machinic generation* as "variables of the assemblage" (91). Focusing on *the way they are produced* rather than on the way they present themselves once in existence exposes the constructed, machinic nature of all "pragmatic, but also semantic, syntactical, and phonological determinations"—as *products* of socio-historically regulated "assemblages of enunciation" (91). Abstract machines explicate such assemblages in ways that make all interventions and acts of production obvious, implicitly rendering grotesque the otherwise smooth exploitative and repressive operations of countless technical or socio-linguistic working machines.

Beckett's stated desire to "drill holes into language" (an image used in a 9 July 1937 letter to Axel Kaun) aptly approximates what abstract machines can achieve:

> [L]anguage is best used where it is most efficiently abused. Since we cannot dismiss it all at once, at least we do not want to leave anything undone that may contribute to its disrepute. To drill one hole after another into it until what lurks behind, be it something or nothing, starts seeping through—I cannot imagine a higher goal for today's writer. (*L1* 518)

This "very desirable literature of the non-word" (520) is defined in even more conspicuously material, grotesque terms in a letter sent to Mary Manning Howe two days later: "I am starting a Logoclasts' League. ... I am the only member at present. The idea is ruptured writing, so that the void may protrude, like a hernia" (521). It is, then, for good reason that Deleuze and Guattari consistently use examples from Beckett's works to set up and explicate their arguments in *Capitalism and Schizophrenia*, and that Critchley deems Beckett's techniques of creating chaos "formalizable" (*Very Little* 196). Beckett's works generate "abstract (writing) machines" that mount methodically destabilizing attacks on "natural" linguistic constructs and, implicitly, on the constitutive logic of language as a component assemblage within larger socio-historical machines. The interrelatedness of these attacks, which bolsters their power, further confirms the highly deliberate character of Beckett's language operations. As a first step in an investigation of these texts' mobilization of affect, let us discuss three such techniques: sabotaging any notion of logical difference *or* logical equivalence, spurring the proliferation of "extensions" (Montague's term covering possible referents *and associated truth values*) through syntactic manipulations and pragmatic clues, and using oblique discursive constructions (sentences linked in non-linear, logically disruptive ways).

"Enough," a story offering manically meticulous and utterly peculiar depictions of a couple's lifelong interactions, is narrated by a voice ostentatiously and subversively constructed, from the beginning, as belonging to a woman—although an *explicit* clue appears only in the last sentence, through the short phrase "my old breasts" (*CSP* 187). Badiou (*In Praise of Love*) reads in this story an obstinate fidelity to love, and Bryden describes it as "a graceful evocation of a cherished communion, and not a sexually ambiguous liaison" (*Women* 152). However, in a reading more focused on Beckett's linguistic "excess," the purported "love" or "communion" translate into an angry denunciation of a lifelong experience of gender-based exploitation, as countless details point to physical and sexual abuse or, at the very least, totalitarian patriarchal control and conditioning.

This corrosive "translation" operates through displacements that compromise the positing of heteronormative relations as universally nourishing and meaningful (implicitly, as "naturally" viable and desirable). (The story is, after all, called "Enough.") One strategy is to unsettle the relation between the abstract and the concrete registers of language by scrambling their functions. In some paragraphs, physicality is emphasized, seemingly, for no logical reason:

> In the beginning he always spoke walking. ... Then sometimes walking and sometimes still. In the end still only. And the voice getting fainter all the time. To save him having to say the same thing twice running I bowed right down. He halted and waited for me to get into position. As soon as out of the corner of his eye he glimpsed my head alongside his the murmurs came. Nine times out of ten they did not concern me. (188)

Abstract descriptions and assessments that might have revealed the content and quality of these communication acts are ostentatiously replaced by a painstakingly concrete depiction of a sequence of bowing and bending movements performed by the woman so she could hear the man—a slapstick-style ritual of submission with sinister undertones, in synch with earlier revelations such as, "I cannot have been more than six when he took me by the hand. Barely emerging from childhood. But it didn't take me long to emerge altogether" (187). In other fragments, conspicuously abstract and repetitive assessments delay the presentation of rather damning concrete examples:

> I did all he desired. For him. Whenever he desired something so did I. He only had to say what thing. When he didn't desire anything neither did I. In this way I didn't live without desires. If he had desired something for me I would have desired it too. Happiness for example or fame. I only had the desires he manifested. But he must have manifested them all. All his desires and needs. When he was silent he must have been like me. When he told me to lick his penis I hastened to do so. (186)

The last sentence caustically clarifies the disjunctive and hierarchical nature of the relationship—in case the eerily redundant and convoluted comments on "desire" hadn't revealed enough: he had always been the order-giver, and she, the service-provider, on any matter, from larger-scope life choices to the unilateral dispensation of oral sex.

The two fragments above offer seemingly redundant and aimless "explanations" only to abruptly switch to final sentences of a different order, whose self-assured and resentful tone translates the apparent confusion and passivity of the previous sentences into repressed anger. Heterosexual communication and love thus incrementally translate into control and abuse, and patriarchal arrangements are debunked as falsely benevolent forms of companionship meant to safeguard men's exploitation and consumption of their partners' energy to the point of physical decrepitude and mental dissolution. The same subversive "explanations" serve to corrode logical notions like equivalency, similarity, or difference. They dispute such notions' logical consistency by stressing that there is always a form of hierarchical thinking and an interested party behind them. Whether the meaning-making machine safeguards the interests of a controlling, egotistical, abusive patriarch or those of a complex of communitarian/ religious/ state structures, the basic mechanisms of subjection are revealed to be similar and the operations used to sabotage them are consistent, as shown here and in the following chapters.

Another strategy used to destabilize the logical consistency and the legitimation strategies characterizing heteronormative assemblages is the ostentatious replacement of productive, goal-oriented discourse based in traditional notions of coherence with linguistic operations based in sets and permutations. Several fragments conspicuously juxtapose improbable mathematical estimations, apparently aimless combinations and permutations, and mock-analytical comments, in stark disregard of linear logic: "He was not given to talk. An average of a hundred words per day and night. Spaced out. A bare million in all. Numerous repeats. Ejaculations. Too few for even a cursory survey. What do I know of man's destiny? I could tell you more about radishes. For them he had a fondness. If I saw one I would name it without hesitation" (192). Here is a longer fragment:

> He sometimes halted without saying anything. Either he had finally nothing to say or while having something to say he finally decided not to say it. ... Sooner or later his foot broke away from the flowers and we moved on. Perhaps only to halt again after a few steps. So that he might say at last what was in his heart or decide not to say it again.
>
> Other main examples suggest themselves to the mind. Immediate continuous communication with immediate redeparture. Same thing with delayed redeparture. Delayed continuous communication with immediate redeparture. Same thing with delayed redeparture. Immediate discontinuous communication with immediate redeparture. Same thing with delayed redeparture. Delayed discontinuous communication with immediate redeparture. Same thing with delayed redeparture. (186)

Deleuze and Guattari see in such combinations and permutations, which proceed through structural repetitions and recurrent rhythms, the corrosive logic of the schizophrenic's inclusive disjunction ("or... or... or..."): "Where the 'either/or' claims to mark decisive choices between immutable terms (the alternative: either this or that), the schizophrenic 'either... or... or...' refers to the system of possible permutations between differences that always amount to the same as they shift and slide about" (*AO* 12). Such elaborately irrelevant permutations and repeatedly sabotaged equivalencies denounce the meaninglessness of human existence not as a given of the human condition but as the *compounded material effect of countless specific, discrete patriarchal injunctions and acts of abuse*. The character-narrator comments, "Given three or four lives I might have accomplished something" (Beckett, *CSP* 187). This deceivingly random use of numerals (*two* lives would not make any difference but "three or four," specifically, might) sarcastically depicts the very perception of a lack of meaning and value (typically arising from predefined quantitative assessments) as a patriarchal shackle. In such fragments, the first-person narrator's falsely flat tone ultimately reads as barely contained anger, while her "explanations" denounce heterosexual male entitlement as a transhistorical scam by debunking both the equivalences *and* the differences it is predicated on as logically inconsistent and self-serving.

In the dramatic works, both the characters' lines and the (seldom merely descriptive) stage directions support this assault on the hierarchical underpinnings of seemingly objective and innocuous logical operations, on multiple syntactic-semantic-pragmatic levels. In Act I of *Waiting for Godot*, Vladimir and Estragon discuss their surroundings, the scriptures, the possibility of hanging themselves, and the relation between the taste of a carrot and the personality of the individual eating it—all to "pass the time" (*CDW* 13). Their conversations are conspicuously filled with failed attempts to establish equivalencies, similarities, or differences that might lead to satisfying explanations. For instance, they discuss the story of Christ's crucifixion and its representation in the scriptures as follows:

> V: It was two thieves, crucified at the same time as our Saviour. One—
> E: Our what?
> V: Our Saviour. Two thieves. One is supposed to have been saved and the other … *[He searches for the contrary of saved.]* … damned.
> E: Saved from what?
> V: Hell.
> E: I'm going. *[He does not move.]*
> V: And yet … *[Pause.]* … how is it—this is not boring to you I hope—how is it that of the four evangelists only one speaks of a thief being saved? The four of them were there—or thereabouts, and only one speaks of a thief being saved. *[Pause.]* Come on, Gogo, return the ball, can't you, once in a way?
> E: *[With exaggerated enthusiasm.]* I find this really most extraordinarily interesting.

V: One out of four. Of the other three two don't mention any thieves at all and the third says that both of them abused him.
E: Who?
V: What?
E: What's all this about? *[Pause.]* Abused who?
V: The Saviour.
E: Why?
V: Because He wouldn't save them.
E: From hell?
V: Imbecile! From death.
E: I thought you said from hell.
V: From death, from death.
E: Well, what about it?
V: Then the two of them must have been damned.
E: And why not?
V: But the other Apostle says that one was saved.
E: Well? They don't agree, and that's all there is to it.
V: But all four were there. And only one speaks of a thief being saved. Why believe him rather than the others?
E: Who believes him?
V: Everybody. It's the only version they know.
E: People are bloody ignorant apes. (13–14)

The passage mocks religious logic in general and institutionalized Christian doctrine in particular by redefining the phrase "our Saviour" through repetition rather than explanatory equivalencies; by reducing the apostles' import to numbers and proportions (note, for instance, the obsessive "one out of four"); by stressing inconsistencies in the crucifixion story (the apostles were all "there—or thereabouts" but offered conflicting accounts); by dismissing Christian claims to universality (see Estragon's "Our what?" and "Abused who?"); and by denouncing the Christian notion of salvation as predicated on a torture threat (Estragon insists to be told "from what" the thieves were or were not saved). The passage also disputes the consistency of logical disjunctions, oppositions, and equivalences in general, exposing them as machinic structures guiding the socio-cultural processes that reduce humans to "bloody ignorant apes."[3] By the end of the

---

[3] In the French version, Estragon says, "Les gens sont des cons." The general assumption in Beckett studies is that censorship concerns may have determined Beckett to avoid the closer translation into English, "People are cunts." However, the fact that the English phrase is more aggressive in general *and more aggressively gender-inflected* than its French equivalent

sequence, Estragon's "thick" questions read as a scathing denunciation of our lazy acquiescence to the repressive oppositions and disjunctions that structure meaning-making. If we register his questions as comically inept, it is because we are fully coupled to language as a repression machine. In fact, his seeming inability to understand is meant to sabotage linguistic-affective indoctrination, as his final verdict clarifies. The stage directions participate fully in this attack. We are told, at some point during the exchange, that Vladimir "searches for the contrary of 'saved,'" but no specific gestures are listed. This condescending authorial note mock-redundantly attaches itself to a line that revolves around "contraries." The text thus offers multiple suggestions that the oppositions, disjunctions, and polarizations allowing us to make sense of the world tend to be perilously reductive and support the formation of stultifying, deadening hierarchies.

The dread of indoctrination and the joy of liberation are encoded into the same linguistic structures—as soon as we grasp the accuracy of Estragon's assessment, a liberatory strategy begins to emerge. Anxiety and joy, bitterness and exultation consistently appear, at several structural levels in Beckett's texts, *in inclusive disjunction* (the logic of the schizophrenic's "either… or… or…" as described by Deleuze and Guattari, which does not imply switching between alternatives or synthesizing opposing terms). Indeed, these texts enact threat and comfort, anxiety and exhilaration as values in a range, and most importantly, outputs regulated by the same machinic "switches." Beckett's destabilizing discursive operations expose consecrated equivalencies, similarities, and differences as logically inconsistent and/or hierarchically inflected. His ostentatious repetitions and reiterations and his destabilizing associations, subtractions, and additions radically impact affect as they denounce and sabotage the functioning of *anxiety* (alongside subordination, exploitation, and repression) as a self-regulating mechanism of the socio-historical machine. In short, these operations trigger our realization that we are socio-linguistically disciplined to fear chaos and seek the safety of machinic structures in a world controlled to the point of dehumanization and ordered to death.

This effect is increasingly built through visual means in Beckett's later plays, where, as Tanaka notes, "even though the actors' bodies, like objects on stage, look stable, the situations they are in seem visually unstable"

may have also played a part in Beckett's decision. This is a defining phrase for Estragon, whose psychological profile seems to exclude both malice and misogyny.

(249). For Tanaka, this mix of immobility and instability instils fear in the audience, especially given Beckett's frequent use of stage darkness and choice to make visible only fragments of bodies (249–50), yet there is also an empowering dimension to this arrangement. In *Not I*, *Play*, as in later dramas, where the visual displaces spoken language further, both the written text and the stage arrangement increasingly stress the mechanical, machinic nature of confinement and repression by translating all levels of abstraction into physical terms. Psychosomatic abuse and trauma (including political repression) materialize as immobility and/or restrained/ repetitive movement. Alongside characters' restrained bodies, what is put on display is humans' readiness to welcome and internalize as beneficial even forms of stability indistinguishable from stasis, forgetting that "habit is a great deadener" (*CDW* 83), as Vladimir rightly warns. Granted, this fear of instability is inscribed into language (and linguistically defined visual representations) as a conservative systemic force, and multiple machinic strata conspire to induce us to perceive ourselves as "naturally" fit to be "coupled" and used. However, the machinic nature of the "societal organism" can never conceal itself fully. Its articulation through language accounts for its ability to camouflage itself even while acting with full power, but it also leaves it permanently exposed to paradox-based attacks.

One of Beckett's recurrent strategies to "uncover the switches," implicitly exposing them to sabotage, is his repeated/ prolonged application of the same violent discursive operation (or violently unnatural visual procedure) until, after a long series of rhythmic convulsions, something of the order of truth emerges. The *comic relief* of Beckett's idiosyncratic-by-the-rule discursive operations always works in tandem with a sort of *cosmic relief*—that of an angry, liberating laughter that indicts anxiety as a conservative systemic force, fully aware that, in its endless progress towards dissolution, the universe will only ever find itself, in Clov's words from *Endgame*, just "nearly" there (*CDW* 93). I will return to this idea in Chaps. 3 and 4 to show that linguistic-based forms of comic relief persist even in texts where the dominant mood appears to be depression or horror. For now, let us retain that socio-historical assemblages can preclude resistance and function effectively only insofar as they can integrate exploitative-repressive disjunctions into seemingly functional and beneficial social organisms (by camouflaging any switches likely to expose their machinic and parasitic nature). Beckett's paradoxical formulations offer a compelling, accessible, and reproducible means to obstruct such disjunctions—a *diagram* or schema for an immediate, action-oriented, energizing, and empowering experience. Again, the process, as discussed by Deleuze and Guattari in several works, consists of *translating* all seemingly "natural," "organic" socio-linguistic structures into assemblages and *dismantling* them in the same move (*K* 47). That is, any perceptual or cognitive dimensions of this process immediately translate into energy discharges inducive of an action-oriented state of becoming. (As Deleuze and Guattari put it, "feelings are introceptive like tools," whereas affects are "projectiles just like weapons," *TP* 400.)

2.3   Humour, Irony, and the Production of Repression

Let us clarify further what makes Beckett's paradox-based texts accessible and attractive despite their obvious complexity and "difficulty," and how they might broadcast liberatory procedures. Again, Deleuze and Guattari define the paradox not as a contradiction but an *attack on the operating principle behind contradictions* (and, by implication, hierarchies). In Deleuze's assessment in the earlier *Logic of Sense*, absurdist language operations generate an "excess" (not a lack) of sense and do not feed into existentialist notions of the absurdity of existence. The same book establishes a sharp contrast between the irony-based perspectives of Platonism, classicism, and romanticism and the humour-based approaches of stoicism, cynicism, and modernity, implicitly correlating existentialism with the *former* series. As Deleuze explains,

> Nonsense and sense have done away with their relation of dynamic opposition in order to enter into the co-presence of a static genesis—as the nonsense of the surface and the sense which hovers over it. The tragic and the ironic give way to a new value, that of humor. For if irony is the co-extensiveness of being with the individual [Plato—my note], or of the I with representation [romanticism], humor is the co-extensiveness of sense with nonsense. Humor is the art of the surfaces and of the doubles ... it is the art of the static genesis, the savoir-faire of the pure event ... with every signification, denotation, and manifestation suspended, all height and depth abolished. (141)

In short, irony operates through disjunction (the core logical operation behind oppositions and reversals), which allows power mechanisms to function and proliferate, thus preserving the hierarchy-based nature of the social machine; in contrast, humour operates through paradoxes—figures of language and thought that, by definition, obstruct attempts to interrupt the flow of affect and thus sabotage machinic processes of subjection, exploitation, and repression.

Deleuze's distinction recalls Adorno's objections to Sartre's representation of the subject and notion of freedom, as briefly discussed in Chap. 1. To bring Adorno and Deleuze's points together, Sartre's *No Exit* didactically represents its characters' fate as a direct consequence of individual "choices," in a traditional psychological framework based in irony and disjunction that does not subvert repression-based socio-historical structures and, as such, follows similar structuring principles as the totalitarian demand.[4] This form of critique can, at best, temporarily reverse disjunctive poles and partially "correct" or "improve" hierarchies. In contrast, Beckett's derelict "creatures" consistently enact the exploitative and repressive effects of machinic disjunctions, rendering grotesque all the hierarchy-based relational modes that failed to prevent or perhaps even paved the way for the catastrophe of genocide, and thus trigger ethical attitudes and actions in readers/ spectators.

Deleuze delineates two laws that govern language and determine sense—a *regressive* law that functions vertically, defining classes/ (sub)categories, and a *disjunctive* law that operates horizontally, separating members/ elements of a category (*LS* 68). Disturbances of these laws produce two types of absurdist excess: "a confusion of formal levels in the regressive synthesis" and "a vicious circle in the disjunctive synthesis" (69).

---

[4] Sartre's character construction in *No Exit* is strikingly linear, disjunction- and irony-based. Granted, some details indicative of socio-political constraints are mentioned (Garcin's execution for his avowed pacifism, Inez's lesbianism, and Estelle's poverty). However, rudimentary disjunctions operate even at this level, stripping characters of individuality and reducing them to "types" in ways that compromise the play's claim to ethical stature (the male intellectual is self-absorbed and ready to walk over dead bodies in his sexual pursuits, the lesbian is sharp but cold and cruel, and the younger woman is vain, self-indulgent, and manipulative in a risibly rudimentary way). On occasion, it is suggested that the characters' interactions are endless rehearsals of the abusive social practices that dominated their lives, but what receives maximum emphasis is their insensitive and exploitative *individual nature*. In depicting these characters as clichéd egotists with hideous personal histories and a penchant for inflicting psychological torture, the play posits their "guilt" as a direct consequence of their choices and any contextual details as background excuses of small consequence. For all its claim to universality captured in Garcin's conclusion, "Hell is other people" ("L'enfer, c'est les autres"), *No Exit* merely offers three unpleasant and somewhat contrived guilty subjects, and its "demonstrative" qualities further weaken its ethical positioning.

Beckett's works are replete with absurdist sabotage of either type, but I shall limit myself to two examples here. When, in *Endgame*, Hamm prays to God (who does not answer) and decides, "The bastard! He doesn't exist"[5] (Beckett, *CDW* 119), a disturbance of the regressive law occurs: the entity named Hamm belongs to a different "class" and lacks the knowledge and ontological status to make such claims concerning the entity named God, so the fact that he does it is a contestation of that classification. When Clov declares he has exterminated "half" (119) of a rat, a disturbance of the disjunctive law occurs—an animate object can be dead or alive (not "half" either way). Clov's word choice can be seen as a paradox-based caustic comment on his own conditions of existence in Hamm's household and in the world. To illustrate what might result from disturbances of the regressive or disjunctive laws—affecting sense ("names" and "classes") or signification (syntactic-semantic-pragmatic composition), respectively—Deleuze further defines four types of paradoxes:

> The paradoxes of signification are essentially that of the *abnormal set* (which is included as a member or which includes members of different types) and that of the *rebel element* (which forms part of a set whose existence it presupposes and belongs to two sub-sets which it determines). The paradoxes of

---

[5] Beckett insisted on preserving this phrase as such in English performances despite resistance from the Lord Chamberlain (Lawrence Lumley, 11th Earl of Scarborough). Several letters reiterate the importance of the phrase, including one dated 5 January 1957 to George Devine, who was meant to direct the London performance at the Royal Court Theatre (*L3* 89), and two dated 9 and 10 January 1958 to Alan Schneider, Beckett's New York director (93–97). In the letter to Devine, Beckett refers to any change as a "grave injury" to his work (89). This was not an authorial whim. Weakening the violence of the phrase might have flattened the paradox-based prayer scene into a mere comedic contradiction (an explicitly ironic comment on Hamm's inadequacy or inflated ego). Beckett needed the word "bastard" because it does not merely express a contradiction but allows us "to be present at the genesis of the contradiction" (Deleuze's definition of the paradox, *LS* 74). Whether it refers to God the father or to Jesus, it is an attack on the basic tenets of religious doctrine (the positing of the former as eternal and the creator of all things and of the latter as his son and earthly representative). Perhaps more importantly, it associates religious authority with illegitimacy and abusive heteronormativity (one can be a "bastard" only within a staunchly patriarchal and heteronormative familial and societal assemblage). In a 7 July 1958 letter to Devine, Beckett concedes that a word like "swine" could replace "bastard" but rejects any change "that will render the line quite inoffensive, i.e., kill it" (*L3* 157). While "swine" does not carry all the connotations of the original choice, it augments the correlation to heteronormativity and adds suggestions of selfishness and (perhaps) malevolence rather than generosity or forgiveness.

sense are essentially that of the *subdivision ad infinitum* (always past-future and never present), and that of the *nomadic distribution* (distributing in an open space instead of distributing a closed space). (*LS* 75)

Even a cursory examination of Beckett's texts can uncover many examples of such paradoxes. I will unpack one example for each type, for clarification, before elaborating on their mobilization of affect.

In *Waiting for Godot*, Vladimir and Estragon, while industriously "waiting," contemplate hanging themselves with at least three suggested aims: passing the time, getting an erection, and/or dying (*CDW* 17–18, 86). This is an *abnormal set*, which "is included as a member or includes members of different types" (*LS* 75)—it consists of elements that either might function as umbrella terms for the rest of the set or could not coexist because they are mutually exclusive/ in other ways incompatible. Through association and disjunction, two groupings emerge: the first two elements (passing the time and getting an erection) on the side of life, in opposition to the third (death); or the last two on the side of intensity and change (solution, energy discharge, change of state) in opposition to a first element of stasis (pointlessness, boredom). If we proceed, instead, through subsumation, other groupings emerge: sexual stimulation and suicide as subcategories of "passing the time"; and passing the time and sexual stimulation as subcategories of acts everyone practices "to death" (in that everyone dies). Whichever the ordering principle, the set remains dysfunctional, as it consists of elements of irreconcilable rank or degree of generality. Two competing associative moves seem possible, and the first and last elements could *each in turn* serve as subsumations of the others. This is not a *lack* of logic but an *excess* of competing and irreconcilable logical operations forging powerful conceptual and affective disruptions. Significantly, even apart from the sophisticated specifics of this disruptive exercise in logical excess, this "abnormal set" places, between life and death, an erect penis—perhaps another mockery of "neo-transcendentalisms" but certainly a disdainful and empowering gesture recognizable as such by anyone whose personal experiences include confrontations with institutional indifference (natural disasters) or cruelty (totalitarian state structures, war, etc.).

Upon first meeting Vladimir and Estragon in Act I, Pozzo offers to entertain them by forcing Lucky to perform. The list of options—"What do you prefer? Shall we have him dance, or sing, or recite, or think, or—" (*CDW* 37)—illustrates the paradox of the *rebel element*, which "forms part of a set whose existence it presupposes and belongs to two subsets which it determines" (*LS* 75). To unpack this definition, the rebel element *presupposes the existence of a set*, but the set does not exist in that element's absence; concurrently, the element creates an artificial, absurd, "excessive" connection between two irreconcilable sets. The verb "think" serves this double function. The other verbs in the series define subcategories of *performance*. Thinking is typically considered an activity of a different "class." Several functional oppositions support this disjunction: mind/ body, private/ public, individual/ collective, essence/ appearance, and so on. In forcing the rebel element "think" into the series, Beckett's text attacks this disjunction, denouncing the machinic character of all human activities. Thinking, in other words, is a social performance, like everything else— one of the many aspects of the subject's coupling to the social machine (as Pozzo explains, Lucky "used to think very prettily once" and "can't think without his hat," *CDW* 37, 39). Thinking, too, is under the control of masters, as Pozzo's frequent jerking of the rope emphatically illustrates. The rebel element destabilizes the social machine by denouncing a powerful and carefully concealed machinic lure: the convenient heroic-masculinist fable whereby exploitation and repression do not incontrovertibly afflict consciousness (see Camus's "happy" Sisyphus).

The many functions of the word "tomorrow" in *Waiting for Godot* illustrate the paradox of *subdivision ad infinitum*, defined by Deleuze as "always past-future and never present" (*LS* 75). Throughout the play, Vladimir and Estragon are waiting for Godot, who has promised to meet them "tomorrow." The events in the two acts occur on different days, but contradictory information is provided as to which days specifically. According to the stage directions, the tree has no leaves in Act I (*CDW* 10) but exhibits "three or four" on the "next day," in Act II (52). The characters appear to have no means of keeping time. Vladimir and Estragon can vaguely recollect having experienced similar events before, and Vladimir becomes increasingly angry at other characters' refusal to acknowledge that. Still, they continue to wait for Godot and plan their time while waiting—towards the end of Act I, they agree to bring a piece of rope "tomorrow," to improve on their suicide exercise, and at the end of Act II, they decide to bring a "good" piece of rope (50, 86). While this continual postponement of the end point may empty the present of substance, it also empties the future of apocalyptic weight, as both the notions of threat and salvation are trivialized by associating the perpetual "tomorrow," concomitantly, with Godot's arrival and/or a better erection and/

or a better chance at suicide. The same elusive "tomorrow" denounces religious discourse as another means to entrap subjects into detrimental forms of social integration: Godot, whose name ostentatiously references but does not quite name God, is depicted as a cross between a bureaucrat (he needs to "consult" his family, agents, correspondents, books, bank account, etc. before offering anyone employment, *CDW* 19) and an abusive land owner (he beats the boy who minds the sheep, as the boy's supposed brother confesses, 48).[6]

Finally, Pozzo's movements within the arid universe of *Waiting for Godot* and Hamm's travels with his chair around the room in *Endgame* illustrate the paradox of *nomadic distribution*, which involves "distributing in an open space instead of distributing a closed space" (*LS* 75). In his first conversation with Vladimir and Estragon, Pozzo claims that they are waiting on his land and implies that his house is at least six hours away (*CDW* 23). During their second meeting, as Vladimir asks, "Where do you go from here?", a blind and confused Pozzo answers, "On!" (81). Hamm abandons himself to the same megalomanic impulse in forcing Clov to push his chair around the room, insisting, "hug the walls, and then back to center again!" and claiming to be going "[r]ight round the world" (104). These scenes betray Pozzo and Hamm's exploitative streak, as their explorations and territorializations occur through the painfully visible—excessive, grotesque—efforts of others (Lucky and Clov). These paradoxical exercises discredit imperialist legitimating discourses—specifically, the use of "exploration" as a machinic tagline advertising openness and benevolence while coupling new territories to the exploitative imperial machine.

Such paradox-based constructs prompt us to register both our everyday social experiences and their mediation through language as process-based

---

[6] Beckett was generally averse to univocal readings of his characters/ settings and particularly irritated by interpretive attempts to equate Godot with a benevolent but absent God. In Chap. 1, I quoted two such examples: "I also told Richardson that if by Godot I meant God I would [have] said God, and not Godot" (letter to Barney Rosset, 18 October 1954, *L2* 507) and "If his [Godot's] name suggests the heavens, it is only to the extent that a product for promoting hair growth can seem heavenly. ... Others, more fortunate, will see in him Thanatos" (letter to Carlheinz Caspari, 25 June 1953, *L2* 391). Beckett's abrasive comments are not surprising. Besides reducing the play's multipronged attack on institutional power to little more than a clichéd religious meditation, such searches for univocal correspondences betray a desire to tame Beckett's linguistic "excess" and forcibly inscribe his works into the more familiar and less unsettling traditions of realism and naturalism or symbolism and expressionism—something Beckett resented.

and purpose-oriented *products*—more specifically, products generated by "statement-producing machinic assemblages" (*TP* 35) more likely to pursue prescriptive and repressive goals than merely transmit information (language as a vehicle for "order words" apt to elicit acts and "instantaneous incorporeal transformations," 78–80).[7] Beckett's paradoxical staging of human interactions makes this repressive function of language manifest in countless ways, on multiple levels—from the linguistic exchange strictly speaking to imagery, symbolic associations, or performance (as I elaborate later, theatricality is a significant attribute of Beckett's *fiction*, too). Again, as Deleuze and Guattari argue in the book on Kafka and as discussed earlier in this chapter, such "translations" of the repressive-machinic character of language can cause component statements to be perceived as immediately collective matters and implicitly also translate "the subject" (stable, individual, localizable, and beneficially integrated into the social machine) into a fuzzy, shifting psychosomatic formation forced into focus, shape, and position at the intersection of various repressive assemblages (Oedipal, economic, social, etc.) and performing social connectivity "on strings." Given their collective dimension, paradox-based discourses "necessarily [act] on semiotic flows, material flows, and social flows simultaneously" (22), sabotaging machinic attempts to use language to interrupt flows of affect and thus neutralize the threat of "becoming" (change). This attack on the pretense of organicity routinely put on by socio-linguistic assemblages always erupts flamboyantly at the level of language, but its primary target is more basal than one might assume. The sophisticated conceptualization of *production* in Deleuze and Guattari's works can help us to unpack this process.

According to Deleuze and Guattari, technical and socio-political machines function *and maintain their relevance and their control* through the same composite process of production. First, in addition to producing *products*, they produce *production* (i.e., the means of perpetuating the process of production) and "miraculating" effects (*AO* 11)—ways to camouflage their products and activities as givens of experience, *naturalizing* them in ways that preclude questioning. At the level of capital, this trans-

---

[7] Deleuze and Guattari define "instantaneous incorporeal transformations" as the immediate acquiring of a socially assigned *attribute* unaccompanied by immediately noticeable corporeal modifications, offering as examples the transformation of a child into an adult, under the law, at a certain age, or of a plane passenger into a hostage during a hijacking (*TP* 80–81).

lates into Marx's contention that the capitalist mode of production per-petuates itself through workers' *alienation* or *estrangement* (Entfremdung) from the products of their labour/ the act of producing a product/ them-selves as human producers. In a larger socio-cultural context, this "natu-ralization" of production determines the internalization of countless socio-linguistic constructs (active, in-process, adaptive structures of cap-ture) as either innocuous or incontrovertible *data* of experience. There are, however, two more components to the process of production: the *production of consumption* at the end of a *production of recording*.

Deleuze and Guattari define one of the revelations brought about by the schizo's dismantling of disjunctive laws as follows:

> the glaring, sober truth that resides in delirium is that there is no such thing as relatively independent spheres or circuits: production is immediately con-sumption and a recording process (*enregistrement**), without any sort of mediation, and the recording process and consumption directly determine production, though they do so within the production process itself. Hence everything is production: *production of productions*, of actions and of pas-sions; *productions of recording processes*, of distributions and of co-ordinates that serve as points of reference; *productions of consumptions*, of sensual plea-sures, of anxieties, and of pain. (*AO* 4)

This translator's note accompanies the passage above in the English edi-tion: "The French term *enregistrement* has a number of meanings, among them the process of making a recording to be played back by a mechanical device (e.g., a phonograph), the recording so made (e.g., a phonograph record or a magnetic tape), and the entering of births, deaths, deeds, mar-riages, and so on, in an official register" (4). It is at this level—of the recording—that Deleuze and Guattari identify a way to block the machines' repressive establishment of an immovable state of "nature," and that is because, in participating in the immediate (unmediated) connection between the production of production and that of consumption, the level of recording constitutes the place of articulation of both language and the subject as fundamentally *unstable* entities re-formed, much like an elec-tronic application, with each update. As Deleuze and Guattari explain, "something of the order of a *subject* can be discerned on the recording surface" (16)—a "strange subject" lacking a fixed identity, "wandering about over the body without organs, but always remaining peripheral to the desiring-machines, being defined by the share of the product it takes for itself, garnering here, there, and everywhere a reward in the form of a becoming or an avatar, being born of the states that it consumes and being reborn with each new state" (*AO* 16). To return briefly to "Enough," the female character who experienced the heterosexual relationship described there is not identical to the character-narrator who, in recording the relationship, denounces its abusive/ pathological nature. As the process of recording incrementally transforms into one of denunciation, the character-narrator extricates her past pain, finally recognized/ recorded as such, from a patriarchal economy of "functional," "organic" sacrifice—and, with every discrete move, experiences successive states of empowerment and regeneration, themselves "recorded" in the incisiveness of her discourse.

From the point of view of our analysis, three aspects are paramount in Deleuze and Guattari's discussion of production in general, and of the production of recording in particular: that language and the subject are coextensive, as both (are made to) coagulate at the level of the recording; that both language and the subject are unfixed, fluctuant, insofar as they have not yet been infected with coupling switches meant to insert them into "organic" processes of production and transform them into fully functioning (read: fully captured) "organisms"; and that, given the *direct* (unmediated), conjoined manifestation of all levels of production once the process is launched, sabotaging the level of the recording halts or hijacks (all levels of) production. These aspects account for the direct and basal manner in which paradoxes may impact affect, as it is on the level of the recording—the most elementary structural level possible, from the point of view of subject formation—that they most decisively act. In stripping bare and de-naturalizing the order of language, they implicitly expose the disjunctive switches that allow the social machine to couple itself to the body, thus forcing the subject to perceive what the machines are trying to hide: precisely how bodies are "subjectified" by being *captured* in a state of being (rather than becoming) and *forcibly positioned* in the "proper" ("natural") place. While the social machine can "program" both language and the subject at the level of the recording—obviously, without the subject's *conscious* contribution, since this operative level structurally predates the fully functioning subject—the paradox *reverses this process* in a mobilization of affect that is, itself, immediate and independent of fully developed and consciously registered processes of "understanding." Vladimir and Estragon's pursuit of suicide *and/or* erections is an example.

I proposed, in Chap. 1, that readers/ spectators of any socio-cultural background and degree of literary expertise ever exposed to repression, confinement, or loss would easily register this play's paradox-based enactment of suicide (and perspective on the bearing of self-determination on the meaning and value of life) as an attack on the social order and on language as its main enforcement tool—since the proscription of suicide is a cross-cultural notion that invariably supports established social structures and the discourses that endorse them. "Honour suicide" notions serve similar functions. Injunctions of this nature—attempts to remove individuals' control over their most basic biological functions—act as "switches" safeguarding the subject's coupling to the social machine, offering it consistency at the expense of freedom. Deleuze and Guattari do not explain this phenomenon as a simple case of "false consciousness" but shift the focus of suspicion from individuals' perception to the *object of their perception*—which is, in their view, a *perceivable*, albeit illusory, product of the social machine (a machinic decoy):

> Society constructs its own delirium by recording the process of production; but it is not a conscious delirium, or rather is a true consciousness of a false movement, a true perception of an apparent objective movement, a true perception of the movement that is produced on the recording surface. (*AO* 10)

Vladimir and Estragon's ostentatious pursuit of death and/or erections sabotages this form of machinic deceit, as it makes obvious instead, on the recording surface, the clockwork movement of the repressive switch—implicitly preventing it from covertly executing its containment function within the machinic process of configuration (production) of the subject.

In sabotaging the production of subjection, paradox-based textual constructs implicitly produce empowering effects. In rendering grotesque all the machinic coupling modes that support our subordination and repression, they denounce machinic production as a *process* that can be sustained or suspended, implicitly blocking the machinic production of "miraculating" effects (*AO* 11) aimed at camouflaging machinic operations as incontrovertible *data* of human nature and experience. Paradox-based discourses thus generate powerful flows of affect rather than momentary states of release. Their attack on machinic means of producing repression offers a *diagram* of a *reproducible* process of removal of repression leading to a state of self-determination that is collective (shared) and accessible rather than remaining an elitist ideal forever beyond reach. Beckett's recurrent paradox-based attacks on the equivalencies and oppositions, similarities and differences, conjunctions and disjunctions that structure our socio-linguistic subordination and repression continually project, strengthen, and illuminate this pathway. The peculiar humour inherent to paradox-based textual constructs is, thus, radically new and utterly corrosive in relation to traditional (religious or philosophical) "revelations," and its liberating power derives from effects best described as *horrific-comic*. The paradox does not promise peace of mind or redemption—on the contrary, it renders such promises (and the implicit/ explicit demands placed on the subject in return) grotesque, denouncing the deceit and cruelty at their core. The means to escape hopelessness that it articulates is radically different: it suspends the "grid" whereby pleasure and plenitude are distributed hierarchically to the haves and have-nots by de-naturalizing the assumption that change/ pleasure can be attained strictly by subjecting others to subordination and exploitation, humiliation and pain. In denouncing all forms of subordination and abuse as *conservative* systemic processes, paradox-based constructs implicitly also enact, in ways that are impossible to ignore, the inscription of abusive practices constitutive of repressive social assemblages (Oedipal, capitalist, fascistic, etc.) into the subject, horrifically emphasizing the subject's active participation in their proliferation. This horrific dimension remains, however, action-oriented and positive rather than paralysing, as it is consistently used to fuel an attack on the countless switches that activate the production of pain, exploitation, and repression at various levels within the socio-historical machine.

2.4   THE PARADOX AND HETERONORMATIVE RULE (MALE *OR… OR… OR…*)

Paradox-based discourses translate subordination, abuse, exploitation, and repression into machinic ruses—mechanisms meant to "plug" everyone (from the bottom to the top of any hierarchy) into place. Their political import is magnified by their *contagious* nature. Paradoxes infect any discourse or process to which they couple themselves with a potential for "becoming" (transformation) by forcibly releasing collective flows of affect previously interrupted by machinic switches on any dried hierarchical attachments. As the San Quentin and other episodes discussed in Chap. 1

show, no degree of reification can thwart the abstract machine. Perhaps more significantly, this trait enables paradox-based literary constructs like Beckett's—"writing machines" apt to generate a plane of consistency that can destabilize any plane of machinic organization—to elicit interpreters' participation in a radically new form of power that does not increase through the subordination and exploitation of others but as it is shared (or as others "catch" it, since it is "communicable"—*contagious*). Deleuze and Guattarri use the term "puissance" for this affect-based, immediately collective and anti-hierarchical form of power, in contrast to "pouvoir"—the power of machinic structures (organizational or institutional).

Disenfranchised Vladimir and Estragon attempt to use their meagre "cord" to uncouple themselves from the social machine and express disgust at Pozzo's use of his much better rope to "drive" Lucky. Their Act II attempt to "play at Pozzo and Lucky" (*CDW* 66) is corrosively inadequate, and their disgusted reactions denounce committing abuse as an utterly unattractive form of empowerment. These supposedly insignificant drifters eager to be granted a place in the social machine (they claim that they are "waiting for Godot" for this purpose) prove conspicuously impervious to machinic coupling. Their rejection of abuse and exploitation as viable and satisfactory means of self-assertion acts as an under-the-radar indictment of patriarchal masculinity both in its heteronormative and economic implications—and their ceaseless sabotage of the machinic order is an exhilaratingly positive enactment of reproducible liberatory procedures.

Beckett's enactment of social interactions, both in his drama and in his fiction, through ostentatiously theatrical means bears heavily on this process. Vladimir and Estragon "play at" multiple consecrated practices denoting social connectedness and find them all unfulfilling. Contrastingly, Pozzo and Lucky enact much more grotesque forms of social connectedness but seem unaware of their hideousness. Equally grotesque enactments of social interactions abound in the two sections of *Molloy*. Pozzo's recurrent comments on his "ties" with Lucky constitute a paradox-based construct of the same horrific-comic and burlesque quality as Molloy's meditation on the relation between "love" and "rubbing up against" women. He repeatedly labels "love" a relationship with an older woman whose "peaceful name" he claims not to remember (Ruth? Edith?); he recalls she suffered of lumbago and asked him to penetrate her as she "bent over the couch" but, in hindsight, suspects her of lying; finally, he claims not to be sure exactly where "she put me" and wonders, "But is it true love, in the rectum?" (*M* 56). Molloy enacts faithful adherence to social conventions defining intimacy and connectivity but grotesquely miscalibrates both his acts and their representation. Like Pozzo, Molloy follows, to some extent, machinic patterns of thought, expression, and behaviour, but he also actively exacerbates them because it suits him—because this allows him to use his past and present discontents to mockingly rationalize his own abusive statements and acts as "organic" occurrences.

Such characters' discourse and actions forcibly foreground, through their horrific-comic outrageousness, the production of subjection and repression—complete with its attendant "benefits"—within the social machine. Most importantly, however, Molloy, Pozzo, as well as other Beckettian "creatures" who internalize machinic means to assert power consistently fail to experience fulfilment. There is a marked political dimension to this failure, as it sabotages implicit machinic claims that one can situate oneself on the "pleasure" side of the switch by "distributing" abuse to others. Machinic claims to the presumably beneficial character of individuals' integration into the social "organism" are thus denounced—through countless "excessive" scenarios—as both ferocious and empty. While the social organism promotes abstraction, positivation, beautification, and closure, Beckett's characters consistently fixate on physicality, inability, disease, and hallucinatory permutations in ways too irresistibly horrific-comic not to elicit a response. Their theatrics and theatricality stage the "mechanics" of being human—the switches and shackles noisily attaching themselves to the subject—to mesmerizing and empowering effects. As Mercier's early assessment of *Waiting for Godot* insightfully puts it, in this play "nothing happens, twice" in a way that keeps audience members "glued to their seats" (29–30).

As discussed briefly here and at length in the following chapters, Beckett's attack on traditional forms of power and his articulation of anti-hierarchical forms of empowerment bear immediate social import, as they may significantly impact flows of affect typically regulated by what we could call the patriarchal or heteronormative machine. In addition, they may have a marked impact on flows coupled to corporate capitalist structures—increasingly active in the second half of the twentieth-century and unprecedently controlling today.

Beckett's work with gender remains underexplored in criticism despite the publication of some salient contributions since the 1990s, such as Ben-Zvi's edited collection *Women in Beckett: Performance and Critical Perspectives*, Bryden's *Women in Samuel Beckett's Drama and Prose: Her Own Other*, or Jeffers's *Beckett's Masculinity*. Earlier essays stress Beckett's sympathetic depiction of women and more or less explicit indictment of male abusers in his postwar works, in contrast to the aggressive misogyny of his early prose (the novel *Dream of Fair to Middling Women*, written in English in 1932 and published posthumously in 1992, and the short story collection *More Pricks than Kicks*, written in English and first published in 1934). Jeffers traces in Beckett's postwar character construction a gradual rejection of heteronormativity, in contrast to some markedly misogynistic/ homophobic depictions from earlier works, showing how Beckett's increasingly disruptive staging of gender dichotomies renders traditional masculinity inadequate, if not grotesque. More recently, in conference interventions at the 2018 Modern Languages Association Convention and London Beckett Seminar, Caselli posits an open discussion of "insufferable Beckett" (focusing on elements of misogyny and other problematic aspects often brushed aside as undesirable topics by Beckett scholars) as vital for the field today.

Beckett's critics concur that Belacqua, the main focalizer[8] of Beckett's early fiction, is misogynistic. As Ackerley, Morin, and others note, Belacqua is not depicted sympathetically,[9] yet not all expressions of misogyny in Beckett's early texts can be ascribed to a compromised focalizer—the love letter received by Belacqua from "the Smeraldina" is a counterexample, and Beckett's transparent use of his real-life early love interests as models for Belacqua's raises some ethical questions ("the Smeraldina" seems to be based on Beckett's cousin Peggy Sinclair, who had died of tuberculosis, at the age of 22, the year before *More Pricks than Kicks* was published). There can be little doubt that Beckett's early prose (up to and including *Murphy*, first published in English in 1938) is in many ways problematic

---

[8] This is Genette's term (188) for the textual instance through whose perceptions/ consciousness the story is narrated. Focalizers could be characters, narrators, or both. Focalization is a useful concept in analyzing Beckett's fiction. Beckett often uses focalization through one main character in third-person narration, compound focalization (through more than one textual instance) in free indirect discourse, and so on. In such instances, ignoring the presence of focalization may lead to the erroneous conclusion that all third-person formulations reproduce "Beckett's" views.

[9] In Ackerley's view, Belacqua "neither seeks sympathy, nor makes it easy for the reader to grant it" ("*Lassata Sed*" 61). He is sexually and emotionally immature, keen to advertise his erudition, and politically inept. As Morin notes, he is "a member of the petty bourgeoisie, a class historically swayed by the messages of Fascism and Nazism; he is portrayed as a keen student of Italian, sporting a 'German shirt'" (53). He also enjoys reading the "Moscow notes" from the Evening Herald (the 'twilight Herald' in the text) but buys it mainly "because the paper itself can be put to many domestic uses" (Morin 53).

from the perspective of gender representations, but I would argue that *Watt* brings about a shift more radical than acknowledged so far.

After the war, Beckett exhibited a deep distaste for his early literary productions. He reluctantly authorized new trade editions of *More Pricks Than Kicks* as late as 1970, after years of mounting pressure from Grove Press and Calder and Boyards,[10] and barred the publication of *Dream* during his lifetime. His repudiation of his early texts may have been aesthetically, ideologically, as well as personally motivated. Ackerley persuasively proposes that, in terms of literary allusions and representational conventions, Beckett's early fiction can be described as an attempted pastiche of "a tradition of misogynistic satire running from Juvenal to Chaucer and Burton," ornate with elements of mockery of "the Provençal tradition of the idealized Lady" (*"Lassata Sed"* 56). The dominant mode in the early works is *irony*—a discursive mode which, as discussed at length earlier, given its disjunctive, opposition-based nature, is highly liable to smack of self-indulgence and to perpetuate the hierarchies and modes of subordination and devaluation it purportedly mocks. A marked imbalance in the abrasiveness of these texts' attack on male vs. female characters (a risk magnified by the disjunctive nature of this discursive mode) dominates these texts, as Bryden (*Women*), Jeffers, Caselli, and others rightly note.

From an ideological perspective, Beckett may have gradually become convinced that aggressive heteronormativity had deleterious psychosexual and social effects. Jeffers notes that Beckett quoted from Alfred Adler's 1917 *Neurotic Constitution* in his mid-1930s "Psychology Notes" and underlined the phrase "masculine protest"—Adler's concept of a neurotic reaction-formation in response to a perceived inferiority relative to dominant forms of masculinity (Jeffers 44–46). She also identifies other components of Adlerian theory in the construction of Murphy from the

---

[10] Beckett repeatedly refused a reprint despite having allowed three stories to be published individually. His loathing of the collection is perhaps best expressed in a 20 October 1964 letter to Rosset: "I have broken down half way through galleys of *More Pricks than Kicks*. I simply can't bear it. It was a ghastly mistake on my part to imagine, not having looked at it for a quarter of a century, that this old shit was revivable. I'm terribly sorry, but I simply have to ask you to stop production. I return herewith advance on royalties and ask you to charge to my account with Grove whatever expenses whatever entailed by this beginning of production" (*L3* 633). In his 31 January 1970 letter to Calder, he finally writes that "pressure on all sides has grown so strong, and I so tired, that I capitulate" but again dismisses the story collection as "this juvenilium" and reasserts that the reprint goes "against my wish" (*L4* 221).

eponymous novel. Indeed, starting with *Murphy*, adherence to heteronormativity is increasingly depicted as pathological in Beckett's works, in terms of self-perception as well as relational patterns. The larger scope societal effects of this pathology become increasingly manifest, as well—specifically, through consistent associations with physical violence and totalitarian control. (More on this in the following chapters.)

Finally, while Beckett's early fiction allows for persuasive biographist readings (his characters and narrators are relatively easy to connect to specific life experiences and people he knew, as Knowlson, Jeffers, and others show), Beckett's later "creatures" and the circumstances of their existence become increasingly unrecognizable and disquieting. The "excess" typical of paradox-based discourse—Beckett's dominant mode starting with *Watt*—manifests itself at this level, too. The violence of postwar Beckett's comments on his early texts indicates that he may have come to perceive those fictional engagements with personal experience as contemptibly immature and frivolous—perhaps as an unethically misdirected expression of frustrated masculinist privilege. Beckett's letters and interviews do not offer, to my knowledge, proof that Beckett ever became interested in feminist, gender, or queer theory and activism. However, as I will show, his works starting with *Watt* systematically treat heteronormativity as one of the major repressive components of the socio-historical machine.

While paradox-based engagements with gender do not emerge fully until *Watt* and *Waiting for Godot*, they make a striking first appearance in *Murphy*. The protagonist of this text is in many ways a "very deep young man" in the Belacqua vein (Ackerley uses the phrase for the "poet" from Beckett's 1929 "Assumption," "*Lassata Sed*" 58), and the character Ticklepenny offers a deeply problematic depiction of homosexual masculinity, as Jeffers and others note. Yet, the novel features elements that anticipate major developments in Beckett's postwar works. The depiction and narrative framing of Murphy's rocking chair routine is an example:

> Seven scarves held him in position. Two fastened his shins to the rockers, one his thighs to the seat, two his breast and belly to the back, one his wrists to the strut behind. Only the most local movements were possible. Sweat poured off him, tightened the thongs. The breath was not perceptible. ...
>
> He sat in his chair in this way because it gave him pleasure! First it gave his body pleasure, it appeased his body. Then it set him free in his mind. For it was not until his body was appeased that he could come alive in his mind, as described in section six. And life in his mind gave him pleasure, such pleasure that pleasure was not the word. (*Murphy* 2)

This procedure recalls the schizophrenic's pursuit of the "body without organs"—all biological functions suspended, so as to offer machinic structures no functioning "organ" or part to which they might couple themselves—as defined by Deleuze and Guattari. Murphy uses the chair and the ties as a support system for his suspended, closed-up body—an ostentatious repurposing of a physical aggregate otherwise associated with repression and pain. Sweat pours out, keeping even his skin pores occupied, and his breathing is reduced to a minimum. The section to which we are unceremoniously directed for more clues—"section six"—further clarifies that, for Murphy, any notion of freedom entails removing the body from the equation. Thus, in a "zone" (state) he defines as "dark," Murphy experiences

> nothing but forms becoming and crumbling into the fragments of a new becoming, without love or hate or any intelligible principle of change. Here there was nothing but commotion and the pure forms of commotion. Here he was not free, but a mote in the dark of absolute freedom. He did not move, he was a point in the ceaseless unconditioned generation and passing away of line. (112)

This experience is typically read in Beckett studies as an approximation of death, and Murphy's obsession with it, as a figuration of the death drive. Yet, if we exit the logic whereby pleasure and vitality are fundamentally rooted in the materiality of the flesh, a different reading emerges.

The novel markedly focuses on the mind-body divide/ connection/ philosophical problem *as it applies to Murphy,* and any allusion to/ mockery of received ideas—from the "forms" of Platonism to the Aristotelian first principles and "prime mover," to the Christian doctrine of divine love, to the mind/body articulation in Descartes or Geulincx, to Kant's thing in itself, to Bergson's *élan vital* (*Creative Evolution*), and so on—is formulated specifically and ostentatiously from this perspective:

> Murphy felt himself split in two, a body and a mind. They had intercourse apparently, otherwise he could not have known that they had anything in common. But he felt his mind to be bodytight and did not understand through what channel the intercourse was effected nor how the two experiences came to overlap. He was satisfied that neither followed from the other. He neither thought a kick because he felt one nor felt a kick because he thought one. Perhaps the knowledge was related to the fact of the kick as two magnitudes to a third. Perhaps there was, outside space and time, a

non-mental non-physical Kick from all eternity, dimly revealed to Murphy in its correlated modes of consciousness and extension, the kick *in intellectu* and the kick *in re*. But where then was the supreme Caress? (109)

The narrator keenly notes, "This did not involve Murphy in the idealist tar. There was the mental fact and there was the physical fact, equally real if not equally pleasant" (108). Notably (and humorously), Murphy does not deny the reality of the body or decry its limitations in any given religious or philosophical logic.[11] He simply—personally and subjectively, but in a manner soon to become contagious—finds the body's attendant pleasures *less pleasurable and satisfying* than his "dark" zone experiences. His routine, then, aims to suspend the body alongside the countless philosophical and religious traditions it has been made to carry, as it were, on its back. Murphy's musings and actions seem to indicate he would rather continue to enjoy his routines for which "pleasure is not the word" (2) than terminate them through death. Death drive-focused readings of this novel cannot fully engage with the verve and joy of its mockery of the (openly stated or carefully hidden) primacy of the body within allegedly divergent religious and philosophical traditions. Thus, while later paragraphs clarify that by "kick" the narrative voice means jolt or impulse, that does not render the word choice less corrosive. The suggestion of physical violence does not just ridicule specific philosophical concepts but sardonically reframes both ontological and epistemological idealism—with their language of impulses, jolts, disjunctions, dichotomies, and incompatibilities—as thinking patterns derived from (and indelibly linked to) physically violent patterns of social interaction.

Murphy's means to subtract himself from this purportedly "natural" circuit of kicks and clashes is dangerous because it is *contagious*. His lover Celia—a sex worker all too familiar with the violent economy underlying patriarchal societal beliefs and interactions—appropriates his suspension procedure and adapts it to her needs once their relationship ends in a fight over Murphy's refusal to seek gainful employment. Alone in the room, Celia

---

[11] Feldman, Uhlmann ("Introduction"), Tucker, and others link *Murphy* to some of Geulincx's ideas, as transcribed in Beckett's philosophy notebooks and invoked in discussions and interviews. Still, while for Geulincx the mind-body divide is the expression of divine will and harmony, and care of the body and the propagation of the species are among humans' primary responsibilities (I.II.II.2, "Inspection of Oneself"), Murphy's primary concerns are different, and the comedic structure of the novel undermines any notion of the character's (or Beckett's) "straight" adherence to Geulincx's principles.

got out of her clothes and into the rocking-chair. Now the silence above was a different silence, no longer strangled. The silence not of vacuum but of plenum, not of breath taken but of quiet air. The sky. She closed her eyes and was in her mind with Murphy, Mr. Kelly, clients, her parents, others, herself a girl, a child, an infant. In the cell of her mind, teasing the oakum of her history. Then it was finished, the days and places and things and people were untwisted and scattered, she was lying down, she had no history. (148–49)

Like Murphy, Celia experiences the suspension of her machinic coupling to systems of Oedipal and economic production as pleasure and plenitude, not as nihilistic abandonment. Unlike him, she does not use the "scarves"— as a woman and a sex worker, she would likely experience them as instruments of sexual exploitation and coercion rather than as obstructions of functionality and productivity. Notably, in her floating state, losing Murphy registers as liberation rather than pain: "It was a most pleasant sensation. Murphy did not come back to curtail it" (149). Warmth and empathy mark the narrative framing of Celia's rocking chair experience and her character construction in general. Conversely, Murphy—in a sexually and economically less threatened position, as a man and the beneficiary of financial help from a Dutch uncle (16)—is framed as self-indulgent, insensitive, and hurtful in dismissing Celia's economic concerns. While many elements in the figuration of the couple function in a reversal-based, ironic mode, as a pastiche of romanticized representations of the "genius" and the "kind-hearted whore," the rocking chair procedure and, especially, the particulars of Celia's engagement in it eerily disrupt that pattern. These disruptions anticipate the more complex anti-heteronormative procedures present in later works, such as Watt and Sam's "dance" within the barbed wire enclosure in *Watt* or Winnie's enactment of traditional femininity in *Happy Days*, analysed in detail in the following chapters.

A major aspect of Beckett's work with gender that does not emerge until the paradox-based *Watt* and *Waiting for Godot* is the role of non-compliance/ false compliance and anger in the representation of gendered attitudes and interactions. Beckett scholars have consistently read the non-compliance of Beckett's "creatures"—in *Not I* and *The Unnamable*, for instance—as the result of a physical or psychological *inability* to integrate socially and/or overcome trauma. In this reading, such characters are sympathetic *victims* of socio-cultural conditioning in general, and gender-based conditioning in particular—a process that may or may not have involved physical and/or sexual violence—and their anger, if at all acknowledged, is a further paralysing symptom of their inabilities. In contrast, I show that Beckett' paradox-based texts support a more positive reading of non-compliance and anger as action- and change-oriented psychosomatic modes apt to prevent the characters' full patriarchal capture and to prompt the development of action-oriented, solidarity-based affects in readers/ spectators.

To date, no critical reading has centred on anger as a major determinant in Beckett's works, with the exception of a recent article by Russell Smith on Moran's section of *Molloy*. Smith persuasively sets up his argument by pointing out that Beckett's claims, in letters and interviews, concerning the emotional intensity of his works have been systematically ignored by critics, who overwhelmingly chose to embrace, instead, Beckett's "proffering of Geulingian quietism as a key to understanding his work" (138). As Smith notes, "if quietism aims at a rationalist mastery of feeling through suspension of the will, the Trilogy involves a steady and remorseless intensification of it, so that it is hard to reconcile Geulincx's doctrine of complete submission to the will of God—'Ubi nihil vales, ibi nihil velis'—with the Unnamable's defiant raging against his 'college of tyrants'" (138). Smith references Fisher and Sloterdijk's recent philosophical attempts to counter the "pathologization of rage in modern Western culture" and "restore to rage its ethical and psychological dignity" (139), connecting these theorists' work to Aristotle's definition of anger as an essential component of virtue in *The Nicomachean Ethics*: being "angry at the right things and with the right people," at the appropriate intensity, when, and for as long as one ought to be (Aristotle, qtd. in Smith 139). However, his focus, in his close reading of Beckett's *Molloy*, is not on delineating positive mobilizations of anger but on exploring, through Moran's character, a specific type of (negative, pathological) neurotic response—the Adlerian "masculine protest." Smith then extrapolates his argument to *Molloy, Malone Dies*, and *The Unnamable* in their entirety, suggesting that the three texts should be read as an expression of "a self-assertion concentrated to the point of its own self-destruction," "the epic of a heroic, impersonal, implacable, and liberated rage" (145). Smith persuasively delineates, in these novels, an attempt to thematize and dramatize negative deviations from the positive, healthy forms of anger theorized by Aristotle. However, while I share Smith's interest in evincing the "political potential and critical value" of representing negative emotions

(Smith 142), my analysis of *Molloy*, *Malone Dies*, and *The Unnamable* (and of Beckett's postwar works, in general) is more concerned with exploring *positive* and more explicitly political mobilizations of anger that are *not* strictly neurotic displacements.

In my reading, the presence of negative emotions in Beckett's works generally inscribes itself into a larger-scope *positive* mobilization of anger largely unacknowledged in Beckett studies. I find Beckett's characters' neurotic displacements too systematic and ostentatious to function as raw, unprocessed expressions of instincts or drives. Instead, they are more or less consciously used by the characters who display them in order to justify their abuse of others or to give a less risky expression to their protestations against Oedipal / social / economic confinement and repression. Repressive socio-economic assemblages systematically and abusively read protestations of whatever order as neurotic displacements as a means to marginalize and control the unruly. However, those systemic means of control are invariably derailed in Beckett's texts through *diagrammatic* procedures (contagious, collective, and reproducible) like Vladimir and Estragon's destabilizing and solidarity-building suicide exercise.

Smith rightly identifies "irritation" (one of the "ugly feelings" discussed by Sianne Ngai in her eponymous volume) as Moran's defining emotion. However, Moran is one of Beckett's most repulsive characters— he lacks all the redeeming qualities displayed, say, by Molloy or Malone, as he is constantly preposterous but never funny, conceited but far less intelligent than he thinks, and manipulative without ever being persuasive. Molloy, Malone, and the speaker(s) from *The Unnamable* display a much wider emotional range, as well as more complex and obviously political expressions of anger, as my analysis in Chap. 4 will show.

Finally, Smith's analysis focuses mostly on momentary bouts of uncontrollable emotion, whereas the expressions of anger I am interested in exploring are more consistent, deliberate, and controlled—corresponding to a self-aware political mobilization of affect rather than a self-indulgent determination to "enjoy one's symptom" (to quote Žižek's famous phrase). In Chaps. 3 and 4, I use some elements of Fisher and Sloterdijk's revaluation of anger and rage to articulate what I hope will be a more comprehensive analysis of the political uses of anger in Beckett's paradox-based texts.

2.5 THE SCHIZOPHRENIC'S STICK AND THE CORPORATE BODY

As briefly suggested in the previous subsection, the experience of empowerment made possible by the paradox might also prove increasingly relevant in today's context of global ascension of *corporate* capitalist models and replacement of the world dominance of a few major nation-states with multinational corporate rule. As I show here and in subsequent chapters, Beckett's obsessive representation of exploitative relations in his works can be translated with uncanny ease into contemporary concerns related to increasingly totalizing means of corporate control of the labour force, labour legislation, and all aspects of the economy worldwide.

Historically, corporations have posited themselves as organically modelled structures of socio-economic cohesion (Lat. *Corpus* = human body, structure, or matter)—social aggregates apt to reconcile multiple human/ social interests (those of employers, employees, and various governing/ administrative bodies). However, in practice, corporate state structures have often served as conservative state-level managerial responses to the threat of progressive thinking and action.[12] For instance, Mussolini's Council of Corporations forcefully coupled all social strata to the fascist state machine under the guise of facilitating wide socio-economic representation. Today's corporate lobbying groups attempt to sell multinational for-profit corporations' growing influence on various countries' labour legislation and economic policies as indispensable in ensuring global economic growth and cooperation. However, Krugman, Piketty, and many others see this development as causing steepening economic divides and threatening the democratic process—their analyses of economic data indicate that corporate allowances (reduced taxation of corporate profits, deregulations, etc.) consistently sharpen exploitation and income inequality rather than stimulate wage growth or even, generally, economic growth. Hardt and Negri—previously hopeful that for-profit multinational corporations' exploitative practices might unwittingly generate liberatory potential, given their constitutive need to distribute knowledge in their pursuit of innovation—now consider corporations perhaps more responsible than institutions like the family or the nation for the "corruption" of the revolutionary drive of the "multitude" (*Commonwealth* 160–63).

---

[12] For a detailed discussion of corporate history and varieties of corporatism, see Williamson.

Deleuze and Guattari's theorization of social assemblages and of the corrosive work of paradox-based literary and artistic constructs aptly explicates the damaging power dynamic propagated socially by corporations and suggests means of resistance unattached to physically violent materializations of affect. Furthermore, Beckett's consistent construction of "social organisms" eerily akin to corporate structures may offer, yet again, powerful liberatory *diagrams.*

Deleuze identifies the profit-driven corporation as a quintessential component of the new "societies of control" that started to coagulate in the early twentieth-century and consolidated after World War II—more insidiously exploitative socio-economic structures apt to remodel all aspects of social living, altering to an unprecedented degree individuals' self-perception and ability to experience authentic forms of connectedness such as solidarity. While "the factory was a body that contained its internal forces at the level of equilibrium, the highest possible in terms of production, the lowest possible in terms of wages" ("Postscript" 4) and offered "bonuses" to spur competition and flaunt systemic fairness, the corporation uses the more damaging systemic lure of a "salary according to merit" to preclude resistance to unfairly low wages by maintaining each member of its labour force both disconnected from the plight of others *and internally divided*:

> the corporation works more deeply to impose a modulation of each salary, in states of perpetual metastability that operate through challenges, contests, and highly comic group sessions. ... The factory constituted individuals as a single body to the double advantage of the boss who surveyed each element within the mass and the unions who mobilized a mass resistance; but the corporation constantly presents the brashest rivalry as a healthy form of emulation, an excellent motivational force that opposes individuals against one another and runs through each, dividing each within. (4–5)

The distinction Deleuze and Guattari make between *machinic enslavement* and *social subjection* may illuminate the implications of this definition. Machinic enslavement—a repressive structure traceable to archaic imperial formation—implies treating humans as (component) machines, alongside animals or tools, whereas regimes of social subjection grant humans the status of *users* of tools/ animals/ machines (*TP* 456–57). In Deleuze and Guattari's view, capitalism—a "worldwide enterprise of subjectification"—technically inscribes itself in the latter category (457) but has recently started to forge a conjunction between the two through such moves as generalized automation and overwhelming control over employees/ customers' personal lives:

> a small amount of subjectification took us away from machinic enslavement, but a large amount brings us back to it. ... [M]odern power is not at all reducible to the classical alternative "repression or ideology" but implies processes of normalization, modulation, modeling, and information that bear on language, perception, desire, movement, etc., and which proceed by way of microassemblages. This aggregate includes both subjection and enslavement taken to extremes, as two simultaneous parts that constantly reinforce and nourish each other. (458)

Profitable conjunctions between social subjection and machinic enslavement are common practice for today's multinational corporations. Their employment practices in wealthier countries with a longer democratic tradition compared to lower-income countries offer a clear example. "Outsourcing" raises profits not just through the exploitation of workers in lower-income states with lax labour and safety legislation but also by pressuring unions and individuals in higher-income democracies to accept lower or stagnant salaries/ benefits and increased workloads for fear of *more* outsourcing. Outsourcing and the erosion of workers' rights in higher-income democracies thus "reinforce and nourish each other," in Deleuze and Guattari's inspired phrase. Multinational corporations' branding and reputation management machines assure us that there are positive global effects to outsourcing, as well, such as increased communication between nations, more access to consumer goods, and a faster circulation of information and innovations. However, this is not a balancing act—corporate power continually attempts to increase machinic enslavement at the level of socio-economic practice while inflating its yearly production of global creativity and well-being at the level of discourse. (To no surprise, the phrase commonly used to designate this process is of technical/ machinic inspiration: "leveraging social media for business.")

Again, historically and by definition, corporations have claimed adherence to principles of organic functioning in reconciling the needs of employers, employees, and the state—and, in the early stages of coagulation of corporate power, a measure of care for the public interest was, no doubt, indispensable in order for this fiction of organicity to grow roots and begin to attract socio-economic allowances. However, matters unsurprisingly evolved towards today's reduction of that concern to an empty advertising slogan. Today's multinational corporations—profit-driven machines that *feign* organic functioning strictly because it is profitable to do so—are the logical consequence of the initial premise on which corporate power was built (a trend insightfully captured by Deleuze's theorization of "societies of control" and by Deleuze and Guattari's language of assemblages and machinic power). They champion "doing more with less"—a seemingly ethical positioning if we relate it strictly to saving energy and raw materials, reducing/ recycling waste, increasing miniaturization, and reducing physical labour through automation, developments with undeniable environmental and quality-of-life benefits. However, in terms of labour practice, "more with less" typically means layoffs, increased workloads unaccompanied by commensurate compensation, the erosion of full-time employment and benefits packages, and union-busting legislative lobbying—even in prosperous, economically stable democratic countries and across economic sectors (from manufacturing to education). To continually increase profits, contemporary corporations also routinely engage in horrific-comic forms of micromanagement, from continually decreasing employees' workspaces (small, exposed desks in a supposedly "social"—read, noisy—open space are touted as more efficient than individual offices) to monitoring employees' coffee and even washroom breaks (a common practice in call centres). Moreover, they attempt to take over employees' free time by pressuring them to contribute to internal/ external social media networks (time-consuming and generally unpaid activities) and to sign up for team-building/ general socializing events (supposedly meant to support work efficiency and the work-life balance but serving mostly to prompt employees to perceive their professional function as the only measure of their human worth, their work as their life, and their state of subordination as their nature).

Within this new context, Franklin aptly recasts Deleuze's notion of a "control society" in terms of digitalization—"[t]he logic under which social systems are reconceptualized as information-processing systems" (xv). He redefines "control" as "a set of technical principles having to do with self-regulation, distribution, and statistical forecasting," positing it as "the episteme grounding late capitalism" (xv), and claiming that its operating principles of continually increased efficiency in fact institute "a system of value production that can produce profit only by exploiting and dispossessing human life" (xviii). Like Deleuze, Franklin identifies powerful procedures of resistance to the control episteme in Beckett's works. He analyses *Watt*, *Endgame*, and *Quad*, which he persuasively correlates to the "theoretical and technical developments of digital computation carried out by Turing and Shannon in the late 1930s ... concerned with the symbolic formalization of experience into algorithms ('enumeration' and 'combination' rather than propositions and syntactical relations)," "the emergence of programming languages and techniques for analog-digital conversion that introduced human-centered layers over the bare algorithmic processes of computing machinery," and "the development of computer graphics in the late 1960s ... [and] the sociocultural construction of the computer as multimedia machine," respectively (119). In Franklin's assessment, Beckett's Watt is institutionalized because he appears to "internalize machinic logic too fully"—he becomes "purely analytical and recursive" rather than productive in his "capture, processing, and communication of data" (124). What Franklin seems to identify here, and what Beckett's human assemblages invariably seem to produce, is a *reductio ad absurdum*—a type of demonstration used in logic and mathematics to invalidate a premise by exposing its less apparent logical/ mathematical implications. (The logical/mathematical opposite of that premise, within the predefined context, is thus proved correct.) Watt's evolution demonstrates—scientifically!—that machinic logic, which may usefully apply to *some* aspects of life, becomes a force against life if given full control over human ecology.

Another text that illustrates Beckett's consistently political use of the *reductio ad absurdum* is "The Lost Ones," commonly read as a take on the unconscious or as an example of Beckett's move towards "exhaustion" and "abstraction" in his late works, but which enacts functional notions of closeness and connectivity in ways that may derail interpreters' acceptance of corporate social assemblages as beneficially constituted, nourishing "organisms." Abbott notes the "stifling inhumanity of engineered lives" in this text, reading it as a general critique of technology (*Beckett Writing Beckett* 138). Welchman comes closer to my argument in seeing a connection to the economic in the text, but for him, too, the threat derives from technological advancement ("machines"—literally): the story enacts the "dissolution of the social under the impact of the economic" through its organization around "a series of terms oriented rhetorically around the concept of the machine: rationalization (Weber); calculation and *technē* (Heidegger); dehumanization" (214). Dowd acknowledges more assuredly the disruptive nature of this text in claiming, in an interpretive framework also derived from Deleuze and Guattari, that it "configures a machinic edifice which on one level stages the human as it interfaces with a cybernetic dystopian terminus" but, on other levels, "provides the immanent conditions for a literary abstract machine" (*Abstract Machines* 127). In my view, the argument can be taken further. While Beckett most likely did not intend the story specifically as an indictment of corporate economic structures, his "cylinder," with its 200 barely human inhabitants (one per square metre), is eerily apt to make obvious the absurdity of corporate demands for a continual application of "more with less" measures.

Beckett's "searchers," who climb ladders to explore "niches and tunnels" and "settle standing" for determined intervals at "level[s] of their choice" (*CSP* 209), follow rules that ensure no one is, at any point, entirely idle. Their oppressive closeness and grotesque "search" dynamic may eerily evoke, for readers, corporate structures like the generally parasitic "outbound" call centre or the more recently emerged e-commerce warehouse. Depictions of the environment and of the rules governing the inhabitants' patterns of movement and behaviour are marked by ostentatious redundancies, scandalous understatements, corrosive explanations, and suspicious caveats. Despite the overwhelmingly industrious character of this generalized "search," its most prominent products, as foregrounded in the text, are *subjection and repression*. This is fully confirmed as the text approximates, towards the end, the progression of this social machine to a stage of total consumption of its human "units," with only *one* climber still active, and ostentatiously connects this final stage to the beginning: "So much roughly speaking for the last state of the cylinder and of this little people of searchers one first of whom if a man in some unthinkable past for the first time bowed his head if this notion is maintained" (223). The iconic image of the bent head, related by Deleuze and Guattari to the idea of blocked, neutralized desire (*K* 3–6), accurately and damningly sums up the functioning logic of this machine, whose purportedly productive and beneficial mobilization of its human units ultimately leads them to exhaustion and dejection.

While not explicitly engaged with corporate or other specific forms of repression and capture, many descriptive passages may horrific-comically evoke, for readers, in the "excessive" manner typical of paradox-based discourses, any number of systemic practices of abuse/ exploitation, from corporate relations (as discussed above) to patriarchal psychosexual violence to, perhaps, racial othering and persecution, exposing their aggregate nature. For instance, climbers and searchers are consistently referenced through masculine singular pronominal forms (he/ him/ his)—and the caveat "if a man" is used, conspicuously, only in the last paragraph, where it appears three times (*CSP* 223), which emphasizes its absence in the rest of the story rather than offering clarification. "The vanquished" and "the sedentary," however, are consistently referenced through non-gender-specific plural pronominal forms, and on the rare occasions when women are mentioned (222, 223), they are part of these groups. Physical/ sexual abuse and exploitation are not as much forbidden as carefully regulated:

> Some searchers there are who join the climbers with no thought of climbing and simply in order to inspect at close hand one or more among the vanquished or the sedentary. *The hair of the woman vanquished has thus many a time been gathered up and drawn back and the head raised and the face laid bare and whole front of the body down to the crutch.* The inspection once completed *it is usual* to put everything carefully back in place as far as possible. *It is enjoined* by certain ethics not to do onto others what coming from them might give offence. This percept *is largely observed* in the cylinder in so far as it does not jeopardize the quest which would clearly be a mockery if in case of doubt *it were not possible* to check certain details. Direct action with a view to their elucidation *is generally reserved* for the persons of the sedentary and vanquished. Face or back to the wall these normally offer but a single aspect and so *may have to be turned* the other way. (221–22, my emphasis)

This is not an abstracted meditation on human relations but a paradox-based indictment of exploitation and abuse as core aspects of heteronormative socialization and perhaps of traditional notions of social "cohesion" in general. The typical "inspection" of "the woman vanquished" is described in terms explicitly indicative of physical and sexual abuse (see the first emphasized fragment). Next comes a conspicuous series of overbearing understatements (ostentatiously set up through impersonal or passive voice verbs) likely to recall justifications of abuse and exploitation we might associate with any number of discrimination-based societal/ state structures.

Critical contributors noted potential references to Nazi camps in this piece, especially in the bureaucratic and dehumanizing description of the "vanquished"; connected the phrase "if a man" to Primo Levi's *If This Is a Man*; and read the delineated "zones" as a reference to Levi's "grey zone" of contagious moral impurity from *The Drowned and the Saved* (Weber-Caflisch 41–43; Rabaté, "Beckett et la poésie de la zone" 80–85; Jones; Katz, "What Remains" 145–46). US segregation laws and the use of the slogan "I Am a Man" in 1968 civil rights demonstrations could also make the list of potential allusions here.[13] I would also add that passages

---

[13] I am grateful to the Palgrave reader for suggesting this connection.

like the one cited above eerily resonate with contemporary realities such as the US "stop and search" laws,[14] the likelihood of harsher legal charges/ sentences for the poor and for people of colour,[15] or the attempt to justify the use of torture in countries otherwise supposedly observant of human rights (see the clarification that "inspections" are reserved for the "sedentary and vanquished" and the gruff aside that "the quest" would be jeopardized and rendered a mockery if intrusive inspections were prohibited). Again, this is not because Beckett "anticipated" such practices or meant to address them specifically but because his paradox-based texts approach exploitation, repression, and abuse in a *diagrammatic* manner. Perhaps this is what dramatist Suzan-Lori Parks hinted at when she said of Beckett, in an interview with Stevens, "he just seems so black to me." Machinic structures couple, use, and abuse us in overwhelmingly various ways, but their functioning processes are always guided by disjunctive switches—and it is at this level that Beckett's "abstract machine" operates, inviting those exposed to it (readers/ spectators) to experience solidarity in an intersectional manner. Beckett's real-life knowledge of/ exposure to twentieth-century realities such as the Nazi offensive, the French atrocities in Algeria, or the violent discrimination against blacks in South Africa have undoubtedly provided the scaffolding for his diagrammatic work, but the *reach* of a diagram produced by an abstract machine, to quote Deleuze and Guattari again, includes "the entire plane of consistency" (*TP* 11).

Like gender issues, class concerns such as poverty, capitalist exploitation, or emerging corporate structures may not have explicitly made the object of Beckett's comments in interviews and letters, but his financial generosity manifested on a number of documented occasions,[16] and his

[14] The New York Civil Liberties Union reports, based on data obtained from the New York Police Department, that between 2003 and 2017, only 10% of the individuals subjected to "stop and frisk" practices were white, and most of the others were black or Latino.

[15] See, for instance, Martinot's analysis of the American justice and prison system as an apparatus of "re-segregation," with 75% of prison inmates represented by persons of colour, who have "a nine to one chance over whites of being incarcerated" (70).

[16] A series of letters to Djuna Barnes from December 1970 and January 1971 show Beckett offering her financial support upon finding out, from an article he had read, that she was struggling (*L4* 242–44, 247). Several letters reveal his artistic, financial, and logistical support for Rick Cluchey and his theatre group (25 February 1974 to Rick Cluchey, *L4* 360; 17 September 1978 to Jocelyn Herbert from the Royal Court Theatre, *L4* 488–89; 26 February 1987 to Barney Rosset and Note 2 of the letter of the same date to Peter Zeisler from the New York Theatre Communication Group, *L4* 687; etc.). Also see Morin for additional details concerning Beckett's donations.

plays and fiction are filled with disenfranchised, struggling "creatures" whose suffering is always rendered in a solidarity-based fashion, though their actions may receive a different treatment. In the following chapters, I analyse several texts by Beckett that may not have been meant as commentaries on corporate economic or state structures but are eerily apt to make manifest the self-serving character of for-profit corporate discourse and the perils of corporate impositions, as well as broadcast effective procedures of resistance. As my analysis shows, such texts always additionally foreground the aggregate, concerted work of other machinic structures—Oedipal, religious, cultural, and so on—equally invested in and responsible for the socio-historical production of repression. Beckett's "cylinder" is a construct of this nature: from the sinister meticulousness of the descriptions to the ominous structural and phrase-level repetitions, it evinces the artifice and inhumanity of multiple social assemblages that claim to connect, order, and nourish but mostly confine, punish, and use. Beckett's horrific-comic, paradox-based humour bolsters the ceaseless motion and mobility needed so that the *diagram* of halting the production of repression can be effectively broadcast.

CHAPTER 3

The Liberating Laughter of "Nearly There": Beckett's Solidarity-Building Dramas

3.1 "PLAYING AT" SOCIAL PRODUCTIVITY AND INTEGRATION

In *Waiting for Godot*, the five characters present on stage, as well as the obsessively discussed but never shown Godot, are explicitly gendered male (Beckett was adamant on keeping them this way in stage representations[1]) and function within a labour-relations framework (Vladimir and Estragon are "waiting for Godot" to offer them employment, Pozzo and Lucky enact a master-slave scenario, and the boy is Godot's sometimes-abused serf). Despite this, little has been said in criticism about gender and class in this play, as if the anti-realistic setup and character construction necessarily dictate that all apparent references to real-life aspects be interpreted metaphorically. As stated earlier, in reading this play as a paradox-based text, I am not suggesting that its meaning is "universal" but *excessive*—composed of countless discrete planes of organization brought

---

[1] Beckett's reiterated refusal to allow any parts to be played by women seems to indicate that gender-specific forms of conditioning and repression had been core concerns of character construction in this play, as in others. In a 11 July 1973 letter to Barney Rosset, Beckett explains, "I am against women playing *Godot* ... . Theatre sex is not interchangeable and *Godot* by women would sound as spurious as *Happy Days* or *Not I* played by men" (*L4* 335–36). Beckett arguably dramatized, in increasingly corrosive ways, traditional *male* socialization and normalization in plays like *Waiting for Godot*, and *women's* subjection to patriarchal exploitation and repression through prominent female characters in other plays.

© The Author(s) 2020
C. Ionica, *The Affects, Cognition, and Politics of Samuel Beckett's Postwar Drama and Fiction*, New Interpretations of Beckett in the Twenty-First Century, https://doi.org/10.1007/978-3-030-34902-8_3

into *diagrammatic association* to enable a multi-pronged, assiduous attack on the analogous and interconnected machinic strata that enforce exploitation and repression at all identifiable levels of our psychosomatic existence. *Waiting for Godot* does not depict relations and mechanisms of repression in a representational mode in any way akin to realism, naturalism, expressionism, or existentialism, but horrific-comically enacts their always unattractive and unsatisfactory effects on the subject, while also broadcasting immediately achievable and reproducible means to destabilize the machinic production of repression. In other words, as theorists as diverse as Adorno, Deleuze and Guattari, Badiou, and Critchley claimed, Beckett's writing does not articulate a diagnostic-based mode of representation (a form of critique) but a *practice*. It is for this reason that Beckett's *Godot* could mobilize, on so many occasions (as discussed in Chap. 1), solidarity- and change-oriented affects in groups of spectators from prison inmates to victims of natural disasters to communities subjected to repressive state machines. The play's paradox-based discourse and structure articulate a model of empowerment based in intersectional solidarity and apt to short-circuit hierarchical distribution on multiple levels in one move.

According to Jeffers, both *Godot* and *Endgame* "write over" any "naturalized" form of traditional masculinity (95) and compromise the notion of a potential return or renewal of the "masculine authoritative tradition" in the postwar context (96). Jeffers suggests reading Godot—depicted in the play as wealthy and in control of his life, as well as those of others—as a sarcastic rendering of the "Western masculine ideal" (97). She quotes from Vladimir and Estragon's Act I speculations on the way their long-awaited meeting with Godot might unfold—Vladimir states that they would have to be "on our hands and knees," Estragon asks, "We've lost our rights?" and Vladimir replies, "We waived them" (*CDW* 19)—and notes that they appear to acquiesce to hegemonic masculinity and the "law of the father" (Jeffers 97–98). However, the scene seems equally likely to evoke economic power relations to readers/ spectators, and Vladimir's seemingly definitive reply is not his last word on the matter of acquiescence. The conversation continues with Estragon's fearful question, "We're not tied?" (*CDW* 19), followed by an interlude concerning turnips and carrots and finally by Vladimir's answer, "To Godot? Tied to Godot? What an idea! No question of it. [*Pause.*] For the moment" (21). (This "walking back" of definitive statements is typical of Beckett's characters' avoidance of machinic coupling, as I show in detail in this and the following chapters.) Following additional remarks on carrots, Lucky enters the stage, and he is *literally* tied to Pozzo—a most grotesquely unattractive materialization of Vladimir and Estragon's prospects under Godot's authority, should he ever arrive and assert it.

My class-based reading is not an alternative to the gender-based interpretation offered by Jeffers but works *in conjunction* with it. The play grotesquely enacts exploitation and repression in a deeply destabilizing manner precisely by connecting diagrammatically multiple ordering planes (Oedipal, economic, and—as briefly discussed in the previous chapter—religious) as part of the heteronormative socio-economic machine. For instance, ropes and cords have a long history of use in both economic production-based and coercive or punitive contexts in human civilization. They are essential in construction—a traditionally male, lower-class occupation—but have also been used in the application of torture and in executions carried out on socio-economic or religious grounds—also male-initiated actions, as a rule (land owners, military leaders, judges, inquisitors, and their subordinates would have been male). Thus, the obsessive presence of ropes, cords, and references to "ties" in the play and their relegation to negative/ grotesque contexts make manifest exploitation and coercion as core components of patriarchal masculinity and point to religion as yet another machinic layer that safeguards patriarchal arrangements. Significantly, while Lucky is "tied" (captured), Vladimir and Estragon are not—"for the moment," and their supposed attempts at social integration sabotage integrative machinic switches on multiple levels.

Let us examine closely, from this perspective, Lucky's speech and Vladimir and Estragon's reactions to it. Lucky's performance starts at Pozzo's violent prodding ("Think, pig!" *CDW* 40) and follows a short, grotesque dancing act called "the net" ("He thinks he's entangled in a net," 38). Lucky stutters and loops through a number of claims, extended explanations, and logical caveats all dealing with *authority*—divine or institutional. He starts by invoking "a personal God quaquaquaqua with white beard quaquaquaqua outside time without extension Who from the heights of divine apathia divine athambit divine aphasia loves us dearly with some exceptions for reasons unknown but time will tell" (40) and then elaborates at length on the "labours" of the "Acacacademy of Anthropopopometry," which has established "beyond all doubt all other doubt than that which clings to the labours of men" that "in spite of the progress of alimentation and defecation" and "in spite of the strides of physical culture the practice of sports," humans appear to "shrink pine waste" (41–42). Alongside obvious scatological jokes, the speech is replete with empty references to scientific studies (the "labours" of "Puncher and Wattman," "Popov and Belcher," "Testew and Cunard," etc.), grotesque clusters of logical transitions ("concurrently simultaneously what is more," "I resume alas alas on on in short in fine on on"), long lists of (existing or made up) sports, stock elements of religious discourse (hell, fire, flames, "the skull," stones, etc.), and ostentatiously simplistic cultural and literary references (to Bishop Berkeley, Shakespeare, etc.) (40–42). Religious, medical, scientific, cultural, and educational discourses are thus stripped of the usual "content" they peddle and exposed in their machinic nature. This is, perhaps, what Pozzo means in expressing regret that Lucky can no longer "think very prettily" (37). Lucky seems to have lost his ability to couple himself seamlessly to the social machine at the level of discourse: instead of smoothly, "prettily" performing subjection, once prompted to start speaking, he industriously recites bare-bones machinic injunctions. (Like Watt in Franklin's assessment, Lucky has internalized machinic logic *too fully* for his performance to remain productive rather than strictly enact the mechanics of production.) Vladimir and Estragon, supposedly bothered by this overwhelming exposé, attack Lucky to shut him up; in a panic, Pozzo quickly instructs them to remove his hat (42).

Oddly enough, the stage directions accompanying the speech are provided all at once at the start rather than gradually as the speech progresses:

> During LUCKY's tirade the others react as follows: (1) VLADIMIR and ESTRAGON all attention, POZZO dejected and disgusted. (2) VLADIMIR and ESTRAGON begin to protest, POZZO's sufferings increase. (3) VLADIMIR and ESTRAGON attentive again POZZO more and more agitated and groaning. (4) VLADIMIR and ESTRAGON protest violently. POZZO jumps up, pulls on the rope. General outcry. LUCKY pulls on the rope, staggers, shouts his text. All throw themselves on LUCKY who struggles and shouts his text. (40)

For readers, this emphasizes the theatricality and artifice Beckett deemed necessary in performance. But while pedantically using numbers to describe the characters' reactions, the directions strangely fail to specify *when exactly*, during Lucky's speech, the other three should change behaviour. It is doubtful that Beckett, whose obsessive attempts "to police the post-textual afterlife of his plays" (Connor, *Repetition* 186) are notorious, "forgot" to clarify that aspect. Rather, the point appears to be—whether one is reading or watching the play—that, since there is no reason to assume that Vladimir and Estragon might react more violently to some parts of the speech than others, their reactions cannot but appear comically haphazard and maladroit. What Vladimir and Estragon's ostentatiously clownish act reveals, then, is that they are not *reacting* as much as *performing a reaction* of sorts—an idea reinforced by Vladimir's claim, after Pozzo and Lucky's departure, that he has merely pretended not to recognize them (*CDW* 45–46).

Vladimir and Estragon's "attack" on Lucky could, in fact, be read as an instance of *playing at* socially sanctioned behaviour—as they do later, in Act II, when they "play at Pozzo and Lucky" (66–69) and then concomitantly at sports and religion (two main topics of Lucky's speech) by praying in ostentatiously self-centred phrasing ("Save *me*! Save *me*!") while doing "the tree" (70). Vladimir and Estragon do not enjoy abusing others and despise those who do. They have meagre means, but Vladimir naturally shares his carrot and turnips with Estragon (Pozzo—who has plenty of food—eats "voraciously" in front of them but allows Estragon to have only some bones he had thoroughly sucked, *CDW* 24, 26), and they thoughtfully plan to use the same cord/ piece of rope to hang themselves.[2] Vladimir and Estragon's performances denounce the emptiness of the game they are expected to play within the heteronormative socioeconomic machine. If there are pleasures or allowances to be had, they can derive only from shared anti-systemic moments. Ultimately, Vladimir and Estragon's performances are more corrosive than Lucky's. Their anxious, industrious act of "waiting"—while removing and putting on smelly boots, exchanging hats, meditating on elusive erections, and searching for a better piece of rope to hang themselves—transforms any notion of (patriarchal) social integration and economic productivity into a damning mockery of itself. Given the corrosive manner in which social integration (or "employment") figures in this play, it is no wonder that spectators tend to find Vladimir and Estragon's strategies both irresistibly comical and empowering.

---

[2] The first time they discuss hanging themselves, they even try to compare body weights to ensure that the heavier one would not be left alone in the world—as Estragon explains, "Gogo light—bough not break—Gogo dead. Didi heavy—bough break—Didi alone. Whereas—" (*CDW* 18). However, they cannot be sure that Vladimir is, as they suspect, heavier, so Estragon concludes, "Don't let's do anything. It's safer" (18).

Godot might as well never come, since all he would offer is capture and exploitation. Yet, Vladimir and Estragon are "waiting"—their corrosive assault on machinic switches remains under-the-radar rather than explicitly drawing attention to itself. They feign inadequacy and inability rather than loudly refusing to comply. The tone of Beckett's exploration of exploitative human relations becomes darker and harsher in *Endgame*, where the Oedipal, economic, socio-cultural, and religious planes of organization are more explicitly aligned as repressive machinic strata and the sabotage of machinic switches begins to rely more noticeably on a mobilization of anger. Within the play's apocalyptic setup, Clov is an old, stiff-legged servant presumably adopted, as a child, by Hamm, a megalomaniacal misanthrope who, blind and unable to walk, routinely orders Clov to push his chair around the room, pretending to be going "[r]ight round the world" (*CDW* 104). From Hamm's falsely benevolent forms of control to his more openly murderous threats to withhold food, the protagonists' burlesque exchanges reveal the predatory nature of their arrangement. Hamm "can't move" (97), while Clov, who "can't sit" or restrain himself from following orders (97, 129), is ceaselessly occupied. Hamm recounts, intermittently and with many asides, a story whereby he hired Clov's biological father as a "gardener," later persuaded him to leave so Clov would benefit from more resources, and finally raised Clov "like a son" and offered him work (110, 116–18, 121, 122, 133). While Clov appears to be the only younger and able-bodied individual alive, Hamm insists that there is no "outside" to their relationship (no other people anywhere, so that if Clov ever left, he would be bound to carry Hamm along). However, when Clov spots a child through the telescope, Hamm suddenly decides to let Clov go (119–20). To no surprise, Hamm uses the word "I" in decision-making contexts (especially when threatening Clov with starvation) but switches to the plural whenever he needs to forestall Clov's departure ("You won't leave us," 110). For today's readers/ spectators, such details may evoke corporate capitalist attempts to colonize employees' free time and imaginary investments and entirely absorb their energy within the purportedly "organic" corporate body. Again, while Beckett could not have "foreseen" such developments, his diagrammatic enactment of economic exploitation appears to make manifest, in a horrific-comic framework—here, in "The Lost Ones," and elsewhere—the ultimate consequences of the machinic "use" of human "units": the extreme of *using them up*—an inhuman development that has become common practice in today's corporate context.

While in *Waiting for Godot* Vladimir and Estragon were able to observe Lucky's psychosomatic deterioration from the outside and resist machinic integration by feigning inability, in *Endgame* that subject position seems no longer attainable, and the master-servant relation becomes central to the dramatic situation. In correlation, the black humour becomes more horrific and—notably—angrier. If Lucky seemed closer to an automaton in his relation to machinic order, Clov performs his duties reluctantly and resentfully, with a cold anger that accumulates to the point of pulling him out of Hamm's exploitative grip. A large part of what fuels the black humour is the play's ostentatious and grotesque translation of subordination and repression into bodily terms—as strained physical movement (Clov), literal confinement and containment (Nell and Nagg, Hamm's parents, are kept in trash bins), disease (Hamm), and starvation:

> HAMM: I'll give you nothing more to eat.
> CLOV: Then we'll die.
> HAMM: I'll give you just enough to keep you from dying. You'll be hungry all the time.
> CLOV: Then we won't die. (*CDW* 94–95)

This paradoxical exchange unsettles the power dynamic by allowing Clov to counter Hamm's sovereign conceit and repurpose Hamm's self-serving use of the I/we opposition. For contemporary readers, it may also connect the functional sadism of the corporate "more with less" to its ultimate consequence—one is persistently pressured to perceive oneself as part of the corporate organism while truly only ever being dead meat. The black humour of the situation is further intensified by the presentation of predatory Oedipal relations, economic exploitation, and socio-cultural conditioning in *diagrammatic association* (as analogous and interconnected machinic strata), complete with the demonstration that, while they support each other in the most insidious, pervasive, and redundant ways, these strata ultimately fail to achieve subjectification-as-subordination without a reminder.

As the examples provided so far show, Hamm acts as a sadistic and exploitative "father" towards Clov—who, in turn, acts as a disenchanted, spiteful, albeit still "bound" son, obeying Hamm's demands but undercutting his discourse. Hamm keeps his parents in trash bins, withholds food, and often reprimands Nagg for having fathered him ("accursed fornicator," "accursed progenitor," 96). Nagg, too, seems to have been a neglectful or abusive father. As Hamm melodramatically asks, "Why have you engendered me?" Nagg sarcastically assures him, "I didn't know it would be you" (116), and he rejoices at the thought that Hamm's old age will render him as helpless as an infant (119–20). The predatory nature of Oedipal scripts transpires through each interaction between these representatives of three generations. Materializations of family relations as ranging from abrasive to predatory are common in the postwar plays of Beckett, Ionesco, or Genet, as well as in earlier expressionist, surrealist, or Dadaist works published in the aftermath of World War I (Apollinaire, Tzara, Artaud, etc.). In fact, many early twentieth-century avant-garde writers employed a programmatic excess of lurid and scatological black humour in an attack on what they saw as previous generations' obscene readiness to sacrifice the young in world conflagrations in order to preserve their nationalist ideals and socio-economic privileges. These works commonly represent the past (and "parents") as *preying on* the present ("children"). Within a similar framework, Beckett's Nagg is a fitting father for Hamm, and the apocalyptic setting of the play ("There's no more nature," *CDW* 97), a fitting consequence of the predatory patriarchal structures Nagg and Hamm inherited and tried to propagate. However, Clov—though separated from his real father and subject to Hamm's indoctrination and abuse since childhood—resists systemic integration. He responds to Hamm's aggression not (in "organic" heteronormative fashion) through increased aggression but through an eerie paradox-based form of *blocking* that consists of sabotaging Hamm's claims through a *reductio ad absurdum*, as in the example analysed above. Clov does not escalate but defuses Hamm's threats by showing that their materialization would imply self-annihilation. He equally dismantles Hamm's promises by revealing their emptiness. Ultimately, Clov does not leave out of a conviction that the "world outside" has promise but because, despite years of indoctrination, his accumulated anger succeeds in corroding the switch connecting capture to safety. The outside may be threatening, but Hamm's house is certainly an exploitation, abuse, and indoctrination machine that can no longer produce illusions of benevolence and nourishment. Clov's departure is not a desperate gesture but a liberated, calculated move apt to mobilize solidarity- and action-oriented affects in readers/ spectators, as it corrodes the most basal systemic maintenance mechanisms of conservative socio-economic assemblages—those meant to ensure that the ties cutting into our flesh invariably "read" as safety nets.

The conflict also supports a cultural history-based reading. Sentimental Nagg and Nell could function as caricatures of a classicist or romanticist world view befittingly thrown into the trash bin of cultural history: "Yesterday you scratched me there!"—"Ah yesterday!" (101). Hamm may mockingly embody realism or naturalism: he dreams to encompass "the world" through his chair-pushing game, deems himself a great storyteller, and obsesses over power relations and bodily fluids. Clov, in turn, might embody a disdainful avant-garde response to this catastrophic cultural tradition whose conceit and self-involvement barred the emergence of viable forms of resistance to the genocidal march of history. (As shown in the examples discussed so far, Clov's lines are the primary generators of paradox-based humour in the play—his corrosive "nearly there," his "half a rat," his many instances of *reductio ad absurdum*, etc.) Finally, in a socio-historical reading, the conflict may grotesquely evoke early capitalism and industrialization anxieties, complete with the typical longing for an idealized past—cleaner, closer to nature, and more sentimental (Nell and Nagg)—alongside a growing culture of regarding capitalist owners (Hamm) as destructive parasites and connecting moral fibre to physical labour (Clov).

All these readings hold horrific connotations, but the *ensemble* is oddly, irresistibly humorous. The four characters are "nearly there" (under total systemic control) but not quite: Nell and Nagg occasionally pop their heads out of the bins; Hamm continues his "travels" and plans to enlist new help; Clov can still move and eventually leaves Hamm's house and "employment"; and only "half" of the ubiquitous rat is exterminated. Threatening as it seems, the end remains in sight without ever coming— and this apparently haphazard and freaky respite renders the text electrifying and uncannily apt to *expel* machinic couplings. This is the margin of respite the schizo uses, in Deleuze and Guattari's conceptualization, to generate a "body without organs," impervious to insertion into processes of production as it has no orifices or individual organs that might permit machinic coupling. Paradox-based discourses like Beckett's are apt to generate abstract machines that do not *represent* subordination, exploitation, and repression but forcefully *spit them out.*

As another embodiment of this necessary uncoupling move, many of Beckett's characters are grotesquely obsessed with excretion: they conscientiously piss, sweat, vomit, and shit machinic switches—or fart in preparation and decry their inability to fart enough, like Molloy: "One day I counted them. Three hundred and fifteen farts in nineteen hours, or an average of over sixteen farts an hour. After all it's not excessive. Four farts every fifteen minutes. It's nothing. Not even one fart every four minutes. … Damn it, I hardly fart at all, I should never have mentioned it. Extraordinary how mathematics help you to know yourself" (*M* 28). While Molloy names mathematics, the logic of *economic productivity* is most directly mocked here (the passage follows a discussion of homeless Molloy's ways to keep warm while sleeping in the park in winter). In Beckett's texts—as in many earlier avant-garde works—scatological humour holds a primarily anti-institutional function. It is meant to affirm in the crudest, most ostentatious and disdainful fashion that institutions and social structures that treat individuals like prey deserve to be treated like *shit*. Only this kind of treatment is apt to illuminate what they are *really* doing under their facade of heightened abstraction, sophisticated planning, and enlightened benevolence, and thus sabotage their inhuman pursuits.

In *Waiting for Godot*, Vladimir refers to Lucky's "dance" (a manifestation of his destructive internalization of machinic logic and requirements) as "The Hard Stool" (*CDW* 38), and one of Lucky's direct references to excrements concerns the word "Academy" ("the Acacacacademy of Anthropopopometry, " 41). In *Endgame*, Nagg and Nell—literally placed in garbage bins—comment that their son and his servant had not "changed [their] sand" in a while (in better days, it used to be "sawdust") (100). The use of scatological humour in contexts related to societal institutions from the family to the school or the police is even more common in Beckett's fiction. Early in *Molloy*, a policeman approaches the title character, accusing him of vagrancy: "Your papers! he cried. Ah my papers. Now the only papers I carry with me are bits of newspaper, to wipe myself, you understand, when I have a stool. Oh I don't say I wipe myself every time I have a stool, no, but I like to be in a position to do so, if I have to. … In a panic I took this paper from my pocket and thrust it under his nose" (17). Here and elsewhere, while the diction mimics bureaucratic objectivity, pedantry, and precision, the subject matter obstinately revolves around processes and products of excretion and their attendant indignities, exaggerated through an emphasis on the mechanics involved and/or the supplies or facilities needed. Building on Beckett's own assessment of the distinction between his characters and narrative and Kafka's, Uhlmann notes that "the order of 'bureaucracy' appears within the form of the narration" and characters "experience it from the inside" in Kafka's texts, while in Beckett's, "the order remains hidden behind the forms it brings into being," so that what we encounter within the text is its shadowy threat (*Beckett and Structuralism* 47). Still, Beckett's consistent use of scatological humour creates an even stronger point of contrast to Kafka's treatment of the social order. Kafka's enactments of institutional power emphasize mostly its ability to generate fear, paralysis, and despair. Mockery and humour are not absent, but while readers might perceive the absurdity of the narrative situation in that key, characters cannot attain that perspective. In contrast, Beckett's characters both fear and mock the shadowy threat of an oppressive order (connected by Uhlmann, for *Molloy* and Beckett's other postwar works, to the manifestation of Nazi power during the occupation of France in World War II), as their ostentatious use of scatological imagery shows.

As Ben-Zvi notes, references to repugnant bodily functions are overwhelmingly frequent in Beckett's early letters (1929–1940), particularly in contexts related to writing and publishing ("Beckett and Disgust"). Ben-Zvi interprets this as a critical reaction to Kantian aesthetics, which associates beauty with value—but, in the context of our discussion, we can consider it proof of Beckett's early intuition of the powerful excretive function of the abstract (writing) machine and of the political value of some forms of textual excess. Focusing partly on Beckett's bodily humour, Dow identifies in his works elements of an anti-Kantian ethics. She reads Beckett's black humour, from a Lacanian perspective, not as an attempt to mitigate the finitude of the human condition (as some post-Kantian critics would have it) but as a means to foreground its excess of "*in*human *in*finitude" (128). In "Kant with Sade," Lacan famously claims that the endless sexual and philosophical incursions into "evil" in the Marquis de Sade's texts expose the deadly and inhuman implications of Kant's ethics—namely (in Lacan's psychoanalytic translation) that the Kantian ethical imperative is a disguise for the superego function and thus operates in service of the death drive. Dow reads Beckett's texts as constructs of the same category, and Beckett's humour, as a means to expose the "accompanying excess" an ethical focus on the "good" might mask (132). In Dow's perspective, "Beckett's comic objects body forth the gap between the phenomenality of the good proffered by pre-Kantian ethics and the noumenality of what Samuel Beckett once dubbed 'the Thing in Itself (God help it!)'" (Dow 134; Beckett, letter to Tom McGreevy from 25 August 1930, *L1* 43). The examples of "excess" from Beckett's works quoted by Dow—Molloy's endless complaints about the nuisance caused him by his foot and balls, Mahood's references to his penis, and other horrific-comic evocations of excessively active but allegedly useless body parts—can indeed be read, as Dow suggests, as destabilizing textual intrusions of the Laçanian "Real" into the supposedly ordered, regulated realm of lived experience. However, this excessive corporeality also constitutes an attack on a history of ethics that is equally one of attempts to anthropomorphize the world and tame the human body—to insert humans and their environment into a logic of Oedipal, social, and economic production.

3.2   DISCHARGING REPRESSION: HUMOUR, ANGER, AND THE MACHINIC SWITCH

To foreground what exactly is humorous in Beckett's works and how this type of humour propagates empowering effects, let us turn to Nell's famous *Endgame* line, "Nothing is funnier than unhappiness" (*CDW* 101). For Weller—one of the few critics to acknowledge the routine extraction of this phrase from its context in Beckett studies and its problematic positing as emblematic of Beckett's take on humour—the phrase appears "in a disintegrating context that places the ethicality of all humour in question" (*Ethics of Alterity* 120). In my interpretation, its context reveals it as an attack on the corrective forms of humour characterizing more traditional comedic modes like the classical comedy, and as a warning against facile disjunctions that can easily be co-opted to support repression and exploitation:

> HAMM: If I could sleep I might make love. I'd go into the woods. My eyes would see … the sky, the earth. I'd run, run, they wouldn't catch me. [*Pause.*] Nature! [*Pause.*] There's something dripping in my head. [*Pause.*] A heart, a heart in my head. [*Pause.*]
> NAGG: [*Soft.*] Do you hear him? A heart in his head! [*He chuckles cautiously.*]
> NELL: One mustn't laugh at those things, Nagg. Why must you always laugh at them?
> NAGG: Not so loud!
> NELL: [*Without lowering her voice.*] Nothing is funnier than unhappiness, I grant you that. But—
> NAGG: [*Shocked.*] Oh!
> NELL: Yes, yes, it's the most comical thing in the world. And we laugh, we laugh, with a will, in the beginning. But it's always the same thing. Yes, it's like the funny story we have heard too often, we still find it funny, but we don't laugh anymore. (*CDW* 101)

Clearly, rather than *claiming* that "nothing is funnier than unhappiness," Nell *delivers a warning* that laughing at unhappiness (even that of an abuser) is a dead end—a momentarily satisfying experience of no *lasting* liberating value. Beckett's literary discourse does not articulate a univocal "comedy of misery" by extracting comedic moments out of some "tragedy of being human." It articulates, instead, a humour of structures and planes of immanence—a far more corrosive attack on ossified, exploitative social structures and the language and "habits" that sustain them.

Nell's circumstance and comments foreshadow the dramatic situation of *Happy Days*, where Winnie and Willie, another married couple, exhibit varying levels of immobility. Winnie is slowly sinking into the ground—at the start of the play, she is "[e]mbedded up to above her waist" (*CDW* 138) in a low mound, centre-stage, and in Act II, "up to [her] neck" (160). Willie, still above ground, is lying down behind the centre-stage mound for most of the play but can still crawl on all-fours. The stage arrangement is ostentatiously contrived:

> Expanse of scorched grass rising centre to low mound. Gentle slopes down to front and either side of stage. Back an abrupter fall to stage level. Maximum of simplicity and symmetry.
>
>   Blazing light.
>
>   Very pompier trompe-l'oeil backcloth to represent unbroken plain and sky receding to meet in far distance.
>
>   Embedded up to above her waist in exact centre of mound, WINNIE. About fifty, well-preserved, blonde for preference, plump, arms and shoulders bare, low bodice, big bosom, pearl necklace. She is discovered sleeping, her arms on the ground before her, her head on her arms. Beside her on ground to her left a capacious black bag, shopping variety, and to her right a collapsible collapsed parasol, beak of handle emerging from sheath. (Act I, *CDW* 139)

Winnie's eerie condition, the "[v]ery pompier trompe-l'oeil backcloth," and the machinic symmetry of the arrangement (the centre mound, the symmetrical slopes, Winnie's centre position, her stretched arms, the two objects on either side, etc.) indicate, from the beginning, that the anti-realistic details of the *mise en scène* are meant to give grotesque, excessive corporeality to a set of supposedly abstract socio-historical constraints.

Kenner identifies in this play a mockery of Englishness—particularly, of the patriotic imperative of "maintaining one's cheer" in confronting adversity (*Reader's Guide* 147). Indeed, Winnie's continual attempts to state reasons for joy are ostentatiously grotesque. The religious imperative to rejoice in one's God-given life might be another target of mockery. In Act I, Winnie starts with a prayer, repeatedly commands herself to "begin [her] day" (138), then launches herself into an endless sequence of apparently pointless attempts to use and reorder objects in her bag, appeals to her husband's attention, and recollections of past events. Marriage as a social institution seems to be another target of this corrosive performance. Willie, hidden behind the mound with his yellow newspaper and barking short, angry replies, is the absentee husband, always too busy to engage with his garrulous wife, who spends her life relentlessly handling "things" (a parasol and a bag full of other symbolic tenets of modern civilization—toothpaste, a comb, a mirror, a revolver) and poring over personal and cultural memory. Childhood obsessions and major life encounters make a truncated appearance in her discourse alongside half-remembered and utterly trivialized lines from Milton, Gray, Wolfe, and others. Her quotations, repeatedly dubbed "wonderful" and "exquisite," sound as follows: "Oh fleeting joys—[*lips*]—oh something lasting woe" (Act I, 141), "something something laughing wild amidst severe woe" (150), or "Go forget me why should something o'er that something shadow fling ... go forget me ... why should sorrow ... bright smile ... go forget me ... never hear me ... sweetly smile ... brightly sing" (Act II, 164). It is doubtful that Beckett's intention, in using these lines in this form, was to express reverence for Milton, Gray, or Wolfe, or to suggest that art gives life value—particularly in light of Winnie's Act II explanation, "One loses one's classics. [*Pause.*] Oh not all. [*Pause.*] A part. [*Pause.*] A part remains. [*Pause.*] That is what I find so wonderful, a part remains, of one's classics, to help one through the day. [*Pause.*] Oh yes, many mercies, many mercies" (164). Winnie's explanations, in this and other passages, are grotesquely keen on finding positivity in obviously confining and torturous situations and redundant to the point of sarcasm—but even if she does find "something something woe" a satisfying rendering of "the classics," readers/ spectators cannot but register it as a scathing mockery. At all these levels, while humour may appear to arise from places of unhappiness, its target is set on the machinic structures that produce unhappiness and pain while continually attempting to mask this process of production.

Gontarski found references to rocket explosions in early manuscripts of this play—specifically, in newspaper headlines of an ostentatiously crude humorous quality read aloud by Willie (*Intent* 80). While Beckett discarded those likes in the final version, the play's *mise en scène* is sufficiently suggestive of an apocalyptic situation, and Winnie's interventions, carefully crafted to point to the patriarchal desire to control as its ultimate cause. One of the most disturbing passages in the play occurs in the second half of Act II, when Winnie, buried in the ground up to her neck, recalls the reactions of a couple who passed by while she was still above ground from the waist up. She had previously mentioned the couple in Act I, reproducing a hostile conversation in which the man had obsessively asked what the "meaning" of Winnie's state might have been and why Willie would not dig her out, posing the problem in sexual terms ("What good is she to him like that?"), and the woman had rebuked him: "And you, she says, what's the idea of you, she says, what are you meant to mean? ... What good is he to her like this?" (156–57). However, in Act II, Winnie provides additional details that present both the man's comments on Winnie's state and the woman's reactions in a darker light:

> Standing there gaping at me. [*Pause.*] Can't have been a bad bosom, he says, in its day. [*Pause.*] Seen worse shoulders, he says, in my time. [*Pause.*] Does she feel her legs? he says. [*Pause.*] Is there any life in her legs? he says. [*Pause.*] Has she anything on underneath? he says. [*Pause.*] Ask her, he says, I'm shy. [*Pause.*] Ask her what? [*Pause.*] Is there any life in her legs. [*Pause.*] Has she anything on underneath. [*Pause.*] Ask her yourself, she says. [*Pause. With sudden violence.*] Let go of me for Christ sake and drop! [*Pause. Do.*] Drop dead! [*Smile.*] But no. [*Smile broader.*] No no. [*Smile off.*] I watch them recede. [*Pause.*] Hand in hand—and the bags. [*Pause.*] (165)

Winnie's eerie state of confinement appears to arouse the man, whose questions are now of a more explicitly sexual nature. He insists on engaging his wife in his sexual inquiry. Her rebuke is harsher than before, yet he does not let go of her hand and they leave together. In conjunction with the passage from Act I, this fragment uses several repetitions with a difference to denounce women's socio-cultural confinement, exposing patriarchal arrangements as pathologically exploitative and irredeemably nonempathic. Winnie's trapped body engenders feelings of indifference or sexual arousal in the two men who can see her rather than a human impulse to ease her suffering. The woman, while apparently scandalized by Winnie's state as well as by her husband's comments and Willie's inaction, seems to be "glued" to her husband's hand and unable to act on her impulses. The account ostentatiously materializes several utterly unattractive aspects of patriarchal coupling, and the two women wield language in ways that further corrode the switches of the patriarchal machine. The "free" woman ridicules her husband's sense of entitlement on both occasions, and her vehemence is compounded by Winnie's corrosive framings (the second iteration makes irrefutable all the more veiled charges apparent in the first, and the ostentatious "he says"/ "she says" stresses both the adversarial nature of gender relations in patriarchy and the hideousness and malignity of male dominance—"he says" appears more often, as the man's offensive comments are more numerous than the woman's rebukes). In case the indictment hadn't been entirely clear, Beckett furnishes the following transition between the couple's conversation and Winnie's rendering of a traumatizing childhood episode that supposedly happened to a girl called Mildred: "And now? [*Pause. Low.*] Help. [*Pause. Do.*] Help, Willie. [*Pause. Do.*] No? [*Long Pause. Narrative.*]" (165). The sequence is likely to elicit a solidarity-building angry laughter in readers/ spectators.

Winnie's gender performance is just as corrosive as Vladimir and Estragon's waiting act. Winnie is sinking into the ground under the weight of repressive switches, but as she is sinking, her words and gestures conspire to incite readers/ spectators to sabotage the social machine that is holding her—and them, too, in various ways—captive. The power of Beckett's texts rests in large proportion on the deceptively unobtrusive, "ordinary," "lowly" nature of their protagonists. Smelly vagrants, garrulous housewives, or traumatized victims of some mysterious turn of fate are more likely to spread their corrosive message and sabotage machinic switches unobstructed by machinic conservation mechanisms, since in a machinic, socio-economically productive logic, their acts would register as pointless or inconsequential. Beckett's "lowly" protagonists thus offer readers/ spectators countless performances—or demonstrations—prompting them to discern and read the *diagram* of their subjection and exploitation and finally start to uncouple themselves from the stultifying self-identity traps generated by repressive machines. The margin of positivity in these texts does not come from an attempted valuation of even the most painful human experiences and strict forms of repression—on the contrary, pain and repression consistently feature as irredeemably consuming experiences in Beckett's texts. The positivity comes, instead, from the comedy of subjection itself—from the grotesquery of processes and structures machinic in nature that never cease to play the pretense of "natural" coupling and growth. Winnie's sinking body puts that grotesquery on display in the most damning and irrefutable manner.

Boulter associates *Happy Days* with "the emergence of the iconic image" (60) in Beckett's plays—the image of the entrapped body as "the compromised embodiment, the crypt, of extinct culture" (64)—noting that this imagery of entrapment becomes progressively more striking in the later dramas. Indeed, in *Play*, a man and two women formerly involved in a love triangle, placed in "three identical grey urns" up to their necks, take turns to speak, with a "spotlight projected on faces alone" (Beckett, *CDW* 307), and in *Not I*, a woman whose body is elevated "about 8 feet above stage level" delivers a fragmented account of her life in the third person, refusing to acknowledge herself as the protagonist, as a stage light illuminates only her speaking mouth (377). Kenner and Kristeva read such dramas as more or less sarcastic representations of divine punishment (for Kenner, *Play* is "Beckett's ultimate version of the Protestant Hell," *Reader's Guide* 153), and Boulter associates them with the compulsion to repeat typical of psychosexual trauma. I would additionally relate the obsessive presence of confinement imagery and the increasingly explicit suggestions of physical and sexual violence in Beckett's postwar drama to Beckett's direct and personal exposure to the Nazi torture and genocide operation during the war. (The correlation to Nazi aggressions has already been made for Beckett's fiction, as I briefly showed in Chap. 2 and will discuss through more critical references in Chap. 4, but Beckett's plays—also produced in the aftermath of the war—continue to be read as less closely related to real-life contexts.) Horrific forms of torture that included sexual violations were systematically used by Nazi forces against the men and women they arrested and/or sent to camps, and Beckett and his partner Suzanne Dechevaux-Dumesnil would have been painfully aware of that—they had lost many friends and fellow Resistance fighters to the German war machine and had been constantly at risk themselves for some time.[3] In a letter dated 11 August 1948 to Georges Duthuit, Beckett describes his partner Suzanne as "inconsolable at living" (*L2* 98), a phrase

[3] Beckett initially translated documents for a Paris-based Resistance cell connected to London but went into hiding in Rousillon when his cell was betrayed and the Gestapo started to arrest its members; he started *Watt* in Paris and completed it while in hiding on the way to Rousillon and while residing there (Knowlson 297–339). All the plays discussed at length in this book and most of the works of fiction were written after the war. In addition to Knowlson, for an account of the Nazi persecution of Resistance members and of the risks taken by Beckett and his partner during this period, also see Harvey (348–49), Uhlmann (the chapter on Molloy and surveillance in *Beckett and Poststructuralism*), Perloff ("Samuel Beckett's War"), Gordon, and Salisbury ("Gloria SMH").

that seems to suggest survivor's guilt, a common traumatic response identified in survivors of catastrophic events. While both this detail and the many references to Beckett's own depression in the same letter can be in part related to the couple's financial problems and to Beckett's creative crisis around that time (he finally started writing *Waiting for Godot* later that year), it would be difficult to exclude the possibility that Beckett and his partner were experiencing symptoms of war trauma—consequences of the deep fear of physical confinement and pain they must have experienced during the war, and of their mourning over lost friends and horror at their fate.

Beckett, who refused to discuss publicly details concerning his experiences as a member of the Resistance, likely became obsessively invested in what Boulter designates as the theme of the "body as liability" (87) during and in the aftermath of the war. Equally likely, postwar Beckett was far more attuned to the sexual and physical risks that marked women's existence than his younger self. Significantly, while both Beckett's male and female characters are typically devoid of options in the postwar plays, women appear more frequently in states of physical confinement, and it is typically in relation to women that allusions to sexual abuse (memories or a fear of sexual abuse or violence) emerge. The negativity of the dramatic situation in these plays is, undoubtedly, striking. Still, what I find more notable are the uncanny ways in which, against all odds, such texts and performances maintain a comedic edge and a margin of positivity, both derived not from a form of reconciliation with the pain and despair of human finitude but from anger-driven and solidarity-based *empowering* effects.

A powerful horrific-comic attack on patriarchal arrangements emerges in *Play*, which features a grotesque version of the bourgeois love triangle, with its sordid little indulgences, concessions, and lies, stressing from the beginning both the man's self-indulgent and dismissive attitude and the two women's (patriarchal) conditioning to resent each other more than they resent their deceiver:

> W1: I said to him, Give her up. I swore by all I held most sacred—
> [*Spot from* W1 *to* W2.]
> W2: One morning as I was sitting stitching by the open window she burst in and flew at me. Give him up, she screamed, he's mine. Her photographs were kind to her. Seeing her now for the first time full length in the flesh I understood why he preferred me.

[*Spot from* W2 *to* M.]
M: We were not long together when she smelled the rat. Give up that whore, she said, or I'll cut my throat—[*Hiccup.*] pardon—so help me God. I knew she could have no proof. So I told her I did not know what she was talking about. (*CDW* 308)

The chronology of the affair soon emerges from such fragmented recollections: M had paid an investigator initially hired by W1 to lie to her that M was faithful; W1, still suspicious, repeatedly threatened M with suicide; afraid of being caught, M revealed his connection with W2; W1 visited W2, threatening to kill her; M "solved" the crisis by convincing each woman of having left her rival; after W1 paid another visit to W2, M exhaustedly concluded, "God what vermin women," and decided, "Finally it was all too much. I simply could no longer—" (311). W1 suspiciously claims, "Before I could do anything he disappeared" (311)—a potential lie, given her previous threats. Later in the play, she alone uses the word "mercy" (312), repeatedly utters the phrase "Hellish half-light" (312, 316), and tries to engage the presence presumably hidden behind the spotlight, obsessing over what "truth" that presence might be seeking (313, 314). However, W2 also obsesses over her state, speculating that "things might disimprove" and asking the hidden presence, "You might get angry and blaze me clean out of my wits. Mightn't you?" (313). Ultimately, M's interventions suggest that he was not killed by W1 but committed suicide or died in some other way, as he insists he could no longer bear the pressure of the affair, claims to have been at peace since, and speculates that the two women might have connected after his death, in their shared grief.

As these details show, throughout the second half of the play, the women feel exposed, obsess over guilt and punishment, and address the presumed hidden presence directly, trying to elicit a response. In contrast, M speaks, mostly to himself, of being at peace, perhaps connivingly expresses pity for the women, and ascribes guilt to all members of the love triangle ("We were not civilized," 317). His lies and subterfuges, grotesquely marked by incessant hiccups, and the two women's poisonous remarks maintain a connection to the vaudeville, as does the gradual emergence of various forms of "untruth" (rather than clarifications) from the characters' lines. A more horrific comedy develops, however, at the level of the characters' machinic adherence to patriarchal assemblages—a level of meaning emphasized through the *speed* at which characters voice their recollections and through their flat tone, as required by the stage directions:

The transfer of light from one face to another is immediate. No blackout, i.e. return to almost complete darkness of opening, except where indicated. Voices toneless except where an expression is indicated. The response to light is immediate. Faces impassive throughout. Rapid tempo throughout. (307)

While equally immersed in a regime of psychosomatic control, the characters offer strikingly different discursive responses. In this "hellish half-light" as in life, for the women, physical immobility and the spotlight generate feelings of discomfort and fear. In contrast, the man sees here an occasion to philosophize. In pitting the women's chilling fear against the man's inane, self-involved, and self-serving musings, the text twists the vaudevillian elements into a grotesque spectacle of gender inequality. The man—the engine of the love triangle—is clearly more comfortable speaking about his sex life and far less tormented by guilt or afraid of physical punishment, confident that, in death as in life, the wheels of the machine would turn in his favour. In contrast, the women act on their lifelong conditioning to internalize guilt and/or ascribe it to other women rather than men—and, while some of their insults may seem to derive from anger and spite, the second half of the play reveals their governing affect as fear. Given their experience of their place in the patriarchal machine, they suspect a male presence behind the spotlight and seemingly fear, specifically, physical torture. There is no "peace" for them even in "death" because they cannot fully trust that even that radical change of state can liberate them from the suffering of the flesh. As W1 puts it in one of her attempts to extract an answer from the presence behind the spotlight, "Bite off my tongue and swallow it? Spit it out? Would that placate you? How the mind works still to be sure!" (314).

In a note on lighting, Beckett specifies that "a single mobile spot" or one "branching into three" should be used, warning that the use of separate spots would be "less expressive of a unique inquisitor than the single mobile spot," and refers to the three characters as "its victims" (318). While the inquisitorial nature of the light and of the entire scenario is conveyed in rather explicit terms, the man finds pleasure in speech and visibility. In fact, his one fear—expressed at the end of the text, just before the repeat—is that there might not be anyone watching:

M: And now, that you are ... mere eye. Just looking. At my face. On and off.
[*Spot from* M *to* W1]
W1: Weary of playing with me. Get off me. Yes.
[*Spot from* W1 *to* M]
M: Looking for something in my face. Some truth. In my eyes. Not even.
[*Spot from* M *to* W2. *Laugh as before from* W2 *cut short as spot from her to* M.]
M: Mere eye. No mind. Opening and shutting on me. Am I as much—
[*Spot off* M. *Blackout. Three seconds. Spot on* M.]
Am I as much as ... being seen? (317)

The women, conversely, fear that the presence is real and active, silently conspiring to enact horrific harm. W1's recurrent line, "Get off me" (313, 317), could be read as expressing fear of sexual violence. W2's nervous laughter (a "wild low laughter," as described in the stage directions, 317) starts after several lines in which she wonders whether she might be going insane and decides that she is not and cannot—with the terrifying implication that she would remain fully conscious of being harmed if her fears materialized:

W2: Am I not perhaps a little unhinged already?
...
W2: I say, Am I not perhaps a little unhinged already? [*Hopefully.*] Just a little? [*Pause.*] I doubt it.
...
W2: A shade gone. In the head. Just a shade. I doubt it.
...
W2: *I* doubt it.
[*Pause. Peal of wild low laughter from* W2 *cut short as spot from her to* W1.] (316–17)

This textual and performative setup does not create humour at the three characters' expense in a mode related to the classical comedy or the vaudeville but uses their memories and obsessions to mount an attack on the patriarchal order as a regime of psychosomatic control that grotesquely extends "beyond death." Far from being a philosophical meditation on freedom, choices, guilt, and due punishment like Sartre's *No Exit*, Beckett's *Play* corrosively denounces guilt and punishment as mechanisms of oppression "organically" integrated into the patriarchal machine.

Beckett's setup is conspicuously similar to Sartre's in some respects. In both plays, a man and two women are trapped in a medium symbolically reminiscent of hell, the women seem more poisonous than the man, a fear of physical punishment is looming, and the scenario appears endless. However, many elements in Beckett's version can be read as sarcastic responses to Sartre's aesthetic and philosophical conceptualization. Sartre's version of hell is a dispiritingly sumptuous, windowless, but otherwise spacious room where one can move around or lie down at ease, while in Beckett's play characters are much more oppressively trapped into urns. In *No Exit*, all characters fear physical punishment (Garcín continually claims he does not but suddenly decides to remain in the room when the door opens), whereas in *Play* only the women do. Thus, *Play* appears to foreground social repression mechanisms relegated to the background in *No Exit* (where the characters' *choices* have primacy), such as the characters' gender-specific psychosexual and economic conditioning and, generally, their acquiescence to an exploitation-based patriarchal regime of signs.

As previously discussed, Sartre's critical mode is irony. In *No Exit*, the pain of the world results from the acts of a number of egotistic and self-indulgent men and, perhaps—one cannot help but snicker, alongside Beckett—twice as many such women. In contrast, in *Play*, countless horrific details conspire to create, as elsewhere in Beckett's works, a sinister humour of machinic structures and strata. Beckett's characters appear to have been unable to break their damaging love triangle precisely because of its smooth integration into the patriarchal machine. Both women sound more insightful and self-aware than M and seem to have been financially independent, yet their sense of value derives strictly from "having" the man who deceived them. M claims to have found the tension of the affair unbearable but proves horrific-comically unable to stop his manipulative and exploitative behaviour—the root cause of that tension. At the end of the text, the stage directions indicate, "Repeat play" (317). The script is then meant to start a third time and abruptly end in a blackout after a few lines. The characters undoubtedly register their condition as horrific and stale, whether or not they are aware of the (presumably eternal) repetition—but readers/ spectators, while being aware of the repetition as repetition, are bound to *experience* it through changing affective states. If, during the first iteration, they plausibly focus more on the characters' "story," the second iteration forces them to acknowledge the sinister implications of the characters' captured state and perceive the characters' speaking bodies as subdued mechanical subunits of the patriarchal machine. Once again, the margin of positivity of this horrific type of humour relates to an active state of contestation that may translate into an *impulse* (not merely a desire) to change. Rather than taking a destructive turn in the form of interpersonal resentment, this impulse is more likely to coagulate into a collective form of anger against the structures keeping everyone in place—all in their tight urns, speaking in turn, and never really living.

Significantly, Beckett describes the placement of the spotlight as follows: "at the centre of the footlights, the faces being thus lit at close quarters and from below"; should the theatre space require a different positioning, the light "must not be situated outside the ideal space (stage) occupied by its victims" (*CDW* 318). In a 26 November 1963 letter to director Alan Schneider, he partly concedes, "I don't mind if the spot hits from above, provided it does not involve auditorium space" (*L3* 584). Clearly, the presence behind the spotlight is meant to come across as part of the scenario in the play rather than as a metaphor of audience voyeurism, implicitly stressing, for audience members, the forceful, punitive, and sadistic nature of the "confession machine" set up on stage. Beckett mentions a further means to cue spectators to the cruelty of this machinic arrangement and invite empathy for its victims in a 9 March 1964 letter to director George Devine. As he explains, during rehearsals of the play in Paris, he and director Jean-Marie Serreau decided that the repeat should be enacted *at a slightly slower pace*: "a slight weakening, both of question and of response, by means of less and perhaps slower light and correspondingly less volume and speed of voice" (594) and "a quality of hesitancy, of both question and answer, perhaps not so much in a slowing down of actual debit as in a less confident movement of spot from one face to another and less immediate reaction of the voices" (595) would provide "an indefinite approximating" towards a "conceivable dark and silence in the end" (595). A complicated laughter erupts at the end of readers/spectators' experience of this absurdly torturous and torturously absurd exercise—one that denounces disappointment, pain, and self-loathing as grotesquely obvious ("illuminated") products of the self-protective mechanisms of the patriarchal machine, and as such, supports the emergence of empowering action- and solidarity-oriented affects in readers/ spectators.

Fisher and Sloterdijk's theorizations of the place of anger and rage, respectively, in the history of culture may offer us additional clues concerning Beckett's political uses of affect. Fisher notes that anger is, typically, delegitimated as a "quaint and archaic" (47) response in contemporaneity, under the concerted influence of the Christian doctrine, psychoanalysis, and an increasingly formalized legal system. However, in Fisher's view, anger in fact founded and then continually reframed the legal system that excludes it: anger orients us towards justice by "discovering or marking out for us unmistakably the contours of injustice and of unjust acts," and the "nuanced legal system" communities produce over time is nothing but the "concrete and ordered form" taken by successive intuitions initially "sponsored by anger" (2). Fisher identifies fear and pity as component passions that insert "a civic component" into our otherwise "self-centered and self-defining" vehement states, and he lists exposure to plays/ films/ novels alongside experiences with the justice system proper as examples (3). Most importantly, he credits such exposure with the power to remind us that the articulation of a fully "objective" and "impersonal" justice system typically entails a problematic elision of the victim's right to an accounting *in the victim's own terms* (179–80, 251). In other words, literature has a civic function directly derived from its ability to furnish anger-based intuitions that may propel us to continually reshape our notions of justice and our legal system.

As Fisher puts it, literature "defends the priority of ... person-centered experiences ... over any idea we might be able to describe of a common world or an objective world or even a world where reciprocity obtains" (251). Indeed, Beckett's peculiar, disquieting, increasingly anti-realistic, *and diagrammatic* "person-centered" accounts grant victims of injustice (exploitation, abuse, or repression) a means to broadcast their unresolved pain and anger—the former, supposedly "healed" through socially integrative processes, and the latter, expelled from the social body as allegedly malignant. These protestations against socially enforced closure facilitate, for readers/ spectators, a transfer of affect that may translate into solidarity-based attitudes and actions. Beckett's anti-realistic ("absurdist") setups support this process by furnishing an "excess" of potential targets for characters and interpreters' anger: all the analogous and interconnected machinic strata that conspire to maintain us in a state of subjectification-as-subordination.

Sloterdijk's historical analysis of rage focuses more on the difficulty of theorizing a positive function for anger given its notorious pathologization in genocidal forms over the course of the twentieth century (Bolshevism, Nazism, Maoism, religiously and economically motivated terrorism, etc.). Sloterdijk designates politicians such as Lenin, Stalin, Mao, or Hitler as founders of "banks of rage" (137), describing their historical impact as the materialization of a carefully planned new "economy of rage" articulated "according to entrepreneurial criteria and controlled by its managers with long-term oversight for its objects," through organizational structures such as an ever-expanding bureaucracy, the single-party system, fixed routines, and so on (26). In other words, these genocidal state machines did not operate on spontaneous collective rage but *forged* rage deposits by "extort[ing] willingness to feign support for the projects of the revolutionary rage bank" (158). Sloterdijk explains the increasingly exploitative direction taken by late capitalism as the result of the contemporary left's failure to extricate rage from such frameworks and mobilize it in pursuit of social justice in a "social-democratic-reformist (and syndicalist)" (145) manner.

Sloterdijk appears to have chosen the German term *Zorn*, meaning "rage" or "wrath," for its suggestion of *extreme intensity* and for its religious associations, and not for its implications of a *lack of control*—the core point of his theory of "rage banks" is that rage was "collected" as "capital" and then *politically employed* in a bureaucratic, carefully planned manner rather than allowed to manifest itself spontaneously in any form at the level of individual sufferers/ small communities. I find Sloterdijk's use of the term *Zorn* for a large number of phenomena of varying levels of intensity, conscious control, and/or malignity problematic, despite his detailed analyses, and his critique of the contemporary left somewhat reductive, especially since he does not discuss in detail what form(s) a positive mobilization of rage might take (how, specifically, it might avoid the dangers of bureaucratic capture). However, Sloterdijk's idea that some forms of anger can and should be employed as an engine for social justice has value in today's context of increasingly paralysing corporate control over all aspects of life. Furthermore, I would argue that Beckett's mobilization of anger in his texts achieves what Sloterdijk stops short of theorizing, as it supports the formation of empowering action- and solidarity-oriented affects in readers/ spectators while remaining impervious to bureaucratic capture—the very development Sloterdijk posits as necessary but does not explicate. This affect-based impulse to change obtains at the contact with the text either through more direct forms of transfer (for instance, we are likely to subscribe wholeheartedly to many of Vladimir, Estragon, Clov, or Winnie's protestations) or through a form of solidarity derived from our *excessive*, stark exposure to the characters' socio-cultural and economic conditioning (as in the case of texts like *Play*, where the setup is even more removed from any recognizable everyday scenario, and the characters are both remote and unpleasant enough to preclude more direct forms of identification).

3.3   "Repetition for Itself" / Recursion-Based Liberatory Practices

As apparent from several examples discussed so far, this process is consistently bolstered by eerie and corrosive forms of repetition that might be better understood in connection to what Deleuze defines as "repetition for itself" or to the mathematical and linguistic notion of recursion. In *Difference and Repetition*, Deleuze defines "repetition for itself," building primarily on Bergson's notion of duration (*The Creative Mind* and elsewhere) and Nietzsche's theorization of the "eternal return," as a form of repetition freed from the concept of an original, self-identical entity, so that each act of repetition is a *repetition of difference*. The mathematical and linguistic notion of recursion, as briefly discussed in Chap. 2, refers to repeatedly applying certain operations to their own output under specific sets of conditions and is therefore a type of repetition that generates difference with each application (in linguistics, it refers to the repeated application of compositional rules to their own output to compose more complex sentences from basic structures). Beckett's repetitions should be understood in this key. Far from functioning as nihilistic reminders of the emptiness, limitedness, and inescapability of the human condition, they constitute linguistic and visual procedures that can corrode repressive structures for characters and readers/ spectators alike. For the former, avoiding total capture may be the only achievable (and not always reached) end, but for the latter, the characters' articulation of this diagrammatic procedure of resistance opens possibilities of action and reveals modes of empowerment prompting positive change. Through their intensity and non-identity, these repetitions generate contagious solidarity-based affects that connect readers/ spectators to the characters' suffering and allow them to shatter machinic repression through their angry laughter. Concurrently, through their ostentatious artifice, these repetitions prevent the formation of uncritical, identification-based attachments between readers/ spectators and characters.

Not I is yet another play whose general tone of depression, anxiety, and passivity may translate into an experience of empowerment for readers/ spectators, and where various forms of repetition serve the multifold purposes described above. The female protagonist systematically refuses to "relinquish [the] third person," as the stage directions indicate (*CDW* 375). She is positioned so that her speaking mouth, "faintly lit from below," appears "8 feet above stage level." The only other character in the play, the Auditor, is placed on an "invisible podium 4 feet above stage level," does not speak, and merely lifts his arms "in a gesture of helpless compassion" (376) on occasion. This ostentatiously odd, disorienting and disturbing visual setup suspends Mouth in a state that cannot be defined through binaries such as dead or alive or easily read in a realistic or symbolic key.

As with *Play*, Kenner (*Reader's Guide*) and other Beckett scholars read this setup as a (perhaps sardonic) version of the Purgatory or Inferno, and Mouth's discourse, as a failed attempt to find peace after a life of suffering. Others see Mouth's measure of patriarchal conditioning as the key to the play. For Gidal, Mouth's fragmented identity allows her to evade, in part, patriarchal capture. For Bryden, Mouth functions (from a Deleuzean perspective) as "the ultimate deterritorialized voice" (*Women* 118). Conversely, Kristeva sees her immersion into a patriarchal regime of signs as complete and inescapable. Sherzer and Diamond identify here the discourse of the female hysteric, whose disruption and critique of patriarchal language and law is "limited by the onus of her disease" (Diamond, "Speaking Parisian" 212). Boulter reads the play as a representation of trauma. Indeed, Mouth's fragmented, redundant, convoluted account revolves around an event that happened somewhere "in a field" as she was "coming up to seventy" and disrupted her otherwise uneventful, dreary, loveless life (Beckett, *CDW* 376). She does exhibit hysterical symptoms, and she shows awareness of a potential witness to her discourse (a therapist? God? Readers/ spectators?). Building on these readings, I propose that the play's peculiar mode of presentation of Mouth's life experiences requires an interpretation involving mutually sustaining machinic strata.

Born, as she claims, of "parents unknown," Mouth has been "spared" any love "such as normally vented on the … speechless infant … in the home," alongside any love "of any kind … at any subsequent stage"—something she describes as a "typical affair" (376). Her sarcastic diction mocks conventional conceptualizations of social connectivity. In addition to implicitly denouncing family relations as generally ("typically") either null or predatory, such details dismiss the very possibility of feeling a connection of whatever kind with other humans as a machinic lure. Indeed, Mouth uses the verb "spared" in one more unusual context, when she mentions that, after the event in the field, "she" had recovered her voice, but not—as, for a moment, she feared—her ability to feel:

gradually she felt ... her lips moving ... imagine! ... her lips moving! ... as of course till then she had not ... and not alone the lips ... the cheeks ... the jaws ... the whole face ... all those— ... what? ... the tongue? ... yes ... the tongue in the mouth ... all those contortions without which ... no speech possible ... and yet in the ordinary way ... not felt at all ... so intent one is ... on what one is saying ... the whole being ... hanging on its words ... so that not only she had ... had she ... not only had she ... to give up ... admit hers alone ... her voice alone ... but this other awful thought ... oh long after ... sudden flash ... even more awful if possible ... that feeling was coming back ... imagine! ... feeling coming back! ... starting at the top ... then working down ... the whole machine ... but no ... spared that ... the mouth alone ... so far ... ha! ... so far ... (379–80)

Besides Mouth's disdainful use of sarcasm, what is consistently apparent here and throughout the monologue is that, as for W2 from *Play*, for Mouth the possibility of feeling is a perpetual threat. The recurrent "so far ... ha! ... so far ..." offers a compact representation of her dizzying, torturous vacillation between disdain and fear, sometimes even over a quick turn of phrase.

Mouth repeatedly interrupts and adjusts her account, in apparent flashes of recollection, but whenever she approaches an admission that she—not someone else—is the subject of her account, she rejects that adjustment: "what? ... who? ... no! ... she! ..." (377, 379, 381, 382). Other instances of non-compliance occur whenever she references Christian doctrine. At the beginning of the play, she twice informs us that, "brought up as she had been to believe ... with the other waifs ... in a merciful ... [*Brief laugh.*] ... God ... [*Good laugh.*]," she is conditioned to interpret life events as instances of sin and punishment, despite being aware of the farcical character of such "vain reasoning" (377). Even apart from her sarcastic sandwiching of "God" between a "brief" and a "good" laugh, her examples of sin and punishment corrode any systemic pretense of benevolence or justice by placing at the core of the arrangement machinic necessity and not human comfort or any legitimate notion of retribution. She might be punished at present, she speculates, because she was meant to suffer in the field and did not, while the episode in the field might have been punishment for not feeling the required pleasure at some earlier point in her life:

she suddenly realized ... gradually realized ... she was not suffering ... imagine! ... not suffering! ... indeed could not remember ... off-hand ... when she had suffered less ... unless of course she was ... *meant* to be suffering ...

ha! ... *thought* to be suffering ... just as the odd time ... in her life ... when clearly intended to be having pleasure ... she was in fact ... having none ... not the slightest ... in which case of course ... that notion of punishment ... for some sin or other ... or for the lot ... or no particular reason ... for its own sake ... thing she understood perfectly ... that notion of punishment ... which had first occurred to her ... brought up as she had been to believe ... with the other waifs ... in a merciful ... [*Brief laugh.*] ... God ... [*Good laugh.*] ... first occurred to her ... then dismissed ... as foolish ... was perhaps not so foolish ... after all ... so on ... all that ... vain reasoning... (377)

While meditating on her inability to feel, Mouth explicitly designates her body as a dysfunctional machine, and her comments on the things she *could not* feel or do are, again, corrosive:

this other thought then ... oh long after ... sudden flash ... very foolish really but so like her ... in a way ... that she might do well to ... groan ... on and off ... writhe she could not ... as if in actual agony ... but could not ... could not bring herself ... some flaw in her make-up ... incapable of deceit ... or the machine ... more likely the machine ... so disconnected ... never got the message ... or powerless to respond ... like numbed ... couldn't make the sound ... no sound of any kind ... no screaming for help for example ... should she feel so inclined ... scream ... [*Screams.*] ... then listen.... [*Silence.*] scream again ... [*Screams.*] ... then listen.... [*Silence.*] ... no ... spared that ... all silent as the grave... (378)

Mouth's hypothetical, yet manifest screams create one of the most terrifying *and* uplifting moments of black humour in the play, as they most stridently denounce the machinic foundations of her predicament. One problematic aspect of even the most insightful readings of *Not I* to date is the assumption that Mouth *should* embrace the "I" but lacks the strength or means to do it. In my reading, Mouth is not *unable* to comply—she is *fighting layers of machinic pressure to do so.* She vehemently refuses to couple herself to the social machine to protect herself from pain, while the social machine is clinging to her memory of her body, eating at her defences. Mouth's screams are both attempts to ward off machinic switches and threatening proof that the switches remain inexorably active. The margin of positivity in this figuration of machinic repression consists, yet again, in the possibilities it opens for a form of resistance that rejects traditional (machinic, falsely beneficial, exploitative) models of social cohesion and allows for the articulation of new forms of solidarity.

Owning the "I" would obviously be required for a move *beyond* Mouth's state, however defined, and towards inner peace and absolution (in an "afterlife" reading) or a means of coping with psychosexual repression and trauma (in a psychoanalytic reading). In refusing to embrace the "I," Mouth expresses revulsion against a mode of social cohesion based on notions of sin, punishment, and sacrifice. She will not grant forgiveness for whatever happened in her past, like a good Christian sufferer, and pursue some soporific state of peace. Instead, she will flatly repeat her denial (Beckett's characters always express their anger, resentment, and pain in a flat, under-the-radar, but implacable tone), barring the social machine from containing and regulating her affects. Additionally, in a post-traumatic perspective, Mouth's discourse sarcastically mimics the psychotherapy session, with the victim of abuse labouring to verbalize trauma while the guilty party (whether an individual perpetrator or society at large) remains entirely outside the process. This, Mouth's discourse implies, is not healing but an attempt to regulate the social environment and reinstate order and peace at the expense of the victim, as if "nothing happened."

Mouth's discourse shows the same mechanisms of containment at work in the religious and the psychotherapeutic logic, denouncing such machinic strata as elements of a general social economy of exploitation, repression, and injustice. The sequence "what? ... who? ... no! ... she!..." appears five times in the play. The first four times, it garners gestures of compassion from the Auditor, but they subside to become "scarcely perceptible at third" (375). The fifth time, no gesture is recorded in the stage directions. Mouth's rejection of the "I" is, then, met with compassion at first and receding tolerance later. The Auditor, as an embodiment of the social order, offers compassion at a price—that of smooth machinic integration. There is an obligation to enjoy, suffer, forgive, and let go, and with each refusal to comply, Mouth forces the Auditor to further reveal the grim machinic economy governing both of their lives.[4]

---

[4] The obsessive image of Mouth and the watching, silent Auditor seemingly came to Beckett's mind before any notion of what Mouth might say. In a 23 February 1972 letter to Barbara Bray, he reports, "Vague image for a short play of a lit face (mouth) with? to say and a cloaked hooded figure, sex unclear, completely still throughout, listening and watching. Latter suggested by an Arab woman all hidden in black absolutely motionless at the gate of a school in Taroudant and by the watching figures in the Caravaggio Malta decollation. Might produce 10 min. strangeness if text found. Only glimmer of consciousness all this time" (*L4* 287). Beckett's reference to the Arab djellaba has been widely referenced in criticism, yet his second stated source of inspiration, Caravaggio's *Beheading of St. John the*

Not I thus offers one of the most damning depictions of suffering in Beckett's texts. Far from granting pain illuminating or redeeming value, it resolutely rejects all social valuations of pain, sacrifice, and acceptance, prompting readers/ spectators' realization that it is this very social mechanism of containment ("God" as a machinic switch) that keeps everyone in place, preventing liberation and change. It is at this level that an affective connection occurs between readers/ spectators and the speaking character, and it is one of *solidarity*—not pity or compassion. This intuition that change comes from anger and a refusal to comply—not from a state of inner peace—may allow readers/ spectators to sandwich their own preconceptions between a "brief" and a "good" laugh and discard them as limiting, stultifying, deadening shackles. This is a positive and valuable form of angry laughter not just because it is solidarity-based and action-oriented but because it strikes at the right object—all the damaging and mutually sustaining mechanisms of exploitation and repression typically shaped as expressions of care and concern for individuals and communities.

Even in some of Beckett's late plays, where the physical violence, abuse, and deprivation haunting his earlier plays becomes increasingly manifest, this margin of positivity survives. *What Where*, Beckett's last play, is a salient example. Weller notes a "darkening of mood" and a "movement away from the comic" within the course of each of Beckett's plays, including in the more obviously comical, earlier *Endgame* (*Ethics of Alterity* 131); a move away from clownish elements in Beckett's contribution to later productions of his plays, offering *Krapp's Last Tape* as an example (132); and a "radical reduction of the comic" in his last works, so that in *What Where* "there can scarcely be said to be anything humorous at all ... despite the use of flagrantly clownish names: Bam, Bem, Bim, Bom" (132). Weller defines this stage in Beckett's work with humour as "posthumorous" (132) and "anethical" (133), since it articulates a position from which it is impossible to determine "whether there is anything

Baptist, far less frequently. It is, however, worth stressing that the latter seems to suggest a disturbingly voyeuristic and not fully benevolent quality to the Auditor's figure. A 15 March 1986 letter to New School for Social Research professor Edith Kern (New York) strengthens this suggestion: "The Caravaggio painting in Valletta shows, outside & beyond the main area, at a safe distance from it, a group of watchers intent on the happening. Before the painting, from another outsidedness, I behold both the horror & its being beheld. This experience had some part in the conception of the Auditor in *Not I*" (671). The figure of the Auditor appears to have been meant as a complex commentary on the social mechanics of victimization and "witnessing" rather than as an unambiguous symbol of compassion.

to laugh at" or "who, if anyone, might have had the last laugh" (133)—a position in which all judgements of value (and, with them, any possibility for divisions such as ethical/ unethical, positive/ negative, self/ other, etc.) are suspended. I would suggest, however, that black humour, empowering displacements of language, and significant elements of socio-cultural anchoring can be identified even in this text.

Beckett seems to have borrowed the names Bim and Bom from a Stalin-era clown duo and to have phonetically derived the other two. The play depicts a succession of seemingly arbitrary episodes of torture purportedly meant to force a confession. The atrocious acts happen off-stage. In the text and on stage, what remains on display is the socio-linguistic genera-tion of conditions of acceptability for those acts. The characters' mechani-cal and sinister dialogue and interactions are replete with black humour. Five characters are mentioned at the start ("We are the last five," *CDW* 471), but two are facets of the leader—V, which in fact designates a mega-phone, is his reflective side, prone to planning, judging, and philosophiz-ing, and the human figure Bam is his active side, who repeatedly orders acts of torture and, towards the end of the play, commits them himself. After a pantomime sequence that previews the interactions in the play, Bom appears on stage to report to Bam that he has tortured an unspecified victim who did not confess:

> BAM: You gave him the works?
> BOM: Yes.
> BAM: And he didn't say it?
> BOM: No.
> BAM: He wept?
> BOM: Yes.
> BAM: Screamed?
> BOM: Yes.
> BAM: Begged for mercy?
> BOM: Yes.
> BAM: But didn't say it?
> BOM: No.
> BAM: Then why stop?
> BOM: He passed out.
> BAM: And you didn't revive him?
> BOM: I tried.
> BAM: Well?
> BOM: I couldn't.

[*Pause.*]
BAM: It's a lie. [*Pause.*] He said it to you. [*Pause.*] Confess he said it to you.
[*Pause.*] You'll be given the works until you confess.

The same conversation later reoccurs with the torturer's role taken by Bim and then Bem, as each former torturer becomes the next victim. It is gradually revealed that victims are expected to confess "what" and "where" (presumably, what happened/ will happen and where), but the specifics of the situation remain undisclosed, permitting countless possible contextualizations. (Some obvious frames of reference might be totalitarian/ police state practices, various sadistic and/or paranoid social interactions, or the Christian hell.) The sinister humour of the play largely derives from its use of corrosive forms of repetition-with-a-difference. V's interventions imply that the events described will be perpetually replayed in the same way. However, while the torturer becomes the next victim three times, not everyone suffers the same fate—Bam is always the one ordering everyone's actions and never the one victimized. In the pantomime version, at the end of the sequence, "Bam enters at W, halts at 3 head bowed" (471), adopting the body posture consistently assigned to future victims throughout the play. However, the ritual ends before he can be victimized, and a recurring fragment concerning each torturer's failed attempt to revive the victim indicates that, by that point in the scenario, everyone else is dead.

What Where does not display, therefore, a cycle of perpetual, perfectly symmetrical permutations but one *rigged to appear* so in order to naturalize torture and victimization as "organic," "natural" aspects of socialization. Always at the top of the hierarchy, Bam "switch[es] off" and "restart[s]" when it is his turn to appear on stage "head bowed." He blandly pontificates, at the start of the sequence, "We are the last five. In the present as were we still. It is spring. Time passes" (470, 471), and at the end: "I am alone. In the present as were I still. It is winter. Without journey. Time passes. That is all. Make sense who may. I switch off" (476). Yet, what he would propose as the tragedy of being human (meaninglessness, impotence, etc.) is but a risible attempt at legitimating sadistic repression as an inevitable fact of life. His recurrent use of ossified language, his obvious perception of his victims as mechanical objects easily reducible to functions like "screaming" and "begging," his subordinates' body language and quasi-monosyllabic interventions, and the conspicuous absence of the victims' suffering bodies from the space of the stage (their confinement to invisibility with the exception of the bowed-head moments) all denounce Bam's inhumanity and tight manipulation of his environment. While what he inflicts on the others is horrific, his attempts to legitimate his pursuits are risible, grotesque, contemptible manifestations of mechanisms of repression at work in any number of exploitative, dehumanizing religious, economic, or political discourses. The self-perpetuating and self-serving character of any *logic of repression* is enacted and ridiculed here, rather than specific instances of it, to the effect of producing, within readers/ spectators, an angry laughter that is *diagrammatic, systemic*, and *enduring*, and may translate into a readiness to act, immediately and in solidarity with any perceived victims, to correct social injustice.

Recursion is used here more ostentatiously, perhaps, than usual in Beckett's works. One character is clearly dead at the end of each "questioning" session, and the "procedure" is reapplied until Bam alone is left alive. The logic of repression is thus shown to rest on the ability of the repression machine to present itself to potential victims as a social cohesion machine, and thus co-opt their support for its repressive practices until their own time to be victimized comes. In fact, perhaps still more corrosively, this predatory and sadistic application of recursion is posited here as the *defining* functional principle in *any* traditional socio-economic assemblage—Beckett uses recursion to demonstrate the total integration, painful consumption, and final elimination of the human "unit" within any machinic socio-economic arrangement. It is not by chance that Beckett's characters use the expression "to give the works" for their acts of torture (a transparent allusion to the common etymology of words designating work and torture in most European languages). Repression, once again, is a product. It requires hard work, and we sacrifice our energy and ethical commitments to it in the name of safety and social cohesion, but texts like Beckett's most corrosively reveal such positive projections as a ruse. We are promised nourishment and fulfilment, but the repression machine can only deliver subjection and pain, neatly packaged as "meaning." Language and the body are laboriously coupled within this process of production—but coupling switches are invariably, to a point, at risk of sabotage.

CHAPTER 4

Under-the-Radar Derision and Anger: Becoming Revolutionary in/through Beckett's Fiction

4.1 Language and the Body

The move towards increasingly horrific but consistently empowering situational sources of black humour discussed so far mostly in relation to Beckett's drama equally characterizes his fiction, which insistently foregrounds countless ways in which social machines can enslave minds and bodies in the guise of "natural," smooth, nourishing processes of integration. Abbott identifies, starting with *Molloy*, a Kafkaesque suggestion of a bureaucracy "too hopelessly involved and secretive to allow any mortal a glimpse of its final cause," reading it as a "commentary on the profound inadequacy of human comprehension" (*Form and Effect* 103). What I hope to prove is that Beckett's black humour reveals his characters' struggles not as symptomatic of a human inadequacy or weakness but as attempts to resist overbearing, overwhelming, painful, and consuming forms of socio-economic exploitation and repression.

Beckett's preoccupation with the impact of violent patterns of social interaction on our language and modes of thinking and being, perhaps first foregrounded through Murphy's meditation on the circuit of "kicks" in nature, gains prominence in *Watt*, written during Beckett's time in the French Resistance. The protagonist, a hyperactive, obsessive-compulsive social reject, becomes, through an incongruous series of events, a servant of Mr. Knott—a man of "very various, very very various" (199) clothing habits and physical shapes, whose behaviour defies understanding. Watt's

© The Author(s) 2020   117
C. Ionica, *The Affects, Cognition, and Politics of Samuel Beckett's Postwar Drama and Fiction*, New Interpretations of Beckett in the Twenty-First Century, https://doi.org/10.1007/978-3-030-34902-8_4

efforts to grasp the logic of Knott's existence (manifested through endless lists of possible causes/ conditions/ objections/ projections for every issue encountered and through increasingly perplexing syntactic structures) are revealed through the mediation of Sam, Watt's fellow resident in a peculiarly organized mental health institution, who provides a stylistically consistent narrative voice. As elsewhere in Beckett, although the content technically befits tragedy, narrative, situational, and linguistic grotesqueries make the reading experience entertaining, energizing, and empowering.

The novel's attack on the logic of language in its reliance on binary (either/or) modalities of reasoning and meaning-making has been widely recognized as a source of humour and a corrosive socio-cultural critique. Additionally, recent readings stress the novel's ostentatious, grotesque coupling of the materiality of language to that of the body—seen as implicitly evocative of the historical conditions of the Second World War. For Hoefer, Mood, and Kenner (*Mechanic Muse*), *Watt* parodies logical positivism, hyper-rationalism, and rational (computational) systems, respectively. For Perloff (*Wittgenstein's Ladder*), its linguistic contortions forge a "language of resistance" modelled after the linguistic codes used by Beckett's Resistance cell, suspending the informational function of language and creating as by-product an alternative poetics. For Rabaté ("Love and Lobsters"), *Watt* denounces rational knowledge as "a machine that barely hides relations of domination, fear, and horror" (167). For Dennis, it depicts the human body as a "machine on the point of collapse" (113), stressing the impossibility of separating language from the speaking body, especially in violent historical contexts. Indeed, *Watt* sutures a stunning mockery of the logic of language to a grotesque representation of the body's participation in and resistance to the act of meaning, attempting to extract both language and the body from repressive assemblages they are often duped to accommodate. My analysis contributes to the field by foregrounding additional aspects implicated in the novel's attack on socio-historical machinic repression, starting with the novel's take on employment.

Watt's first of many perplexing experiences in Knott's house consists of witnessing former employee Arsene's parting statement. As Arsene explains, each Knott employee starts on the ground floor, is next promoted to the first floor, and is dismissed when a new hire assumes the ground floor position. While some elements of Arsene's statement seemingly exalt the benefits of belonging to a social assemblage and bemoan being discarded, its tone and composition reveal, instead, an angry, however seemingly collected, denunciation of the systemic and soul-crushing work of the socio-economic machine.

As Arsene sarcastically notes, from birth, the individual is socially conditioned to conceive of any form of exchange in a deviously self-interested, predatory manner—all the better to be "integrated" into economic circuits that naturalize exploitation: "For the first time, since in anguish and disgust he relieved his mother of her milk, definite tasks of unquestionable utility are assigned to him. Is not that charming?" (39–40). He assures Watt that his "indignation" towards menial work disappeared some months into the job, as he realized he was working "not merely for Mr Knott in person, and for Mr Knott's establishment, but also, and indeed chiefly, for himself," but describes that supposedly positive state as a renunciation of mobility and growth for the sake of stability ("that he may abide, as he is, where he is, and that where he is may abide about him, as it is") and a dense acceptance of a perpetual deferral of benefits (he had acquired "the celebrated conviction that all is well, or at least for the best") (40). A key sentence defining his state of mind as "calm and glad" and his work experience as "witnessing" and "being witnessed" references excrements: "calm and glad at last he goes about his work, calm and glad he peels the potato and empties the nightstool, calm and glad he witnesses and is witnessed" (40). A most explicitly angry section presents the process whereby a servant replaces another. Here, Arsene notably uses female servants as examples: "Mary" (recently fired) and "Ann" (recently hired). As he flatly informs Watt, the household economy dictates that the replacement be provided extensive information about the former servant—mainly, his example reveals, in the form of an overblown denigration. This procedure is undoubtedly meant to attest that servants are always fired for cause, reaffirming the fairness of the system and facilitating the vicious exploitation of new hires. The master randomly refers to Ann as Ann or Jane and describes Mary as hyperbolically stupid, lazy, dirty, promiscuous, and voracious—she apparently never spoke because her mouth was always "overflowing" with "partially masticated morsels of meat, fruit, bread, vegetables, nuts and pastry," which invariably fell on the floor

in places as remote in space, and distinct in purpose, as the coal-hole, the conservatory, the American Bar, the oratory, the cellar, the attic, the dairy and, I say it with shame, the servants' W.C., where a greater part of Mary's time was spent than seemed compatible with a satisfactory, or even tolerable, condition of the digestive apparatus, unless we are to suppose that she retired to that place in search of a little fresh air, rest and quiet, for a woman more attached to rest and quiet I have never, I say it without fear of exaggeration, known or even heard of. (53)

As the defamation—verbose, lurid, and mean to exhaustion—extends over several pages, Mary's identity begins to blur and the master's sadistic, devious, and exploitative nature emerges fully. This depiction of the master's discourse may seem disconnected from Knott and his household—Knott, after all, does not speak and has no female servants. However, he also does not pay his employees, and, as Arsene sarcastically specifies, he likes them "seedy and shabby and few in number, for to seediness and shabbiness and fewness in number he is greatly attached" (58).

Arsene's "short statement" (37) represents almost one tenth of the novel. This blatantly facile joke signals the paradoxical character of his ostentatiously lengthy and subjective descriptions, divagations, and speculations, which produce—concisely enough, after all, given their affective and political weight—a *diagram* of the suspension of exploitation and repression. Mary's story (which foregrounds female servants' exploitation and abuse) features prominently in a statement otherwise focused on Arsene's recollections and *male* servants' concerns because it supports the emergence of the diagram by allowing Arsene's account to cover the entire plane of consistency (Deleuze and Guattari's condition for the generation of an abstract machine). The juxtaposition of Mary and Arsene's experiences denounces the aggregate and mutually sustaining nature of economic and socio-cultural systems of exploitation and abuse. Upon his departure from Knott's house, Arsene has gained the ability to sabotage the repression work of all these strata—he has built his own abstract machine, and his statement effectively broadcasts its diagram.

If Arsene speaks with anger and sarcasm of Knott's need for servants "eternally turning about [him] in tireless love" (61), Watt maintains his dedication to the idea of belonging and to unintelligible Knott as he is attempting, through increasingly desperate displacements (reversing the order of his words in sentences, of the letters in words, the sentences in the period, and all possible combinations thereof), to communicate his experiences to Sam. With near-religious fervour, he laments, "Of nought. To the source. To the teacher. To the temple. To him I brought. This emptied heart. These emptied hands. This mind ignoring. This body homeless. To love him my little reviled. My little rejected to have him. My little to learn him forgot. Abandoned my little to find him" (164). His reverential meditation on Knott's need to be witnessed strongly contrasts Arsene's disdain:

> And Mr Knott, needing nothing if not, one, not to need, and, two, a witness to his not needing, of himself knew nothing. And so he needed to be witnessed. Not that he might know, no, but that he might not cease. ...
> But what kind of witness was Watt, weak now of eye, hard of hearing, and with even the more intimate senses greatly below par?
> A needy witness, an imperfect witness.
> The better to witness, the worse to witness.
> That with his need he might witness its absence.
> That imperfect he might witness it ill.
> That Mr Knott might never cease, but ever almost cease.
> Such appeared to be the arrangement. (202–3)

A version of Beckett's omnipresent and horrific-comic "nearly there," this expression of Watt's pain and confusion likely mobilizes solidarity-based anger rather than mere empathy in readers—especially given the powerful effect of the closing word "arrangement," which foregrounds Watt's coupling to exploitative machinic structures and must belong to Watt's protector and "translator" Sam, an external observer of Watt's predicament. Subsequently, Sam painstakingly builds, for both of their benefit, a liberating assemblage apt to become an abstract machine.

During the period of Watt's linguistic shifts and most substantial Knott-related accounts, Sam and Watt live in different pavilions, separated through a system of barbed wire fences of "a striking irregularity of contour," "[n]ow converging, now diverging" (154). One day, Sam sees Watt walking towards him (back turned, as was his preference), discovers two holes in the fences on either side, and brings Watt into the space in between. The setup of the encounter corrosively depicts religious and economic logic as analogously structured, mutually sustaining strata of the socio-historical exploitation machine. Watt repeatedly falls on his back and injures himself, yet

> without murmur he came on until he lay against the fence, with his hands at arm's length grasping the wires. Then he turned, with the intention very likely of going back the way he had come. ... His face was bloody, his hands also, and thorns were in his scalp. (His resemblance, at that moment, to the Christ believed by Bosch, then hanging in Trafalgar Square, was so striking, that I remarked it.) (157)

The obstinacy and abnegation of the dedicated worker *and* fervent believer seemingly drive Watt here, as in his general attitude towards Knott: he performs his "duty" to self-effacement. The narrator further stresses the conjunction between religious and socio-economic strata through a deceitfully random cultural reference: Watt resembles, specifically, Christ as depicted in a famous painting (a *product* of high economic value). Next, as Sam intercepts Watt, the denunciation mutates into an under-the-radar sabotage operation:

> with a cloth that I had in my pocket [I] wiped his face, and his hands, and then taking a little box of ointment that I had in my pocket from my pocket I anointed his face, and his hands, and then taking a little handcomb from my pocket I straightened his tufts, and his whiskers, and then taking a little clothesbrush from my pocket I brushed his coat, and his trousers. (161)

Sam subversively moves from "anointing" Watt (with ointment...) to brushing his clothes, equivalating the effects of religious martyrdom and exhausting physical labour. His mechanical operations and redundant "explanations" expose the machinic *and reversible* nature of exploitation and subjection, sabotaging what Deleuze and Guattari designate as the "miraculating" effect (*AO* 11) of religious, socio-economic, and other machinic systems whose preservation hinges on persuasively posing as spontaneous emanations of "(human) nature."

These operations merely *initiate* the process of disentangling Watt from the "knot" of exploitation and subjection. To *advance* it, Sam attaches himself to Watt to produce a liberating walking machine:

> I placed his hands, on my shoulders, his left hand on my right shoulder, and his right hand on my left shoulder. Then I placed my hands, on his shoulders, on his left shoulder my right hand, and on his right shoulder my left hand. Then I took a single pace forward, with my left leg, and he a single pace back, with his right leg. ... Then I took a double pace forward with my right leg, and he of course with his left leg a double pace back. And so we paced together between the fences ... until we came to where the fences diverged again. And then turning ... we paced back the way we had come, I forwards, and he of course backwards, with our hands on our shoulders, as before. (161)

These movements create the perfect medium for Watt's linguistic shifts and Sam's "translations." In their exchanges, Watt pulls "backwards" in one way or another, and Sam effects recuperative, arguably "forward-looking" operations. However, the latter are not simply meant to produce the "reverse" of Watt's actions and "return" him to the light of reason.

Sam and Watt's "walking machine" translates Watt's desperate discourse of repression not to make it intelligible in some transcendental logic whereby human failings render meaning elusive but to discard it with each move. Watt cannot grasp Knott's logic because there is no logic to be grasped—only parasitic perversions of thought meant to maintain their victims too obsessed with their state of unknowing to notice their state of exploitation. Sam and Watt's "walking machine" enacts their full psychosomatic disengagement from productivity and conservation-based social assemblages meant to capture, pervert, and exploit human "units." In their embrace, walking within the confines of a no man's land generated between two enclosures, and rotating at times, so that each may walk in his preferred fashion, Sam and Watt enact a perpetual dance along the schizophrenic's stick—a liberating meaning-making and transmission operation that invites readers to internalize, in a solidarity-based move, the *diagram* of halting the production of repression.

Again, Sam, Watt, and Arsene's liberatory procedures aim to disable exploitative assemblages whose power rests on their ability to colonize their victims mind and body, remain ubiquitous and obscure, and pose as emanations of "nature." While some solutions offered may appear horrific-comically asocial, inadequate, and/or futile, Sam, Watt, and Arsene's struggles forcefully communicate that the value of belonging to a community is only as high as the nourishing character of the exchange processes involved. Communitarian integration for its own sake or as a noble sacrifice for "humanist" ideals is denounced as a repressive lure, and the mechanisms of individuals' participation in their own exploitation alongside that of others are sabotaged throughout, particularly through the novel's humour. The following much-quoted—and an emphatically theatrical—philosophical musings on laughter appear in Arsene's statement:

> Of all the laughs that strictly speaking are not laughs, but modes of ululation, only three I think need detain us, I mean the bitter, the hollow and the mirthless. They correspond to successive, how shall I say successive... suc... successive excoriations of the understanding, and the passage from the one to the other is the passage from the lesser to the greater, from the lower to the higher, from the outer to the inner, from the gross to the fine, from the matter to the form. ... The bitter laugh laughs at that which is not good, it

is the ethical laugh. The hollow laugh laughs at that which is not true, it is the intellectual laugh. Not good! Not true! Well well. But the mirthless laugh is the dianoetic laugh, down the snout—Haw!—so. It is the laugh of laughs, the *risus purus*, the laugh laughing at the laugh, the beholding, the saluting of the highest joke, in a word the laugh that laughs—silence please—at that which is unhappy. (46–47)

Ackerley relates this typology to Aristotle's hierarchy of ethical, intellectual, and dianoetic virtues, as listed in Beckett's philosophy notes (*Obscure Locks* 75). However, as Dennis points out, the passage translates these categories into "involuntary bodily response[s] born of emotion rather than reason," challenging "the kind of dualist thinking that would distance the thinking mind from the body" and warning against an overreliance on reason (110). In my reading, this typology of laughter—conveyed, significantly, by Arsene, who shows himself fully aware of the theatrical value and participative impact of his claims—invites full affective participation in the text's rejection of the mechanisms of exploitative psychosomatic coupling that enslave us to ossified socio-historical structures. It does so by emphasizing that, to effectively use humour as a liberatory mechanism, one needs to set the target on the *machinic production* of unhappiness, exploitation and repression, and by detailing the necessary steps in this process. Thus, Arsene's three types of laughter correspond, as emphasized through his stumbling (likely feigned for dramatic effect), to successive and interdependent psychosomatic stages of liberation achieved through positive transformations that may appear damaging ("excoriations") in a traditional, productivity and conservation-based perspective. These transformations carry the promise of revolution—an idea I develop fully later. For now, let us reemphasize the violence of Beckett's consistent attempts to extract from the domain of tragedy manifold elements traditionally associated with it and integrate them into the domain of humour. This predilection becomes increasingly evident in Beckett's later prose, as his black humour more emphatically attempts "reterritorializations" of the horrific.[1] The point is never to deride victims' suffering but to corrode the mechanisms that facilitate the production of pain, and thus generate powerful affects that may transform the acquiescence or paralysis of tragedy or horror—implicitly denounced as meaning formations readily disposed to accommodate machinic repression—into the collected, focused, action-oriented, and solidarity-based anger of liberating laughter.

---

[1] For an extended discussion of *terror* in relation to Beckett's writing, see Langlois.

4.2 Feigning Impotence and Repurposing Language, or, Sharing the Diagram

Beckett's later prose features images of increasingly horrific-comic corporeality. The psychosomatic human assemblage becomes, explicitly and obsessively, a site where machinic structures exercise growing force but still fail to acquire total control. Increasingly diseased, decaying "creatures" afflicted with malfunctioning and oppressive appendages they supposedly cannot discard interact in almost exclusively predatory fashion—including, or perhaps especially, within the family. Simultaneously, they become increasingly creative in their pursuit of empowerment—some painstakingly walking a vaguely ethical line, others ruthlessly pursuing power at others' expense. The perpetrator of abuse as a committed, sadistically participative machinic tool progressively gains prominence within Beckett's comedy of structures, as successive texts broadcast increasingly powerful under-the-radar procedures to resist both the types of conditioning and the forms of interested participation they enact.

Molloy juxtaposes two first-person accounts seemingly completed under pressure: one by Molloy, a drifter living in his (presumably dead) mother's house and visited each Sunday by a man who pays him for any new pages written; and the other by Moran, a detective hired for unspecified reasons to locate Molloy and submit a report. Both men purportedly write their stories under orders, in a weak psychosomatic state. Molloy complains, "What I'd like now is to speak of the things that are left, say my goodbyes, finish dying. They don't want that" (*M* 3). Moran worries that he might fail to complete his report despite his superiors' insistence (95, 183). However, once they start recounting their (mostly abusive) pursuits, both promptly abandon their initially flat and reluctant tone, adopting the animated theatrical personae typical of Beckett's "creatures" in plays *and* in fiction.

Both accounts foreground the predatory nature of Oedipal attachments. Molloy claims, "[my mother] brought me into the world, through the hole in her arse if my memory is correct. First taste of the shit" (13)—and he is not merely making a crude joke. He experiences physicality (his own and others') as a barely disguised variety of *refuse*, as his obsessive poring over excretions, garbage dumps, and festering organic matter reveals. He is repulsed by the affection he feels for his mother and depicts her in ostentatiously disparaging terms:

with this deaf blind impotent mad old woman … and with her alone, I—no, I can't say it. That is to say I could say it but I won't say it, yes, I could say it easily, because it wouldn't be true. What did I see of her? A head always, the hands sometimes, the arms rarely. A head always. Veiled with hair, wrinkles, filth, slobber. A head that darkened the air. (16)

He explains that, since she became deaf in her old age, he "got into communication with her by knocking on her skull. One knock meant yes, two no, three I don't know, four money, five goodbye" (14)—a method indistinguishable from abuse that soon becomes (for mathematical reasons!) *more* abusive. As she had also lost "the faculty of counting beyond two" and "must have thought I was saying no to her all the time," he had to replace "the four knocks of my index-knuckle by one or more (according to my needs) thumps of the fist, on her skull"—and "That she understood" (15). This is not the only time when Molloy uses mathematics to justify abusive performances, or when he exploits and/or denigrates older women with whom he is supposedly close (see his accounts of interactions with Ruth/Edith and Sophie/Lousse). On all these occasions, Molloy's grotesquely inadequate comments and deeds horrific-comically reveal his recourse to various mitigating discursive modes in justifying his acts (his being a victim of circumstance, at the bottom of the social hierarchy, in no position to make choices or act but merely *react*, etc.)

The grotesque comedy of Molloy's physical movements is on a par with his discursive dance. He reviles his stiff leg and supposedly oversized, ever-dropping testicles—useless appendages whose excision would markedly improve his quality of life:

Now my sick leg, I forget which, it's immaterial here, was in a condition neither to dig, because it was rigid, nor alone to support me, because it would have collapsed. … I was virtually one-legged, and I would have been happier, livelier, amputated at the groin. And if they had removed a few testicles into the bargain I wouldn't have objected. For from such testicles as mine, dangling at mid-thigh at the end of a meagre cord, there was nothing more to be squeezed, not a drop. … And, worse still, they got in my way when I tried to walk, when I tried to sit down, … and when I rode my bicycle they bounced up and down. (33–34)

However, apart from clearly not preventing him from riding a bicycle or acquiring sexual partners, these allegedly useless appendages also do not make him less lethal on occasion, as his account of a vicious beating inflicted on a "coal burner" who propositioned him sexually shows:

> I contented myself with giving him a few warm kicks in the ribs, with my heels. ... I carefully chose the most favourable position, a few paces from the body, with my back of course turned to it. Then, nicely balanced on my crutches, I began to swing, backwards, forwards, feet pressed together, or rather legs pressed together, for how could I press my feet together, with my legs in the state they were? ... What can that possibly matter? I swung, that's all that matters, in an ever-widening arc, until I decided the moment had come and launched myself forward with all my strength and consequently, a moment later, backward, which gave the desired result. ... I rested a moment, then got up, picked up my crutches, took up my position on the other side of the body and applied myself with method to the same exercise. (85–86)

Here and elsewhere, Molloy's comedic verve in recounting violent acts undermines his claims concerning his misadventures and psychosomatic condition—claims whose questionable veracity he otherwise keeps flaunting, either by complaining of a weak memory or by admitting to have lied. The same comedic verve evinces a strong undercurrent of anger originating, as already revealed in earlier passages, in his lifelong subjection to conditioning and abuse.

Molloy prefaces his "idyll" with Ruth/Edith by asking himself if a woman might ever "have stopped me as I swept towards mother," and then elaborates as follows:

> was such an encounter possible, I mean between me and a woman? Now men, I have rubbed up against a few men in my time, but women? Oh well, I may as well confess it now, yes, I once rubbed up against one. I don't mean my mother, I did more than rub up against her. ... But another who might have been my mother, and even I think my grandmother, if chance had not willed otherwise. ... It was she made me acquainted with love. She went by the peaceful name of Ruth I think, but I can't say for certain. Perhaps the name was Edith. She had a hole between her legs, oh not the bunghole I had always imagined, but a slit, and in this I put, or rather she put, my so-called virile member, not without difficulty, and I toiled and moiled until I discharged or gave up trying or was begged by her to stop. ... I lent myself to it with a good enough grace, knowing it was love, for she had told me so. She bent over the couch, because of her rheumatism, and in I went from behind. ... It seemed all right to me, for I had seen dogs, and I was aston-

ished when she confided that you could go about it differently. I wonder what she meant exactly. Perhaps after all she put me in her rectum. A matter of complete indifference to me, I needn't tell you. But is it true love, in the rectum? That's what bothers me sometimes. Have I never known true love, after all? (55–56)

In this key passage, Molloy mentions explicitly, though supposedly in passing, sexual contact with men, insistently compares his mother to Ruth/ Edith, whose exact name he claims not to remember, and obsessively uses the word "love" in horrific-comically inadequate contexts. The sequence bears conspicuous traces of psychosexual conditioning and anger. Most critical contributions integrate such aspects of Molloy's psychosexual makeup into larger discussions of his erudition, taste for scatological humour, problematic relationship with his mother, and/or misogyny, usually without acknowledging him as a queer subject.[2] Yet, many details support this reading. Molloy seems to have been subjected to psychosexual and socio-cultural normalization to the point of perceiving his sexual inclinations as abject. An intense and generalized hatred of others, in conjunction with deep feelings of self-loathing, dominates his attitude and interactions. The black humour of his detailed accounts of abusive pursuits derives from his ability to put himself on display as a *working machine* industriously transforming received conditioning into inflicted abuse. The target of the mockery is neither Molloy's suffering nor that he inflicts on others but the mechanics of its social transmission.

Reading Beckett's *Molloy, Malone Dies*, and *The Unnamable* through Michel Foucault's *Discipline and Punish* and within the historical context of the Second World War, Uhlmann deems Becket's characters' "ill-discipline and failure" as "not necessarily intentional" but effective means to oppose surveillance, order, and ultimately, subjectification (*Beckett and Poststructuralism* 54, 55). I would suggest, however, that the impotence

---

[2] To date, few studies define Beckett's postwar male characters as queer. Bersani and Dutoit explore Beckett's use of homoeroticism to destabilize consecrated relationship patterns. More recent studies by Ackerley, Boxall, Jeffers, and Stewart advance this line of argumentation. For instance, Jeffers identifies, in Molloy and other male characters' "indifference" towards "heterosexual masculine norms," a means to "upend the very logic" of heteronormative impositions (78–79). Noting that most of Beckett's characters interact violently (whether they follow their inclinations or are "normalized") and/or end up *alone*, Stewart concludes that Beckett may have considered solitude "preferable to a relation predicated on violence" (113).

and failure are always partly feigned, and the opposition, generally intentional. Molloy's presumably deteriorating body does not prevent engagement in sexual or aggressive acts, and his discursive combination of erudition and scatological humour is not random but exceedingly meaningful and corrosive, revealing barely contained anger. Moran, less intelligent and self-aware than Molloy and to a larger extent a machinic tool, also mostly feigns his inability and weakness—because he is a dissatisfied tool, constantly spouting angry remarks that betray his (and the system's) predatory nature.

Molloy's sarcastic verve broadcasts transformative anger rather than resigned bitterness. Still, Molloy does not achieve liberation by the end of his experience, as the coal burner incident foretells. The following painful confession prefaces the beating:

> I might have loved him, I think, if I had been seventy years younger. ... I never really had much love to spare, but all the same I had my little quota, when I was small, and it went to the old men, when it could. And I even think I had time to love one or two, oh not with true love, no, nothing like the old woman ... but all the same, how shall I say, tenderly, as those on the brink of a better earth. Ah I was a precocious child, and then I was a precocious man. Now they all give me the shits, the ripe, the unripe and the rotting from the bough. He was all over me, begging me to share his hut, believe it or not. A total stranger. Sick with solitude probably. (84–85)

In light of this confession, Molloy's brutal treatment of the coal burner reveals self-loathing and self-denial while corrosively enacting what "successful" normalization entails. The beating scene—remarkably grotesque even in an account where excrements are thrown at mathematics, logic, literature, philosophy, and religion on every page—matches the viciousness of the normalization pressures that have plagued Molloy's life. Horrific-comically, in internalizing this viciousness and becoming a "kicking assemblage," Molloy finally comes to deserve to be saved: he is recuperated from a ditch (93), presumably by "agents" working for the same "organization" as Moran, and restored to a form of gainful employment whereby the last remnants of his lifelong rebellion can be contained in a written text. Remnants, however, prove unruly here, as elsewhere in Beckett. Molloy's horrific-comic verve and underlying anger are contagious and cannot be contained. He may be defeated, but the action and change-oriented anger emanating from his confession is likely to "infect" readers, whose exposure to his claims and misadventures might prompt them to reassess disruptive displacements of anger and target, through intense flows of affect, the core causes of repression instead.

Moran's section initially appears to override Molloy's as an objective account apt to contextualize events and justify systemic actions—yet, it proves no less subjective than Molloy's and far less persuasive: dull, self-important, and hollow. Moran appears, in principle, as Molloy's opposite: if Molloy is the epitome of restlessness, unpredictability, and excess, as Moran claims (117–18), Moran is a model of planning and poise. However, these oppositions consistently fail to function in Moran's favour, so that his report compromises (instead of supporting) systemic claims to benevolence.

While Molloy's relationship with his mother is ambiguous, Moran—a caricature of Victorian parenting—confirms Deleuze and Guattari's claim that Oedipal relations originate in parents' paranoid projections rather than being givens of child development (*AO* 275). He randomly reads "unimaginable effrontery" (*M* 113) in his son's tone and exalts the pedagogical merits of parental abuse:

> I was sometimes inclined to go too far when I reprimanded my son, who was consequently a little afraid of me. I myself had never been sufficiently chastened. ... Whence bad habits ingrained beyond remedy. ... I hoped to spare my son this misfortune, by giving him a good clout from time to time, together with my reasons for doing so. (98–99)

On the evening preceding his journey in search for Molloy, he sends his seemingly ill son to fetch the thermometer, asking him, "You know which mouth to put it in?" (122). Next, he elaborates on the developmental value of his utterance, in case anyone missed it:

> I was not averse ... to jests of doubtful taste, in the interests of his education. Those whose pungency he could not fully savour at the time ... he could reflect on at his leisure or seek in company with his little friends to interpret as best he might. ... And at the same time I inclined his young mind towards that most fruitful of dispositions, horror of the body and its functions. But I had turned my phrase badly, mouth was not the word I should have used. (122)

The evening ends with a forced enema ("He struggled, but not for long," 119).

While Molloy craftily alternates discursive modes to paint his acts of exploitation and abuse as logical or unavoidable, Moran's sanctimonious and paranoid rants fully denounce his sadism. Molloy reports some affectionate interactions, but Moran's exploits are purely predatory. He claims to avoid showing affection towards his son for purposes of "character-building," but only sadism, bigotry, and spite transpire from his words and acts. A chat with his priest (103–5) reveals his attachment to rule and ritual in their punitive aspects and contempt for compassion. During his search for Molloy, he professes fairness and benevolence—a readiness to sacrifice money and pride to preserve peace and order—but repeatedly betrays his true character, as in this falsely hazy and deeply conceited account of a violent incident:

> He thrust his hand at me. I have an idea I told him once again to get out of my way. I can still see the hand coming towards me, pallid, opening and closing. As if self-propelled. I do not know what happened then. But a little later, perhaps a long time later, I found him stretched on the ground, his head in a pulp. I am sorry I cannot indicate more clearly how this result was obtained, it would have been something worth reading. (158)

By the time the search is abruptly suspended by another "agent," who declares the problem solved, Moran's sadism and malice have been fully revealed.

Several occurrences in Molloy's and Moran's travels seemingly reference John Bunyan's *Pilgrim's Progress* (Fletcher 132–33), and the names Gaber (another agent of the "organization") and Youdi (the "chief") may point to Gabriel and Yahweh (147–48). Since "Youdi" is also a French slang term for "Jew," Uhlmann wonders at its effect on French readers after the Holocaust revelations (*Beckett and Poststructuralism* 48). It may be tempting to interpret such elements as expressions of human powerlessness and hunger for transcendental justice and meaning. I would suggest, however, that neither Beckett's grotesque rendering of Molloy and Moran's bicycling, walking, and crawling, nor what could alternately be read as neighbourhood gang versions of deities' names seem ideal methods if Beckett indeed meant to stress the tragedy of the human condition. Not abnegation and resignation but sarcasm and anger dominate the text. Molloy and Moran's "confessions" reveal (one deliberately, the other against itself) not the enlightening virtues of suffering but its utter cruelty and destructiveness as a maintenance mechanism of the socio-historical

machine. As these confessions show, multiple strata of Oedipal, communitarian, cultural, economic, and religious conditioning conspire to extract
full acquiescence from the human assemblage—but conditioning and
repression, forever dependent on language, fail to efface their places of
articulation and remain vulnerable to attack.

Malone Dies is framed, like *Molloy*, as a forced writing exercise—
although it first appears that Malone is not coerced by an external entity
but that, his death approaching, he is attempting to appease its dread with
stories. His opening claim, "I shall soon be quite dead at last in spite of
all" (*MD* 3), reiterates Beckett's horrific-comic "nearly there." Like
Molloy, Malone first adopts a deceivingly flat, exhausted, prostrate tone—
"While waiting I shall tell myself stories, if I can. … They will be neither
beautiful nor ugly, they will be calm, there will be no ugliness or beauty or
fever in them any more, they will be almost lifeless, like the teller" (4)—
but soon veers into a vividly paced, intensely dramatized account. A
humour of structures emanates from a variety of otherwise sordid affairs
involving him and several (other) characters—some of them, seemingly
fictionalized younger versions of himself.

Malone ostentatiously uses his writing to relive the venom and anger of
his past rather than find peace: "I forgive nobody. I wish them all an atrocious life and then the fires and ice of hell and in the execrable generations
to come an honoured name" (4). He obsessively readjusts a writing "programme," finally settling on "five" steps: "Present state, three stories,
inventory, there. An occasional interlude is to be feared. A full programme.
I shall not deviate from it any further than I must" (6). Whatever purpose
of containment this confession had been assigned, it will clearly be sabotaged at every turn by the usual "stirrings" that render Beckett's characters horrific-comically impervious to machinic coupling:

> There it is then divided into five, the time that remains. Into five what? I
> don't know. Everything divides into itself, I suppose. If I start trying to
> think again I shall make a mess of my decease. I must say there is something
> very attractive about such a prospect. But I am on my guard. For the past
> few days I have been finding something attractive about everything. (6)

Malone derives pleasure from his writing and repeatedly admits it (usually,
as above, by mockingly condemning the vivifying effects of the
experience)—a pleasure, assumedly, not sanctioned by the "powers that
be" (6) mentioned as though in passing. It is, perhaps, for this reason that,

in the functionally sadistic and crude fashion in which institutional repression operates in Beckett's works, in the late stages of his "stay" at the House of Saint John of God, Malone no longer receives food or has his chamber pot emptied. The risible redundancy in the name of the charity institution is compounded by the fact that, upon arrival, Malone's avatar Macmann is reassured, "Fear nothing, you are among friends. Friends! Well well. Take no thought for anything, it is we shall think and act for you, from now forward. We like it. Do not thank us therefore" (84). Residents must renounce all thinking and mobility in exchange for a place in a presumably well-structured charity machine. Once he signs the agreement, Macmann is confined to a bed and brutally punished if he leaves his room without permission.

Macmann is first placed in the care of Moll, an old woman. Their sexual interactions generate explosive moments of black humour. Moll has earrings shaped like crucifixes and "a long yellow canine bared to the roots and carved, with the drill probably, to represent the celebrated sacrifice" (93). The lovers' discussion of these adornments is perhaps the most iconoclastic episode in a novel replete with religious irreverence. Macmann asks, "Why two Christs?"—and Moll replies, "Why two ears? ... Besides they are the thieves, Christ is in my mouth" (93). As the narrative voice specifies, "in the pleasure [Macmann] was later to enjoy, when he put his tongue in her mouth and let it wander over her gums, this rotten crucifix had assuredly its part" (93). Notions of forgiveness, sacrifice, and redemption are systematically placed in hyperbolically prurient, sadistic, and/or otherwise disparaging contexts in Beckett's works, as their integrative function is denounced as a containment and repression tool. Unsurprisingly, Macmann's refusal to integrate body and mind into the charity machine attracts Moll's replacement (supposedly due to her sudden death) with a different enforcer: Lemuel—a man equally partial to inflicting self-harm and harming others with his sticks, hammer, and hatchet. Subsequently, Macmann is repeatedly punished for exiting his room and roaming the grounds. While on an approved outing, Macmann witnesses Lemuel killing several residents and loses consciousness, perhaps after a blow to the head. Both Moll (87) and Macmann (111) refer to the residents as "inmates," and Macmann, also as "prisoners" (108). The House of Saint John of God reveals itself as a functionally sadistic repression machine within the larger, functionally sadistic socio-historical machine. Everyone is "coupled" to it in a mode ranging from feigned benevolence to barefaced cruelty—yet the former fails to be entirely persuasive, and the latter, entirely effective.

Malone is generally discussed in Beckett studies as a composite character sharing various traits with his avatars Macmann and Sapo, as with characters from *Molloy* and earlier works (physical appearance, clothing, physical ailments, preferred travel routes, sexual inclinations and experiences, personal obsessions and possessions, etc.). Besides destabilizing traditional narrative conventions, these ostentatious yet inconsistent correspondences and connections support Beckett's omnipresent and empowering humour of structures. Malone sarcastically comments, "When I have completed my inventory, if my death is not ready for me then, I shall write my memoirs. That's funny, I have made a joke" (8). Clearly, he has been tasked to recall, rethink, and record his experiences in a teleological and redemptive manner. Instead, he *feigns* compliance and uses fictionalization, sarcasm, and anger to render memory and invention indiscernible and blur his contour enough to preclude totalizing control.

Malone's anger, like Molloy's, may derive from lifelong heteronormative, masculinist conditioning. In his youth (as Sapo), he apparently witnessed an endearing neighbour's relentless abuse by her husband, Mr. Lambert, the local "bleeder and disjointer of pigs," an older man at his "third or fourth" marriage (25) who also abused his children and may have caused his previous wives' deaths. Mrs. Lambert

> had abandoned all hope of bringing him to heel, by means of her cunt, that trump card of young wives. For she knew what he would do to her if she did not open it to him. And he even insisted on her making things easy for him, in ways that often appeared to her exorbitant. And at the least show of rebellion on her part he would run to the wash-house and come back with the battle and beat her until she came round to a better way of thinking. All this by the way. (26)

In such fragments, where the abuser's perspective seemingly crushes the victim's, the collected sarcasm that dominates most of the text mutates into uninhibited solidarity and compassion-based anger. Mr. Lambert's sadism and Mrs. Lambert's psychosomatic disintegration likely galvanize readers' action-oriented anger, as does the black humour of the power dynamic. In the Oedipal-familial logic, self-sacrificial submission to the Father's rule is the "better way of thinking," and the slightest refusal, a threat meriting extreme punishment. Those at the bottom of the hierarchy quickly become little more than broken machines, as Mrs. Lambert's fits reveal:

> The woman, pausing an instant between two tasks, or in the midst of one, flung up her arms and … unable to sustain their great weight, let them fall again. Then she began to toss them about in a way difficult to describe, and not easy to understand. The movements resembled those, at once frantic and slack, of an arm shaking a duster, or a rag, to rid it of its dust. And so rapid was the trepidation of the limp, empty hands that there seemed to be four or five at the end of each arm, instead of the usual one. (27–28)

Language itself seems flattened and defeated here. Yet, the Lamberts' story still sustains Beckett's horrific-comic humour of machinic structures, as it is implicitly posited as the real face of heteronormativity rather than a random episode of sadistic excess, and as a formative experience for Sapo. Macmann's relationship with Moll is a collection of grotesqueries. Malone mentions that five male lovers found his character "disgusting" (45) and dreams, in his final days, of coercing "a little girl" to meet his physical and sexual needs (103). Sapo's "socialization" must have involved acquiring some of Mr. Lambert's habits—which may explain Malone's intense self-loathing. While, individually, these occurrences are horrific, their articulation into a "functional" heteronormative political economy is corrosively horrific-comic, as any systemic pretense of benevolence or functionality is diagrammatically enacted as a maintenance mechanism safeguarding masculinist sadistic enjoyment.

Both Malone and Macmann recall losing consciousness, for blurry reasons, at key points in their lives. Both wake up in the House of Saint John of God after such events. Later, Macmann presumably receives a blow to the head from Lemuel on the trip, and Malone, from a "visitor" who resembles Moran. These conspicuous occurrences denote a machinic presence behind the events that befall Malone and the "others," as does Malone's obsessively revised "programme": "Visit, various remarks, Macmann continued, agony recalled, Macmann continued, then mixture of Macmann and agony as long as possible. It does not depend on me, my lead is not inexhaustible, nor my exercisebook, nor Macmann, nor myself in spite of appearances" (98–99). This fearfully redundant expression of powerlessness starkly contrasts Malone's self-assured earlier claim that, with his imminent demise, "it will be all over with the Murphys, Merciers,

Molloys, Morans and Malones" (63). Malone has seemingly concluded that the game (he often uses the word "play") is rigged to continue for as long as he refuses to unify his experiences into a redeeming story of soporific machinic coupling and social functionality—and, corrupt as he is, Malone will not do it. He will not forgive or be forgiven. He will not allow whatever he perceives now as himself, in his ever-(un)ending and cruel last moments, or any of his twisted, fragmented avatars to be reduced to docile souls at peace.

While Malone and his avatars' actions and experiences have mostly been abusive and exploitative, in blocking his avatars' merger and rejecting redemption, Malone prevents the socio-historical normalization, exploitation, and repression forces that have maimed him (in part, as he acknowledges, with his cooperation) from claiming overall benevolent designs. This move may trigger solidarity-based flows of affect in readers. He deviously—writerly—seals his case through an ending that seemingly fulfils machinic requirements for cleansing containment while exploding the assemblage from within:

> Lemuel is in charge, he raises his hatchet on which the blood will never dry, but not to hit anyone, he will not hit anyone, he will not hit anyone any more, he will not touch anyone any more, either with it or with it or with it or with or
> or with it or with his hammer or with his stick or with his fist or in thought in dream I mean never he will never
> or with his pencil or with his stick or
> or light light I mean
> never there he will never
> never anything
> there
> any more. (119)

Given Malone and Macmann's fluctuating, agonizing, yet ostentatious connection, Macmann could have "died" only to "become" Malone. This "execution"—nightmarish but clearly fake or failed—likely ends the text partly due to Malone's self-loathing but mostly due to its theatrical value and ability to obstruct closure. Lemuel's flamboyant killing spree has maximum dramatic impact and symbolic value: Macmann and the others appear to succumb to an implacable and tragic stroke of fate—purportedly an awe-inspiring closure. However, sadistic Lemuel "the Aryan," with his legs full of self-inflicted bruises, with his sticks, hammer, hatchet, and brutish way of speaking, is a caricature of machinic precision—sufficiently grotesque to be horrific-comic rather than strictly frightening. The trip itself is a subversive collection of grotesqueries, as the narration ostentatiously juxtaposes other residents' disturbed behaviours to Macmann's protestations to being restrained (114–15). Macmann's demise theatrically denounces the system rather than confirming its natural or "fated" functioning. The system treats Macmann's need for freedom as a variety of "madness" and would have us read Lemuel's psychotic attack as a symptom of the victims' unhealthy, failed lives rather than an instance of criminal institutional indifference. The screaming artifice of the episode, however, spotlights the switches that set this semantic reassignment charade into motion. (Malone throws in a cute link between Lemuel's weapons and his pen, and between murder and the act of writing, for good measure.)

Molloy ends with Moran's self-pityingly tragic, "Then I went back into the house and wrote, It is midnight. The rain is beating on the windows. It was not midnight. It was not raining" (*M* 184). The ostentatiously dramatic and deceitfully "round" ending of *Malone* similarly mutates tragedy into angry, action-oriented laughter. Always in collusion, always excessively invested in precluding resistance, the Oedipal, socio-economic, religious, and militaristic machinic strata at work in these novels have seemingly succeeded only in depressing and/or rendering criminally insane their own "agents." Corrupted, mutilated, and in pain, Beckett's Molloys and Malones "go on," flaunting their wounds and using their composite nature to resist machinic coupling, denouncing even their recurring "deaths" as loops in a deranged machinic economy. Cohn places Beckett's subsequent work, *The Unnamable*, in the category of the tragicomic (139). Weller responds that the novel enacts "precisely the disintegration of even this most hybrid of genres" (*Ethics of Alterity* 119). In my reading, more importantly, with *The Unnamable*, the focus shifts from comedically sabotaging the repressive underpinnings of tragedy to attacking those of horror. Beckett's critics noted the increasing disembodiment of the narrative voice starting with *The Unnamable*. What I would emphasize, instead, is that this disembodiment is paradoxically accompanied by the persistent presence (or threat to return) of the suffering flesh, in an increasingly powerful and more explicitly political denunciation of abstract systems' reliance on the physical threat as their ultimate maintenance procedure.

The speaker from *The Unnamable* claims to be unable to define his environment and body position, control his body, or use anything but "the words of others" (*U* 4–5, 14–16, 25). While his conditions of existence are notably more precarious and less recognizably human than those inflicted on Molloy or Malone, he, too, has seemingly been tasked with a confession. Like the others, he first seems tentative, dispirited, and passive, but his caveats, qualifications, and negations are eerily infused with vigour. In the opening passage, basic expressions of alienation and powerlessness ("Where now? Who now? When now? Unquestioning," "I seem to speak, it is not I, about me, it is not me," or "what shall I do, what should I do?") are conspicuously undercut by second-person inserts ("call that going, call that on," or "It, say it, not knowing what") that become increasingly disquieting as they proliferate (1). The speaker follows his fluctuant first comments with the pedantic line, "These few general remarks to begin with," wondering whether to proceed "[b]y aporia pure and simple" or "by affirmations and negations invalidated as uttered (or sooner or later)," only to then pretend not to know what "aporia" means (1). Next come an instance of sophisticated persiflage ("Can one be ephectic otherwise than unawares?"), a deadpan dismissal ("I don't know. With the yesses and noes it is different: they will come back to me as I go along"), and, finally, the usual scatological exorcism ("And now, like a bird, to shit on them all without exception") (1). While seemingly thematizing human powerlessness, unawareness, and incomprehension, the opening already introduces elements of mockery meant to destabilize such notions and implicitly sabotage the repressive potential of any social and institutional assemblages wired to them. Still, readers less familiar with Beckett's works might not perceive the meaning and direction of this comedic attack until later, when the Unnamable begins his more straightforward sabotage of "masters," "gods," "tyrants," and their sadistic pastimes—enforcing language, complacency, and pain.

In a passage where he keenly elaborates on the "pensum" he had been given at birth "as a punishment for having been born perhaps, or for no particular reason, because they dislike me," the Unnamable defines the "masters," with increasingly iconoclastic sarcasm, as follows: "there may be more than one, a whole college of tyrants, differing in their views as to what should be done with me, in conclave since time began or a little later, listening to me from time to time, then breaking up for a meal or a game of cards" (21). The same passage vividly denounces the masters' controlling and exploitative imposition of language: "when I have finished my pensum I shall still have my lesson to say, before I have the right to stay quiet in my corner, alive and dribbling, my mouth shut, my tongue at rest, far from all disturbance, all sound, my mind at peace, that is to say empty" (21–22). Far from being allowed to function as a means of communication at individuals' disposal, language is, then, a machinic assemblage masters use to set bodies in motion, engage them in processes of production (a "pensum" here, a "lesson" there), and exploit their physical and mental labour to exhaustion. Here and elsewhere, the Unnamable's stated longing for "emptiness" is not nihilism but a corrosive denunciation of that exploitation as a prolonged act of torture and of machinic claims to benevolence as increased-efficiency procedures meant to extract declarations of consent and contentment, with the last drop of energy and life, from those coupled and used.

God, in the Unnamable's description, is a "fomenter of calm"—a spiteful definition paired with a categorical negation of the benevolent metaphysical foundation of social arrangements: "I never believed. Not for a second" (16). The Unnamable is not *unable* to find peace—he adamantly rejects acquiescence, and if he often feigns impotence and confusion, it is for fear of punishment (his "delegate" Mahood's stories are all about that, but I will return to this later). He at times references "my master" as a separate being from "god," but only to engage in more vividly iconoclastic mockery:

> The master in any case, we don't intend ... to make the mistake of inquiring into him, he'd turn out to be a mere high official, we'd end up by needing God, we have lost all sense of decency admittedly, but there are still certain depths we prefer not to sink to. Let us keep to the family circle, it's more intimate, we all know one another now, no surprises to be feared, the will has been opened, nothing for anybody. (91)

Gods and masters, under whatever name, are machinic safeguards in a generalized exploitation assemblage that endlessly puts on a show of fulfilment and belonging the Unnamable and his "delegates" resent, as they see such notions as injunctions to embrace exploitation—to exalt their bondage as connectedness and their exhaustion as self-realization, without a reminder.

Unequivocally indicting this "happiness" as a barely disguised form of forcing, the Unnamable reports that, since his birth, his master has been "commanding me to be well, you know, in every way, no complaints at all" (24)—and reasserts the point ad nauseam, ostentatiously vacillating between emphatic disdain and false reverence:

> My master then ... wishes me well, poor devil, wishes my good, and if he does not seem to do very much in order not to be disappointed it is because ... there is nothing to be done, otherwise he would have done it, my great and good master, that must be it, long ago, poor devil. ... I want all to be well with you, do you hear me, that's what he keeps on dinning at me. To which I reply, in a respectful attitude, I too, your Lordship. ... What he means by good, my good, is another problem. He is capable of wanting me to be happy, such a thing has been known, it appears. Or to serve a purpose. Or the two at once! A little more explicitness on his part, since the initiative belongs to him, might be a help. ... In a word let him enlighten me, that's all I ask, so that I may at least have the satisfaction of knowing in what sense I leave to be desired. If he wants me to say something, for my good naturally, he has only to tell me what it is and I'll let it out with a roar straight away. (23–24)

The diction, tone, and content of this "meditation" on divine intent, supreme good, free will, divine grace, and divine punishment is not tentative and accommodating but defiant and corrosive. Moreover, it is not merely a deconstruction of religious conditioning and repression but a scathing attack on any modes of social connectivity similarly based in circular logic and a need to contain and control.[3]

We again see Beckett's humour of structures at work in this attack. In previously quoted passages as elsewhere in the novel, the Unnamable denounces the machinic connections between religious commandments, parental conditioning, social containment, and economic exploitation. Typically, the notion of an absolute, divine authority smoothly couples itself to that of mandatory filial piety within the family, to an ideal of organic communitarian connectivity complete with benevolent hierarchical arrangements within social interactions, and to a requirement of ever-increasing efficiency/ speed in terms of economic productivity—all the better to legitimize the subject's coupling to this totalizing assemblage. However, the Unnamable's "meditation" denounces the operating logic

---

[3] As Adorno notes, anti-representational modernist art often denounces structures of authority in this manner and is often subjected to censorship for this reason: "Art, even as something tolerated in the administered world, embodies what does not allow itself to be managed and what total management suppresses. Greece's new tyrants knew why they banned Beckett's plays, in which there is not a single political word" (*Aesthetic Theory* 234).

of this purportedly munificent, bountiful system as "nothing for anybody" (91). Part of what enables this exploitative assemblage to operate with impunity is, undoubtedly, *language*—and it is in this logic and from this perspective that the Unnamable's linguistic contortions should be understood.

The problem with language, as the Unnamable knows all too well, is not that it is poor and imprecise, but on the contrary, excessively defined and heavily anchored—words are rigid, overcharged, and confining. Consequently, his logical and grammatical contortions, while seemingly expressing powerlessness and doubt, are in fact elaborate, vivid, dramatic attempts to forge connections with assumed interlocutors and perhaps establish an alternate socio-linguistic community. The "binary-turned sentence" (a redoubling of the subject/ direct object characteristic of colloquial French) is an example. Astbury notes that Beckett uses this syntactic structure extensively in the French texts starting with *Molloy* but does not mimic it in his English translations until *The Unnamable*—from which point all his texts dislocate syntax more radically (452). In my assessment, Beckett's syntactic operations also become increasingly aggressive and focused—more obviously *diagrammatic*, generating increasing volumes of affective energy and approximating clearer paths to transformative action through their unbridled connective theatricality. One binary-turned English sentence Astbury identifies—"But perhaps I malign him unjustly, my good master" (*U* 24), which she connects to Beckett's characters' presumed anxiety concerning their ability to make themselves understood (Astbury 447)—suggests, through its sarcasm, disdain and anger rather than apprehension or doubt. The direct object is redoubled so it can be *nullified* rather than clarified—the Unnamable uses the masculine singular pronoun to invoke the master and the derisive noun phrase to disgustedly spit him out.

Such under-the-radar angry reactions characterize most of Beckett's postwar "voices," in his dramas *and* fiction, indicating an eerie awareness of being witnessed by a potentially sympathetic audience alongside being under surveillance by "masters." Gontarski identifies a "direct and fundamental dramatic quality of which Beckett was fully aware" even in the "disembodied voices" and "dehumanized immobility" of the late prose ("Unabandoned" xvi). He discusses Beckett's correspondence with directors interested in staging his fiction, noting his rejection of "adaptations that posited a unity of character and narrative that the monologue form suggests" and insistence that all dramatizations stress the "immediacy and emotional power" characterizing even his most philosophical or experimental texts (xviii). Beckett's fictional speakers' dramatized mode of expression is paramount for my argument, as it accounts for much of the astonishing energy of his texts. These speakers tend to be in some way captive and to perform at the injunction of an abuser/ "college" of abusers with pretend-benevolent designs. Increasingly disembodied yet acutely preoccupied with the threat of physical pain, they live in isolation and often adamantly claim to loathe human connections, but many elements in their discourse are addressed to an audience—corrosively angry, humorously contagious appeals to solidarity in the face of exploitation and oppression. Their tone and diction indict social performance as a function of aggregate, machinic performativity, as they struggle to clear language of repressive micro-assemblages so that it may function, despite its history of use as a conservative systemic tool, as a receptacle for affective energy and an incitement to transformative action.

Salisbury describes Beckett's characters' cautiously insubordinate attitude in *Molloy, Malone Dies*, and *The Unnamable* as follows: while they are "constantly force-fed" words, social norms, and physical nourishment of varying degrees of repugnancy, this merely trains them to avoid absorbing "what is … served up" (100). This peculiar treatment of language generates "a formal gag reflex within the artwork itself"—Beckett's notoriously endless caveats, justifications, partial negations, and qualifications (Salisbury, *Laughing Matters* 104). In discussing the obsessive co-presence of matters of corporeal excretion and linguistic expression in these novels, Salisbury references Beckett's 1934 reading notes on psychoanalytic works by Ernest Jones, defining the "obligation to express" discussed by Beckett in his dialogues with Georges Duthuit as a compulsion as inescapable as the anal neurotic's "gathering [of] matter together, speech, writing, and faeces" (*Laughing Matters* 87–90). I would suggest, instead, that Beckett consistently enables his speakers to use the excretive function of language in a *diagrammatic* manner—to broadcast a deliberate and reproducible procedure that involves *feigning compulsion to hide intentionality* while sabotaging the socio-linguistic machine.

As the Unnamable is aware, sabotaging the repressive function of language is difficult for two major reasons. First, repressively-focused language has historically formed the basis of identity for any socially connected human being: "Not to be able to open my mouth without proclaiming them, and our fellowship, that's what they imagine they'll have me reduced to. It's a poor trick that consists in ramming a set of words down your gullet on the principle that you can't bring them up without being branded as belonging to their breed" (37). Second, historically, in any exploitative socio-economic assemblage, confessional, fully acquiescent language has been peddled as an ideal means to evade exclusion and pain—and, while submission might not preclude suffering, straightforward resistance would certainly attract punishment:

> If they had told me what I have to say, in order to meet with their approval, I'd be bound to say it, sooner or later. But God forbid, that would be too easy, my heart wouldn't be in it! I have to puke my heart out too, spew it up whole along with the rest of the vomit. It's then at last I'll look as if I mean what I'm saying, it won't be just idle words. (49)

A frontal attack on language or the repressive circuits it maintains would be doomed to failure, even apart from comporting serious risks, as these passages suggest. The solution, then, is to pretend to be playing the game while sabotaging it from within:

> First I'll say what I'm not, that's how they taught me to proceed, then what I am ... I am neither, I needn't say, Murphy, nor Watt, nor Mercier, nor— no, I can't even bring myself to name them, nor any of the others whose very names I forget, who told me I was they, who I must have tried to be, under duress, or through fear, or to avoid acknowledging me, not the slightest connection. I never desired, never sought, never suffered, never partook in any of that, never knew what it was to have things, adversaries, mind, senses. ... There's no getting rid of them without naming them and their contraptions, that's the thing to keep in mind. I might as well tell another of Mahood's stories ... to be understood in the way I was given to understand it, namely as being about me. (38)

The Unnamable alternates between refusals to identify with his "delegates" (or bitter claims that identification would occur under duress) and vivacious first-person accounts of their experiences. While posing as an effect of confusion and weakness, this vacillation sabotages unified notions of identity—"they" cannot be univocally identified as real people the Unnamable knew, past/ future selves, states of mind, or figments of his imagination. Telling the stories of his "delegates"—especially Mahood's horrific-comic tales of dispossession, pain, and ultimately disembodiment—enables the Unnamable to build momentum for an affect-based transformation of language from a vehicle of oppression into an unstoppable liberation machine.

For Adorno, Beckett's postwar works produce "the negative imprint of the administered world," questioning a long history of "pseudoconcreteness" in art and indicting realism as a representational mode supportive of a "total society," whereby individuals and objects, "by being in some way distinct, can be identified, possessed, and sold" (*Aesthetic Theory* 31). In Adorno's view, Beckett designates his narratives as novels "sardonically" (30) and "put[s] out of service" both the concepts of the realistic and the symbolic (31). The mockery of character development in *The Unnamable* supports this assessment. The Unnamable first refers to Mahood as Basil—an appropriate generic name for the upper-middle-class protagonist of a realist novel—and abruptly switches to Mahood in a passage additionally meant to "clarify," in the Unnamable's falsely tentative, sarcastic style, their relationship:

> Basil is becoming important, I'll call him Mahood instead, I prefer that, I'm queer. It was he told me stories about me, lived in my stead, issued forth from me, came back to me, entered back into me, heaped stories on my head. I don't know how it was done. I always liked not knowing, but Mahood said it wasn't right. He didn't know either, but it worried him. It is his voice which has often, always, mingled with mine, and sometimes drowned it completely. Until he left me for good, or refused to leave me any more, I don't know. (20)

The transparent reference to "manhood" in the new name signals the presence of Beckett's humour of structures. Mahood (like Macmann before him) is Beckett's "queer" version of the generic male protagonist of a respectable novel—or, indeed, of contemporary man: obsessed with knowledge, self-reflection, and his penis (not necessarily in that order), used and abused to exhaustion, and brutally pressured into unqualified, self-denying acquiescence to a higher power.

In purportedly "channelling" Mahood—who embodies the condition of being fully wired into the social machine (Adorno's "total society" as defined above)—the Unnamable steadily undermines enslaving machinic structures. He slyly decodes and appropriates machinic procedures that had repeatedly been used on him. His delegates, he tells us,

> gave me courses on love, on intelligence, most precious, most precious. They also taught me to count, and even to reason. Some of this rubbish has come in handy on occasions, I don't deny it, on occasions which would never have arisen if they had left me in peace. I use it still, to scratch my arse with. Low types they must have been, their pockets full of poison and antidote. (8)

The Unnamable has been bombarded with falsely beneficial, "necessary" remedies for machinic-generated problems long enough to recognize the very philosophical notion of the "pharmakon" as an enslavement tool. Remedies produced within the socio-linguistic machine are *always*, ultimately, poison. Machinic assemblages do not kindly grant some measure of indeterminacy, translatable into appropriation and repurposing; on the contrary, they keenly obstruct such possibilities. The only means to sabotage the machine is to "hack" its socio-linguistic assemblages so that, instead of distributing their poison to their human components, they reabsorb it and damage themselves.

The story of Mahood's one-legged return to his family after a "world tour"—a grotesque representation of machinic enslavement and conditioning—compellingly exemplifies this "hacking" process. Having reached the "yard or campus" surrounding his family home, Mahood advances in a spiral trajectory, as seasons change and his relatives age (28–32). Before his arrival, they all die of food poisoning (33–34)—at which point the stories diverge. Mahood claims that his family members' dying screams and stinking corpses forced him to reverse course (33). The Unnamable insists he reached his destination and "completed my rounds, stamping under foot the unrecognizable remains of my family, here a face, there a stomach, as the case might be), and sinking into them with the ends of my crutches, both coming and going" (35–36). He also protests to being represented, in Mahood's version, as "upset at having been delivered so economically of a pack of blood relations, not to mention the two cunts into the bargain, the one for ever accursed that ejected me into this world and the other, infundibuliform, in which, pumping my likes, I tried to take my revenge" (35). His disparagement of any notion of family love or even basic human empathy remains remarkably atrocious throughout: "I like to fancy, even if it is not true, that it was in mother's entrails I spent the last days of my long voyage, and set out on the next. No, I have no preference, Isolde's breast would have done just as well, or papa's private parts, or the heart of one of the little bastards" (36).

This grotesque family story, with its dark comedic verve, participates in Beckett's humour of structures. In a mockery of narratives of male accomplishment from the Ancient Greek epic to colonialist British travel literature, the protagonist's "world tour" supposedly lasted "two or three centuries"—so he forgot, specifically, in the waters of which ocean he "had left [his] leg behind" (29). His return is not driven by family love but represents a logical (mechanical) occurrence within a larger-scale curvilinear movement: "Having set forth from that place, it was only natural I should return to it, given the accuracy of my navigation" (34). Mahood's spiral trajectory around his family's house, is, then, an organic continuation of that "world tour"—its localized, cut-to-size, "familial" reflection—and it is not at random that the Unnamable insists he must have "completed [his] rounds" (35). Faraway travels and family dealings are part of a machinic assemblage meant to maintain its human components in perpetual motion until fully spent—exhausted, worn down, consumed.

Mahood is already missing a leg in this story, and perhaps an arm, too, as suggested in passing (33). The next time the Unnamable channels him, he has no limbs, can no longer speak, and is "[s]tuck like a sheaf of flowers in a deep jar" (39), yet remains grotesquely productive. His caregiver/ employer/ owner uses his excretions to fertilize her "kitchen garden" (40), and his body, as an advertising prop—she has mounted his jar on a "pedestal" and has attached to it the menu to her chophouse (41). She covers him with "a tarpaulin still watertight in places" only during heavy show (41–42). Hoping to be covered more often, he resorts to "dashing my head angrily against the neck of the jar" and "let[ting] my spittle flow over" (42)—to no avail. Most disturbingly, his habit of lowering his body into the jar and popping his head out unexpectedly

> has cost me dear … It is true one does not know one's riches until they are lost and I probably have others still that only await the thief to be brought to my notice. And today, if I can still open and close my eyes, as in the past, I can no longer, because of my roguish character, move my head in and out, as in the good old days. For a collar, fixed to the mouth of the jar, now encircles my neck, just below the chin. And my lips which used to be hidden, and which I sometimes pressed against the freshness of the stone, can now be seen by all and sundry. (45)

Such passages have persuaded Adorno to read Beckett's postwar works as a response to the Holocaust.[4] The subjection of systematically abjected

---

[4] Several other critics make this argument. Garrison identifies allusions to concentration camps in Mahood's first story and reads the frequent references to tormentors and testimony as references to the Nazi treatment of prisoners and to survivors' "ethical responsibility of testimony at the limit of fact" (102–3). Bryden relates the unnamed "them" to the Nazi regime ("Pain and De-paining"); Adelman connects numerous details to survivors' testimonies at the Nuremberg trials; and Kennedy interprets characters' "failing" bodies as a denunciation of degeneration theories (popular in Anglo-Irish circles after independence, in Hitler's Germany, and in Vichy France).

groups to abject treatment to prove their abject character is a defining component of the Nazi exploitation, torture, and genocide operation, and echoes of this circular-logic procedure make themselves heard in Mahood's grotesque abuse. As elsewhere in Beckett's works, what makes such situations most horrifying is the removal of death from one's control—the possibility of its perpetual deferral by machinic structures, with or without the direct mediation of sadistic human components. There is always more pain and loss to be inflicted on victims, and "microfascisms just waiting to crystallize" can be found within all social interactions, as Deleuze and Guattari emphasize (*TP* 9).

Yet, amidst this utter negativity, Beckett's humour of structures remains active and apt to generate empowering effects—precisely at the level of the switch that transforms previously neutral or mildly comforting elements into riches and pleasure *in retrospect*, as bodily functions are lost to confinement and/or dismemberment. The procedure is meant to erase all remnants of a will to freedom—to instil into the victim's weakened, abused psyche the perception of further punishment as a logical correlate of the slightest attempt at self-assertion or self-preservation. However, the Unnamable poisons Mahood's acquiescent language enough to allow an intense, angry mockery to transpire. Even as Mahood supposedly blames his misfortunes on his "roguish" character, the mechanisms of his enslavement fail to fade smoothly into the background, allowing an organic narrative of social integration or a self-congratulatory metanarrative of the "tragedy of the human condition" to emerge. Instead, they make a grotesque spectacle of themselves. The socio-economic machine is sabotaged by preventing its repressive switches from quietly completing their work.[5] This does not mean that Mahood can break free; it does, however, prevent his experience from being smoothly integrated into the annals of "organic," glossy, undisturbed machinic history, in a darkly comedic system-hacking move apt to elicit readers' angry, action-oriented laughter.

While the Unnamable flaunts his imprecision and hesitations as effects of inability and weakness, his discourse skilfully (and comedically) maintains any coagulation of identifying traits elusive enough to evade machinic integration, forcing all procedures of machinic capture to overexert themselves and expose their grotesquely sadistic and exploitative nature. He

---

[5] In Garrison's words, in bearing testimony, the voice "jams the machine of language" (105).

does not identify with Mahood because that would imply integrating Mahood's pain as his own and fully acquiescing to machinic capture. His atrocious mockery of family love alongside piety or empathy in channelling Mahood's first story is, then, an attempt to sabotage machinic coupling by blocking the routine alignment of machinic strata (Oedipal, communitarian, socio-economic, etc.). While rememorating his supposed stomping over his family members' remains, the Unnamable lists his mother's entrails, his wife's breasts, his father's genitalia, and his children's hearts (36). Thus, for each family member, he *hacks the coupling switch*—he desecrates the body part symbolically representative of each individual's *function* within the family assemblage and the larger social machine (the engendering parental couple, the nourishing wife, and children as the "heart" of the assemblage). The Unnamable places in the shadow of his vivid desecration scene (and immediately abandons) the question, "Would I have not been more likely, in a sudden access of independence, to devour what remained of the fatal corned-beef?" (36). As elsewhere in Beckett's texts, suicide is not an available option. Perhaps that is why Mahood, the "actual" experiencer of the story, "decides" to leave before having reached his family members' bodies and, implicitly, the table with the deadly food.

The Unnamable is aware of sabotaging machinic capture in refusing to identify with his "delegates": "I am he who will never be caught, never delivered" (52), he reports as he begins to describe Worm, alleged future avatar of Mahood. Worm is meant to be "inexpugnable" (61) and thus impervious to machinic capture—"feeling nothing, knowing nothing, capable of nothing, wanting nothing" (63)—but the Unnamable can see the precarity of this state. As a protective measure, the section following Worm's introduction tenaciously disrupts the logical relation between beginning and end, birth and death, development and decay, sabotaging any notion of *progress* propagated by the social machine (and posited as beneficial to human development) by exposing this *sense of direction* as a laughable ruse:

> Mahood I couldn't die. Worm will I ever get born? It's the same problem. But perhaps not the same personage after all. The scytheman will tell, it's all one to him. But let us go back as planned, afterwards we'll fall forward as projected. The reverse would be more like it. But not by much. Upstream, downstream, what matter, I begin by the ear, that's the way to talk. Before that it was the night of time. Whereas ever since, what radiance! (66–67)

In continually linking his avatars only to promptly sabotage any connection, the Unnamable precludes them from acquiring enough stability (in themselves or in relation to each other/ to him) to be fully captured and organically integrated into progress- and productivity-based machinic structures. (Throughout the text, expressions like "making headway," "getting on," "moving forward" recur in stagnant or otherwise inappropriate contexts.) However, his acts of resistance must remain covert to effectively ward off the pain and exploitation propagated by these machinic arrangements.

Worm is, at times, smoothly brought to action through light and sound—or violently, through pain. The Unnamable channels his perceptions in the same convulsive manner as he did Mahood's, concurrently mimicking and rejecting identification. One of the novel's starkest condemnations of the supposedly enlightening value of pain appears here:

> let him toss and turn at least, roll on the ground, damn it all, since there's no other remedy, anything at all, to relieve the monotony, damn it all, look at the burnt alive, they don't have to be told, when not lashed to the stake to rush about in every direction, without method, crackling, in search of a little cool, there are even those whose sang-froid is such that they throw themselves out of the window. No one asks him to go to those lengths, but simply to discover, without further assistance from without, the alleviations of flight from self ... it's the least he might do. No one asks him to think, simply to suffer, always in the same way, without hope of diminution, without hope of dissolution, it's no more complicated than that. No need to think in order to despair. (83)

This ostentatiously physical, crude, and grotesque depiction denounces a long cultural tradition of defining pain as a prerequisite for knowledge/ plenitude as a millenary sadistic project. These discursive traditions generally glorify more or less "abstract" forms of pain (suffering for love), or more or less "practically oriented" forms (suffering deprivation/ sacrificing oneself for one's family/ community)—but, in the Unnamable's implicit assessment, these are mere sublimations of deep-rooted sadistic impulses that will seldom be satisfied by anything less than atrocious physical torture. The novel's supposedly disembodied narrator is suspiciously wary of physical threats: "And sometimes I say to myself I am in a head, it's terror makes me say it, and the longing to be in safety, surrounded on all sides by massive bone" (65). He is *not* in a head—no one fully is, in

Beckett's works. There is no such safety, and the mere thought of it could only be met with derision: "It's a head, I'm in a head, what an illumination, ssst, pissed on out of hand" (88). Multifaceted, hyperactive, and unyielding despite being wary of additional pain, the Unnamable likely infects interpreters with his strategies of self-fragmentation, redoubling, and evasion, alongside his anger against machinic structures and associated "masters."

"Masters" manipulate the relation between knowledge and pain as they please, to instil knowledge that meets their approval or punish knowledge that threatens their privilege, as an early passage warns:

> The fact that Prometheus was delivered twenty-nine thousand nine hundred and seventy years after having purged his offence leaves me naturally as cold as camphor. For between me and that miscreant who mocked the gods, invented fire, denatured clay and domesticated the horse, in a word, obliged humanity, I trust there is nothing in common. But the thing is worth mentioning. (13–14)

The only constant is the masters' readiness to satisfy their sadistic cravings. "The thing" is, indeed, "worth mentioning"—and serious precautions are required for the Unnamable to pass for an inconsequential creature unworthy of the masters' more elaborate attentions. His sabotage of the socio-linguistic assemblage needs to be skilfully coded as weakness, inability, and ineffectiveness, so that it can continue to perform its subversive affective work. Perhaps this is what Beckett's "syntax of weakness" (Harvey 249) really means—a low-profile, high intensity linguistic intervention arising not out of confusion and powerlessness but an effort to avoid detection and capture:

> you must go on, I can't go on, you must go on, I'll go on, you must say words, as long as there are any, until they find me, until they say me, strange pain, strange sin, you must go on, perhaps it's done already, perhaps they have said me already, perhaps they have carried me to the threshold of my story, before the door that opens on my story, that would surprise me, if it opens, it will be I, it will be the silence, where I am, I don't know, I'll never know, in the silence you don't know, you must go on, I can't go on, I'll go on. (*U* 134)

The end of the Unnamable's "confession" craftily loops to the beginning, barring the integration of his discourse into any schema of logical progression or narrative closure. While vacillating between the first and second person as in the first lines, his tone becomes deceivingly tentative and tragic. The recurrent "you must go on, I can't go on, I'll go on" feigns sacrificial perseverance and noble defeat while denouncing machinic forcing (it can be read as a corrosive depiction of a machinic injunction followed by the human component's initial refusal and subsequent acquiescence, presumably under duress). It also gives veiled expression to the powerful affect generated by the text, as it can equally be read as a vow to action exchanged between the Unnamable and his projected audience despite machinic attempts to interrupt and control this flow. Thus, the Unnamable seems to be using a feigned expression of acquiescence to sacrificial patterns of behaviour as a means of masking his sabotage of the socio-linguistic assemblage, so that he can continue to broadcast his empowering call to transformative action. The subversive work of this passage and, indeed, of the entire novel is bolstered by the theatrical dimension of the text, with its corrosive, contagious appeal to human solidarity in the face of pain, exploitation, exclusion, and repression.

4.3   The Flesh as a Machinic Imposition

Texts for Nothing upholds Beckett's practice of developing a new diagram from an earlier diagrammatic text. The first text starts, "Suddenly, no, at last, long last, I couldn't any more, I couldn't go on" (*CSP* 100)—an ostentatious "continuation" to *The Unnamable*. Kenner insightfully describes these thirteen texts as "fantasies of non-being" (*Reader's Guide* 119). Notably, however, the spectral voices featured in these texts are not entirely disembodied and communicate sarcasm and anger rather than tragic, meditative acquiescence. The speaker from Text 1 is crawling through mud, seemingly incapable of basic motor operations, but the account is eerily lively: "I say to the body, Up with you now, and I can feel it struggling, like an old hack foundered in the street, struggling no more, struggling again, till it gives up. I say to the head, Leave it alone, stay quiet, it stops breathing, then pants on worse than ever" (*CSP* 100). After some resentful comments on a number of "others" who might be dead or in hiding, watching him, he comments,

> Sometimes it's the sea, other times the mountains, often it was the forest, the city, the plain too, *I've flirted with the plain too, I've given myself up for dead all over the place*, of hunger, of old age, murdered, drowned, and then

for no reason, of tedium, *nothing like breathing your last to put new life in you*, and then the rooms, natural death, tucked up in bed, *smothered in household gods*, and always muttering ... the same old stories, the same old questions and answers, no malice in me, hardly any, stultior stultissimo, never an imprecation, not such a fool, or else it's gone from mind. (103, my emphasis)

These are not merely comments on the frailty of human existence or the nature of fiction. Given the virulent and contagious humour in the phrases emphasized above, the references to malice, stupidity, and memory, and the delirious list of "deaths," the passage seems primarily meant to destabilize notions of death and sin as coagulating mechanisms within the socio-historical machine. If death is serial, omnipresent, and randomly varied rather than singular and mobilized in given forms, at given moments, following set rules, then much of its ontological weight (and attendant terror) is lost, and its repressive function weakened. The subdued anger underlying this passage intensifies in other texts. After first feigning a meditative tone, the voice in Text 5 angrily spouts, "long live all our phantoms, those of the dead, those of the living and those of those who are not born ... prayers will be offered for my soul, as for that of one dead, as for that of *an infant dead in its dead mother*, that it may not go to Limbo, sweet thing theology" (120, my emphasis). The disdainful repetition in the emphasized phrase and the references to Limbo and theology have a dramatic and angry quality apt to generate intense, contagious affect-based energy in interpreters.

The speaker in Text 1 further attacks repressive functions derived from biological constraints, like Artaud in his 1947 violent self-epitaph "Ci-gît" ("Here Lies"), by rejecting parental and other social forms of authority/connectivity and claiming to have conceived and to relate only to (avatars of) himself:

I was my father and I was my son, I asked myself questions and answered as best I could, I had it told to me evening after evening ... or we walked together, hand in hand, silent, sunk in our worlds, each in his worlds, the hands forgotten in each other. That's how I've held out till now. And this evening again it seems to be working, I'm in my arms, I'm holding myself in my arms, without much tenderness, but faithfully, faithfully. (CSP 103–4)

The speaker feigns weakness and humility, in a move reminiscent of the Unnamable's sabotage of machinic structures, while meticulously, comically circumventing potential dismissals of self-involvement as a masturbatory-narcissistic exercise and diagrammatically demonstrating the potential of this exercise to sabotage systemic repression.

However, machinic structures register this "body without organs" as an aggressive—inherently political—abdication of biology (the foundational aggregate of social functionality) and continually work to break it into manageable subunits. The speaker in Text 3, similarly preoccupied with memories, relations, and identity, perceives being alive as an undesirable machinic imposition: "Start by stirring, there must be a body, as of old, I don't deny it, no more denials, I'll say I'm a body, stirring back and forth, up and down, as required. With a cluther of limbs and organs, all that is needed to live again, to hold out a little time, I'll call that living, I'll say it's me" (109). With body parts and organs come repressive switches and their "work of connectivity" (read: exploitation). The voices in *Texts for Nothing* may not refer to "masters" as often as the Unnamable does, but they are fully aware of their presence. In Text 6, the speaker comments,

> Do my keepers snatch a little rest and sleep before setting about me afresh, how would that be? That would be very natural, to enable them to get back their strength. ... My keepers, why keepers, I'm in no danger of stirring an inch, ah I see, it's to make me think I'm a prisoner, frantic with corporeality, rearing to get out and away. (122–23)

The dramatic verve and thematic obsessions of the Unnamable's diatribes survive here, alongside the corrosive humour of structures apt to sabotage the repressive alignment of Oedipal, socio-economic, and religious/metaphysical machinic strata. The indoctrinating content peddled by these structures is as self-serving, exploitative, and sadistic as ever, and the speaker still feigns incomprehension and weakness while blasting repressive switches. These structures seem to have become, however, more devious if not also more forceful—a distinction historically relatable to the danger of indoctrination taking precedence over the death threat as the horrors of the war gave way to less immediately lethal forms of exploitation in postwar capitalism—launching the speakers into a search for new liberatory countermoves.

One example of this deviousness and its consequences appears in Text 4, which combines a meditation on the split subject of modernity with an unsettling dramatization of the danger of contamination between the act of writing and processes of socio-historical capture:

> he's looking for me to kill me, to have me dead like him, dead like the living. … He protests he doesn't reason and does nothing but reason, crooked, as if that could improve matters. He thinks words fail him, he thinks because words fail him he's on his way to my speechlessness … he would like it to be my fault that words fail him, of course words fail him. He tells his story every five minutes, saying it is not his, there's cleverness for you. He would like it to be my fault that he has no story, of course he has no story, that's no reason for trying to foist one on me. … He has me say things saying it's not me, there's profundity for you … If at least he would dignify me with the third person, like his other figments, not he, he'll be satisfied with nothing less than me, for his me. (114–15)

The speaker begins by denouncing machinic integration ("living") as total consumption (being "dead like the living")—a reality made revoltingly apparent by what Deleuze and Guattari designate as a "writing machine." (Concerns with the effects of such denunciations undoubtedly drive state-level attempts at censorship of the arts.) Next, the speaker stresses a danger inherent to the writing process. Though the "living" author may attempt to resist socio-historical conditioning by feigning failures of thought and expression ("crooked" reasoning, speechlessness, etc.), unconsciously internalized machinic strategies might permeate the text, reproducing machinic divisions/ disjunctions and ultimately sabotaging the author's generation of a writing machine. Hence, *even as he is being created*, the speaker denounces his relation to the writing "other" as adversarial, aiming to block the ways in which literary discourse might, itself, perform repressive work, delivering new human components (interpreters of the text, too, alongside the speaker) to the social machine. He clears the text of such machinic impositions through a diagrammatic humour of instability. His endless protestations highlight new switches, unsettle them briefly, and move on to others, throwing machinic disjunctions into disarray and preventing them from becoming productive, as he proves to be a subject too quickly and too often decomposed and reconfigured for machinic switches to attach themselves to exposed appendices/ organs.

What all these voices abhor is the "committal to flesh, as the dead are committed to the ground" (Text 10, *CSP* 142). Embodiment is nothing but a repressive operation of insertion into the machinic order—and language, both its site *and* the means to reverse it: "No, no souls, or bodies, or birth, or life, or death, you've got to go on without any of that junk, that's all dead with words, with excess of words" (142). Demonstrations of this two-sided weaponization of language come on nearly every page and can be deliriously funny:

> I let them say their say, my words not said by me, me that word, that word they say, but say in vain. ... But peekaboo here I come again, just when most needed, like the square root of minus one, having terminated my humanities ... caput mortuum of a studious youth, ears akimbo, eyes back to front, the odd stray hair, foaming at the mouth, and chewing ... a gob, a prayer, a lesson, a little of each, a prayer got by rote in case of emergency before the soul resigns and bubbling up all arsy-versy in the old mouth bereft of words, in the old head done with listening, there I am old, it doesn't take long, a snotty old nipper, having terminated his humanities, in the two-stander urinal on the corner of the Rue d'Assas was it, with the leak making the same gurgle as sixty years ago, my favourite because of the encouragement like mother hissing to baby on pot, my brow glued to the partition among the graffiti, straining against the prostate, belching up Hail Marys, buttoned as to the fly, I invent nothing ... or one-armed, better still, no arms, no hands, better by far, as old as the world and no less hideous, amputated on all sides, erect on my trusty stumps, bursting with old piss, old prayers, old lessons, soul, mind and carcass finishing neck and neck, not to mention the gob-chucks, too painful to mention, sobs made mucus, hawked up from the heart, now I have a heart, now I'm complete, apart from a few extremities, having terminated their humanities, then their career, and with that not in the least pretentious, making no demands, rent with ejaculations, Jesus, Jesus. (Text 11, *CSP* 145–46)

It is an organized delirium, however, meant to sabotage the many ways in which the flesh might be productively inserted into the socio-historical machine. In perhaps the longest sentence in the thirteen texts (the "peekaboo" sentence above), with commas expertly used—as in *The Unnamable*—to replace machinic organization with the schizophrenic's "inclusive disjunction," the speaker industriously and theatrically wriggles between youth and old age, abstractions and bodily functions, the university and a "two-stander urinal," never settling long enough to allow machinic capture in the form of a stabilization or unification of identity/ experience. His ostentatiously obscene juxtapositions expose the alignment of strata within the socio-historical machine (he family, the school, the church, etc.), with their insistence on inserting the body into processes of social productivity, as a congregation of grotesqueries. The liberating humour of this refusal of social insertion may erupt less often here than in Beckett's earlier works, but rather than being overridden by the meditative tone of some segments, it lends an eerie energy to a collection of texts presumably in search of total motionlessness and silence—beyond the flesh, machinic coupling, and conceptualization.

4.4   COMPANY AS A MACHINIC RUSE

The far more disturbing *How It Is* articulates, according to Rada, an "aftermath" of laughter and parody (151–52)—a humour of critical self-awareness and aesthetic exhaustion "almost indistinguishable from non-sense, torture, and the torturously senseless reading experience it entails" (159). Salisbury identifies here a residual humour derived from the *doubt* regarding the target of the "comic aggression"—one can no longer distinguish if the tortured or the torturer is the main target, mainly due to the "cruelly rational and mathematically perfected reversibility of their systems" (51), which ultimately leads to an "indefatigable interrogation of the comic" (150) as a value fundamentally marked by uncertainty. Indeed, Beckett's figuration of a "torture society" of sorts in *How It Is* appears to produce significant mutations of the comic. However, a reading focused on Beckett's humour of structures may allow us to identify a powerful mobilization of action-oriented forms of angry laughter even in this text—especially given its ever-intensifying horrific-comic sabotage of naturalized linguistic and relational structures.

The speaker claims to be "quoting" confusing scraps of thought dictated by an unspecified entity: "how it was I quote before Pim with Pim after Pim how it is three parts I say it as I hear it" (7). However, these supposedly disjointed fragments, voiced in between moments of panting as he is crawling through mud in a dark and otherwise undefined space, inescapably—indeed, *comically*, in a dark but eerily tonic mode—fall into sense on multiple levels. Several fragments from Part 1 seemingly focused on the straining, desperate mechanics of the speaker's forced voicing of recollections covertly evoke an incompletely sublimated form of masturbation:

to my hand that is free rather than some other part I say it as I hear it brief
movements of the lower face with murmur to the mud
    it comes close to my eyes I don't see it I close my eyes …
    if that is not enough I flutter it my hand we're talking of my hand ten
seconds fifteen seconds close my eyes a curtain falls
    if that is not enough I lay it on my face it covers it entirely but *I don't like
to touch myself they haven't left me that this time*
    *I call it it doesn't come I can't live without it I call it with all my strength
it's not strong enough I grow mortal again*
    my memory obviously the panting stops and question of my memory
obviously that too all-important too most important. (15–16, my emphasis)

The pronoun "it" is supposedly meant to designate, throughout, either
the speaker's hand or (content from) his memory, but phrases like "some
other part" or "I flutter it" deviously suggest another referent. The first
fragment emphasized above—an allusion to previous Beckettian heroes'
presumably more successful masturbatory pursuits—leaves us little choice
in interpreting the second. The speaker does pause after such segments to
clarify what "it" means ("my hand we're talking of my hand" or "my
memory obviously"), but since our work of meaning-making has already
followed its course, such "clarifications" seem comical rather than informative—a mockery of the machinic nature of language.

The speaker's statements consistently prove unreliable. He claims to
quote something spoken in his ear, but the source appears to be his memory. He complains of powerlessness and immobility, but in Part 2 he man-
ages to find Pim, overpower him, and move enough to cause him atrocious
physical pain. He also claims that his effort to speak causes him discomfort
but seems to enjoy blasting his religious mother and oppressive upbring-
ing in Part 1, detailing his torture of Pim in Part 2, and mulling over torture and immobilization-related probabilities and combinations in Part 3.
He is neither simply lying nor entirely oblivious—and we are, by now,
used to the jarringly fluctuating identities of Beckett's speakers, impossible
to tame into realistic coherence, plausibility, and predictability. What is
further radicalized in this text is Beckett's stark, anxiety-producing, yet
ultimately empowering comical hijacking of elements more properly pertaining to the horrific, so that they can be used to activate powerful affects
in readers.

The most vivid images of the speaker's interactions with his mother
appear in the following sequence:

we are on a veranda *smothered* in verbena the scented sun dapples the red tiles yes I assure you

the *huge* head *hatted with birds and flowers* is bowed down over my curls the eyes *burn* with *severe* love I offer her mine pale upcast to the sky whence cometh our help and which I know perhaps even then with time shall pass away

in a word *bolt upright* on a cushion *on my knees whelmed* in a nightshirt I pray according to her instructions

that's not all she closes her eyes and *drones a snatch* of the *so-called* Apostles' Creed I steal a look at her lips

she stops her eyes *burn* down on me again I cast up mine *in haste* and repeat *awry*. (16–17, my emphasis)

A black comedy of machinic strata is enacted here. Two episodes appear to be depicted—one spatially located on a verandah, the other in the child's bedroom—but they are melded through an eerie vertical-axis exchange of glances, with the mother's "burning eyes" above the child's and the all-seeing eyes of God presumably higher. The tone and diction (see especially the emphasized phrases) suggest that, in the speaker's assessment, all that his mother and her God had to offer was oppression poorly disguised as love. The child obeys, "whelmed" in intimidation and fear, and the speaker reports the events whelmed in resentment and anger. The comedy of this vertical alignment of Oedipal and religious strata is horrific in its implications but empowering in terms of energy discharge, as it can galvanize readers' angry, action-oriented laughter at the crushing, but ultimately crude and ludicrous indoctrination and oppression strategies routinely applied within the socio-historical machine. While Parts 2 and 3 of *How It Is* radically complicate matters on multiple levels, they continue to facilitate such constructive affective discharges.

In Part 2, the speaker details his torturous treatment of Pim, whom he encounters during his mock-Sisyphic crawling (grotesque rather than tragic, socially productive in sinister ways, rich in sadistic pleasures, and not exactly heroic). He glibly mentions "the day … when clawed in the armpit instead of crying he [Pim] sings his song" (70), then details his sadistic enjoyment and dehumanizing perception of the other's body in pain: "that's not all he stops nails in armpit he resumes cheers done it armpit song and this music as sure as if I pressed a button I can indulge in it any time henceforward" (71–72). The passage foregrounds the enlisting of language in the social production of pain. The narrator redefines torture as a means to produce "music," and the victim's broken body, as a (button-activated) music-making machine. He further inserts his production of pain into a more general framework of social production—he communicates his orders to Pim by scratching "Roman capitals" on his back "from left to right and top to bottom as in our civilisation" (77) and defines his acts of torture as necessary and thoroughly regulated "training":

> training continued no point skip
>   table of basic stimuli one sing nails in armpit two speak blade in arse three stop thump on skull four louder pestle on kidney
>   five softer index in anus six bravo clap athwart arse seven lousy same as three eight encore same as one or two as may be. (76)

While the pain he inflicts on Pim is horrific, there is plenty of sinister humour in the ways in which language both supports his attempt to legitimate his pursuit and sabotages its pretenses, producing in interpreters not mere revulsion but anger.

The speaker's obsessive claim to report events in "natural order" is consistently belied through destabilizing qualifiers: "more or less," "my life last state last version what remains bits and scraps," "not all a selection," etc. (7). Frequently, fragments that "naturally" belong in other sections are revealed too early or much later—and, presumably upon realizing it, the speaker interrupts them with "something wrong there" (8, 9, 10, 15, and elsewhere). Some memories extracted from Pim appear, in first-person narration, in the wrong section or in contexts that conceal whose experiences are relayed. Thus, the speaker deflects machinic control both through his fragmented, destabilizing use of language and by preventing his identity from coagulating fully (it never follows a logic of cumulative experience, and it is never free of heterogeneous elements).

This play of identities is taken to a different level in Part 3, where the speaker—who, since his interactions with Pim, has been calling himself Bom—provides a larger-perspective presentation of his "world" while meditating on its justice, practicality, and logical consistency. As Dowd notes, the three sections feign a grotesque, muddy transversal movement across "prehistory, ancient Greece, and ... the Enlightenment" (*Abstract Machines* 184), and the talk of community and justice in Part 3 is a ruse meant to maintain the narrator's identity too "porous" to permit the return of any notion of transcendence (187). Indeed, the remarkably lengthy depictions of grotesquely sadistic acts and the suggestion that large numbers of inhabitants of this "underground" space practice them unceasingly and unquestioningly do not function as a philosophical meditation on community/ justice but horrific-comically destabilize such coagulants meant to entrap us in sadistic and exploitative socio-historical arrangements. Bom's Part 2 treatment of Pim is horrifically sadistic in its toll on the victim and comically grotesque in its machinic setup and discursive justifications. In Part 3, both the horror and the grotesquery escalate. Pim escaped, Bom claims, and he himself has been captured and tortured by someone else—but he eerily places his victimization at times *after*, and at times *before* his abuse of Pim. Next, he clarifies that, in fact, a cyclical experiential sequence defines his "world"—any number of individuals might be engaged in such "exchanges" at any given moment, alternately as victims and torturers. He estimates the population number at "one hundred thousand strong," "one million strong," or "millions" (121, 124, 123). This population's unity of experience partly explains the confusion of voices, identities, and timelines in the text: "the same voice the same things nothing changing but the names and hardly they two are enough nameless each awaits his Bom nameless goes towards his Pim" (124). Several elements reveal the account as more than a mere variation on the theme of the Inferno: a horrific-comic preoccupation with logic and mathematics, conspicuous references to justice and regulations *alongside economic measurements*, and many passages where acquiescence is meticulously transcribed as conditioning under torture.

Bom describes the population's lifestyle through a four-member sample, with the "travelers" moving along "a closed curve" (127):

> two tracks only of a semi-orbit each say how shall we say AB and BA for the travellers
> let me for example be numbered 1 ... and at a given moment find myself abandoned that is to say again abandoned at the extremity A of the great chord and assuming we turn deasil
> then before I can find myself again at the same point and in much the same state I shall have been successively
> victim of number 4 at A en route along AB tormentor of number 2 at B abandoned again but this time at B victim again of number 4 but this time at B en route again but this time along BA tormentor of number 2 again but this time at A and finally abandoned again at A and all set to begin again
> correct. (127–28)

While accurate from a geometrical, logical, or algebraic viewpoint, this description is not primarily informative—rather, it is meant to demonstrate the infallible logic of the system and generate feelings of confinement and terror. The carefully calculated, geometrically distributed economy of pleasure and pain of this arrangement horrific-comically denounces the machinic nature and sheer ferociousness and negativity of societal structures that operate with dehumanizing notions of equity strictly meant to ensure systemic functionality, with no concern for the individual human component beyond basic (or rather, base) maintenance.

There are no direct references to "masters" in this text, but Bom repeatedly alludes to a machinic system that regulates the slightest "stirrings." While meditating on the provenance and nature of the "sack" of canned goods each individual possesses, Bom begins to discern the exploitative economy governing his world: "a sack no doing without a sack without food when you journey ... it's regulated thus we're regulated thus" (120)—the journey "would otherwise be brief and is not brief" (121). He concludes, "more sacks here then than souls infinitely if we journey infinitely and what infinite loss without profit there is that difficulty overcome"—but his dangerous ratiocination is abruptly discontinued through the corrective "something wrong there" (121). In a subsequent passage, references to regulations, justice, and mathematics appear in horrific-comic conjunction, and a list of torture methods ends with "all the needful" in lieu of *et cetera*:

> at the instant I reach Pim another reaches Bem we are regulated thus our justice wills it thus fifty thousand couples again at the same instant the same everywhere with the same space between them it's mathematical it's our justice in this muck where all is identical our ways and way of faring right leg right arm push pull
>
> as long as I with Pim the other with Bem a hundred thousand prone glued two by two together vast stretch of time nothing stirring save the tormentors those whose turn it is on and off right arm claw the armpit for the song carve the scriptions plunge the opener pestle the kidney all the needful. (121)

As Bom concludes, everyone is maintained in perpetual motion "by the mere grace of our united net sufferings" (156), and "for the likes of us ... there is more nourishment in a cry nay a sigh torn from one whose only good is silence or in speech extorted from one at last delivered from its use than sardines can ever offer" (157). The machinic logic of exploitation and repression ascribed to "masters" and only partly internalized in earlier works has seemingly permeated the subject fully here: everyone perpetually loops through cycles wherein profit equals extracting pain and equity means forcing the other to suffer whatever one has suffered. However, while Bom often voices his sadistic pleasure and speculates on that of others, in his only attempt to imagine an ideal world, he depicts a space entirely devoid of human contact:

> if it is still possible at this late hour to conceive of other worlds
> as just as ours but less exquisitely organized
> one perhaps there is one perhaps somewhere merciful enough to shelter such frolics where *no one ever abandons anyone and no one ever waits for anyone* and *never two bodies touch.* (156, my emphasis)

The formulation is subversive: the first fragment emphasized above suggests that Bom's ideal projection might be a world of fixed positions with him in the torturer's role, but the second summarily repudiates his world's social arrangements altogether.

The text ends in a lengthy "transcription" of torture:

> if all that all that yes if all that is not how shall I say no answer if all that is not false yes
> all these calculations yes explanations yes the whole story from beginning to end yes completely false yes
> that wasn't how it was no not at all no how then no answer how was it then no answer HOW WAS IT screams good (157–58);
> alone in the mud yes the dark yes sure yes panting yes someone hears me no no one hears me no murmuring sometimes yes when the panting stops yes not at other times no in the mud yes to the mud yes my voice yes mine yes not another's no mine alone yes sure yes when the panting stops yes on and off yes a few words yes a few scraps yes that no one hears no but less and less no answer LESS AND LESS yes
> so things may change no answer end no answer I may choke no answer sink no answer sully the mud no more no answer the dark no answer trouble the peace no more no answer the silence no answer die no answer DIE screams I MAY DIE screams I SHALL DIE screams good
> good good end at last of part three and last that's how it was end of quotation after Pim how it is. (160)

Scarry explains the linguistic effects of the radical power imbalance between the torturer and the victim as follows: "The question, whatever its content, is an act of wounding; the answer, whatever its content, is a scream" (46). At the end of *How It Is*, the torturer and the victim compliantly perform their parts, but "yes" and "no" lose meaning, making the veracity of the story (whether or not "that's how it was") irrelevant. The only truth is that everything is voiced under duress, as language absorbs machinic poison to the point of implosion. Yet the horror of this state of being and language may, again, translate into an action-oriented, angry laughter, as readers witness the repression machine gripping the text collapsing under its own weight.

As elsewhere, what supports this effective circulation of affect is Beckett's humour of structures. All residents of this dark world are male, and their occasional thoughts on the female gender are grotesquely sex-driven. Bom dreams to have "tasted of love of a little woman," but "failing kindred flesh," he happily considers an "emergency dream an alpaca llama" (14–15). Pim recalls that his wife (who might have committed suicide) always "shaved her mound," and wonders, "she must have been dark on the deathbed it grew again" (84–85). They obsess over issues of control, alternately extract/ are forced into "confessions," and otherwise interact in strictly torturous ways. This grotesque social aggregate evokes repressive political/ military/ religious regimes and their pervasive acts of brutality alongside religious and psychoanalytic "confessions" and economic notions of convenience and efficiency: the mud in which Bom and the others lie and crawl and the canned food they eat evoke military training and rations[6]; pilgrims, with their sacks and ritual crawling, may be another target of mockery; finally, Bom's stated reason in torturing Pim is to extract his life story, and he repeatedly references accessibility and convenience in rationalizing his torture methods. This grotesque assemblage of allusions to Oedipal, socio-economic, religious, and state-level conditioning reveals Beckett's perception of the patriarchal system and its "contribution" to human civilization: there is nothing positive about it, and if allowed to follow its inherent logic, it will reduce humanity to a sea of mud populated by crawlers who take turns stabbing each other's butt cheeks with can openers. The slapstick quality of this scenario is undeni-

---

[6] Morin identifies in this text echoes of "contemporaneous testimonies of conscription, pacification, torture and desertion" and of "reports documenting Algerian methods of guerrilla war" (233).

able, in spite of its countless sinister features and predominantly dark tone. Ultimately, its mud, blood, and screams paradoxically generate a flux of angry, action-oriented laughter likely to arrest machinic capture by motivating readers to reject anything resembling the machinic connectivity and reciprocity it has made manifest.

For Salisbury, the low-energy "comic embers" (*Laughing Matters* 168) of Beckett's late fiction denounce traditional forms of representation based on *seeing* as constitutively abusive—an exhausted reaction to "a century in which vision and Enlightenment accounts of knowledge and representation ... had been philosophically implicated with the most systematic forms of violence humans had yet perpetrated" (180). She is referring to the idea often expressed in early avant-garde works, dominant in critical theory after the 1950s, and perhaps best synthesized by Horkheimer and Adorno in their 1947 *Dialectic of Enlightenment* that monstrous twentieth-century occurrences such as chemical warfare or the Nazi pseudoscience and "final solution" can be logically traced back to the Enlightenment model of knowledge and understanding of otherness—that they took that logic to its ultimate consequence: a need to assimilate all forms of otherness deemed worthy and eliminate anything falling outside of that self-servingly defined category. Indeed, Beckett's preoccupation with the implications and consequences of being seen intensifies in his late works. Memorably disturbing eye imagery haunts the *Nohow On* texts:

> There is of course the eye. Filling the whole field. The hood slowly down. Or up if down to begin. The globe. All pupil. Staring up. Hooded. Bared. Hooded again. Bared again (*Company, NO* 16);
>
> Not possible any longer except as figment. Not endurable. Nothing for it but to close the eye for good and see her. ... Close it for good and see her to death. ... Close it for good this filthy eye of flesh (*Ill Seen Ill Said, NO* 74);
>
> "Clenched staring eyes. Clenched eyes clamped to clenched staring eyes." (*Worstward Ho, NO* 105)

The tone and imagery in these examples—consistently dark, suggestive of confinement, and tainted with disgust—confirm Salisbury's assessment. Yet there is also anger brewing under that seemingly placid tone, as the emphatic phrases ("of course"), repetitions with a difference ("close the eye for good and see her"/ "see her to death"), and logically unnecessary explanations ("Or up if down to begin") suggest. Such rhetorical markers perpetuate, against all odds, the energetic theatricality of previous works, allowing these late texts to continue the affective work of forging connections with readers even as the voice is supposedly nearing its demise. Finally, a layer of dark humour persists in the depiction of the physicality and movements of the eye—heavy, awkward displacements of graceless, machinic chunks of flesh, contrasting the usual beautifications and abstractizations of representational art.

Corrosive elements of phrase-level humour alongside a humour of structures continue to emerge from such syntactic and semantic convulsions. *Company*, generally described in Beckett studies as a meditation on ageing and solitude, is replete with sarcastic comments revealing *disgust* with the sadistic and tyrannical forms generally taken by companionship or community within the socio-historical machine:

> In order to be company he must display a certain mental activity. But it need not be of a high order. Indeed it might be argued the lower the better. Up to a point. The lower the order of mental activity the better the company. Up to a point (9);
>
> Crawling on all fours. Another in another dark or in the same crawling on all fours devising it all for company. Or some other form of motion. The possible encounters. A dead rat. What an addition to company that would be! A rat long dead. (21–22)

In one passage, the definition of an "improved" and "more companionable" individual insidiously introduces distress as a requirement: "Might not the hearer be improved? Made more companionable if not downright human. Mentally perhaps there is room for enlivenment. An attempt at reflexion at least. At recall. At speech even. Conation of some kind however feeble. A trace of emotion. Signs of distress. A sense of failure" (22). In another, the hearer is prompted to "chart the area" (39) by travelling on all fours in the dark "till he drops" (40). The necessary movements are described in a dehumanizing fashion reminiscent of *How It Is*: "Hands and knees angles of an oblong two foot long width irrelevant. Finally say left knee moves forward six inches thus halving the distance between it and homologous hand. Which then in due course in its turn moves forward by as much. Oblong now rhomboid. But for no longer than it takes right knee and hand to follow suit. Oblong restored" (*NO* 39–40). Finally, lying face down in the dirt—the consecrated position of total acquiescence to religious, military, or aristocratic authority throughout history—is declared the most "endearing" and "companionable" body position:

> Which in other words of all the innumerable ways of lying is likely to prove in the long run the most endearing. If having crawled in the way described he falls it would normally be on his face. ... But once fallen and lying on his face there is no reason why he should not turn over on one or other of his sides or on his only back and so lie should any of these three postures offer better company. ... The supine though most tempting he must finally disallow as being already supplied by the hearer. With regard to the sidelong one glance is enough to dispel them both. Leaving him with no other choice than the prone. But how prone? Prone how? How disposed the legs? The arms? The head? Prone in the dark he strains to see how best he may lie prone. How most companionably. (45–46)

As elsewhere, acquiescent language is hijacked to support the emergence of a humour of structures—here, that of the alignment between communitarian, religious, economic, and state-level means of repression. The description of the "betterment project" quoted earlier in this paragraph horrific-comically mimics conformity so as to sabotage the socio-historical legitimation of sadistic practices through falsely benevolent claims; the depiction of the "mapping" work grotesquely mimics machinic economic integration while rebuking its exploitative, dehumanizing nature; and the description of the search for the best "position" mimics acquiescence while denouncing the grotesquery of subjection and repression alongside the emptiness of whatever forms of companionship are available within the social machine.

The text ends with the speaker moving "on from nought anew" (50), "[w]ith every inane word a little nearer to the last" (51), "[a]lone" (52). While perhaps not humorous in itself except through the presence of Beckett's trademark "nearly there," this ending works in conjunction with earlier humorous convulsions to offer an empowering rejection of company for company's sake. Beckett's purported meditation on ageing and companionship thus reveals itself as an under-the-radar attack on the fake benevolence of societal mechanisms that take advantage of humans' need for contact and emotional exchange to couple them to exploitative machinic structures and use them to decrepitude.

While the male character from *Company* is engulfed in darkness, the woman from *Ill Seen Ill Said* occupies a space where the day-and-night cycle abides, and she resents this regime of visibility: she "rails at the source of all life" (the sun) and, in the evening, "savours its star's revenge" (*NO* 57). She can be seen, intermittently, by 12 entities—presumably spectres from her past, one of which might be her dead husband. In addition, an unattributed "eye" follows her every move—perhaps the eye of the narrator, identity unspecified, clearly gendered male, whose self-incriminating display of sexually predatory masculinity is likely to galvanize angry, solidarity-based and action-oriented forms of laughter in readers.

From the start of the text, this narrative voice of stark consistency in style, interests, desires, and obsessions vacillates between discontent and hostility in describing the woman's physicality, environment, and level of exposure. The woman is, as Bryden notes, "far from being the hapless plaything of the narrative voice" (*Women* 157)—and her uncooperative attitude is met with an angry perplexity suggestive of masculinist entitlement. Passages in which she is inspected voyeuristically abound, and the only variables are the degree of eroticization and the speaker's level of anger.

The voice haughtily posits a bucolic paradise as the most suitable environment in which the woman should be "seen" (that is, voyeuristically examined and objectified): "A moor would have better met the case. Were there a case better to meet. There had to be lambs. Rightly or wrongly. A moor should have allowed of them. Lambs for their whiteness. And for other reasons as yet obscure" (60). While maniacally watching her—"She raises her eyes and sees one. Turns away and sees another" (63)—the "specters" bemoan being unable to reduce her entirely to an object of fantasy and consumption (a "figment" easily categorized and assimilated): "Already all confusion. Things and imaginings. As of always. Confusion amounting to nothing. Despite precautions. If only she could be pure figment. Unalloyed. This old so dying woman. So dead. In the madhouse of the skull and nowhere else. Where no more precautions to be taken" (67). Unlike her male observer(s), she appears impervious to desire-based machinic capture—something the voice resents and dismisses as an effect of old age: "What is it defends her? Even from her own. Averts the intent gaze. Incriminates the dearly won. Forbids divining her. What but life ending. Hers. The other's. But so otherwise. She needs nothing. Nothing utterable. Whereas the other. How need in the end?" (64). Elsewhere, her eyes are intently observed in hopes of capturing traces of confusion and vulnerability, and her mouth examined for any speck of sensuality while also craftily dismissed as no longer attractive:

Hidden from chin to foot under a black covering she offers her face alone. Alone! Face defenceless evening and night. Quick the eyes. The moment they open. ... One staring eye. Gaping pupil thinly nimbed with washen blue. No trace of humour. None any more. Unseeing. As if dazed by what seen behind the lids. The other plumbs its dark. Then opens in its turn. Dazed in its turn (81);

> The thin lips seem as if never again to part. Peeping from their join a suspicion of pulp. Unlikely site of olden kisses given and received. Or given only. Or received only. (89)

The observers' "tragic" lamentations are in fact horrific-comical—what they peddle as meditative depth achieved as a result of tragic deprivation looks more like a predator's bout of self-pity at being able to watch very little and touch nothing at all.

In perhaps the most striking such passage, halfway through the text, the sexual frustration and resentment slowly brewing in other fragments uncontrollably gush out:

> The hands. Seen from above. They rest on the pubis intertwined. ... They tighten then losen their clasp. Slow systole diastole. And the body that scandal. While its sole hands in view. On its sole pubis. Dead still to be sure. ... Tightening and loosening their clasp. Rhythm of a labouring heart. Till when almost despaired of gently part. Suddenly gently. ... Then after a moment as if to hide the lines [the hands] fall back pronating as they go and lying flat on head of thighs. Within an ace of the crotch. It is now the left hand lacks its third finger. A swelling no doubt—a swelling no doubt of the knuckle between first and second phalanges preventing one panic day withdrawal of the ring. The kind called keeper. Still as stones they defy as stones do the eye. Do they as much as feel the clad flesh? Does the clad flesh feel them? Will they then never quiver? This night assuredly not. For before they have—before the eye has time they mist. Who is to blame? They? The eye? The missing finger? The keeper? The cry? What cry? All five. Six. And the rest. All. All to blame. (75–76)

The words "pubis" and "clad flesh" are used twice, and "thighs" and "crotch" once each. Based on details such as the "[t]lightening and loosening" of the clasped hands, the "[r]hythm of a laboring heart," or the supposedly lacking "third finger," several essays included in Ben-Zvi's collection *Women in Beckett* identify here a depiction of masturbation. However, other details suggest that the voice may be attempting to *fanta-*

size that occurrence and is systematically undermined by the woman's uncooperative "dead still" body, hands that "defy as stones do the eye" (a phrase used twice), and fingers that "never quiver." (Also note the verbose and dubious explanation provided for the way she might have lost—specifically—her "third finger.") The passage conspicuously ends in a commentary on "blame" in which accusations are thrown at anyone and anything except the speaking voice.

Such passages horrific-comically depict gender relations as inherently and inescapably adversarial, indeed *predatory*, within a patriarchal psychosexual setup. The male "spectres" cannot physically interact with their female object of obsession but control the voice and continually try to manipulate whatever images they can perceive so that, once fantasy-enhanced, those images might better suit their needs. They see the woman "ill"—conveniently so—and depict her as such, justifying their continued voyeuristic abuse as the effect of a burning, inescapable need. Twelve spectres are mentioned early in the text, but there is only one voice, and only one ever-intrusive, voyeuristic "eye." Perhaps Beckett wanted to put on display the voice and the eye of the phallus—crude joke arguably intended.

A grotesque humour of structures apt to galvanize readers' action-oriented laughter again emerges here. As the voice frantically switches between lyrical, pretend-empathetic, and unrepentantly abusive depictions of the woman, its true intentions transpire alongside the socio-historical foundations of its power. While many melancholy fragments mark a slow advancement towards dissolution, the text repeatedly reveals itself as a predator's frustrated lamentation, its slow pace comically disrupted by crude illustrations of patriarchal entitlement. In the last lines, in a horrific-comic spectacle of gluttony (note the ostentatiously colloquial and luridly material terms emphasized below), "grace" and "happiness" are equated with the total consumption of the "void" alongside organic life and inorganic matter: "Grant only enough remain to *devour* all. Moment by glutton moment. Sky earth *the whole kit and boodle*. Not another *crumb of carrion* left. *Lick chops and basta*. No. One moment more. One last. Grace to breathe that void. Know happiness" (97, my emphasis). The ending thus denounces the violent and exploitative underpinnings of patriarchal religious and philosophical abstractizations, and the dominant mood remains angry laughter at the monstrosity of the patriarchal system rather than sadness at the tragedy of the human condition.

Worstward Ho exhibits Beckett's language at its most successful in attempting to erase characters, elements of situational humour, and perhaps even itself as a viable vehicle for fiction:

> Say a body. Where none. No mind. Where none. That at least. A place. Where none. For the body. To be in. Move in. Out of. Back into. No. No out. No back. Only in. Stay in. On in. Still.
>   All of old. Nothing else ever. Ever tried. Ever failed. No matter. Try again. Fail again. Fail better. (*NO* 101)

Yet even in such passages, where language seemingly names elements of character construction, setting, and chronology only to negate them, the comedy of structures survives, alongside that of language. Few critics see traces of humour here—faded to the point of disappearance or aborted not yet fully formed (the typical reading of the recurring "missaid"). I propose, instead, that, here, Beckett's humour is much more radically compressed but also singularly intertextual (passages/ sentence fragments/ word units become cores of compact meaning articulating extensive connections to previous works), and thus still apt to propagate action-oriented affects.

In the fragment above, as the voice posits a body and a place for it, an exploitation machine arises from the rudiments of language used, despite the absence of other stabilizing or connecting elements: once "in" place, the body can no longer move "out" or "back"—it is captured. This is a condensed generalization of countless machinic scenarios at work in Beckett's earlier texts. In acknowledging that previous attempts ("[a]ll of old") at whatever it is currently pursuing failed, the voice uses an eerie negation, suggesting that something "else" could still be attempted: "Nothing else ever. Ever tried. Ever failed" (101). Next, in discussing its current attempt, it posits a desirable affective dimension to failure, radically redefining it: "Try again. Fail again. Fail better" (101). Beckett's characters/ voices routinely fail at social integration but do so in ways that sabotage or at least denounce most operating notions of social integration as barely disguised exploitation lures. They also fail to "change the system" in some sweeping way, but even this failure mobilizes affect as it questions inherited notions of what constitutes desirable change, perhaps suggesting that traditional notions of "revolution" are mere instances of machinic reversal and renewal. (More on this shortly.) Failure thus defined surely is worth pursuing—as a decidedly *positive* category. The phrase "fail better" becomes humorous in an entirely different way if read in this key—no longer a facile word game based on a rudimentary semantic reversal but a paradoxical formulation functioning as a *diagram* for Beckett's relentless discursive sabotage of repressive structures.

The passage previously quoted posits a body but not also a mind, and the voice comically (redundantly) expresses relief at this realization: "No mind. Where none. That at least" (101). Yet, allowing for a body insidiously draws the mind into existence—positing it as an absence creates a locus for it within language and the exploitation machine, as the voice quickly grasps:

Say bones. No bones but say bones. Say ground. No ground but say ground. So as to say pain. No mind and pain? Say yes that the bones may pain till no choice but stand. Somehow up and stand. Or better worse remains. Say remains of mind where none to permit of pain. Pain of bones till no choice but up and stand. Somehow up. Somehow stand. Remains of mind where none for the sake of pain. Here of bones. Other examples if needs must. Of pain. Relief from. Change of. (102)

The passage recalls the Unnamable's angry depiction of the masters' extraction of Worm from his protective state of unknowing. No sooner attached to the body, exploitation and repression machines insert it into a system that consistently dispenses knowledge alongside pain. Subjectification is achieved by exposing the body to varieties of pain ("other examples"). Change itself becomes a function of pain, defining the subject's condition of captivity.

To counter this, the voice takes over all second-person injunctions to engage in the use of language ("Say a body," "Say bones," etc.), diligently sabotaging their aims:

First the body. No. First the place. No. First both. Now either. Now the other. Sick of the either try the other. Sick of it back sick of the either. So on. Somehow on. Till sick of both. Throw up and go. Where neither. Till sick of there. Throw up and back. The body again. Where none. The place again. Where none. Try again. Fail again. Better again. Or better worse. Fail worse again. Still worse again. Till sick for good. Throw up for good. Go for good. Where neither for good. Good and all. (101–2)

Beckett's characters' obsession with excretion survives even in the context of this disembodied voice—serving, as always, anti-institutional, antimachinic functions. What the voice is trying to "throw up" is not just constricting character development/ representational conventions but also conjunction and disjunction ("both"/ "either") as logical operations backing the functioning of machinic switches. The final aim is to expel all elements of machinic coupling ("Throw up for good") alongside benevolent machinic pretenses ("Good and all"). Yet, as the voice anticipates, while repetition of the evacuation act is partly effective, an end to this process is unlikely ("Where neither for good"). The affective import of this procedure rests on industrious repetition. There is a slapstick-style quality to this take on the subject as perpetually assaulted and infested by machinic switches and diligently throwing them up. As elsewhere in Beckett's late texts, this paradoxical, diagrammatic slapstick-style figuration extracts comedic material from the domain of the horrific.

After the opening remarks, the text approximates an authorial figure that might have generated it ("Head sunk on crippled hands. Vertex vertical. Eyes clenched. Seat of all. Germ of all," 103) and three potential characters ("One old man and child" and a woman, 105, 120) only to sabotage the coagulation (and potential capture) of each in turn. The head is described through nested-doll imagery: "On back better worse to fail the head said seat of all. Germ of all. All? If of all of it too. Where if not there it too? There in the sunken head the sunken head" (109). This use of recursivity sabotages machinic capture by multiplying the entity to be captured and engaging the machine in a self-perpetuating non-productive loop. Furthermore, the creative mind is ambiguously designated as a "germ," implicitly denouncing representational art as a machinic disease (a means to "infect" the subject with machinic switches).

The old man and the child are still, yet stirring—"At rest plodding on" (105)—and indistinct, yet special, with a tint of Beckett's trademark "nearly there": "Any others would do as ill. Almost any. Almost as ill" (105). The old man, dressed similarly to Beckett's earlier vagrants, is ostentatiously shown only from the back ("Vertex vertical in hat. Cocked back of black brim alone. Back of black greatcoat cut off midthigh," 107), as is the child. Repeatedly called "the one" and "the twain" (105–7), they disappear and reappear, slapstick-style (106–7). These are not human characters but, like the authorial figure, lures for machinic switches—composite, slippery creatures meant to lock machinic structures in an endless chase, precluding the coagulation and individuation required for machinic coupling. The woman is even more so. Besides lacking consistency, she is explicitly described as "oozing" from the "soft" parts of the (male) creative mind, occasioning another indictment of patriarchal imagination as voyeuristic and predatory: "Somehow again on back to the bowed back alone. Nothing to show a woman's and yet a woman's. Oozed from softening soft the word woman's. The words old woman's" (120).

Beckett's contorted use of language intensifies this sabotage of machinic structures. Instead of smoothly varying sentence types, style, and pace with the subject matter, drawing the reader into the typical identification games of representational art and facilitating machinic capture, the voice offers a disruptive staccato of sentence fragments and single words stubbornly punctuated as sentences, repeatedly using this rhythm to empty the void and its correlate, death, of threatening qualities. Rather than meditating on their imminence or terror, the voice comically expresses either full-blown anger or half-hearted resignation at *unsuccessfully chasing* them:

> Say child gone. As good as gone. From the void. From the stare. Void then not that much more? ... No. Void most when almost. Worst when almost. Less then? All shades as good as gone. ... Less worse then? Enough. A pox on void. Unmoreable unlessable unworseable evermost almost void (125);
>
> Same stoop for all. Same vasts apart. Such last state. Latest state. Till somehow less in vain. Worse in vain. All gnawing to be naught. Never to be naught. (127)

The threat of the void is thus denounced as overblown—a way for the social machine to tame potential escapees by positing its exploitation practices as acceptable alternatives to a horrifying "beyond." These and other staccato passages yank, with theatrical verve, control of the disjunction switches from the machine, diligently disrupting each component operation of each machinic cycle of exploitation and oppression. This may be achieved by obstinately depicting the subject as a grotesque aggregate of worn-out parts capable only of defective, partial operations: "What were skull to go? As good as go. Into what then black hole? From out what then? What why of all? Better worse so? No. Skull better worse. What left of skull. Of soft. Worst why of all of all. So skull not go. What left of skull not go" (128). Another procedure involves pretending to depict, through approximations and negations, states of annihilation of the subject, only to then allow its remnants to strike from places posited as nonexistent (note the verb "said," unaccompanied by a grammatical subject, in the closing line of the text):

> Enough. Sudden enough. Sudden all far. No move and sudden all far. ... In dimmost dim. Vasts apart. At bounds of boundless void. Whence no farther. Best worse no farther. Nohow less. Nohow worse. Nohow naught. Nohow on.
>   Said nohow on. (128)

Approximations, negations, and recursivity are operations consistently used in this attack. As discussed before, the primary goal seems to be the erasure of what Deleuze and Guattari define as "microfascisms just waiting to crystallize" (*TP* 9). An effect of a higher order, however, emerges: the articulation of a revolutionary model no longer predicated on hierarchical reversals and the capture of the state but a never-ending vibration, a continual stirring (to no surprise, Beckett titled his last work of fiction, published in 1988, "Stirrings Still").

4.5   REVOLUTION

My insistence to delineate a revolutionary model in Beckett's works may seem problematic given Beckett's disenchanted or, at best, cautious engagement with such political notions as "revolution" throughout his career. In 1937, after Beckett's trip through Nazi Germany, Nancy Cunard, editor of the *Left Review*, asked him to contribute to a pamphlet called *Authors Take Sides on the Spanish Civil War*. His response was, "¡UPTHEREPUBLIC!"—interpreted by McNaughton to mean that "for Beckett the political integrity Cunard demanded was trumped by the need for an astute analysis of political language" ("*Utopian Scrap-heap*" 2). For McNaughton, Beckett's reaction reflects his disillusion with the Irish republican movement, which "since 1922 had changed its ideological basis in socialism, feminism, and artistic liberty for the emptiness of an increasingly nationalist and conservative rhetorical prop" (5). It also "acknowledges that facile conceptualization and political cliché—even expressions that ostensibly support positions for which one has sympathy—exacerbate the political crises facing Europe by further disconnecting language from any meaningful relationship to experience" (6). The phrase "UpTheRepublic" reappears in *Malone Dies* (in English in the French version, too), indicating a continued preoccupation with the unpropitious reversals often brought about by initially promising revolutionary movements.

While acknowledging Beckett's resistance to traditional notions of "revolution" on these grounds, I propose that the *diagram* of halting the production of repression consistently emerging from his texts resonates with theorizations of contemporary revolutionary forms, which often rely on Deleuze and Guattari's discussion of revolutionary potential and practice from *A Thousand Plateaus*. As Nail notes, most contemporary theorists favour "more heterogeneous and non-representational directions" in defining "revolution," discarding the traditional tethering of the term to "the capture of the state, the political representation of the party, the centrality of the proletariat, or the leadership of the vanguard"—largely in response to "the failure of such tactics over the last century" and "the socio-economic changes brought by neoliberalism in the 1980s" (1). Nail deems Deleuze and Guattari's work vital to any analysis of contemporary revolutionary practices like the "leaderless and networked horisontalism" of the "Occupy" movement (3), emphasizing that, in *Capitalism and Schizophrenia*, "revolution is consistently valorised and juxtaposed against state-capitalism as well as state-socialism and the party/union bureaucracy, heavily criticized in France and around the world in the 1960s and 1970s" (3).

Nail sees Deleuze and Guattari's theory of revolution as *constructivist*—an "arrangement and distribution of heterogeneous elements or singularities without vanguard, party, state, or capital" and "a politics based on autonomy and the self-management of political problems" instead of "a utopian programme laid out in advance" (21). Nail defines "reterritorialization" as Deleuze and Guattari's concept of *change* and their "absolute positive deterritorialization" as the only type of revolutionary development that can disrupt the logic of power, "connect up to other such ruptures and create a collective alternative to representational politics" (Nail 84–85). This type of deterritorialization generates revolutionary events whose main defining trait is the future anterior—a state of becoming that is not a synthesis of past, present, and future (85) or a privileging of a "pre- or post-evental intervention" (87) but a delineation of a new present (89). Thus, revolution "is not an opposition nor an *ex nihilo* insurrection, it is a prefiguration in the sense that it creates a new world parallel to the old one" through "the direct action of that particular world within the present" (90). This phenomenon involves what Deleuze and Guattari call "reverse causalities"—in Nail's interpretation, "what is to come already acts upon 'what is' before the future can appear, insofar as it acts as a limit or threshold continually being warded off by the past's attempt to preserve itself. But once a new present emerges it is seen to have been on its way the entire time" (98). The work of prefiguration thus consists of "bring[ing] the imperceptible to perception" (*TP* 267) by connecting different lines of deterritorialization: "by conjugating, by continuing with other lines, other pieces ... one makes a world that can overlay the first one, like a transparency" (280). A *diagram* emerges here not as a mere indication of revolutionary potential but as the active, transformative prefiguration of a practice already in motion once it begins to be perceived.

Another key term Nail employs in this context is "consistency," also used by Deleuze and Guattari to define revolutionary practice. Nail emphasizes that "consistency" does not designate stasis or predictability but a "constructive rupture" from intersections of machinic strata that is meant to connect to/ consolidate assemblages of similarly deterritorialized "collective practices or capacities for action" and to facilitate acts of "mutual and conflictual transformation" within the "participatory political body" (116). Nail further theorizes a related "singular-universal" solidarity different from traditional forms like charity, altruism, duty, or the political alliance, which foreground individual responsibility without radically undermining the conditions that allow inequality, pain, deprivation, and injury to occur, and/or hinge on narrow definitions of group needs and interests (159–60). In contrast, "singular-universal" solidarity mobilizes global connections through what Deleuze and Guattari designate as "a constructivism, 'diagrammatism,' operating by the determination of the conditions of the problem and by transversal links between problems" (*TP* 473).

This revolutionary construct can be traced throughout Beckett's works. Varieties of deterritorialization are industriously exercised by all of Beckett's characters, and whether, in immediate narrative terms, the result is some version of failure or some rate of success, the emerging diagram invariably performs affective work at the contact with interpreters. Consequently, a "singular-universal" form of solidarity emerges from each text as a "future anterior" ready to take root in interpreters' present and begin to manifest its transformative power. The diagrammatic character of the process ensures the *transmissibility* and *consistency* of the message—the bypassing of traditional models of understanding and the consolidation of a state of mutability allowing for immediate and continual transformation at the contact with others' struggle and pain.

As we have seen, Beckett's texts enact countless forms of repression and pain inflicted by socio-historical machinic structures with the full, partial, or reluctant participation of human components, and they insistently construct procedures meant to sabotage or at least hinder such impositions, including all the partial and deceitful forms of solidarity promoted by those structures (duty, charity, altruism, and the other traditional forms discussed by Nail). What they articulate instead are authentically and reciprocally nourishing forms of connection. The unstable identity of all textual instances (characters/ narrators/ implied authors/ "instigators" who presumably force characters to voice, write, or in other ways "confess" or record their experiences) fuels an attack on the subject but also creates the conditions for new forms of contact/ connectivity—it fosters the emergence of complex affective networks at interpreters' contact with the text. Thus, interpreters can establish mutable points of connection with these textual instances without being forced into some version of the wholesale identification with fictional instances (and implicit acquiescence to attendant ideological values) often encouraged by more traditional dramatic/ narrative forms. This instability and fragmentation at the level of textual instances' identity is immediately contagious—it translates, for interpreters, into a perception of the self as no longer coherently captured within the social machine and perfectly fitted for use, and into the realization that this is a *liberating* rather than a perilous position.

In examining various possibilities of *halting the production* of repression, some of which clearly rest on such unstable and composite notions of identity, interpreters may discover an exhilarating form of self-awareness and self-determination: a state of heightened perception of the flows that constitute the self as always in motion, always *becoming*—an entirely positive experience of a degree of intensity comparable to that of the schizophrenic's creation of a "body without organs," as defined by Deleuze and Guattari, but also markedly different, in that instead of merely extracting the body from machinic assemblages of repression, it enables it to connect to a participatory political body in ways that strengthen that network's revolutionary consistency. Beckett's humour of structures continually elicits this response by emphasizing the grotesquely excessive and redundant redoubling of mechanisms of repression on multiple planes—Oedipal, communitarian, cultural, religious, economic, and so on—all striving to convince us that the binding ties that cut into our flesh aim to prevent our falling into some consuming abyss.

While language "naturally" (traditionally, through habit) codifies that redundancy as a necessary reiteration of power meant to build and maintain universally beneficial forms of social cohesiveness, Beckett's paradox-based linguistic mischief translates it into an exploitative and sadistic recursive operation meant to progressively eliminate all traces of resistance and ensure the perpetual high-efficiency functioning of repressive social machines. In this transgressive translation, fear and pain, coercion and exploitation are no longer data of experience but exquisitely designed, frequently updated, and carefully managed *products* of the repressive structures they, in turn, support. This use of language prompts interpreters, often through the affective mediation of angry forms of laughter, to connect to networks of "singular-universal" solidarity, reinforcing these networks and sustaining their generation of a state of revolutionary consistency. It is for these reasons that a play like *Waiting for Godot* can be perceived as a liberating, hope- and life-giving call to action by audiences of unrelated backgrounds and conditions of existence, as shown. The play diagrammatically generates an irresistible, contagious, immediately productive future anterior already at work on interpreters' present before the reading process/ dramatic performance ends. The experience of "singular-universal" solidarity elicited by the play—liberating due to its composite nature and perpetual mutability—may account for both the overwhelming positivity of audience reactions and the registered long-term transformative effects of this positivity. This is because it prefigures a positive future characterized by increased freedom/ self-determination and non-exploitative forms of exchange and connectivity—and, as such, it begins to project a new mode of living: engaged, liberated, and equitable. Such experiences consistently emerge at interpreters' contact with Beckett's texts, as my discussion in this and the previous chapters shows. The following chapters explore more in-depth the possible consequences of repeated exposure to Beckett's texts on interpreters' cognitive processing experiences and abilities.

Script Evaluation and Enrichment: Evolutionary Beckett

Beckett's "Script Multiplication and Enrichment": Rejecting Toxic Disjunctions and Seeking Inclusivity

5.1   Interpretation, Cognitive Encoding, and the Paradox

Cognitive narrative theory and the more recent "postcognitivist" approaches that place additional emphasis on cognition as an embodied, enactive, and emotively inflected process provide another framework apt to approximate the profound effects of repeated exposure to Beckett's paradox-based texts. As briefly outlined in Chap. 1, Herman's cognitive narrative interpretive model, which integrates linguistic, discourse analysis, cognitive theory, and artificial intelligence concepts, offers a flexible, sophisticated, and scientifically relevant conceptualization of the relation between narrative texts, their interpreters, and the world(s) they inhabit. Herman prefers the term "storyworld" to "story" (which is used in opposition to *discourse* in narratology to define the "what"/ the "matter" of the narration vs. the "how"/ the "manner" of narrative presentation, in Gerald Prince and Seymour Chatman's definitions) for two main reasons. First, "storyworld" better captures the notion that interpreters decode narratives by attempting to reconstruct "not just what happened—who did what to or with whom, for how long, how often and in what order— but also the surrounding context or environment embedding existents, their attributes, and the actions and events in which they are more or less centrally involved" (*Story Logic* 13–14). Second, "storyworld" better describes the specificity of interpretive activities, which proceed "not just

© The Author(s) 2020   181
C. Ionica, *The Affects, Cognition, and Politics of Samuel Beckett's Postwar Drama and Fiction*, New Interpretations of Beckett in the Twenty-First Century, https://doi.org/10.1007/978-3-030-34902-8_5

additively or incrementally but integratively or 'ecologically'"—that is, the term implies that interpreters additionally assess narrative developments and ensuing timelines against other possible courses of action and developments within the same and/or different environments (14). According to Herman, narrative discourses always contain identifiable cues that prompt interpreters to establish connections between these discourses and the *contexts* in which they are interpreting them (anything from an awareness of narrative/ genre conventions to interpreters' perception of the world)—a phenomenon he designates as "contextual anchoring" (8).

Another basic premise of Herman's model is that interpreters' perception of socio-cultural and economic determinations, in synchrony and diachrony, is a function of their lived experience—more specifically, this perception, as argued in cognitive and artificial intelligence studies, coagulates into cognitive "frames," "scripts," and "schemata" used and reshaped in successive lived experiences (85). Herman emphasizes interpreters' mediation in the implementation of *reciprocal changes* in scripts and stories: social changes modify individuals' interpretation of stories, while changing narrative conventions (typically caused by a growing perception of certain storytelling modes as hollow/ contrived/ stereotypical) prompt interpreters to multiply and enrich the frames, scripts, and schemata defining their perception of the world (85, 108). Thus, texts like Kafka's *Metamorphosis*—which "subverts expected coding strategies" in reconfiguring "a predicate that normally operates in binary fashion (human/ inhuman or ±human)," as the protagonist Gregor Samsa remains consistent as a discursive entity while his body presumably undergoes an abrupt and radical physical change—consistently generate "shock effects" that prompt interpreters' reassessment of those frames/ scripts/ schemata (45). Herman further connects such interventions at the level of expected coding strategies with the subversion of repressive social models of power at the level of their place of articulation within language. In discussing stylistic shifts, he describes fictional styles as "jointly formal and social phenomen[a]" insofar as they "invite reflection on how discourse is an instrument that can either work against or reinforce patterns of conflict—more or less unquestioned hierarchies and antagonisms—operative in society at large" (207). Deleuzian theory concurs on this—as Lecercle puts it, it systematically supports a "political concept of style" (246).

Both Beckett's drama and his fiction confirm this assessment, as they repeatedly reveal to what extent stories participate in repressive circuits of power but also threaten such aggregates' consistency, exposing them to attack. In its systematic reliance on the paradox—by definition, an assault on binary and linear operating modes/ principles—Beckett's discourse relentlessly generates shock effects that prompt interpreters to reassess particular situations, connect those situations to larger organizational patterns/ principles that are, then, themselves reassessed, make predictions, and ultimately redraw (rearrange, reshape, restrict/ enrich, eliminate/ multiply, etc.) the frames/ scripts/ schemata they live by. In so doing, Beckett's works foreground the narrative nature of cognitive processes, prompting interpreters' engagement in sustained mental work aimed at questioning and enriching inherited cognitive patterns. This questioning work ultimately allows for more ethical means of articulating environmental judgements and predictions—a process of major import for interpreters' reshaping of their connections to others within a multiplicity of local and global environments.

The transformative work of the paradox, discussed in detail in terms of its mobilization of affect in previous chapters, easily translates into cognitive terms, as well. I will explicate its basic cognitive import here and illustrate it briefly through examples from Beckett's *Waiting for Godot* before delving, in this and the following chapter, into a more detailed examination of several works by Beckett from a (post-)cognitivist perspective.

The frames, scripts, and schemata we use and reshape through lived experiences (from direct human interactions to our exposure to cultural products) tend to rely on functional distinctions of a binary order—and, whether or not this is in part a biologically predetermined brain functioning trait, it must also result from millennia of *socially inflected cognitive framing*. As discussed in earlier chapters, functional disjunctions such as male vs. female, mind vs. body, white vs. black, good vs. evil, once accepted and used as organizational principles, tend to acquire a definitiveness they do not objectively possess, form paradigms through associations that are not inherently logical, and become "naturalized"—as do the hierarchies emerging from these associations. The uncomplicated, "common-sensical" appearance of such formations makes them ideal indoctrination and repression tools. Given the brain's property of plasticity, once "wired" into neural pathways, binary-structured cognitive frames become exceedingly resilient—for instance, as commonly acknowledged in today's political context of ascension of "alt-right" doctrines and politicians even in countries with long democratic traditions, certain cognitive frames can be peculiarly resistant to *facts*.[1]

The phenomenon is not, however, restricted to holders or promoters of "extremist" views. Support for the late-capitalist (corporate) socio-economic establishment routinely manifests itself in the form of well-crafted disjunctions meant to further entrench and ossify norms and values detrimental to most of those who adopt them. For instance, opposition to the status quo is systematically drained of positive meaning through two apparently antipodal but artfully intertwined moves. On the one hand, significant changes aimed at increasing the fairness of the system (by eliminating or even just reducing class, racial, and gender discrimination) are disjunctively framed as equivalent to instability, chaos, and/or violence, in opposition to "stability" and "safety"—late-capitalist political establishments' mendacious discursive disguises for stasis. On the other hand, the system's consistent pull *backwards*—its reactionary and financially motivated attack on fairness and rights—is framed as a desirable form of change through another well-crafted disjunction: that between freedom/ flexibility and restriction/ inflexibility. Thus, the withholding of government measures that might abate corporate exploitation is framed as care not to encumber the "free market"; homophobic policies and actions, as preserv-

---

[1] Many cognitive and neurological studies published in the last decades explore this problem, from various perspectives. Ronquillo et al. show, through an analysis of functional magnetic resonance imaging scans (fMRI), that the amygdala, essential in regulating strong emotions like fear, activates to a higher degree in white study participants when shown black faces as compared to being shown white faces—which suggests that racist stereotypes assimilated through social exposure typically evolve into neural pathways categorizing people of colour as threatening. Activists fighting extremist violence and prejudice like Angela King, co-founder of *Life After Hate*, confirm that individuals with extremist views encounter major difficulties in changing their thinking patterns even if they are strongly committed to change (King, interviewed in Hayasaki). Kraft et al. discuss "motivated reasoning" (a strong investment in long-held values/ ideologies) as a barrier against some individuals' acceptance of scientific facts. Ecker et al. show that false information presumed true at initial decoding influences memory and reasoning even after being debunked, despite most strategies used to eliminate that influence. Chang confirms the difficulty of correcting false information once it has been stored in one's memory. De Keersmaecker and Roets show that individuals with lower cognitive abilities are significantly less likely to adjust their attitudes after "explicit disconfirmation of the false information" (107) than individuals with higher cognitive ability, who typically adjust to attitudes fairly close to those of the control group (not exposed to misinformation). As confirmed by these and other studies, the formation of biased frames/ scripts/ schemata (racist, sexist, homophobic, etc.) appears to lead to *a priori* judgements that may sidestep the processing of new/ corrected information.

ing religious freedoms; legal protections for women and people of colour, as attempts to restrict the rights of white men (or, at best, as "rushed" and "unnatural" interventions into the organic development of the social body); etc. The furthest-right grouping within the U.S. House Republican Conference unironically calls itself "The Freedom Caucus." European extreme right movements revived starting in the 1960s call themselves "new" (*La Nouvelle Droite, Neue Rechte, Forza Nuova*, etc.). Recep Tayyip Erdoğan's religiously conservative, authoritarian, and corrupt political rule is safeguarded, in Turkey, by the "Party of Justice and Development."

Paradox-based textual constructs make forcibly manifest both the fraudulent and perfidious nature of such disjunctions and their habitual "scaffolding" to reinforce analogous, interconnected, and mutually sustaining cognitive frames/ scripts/ schemata. Thus, Vladimir and Estragon's iterative suicide exercise forcibly removes suicide from its *morality-based* cognitive framing as a matter of irresponsibility and cowardice (in opposition to responsibility and courage—"manly" and "moral" attributes strongly supportive of economic and other forms of patriarchal exploitation) and bafflingly reframes it as a matter of sexual gratification, *or* a way to pass away the time, *or...*, *or...*, *or...* The point is not to suggest, in keeping to binary frameworks, that committing suicide is a *courageous* act, and that one *should* attempt it, but to put on display the structural causes behind the potential temptation to commit suicide, as well as enact the encoding of the suicide interdiction into countless cognitive frames/ scripts/ schemata that facilitate exploitation—whose injunction to live is really not enlightened and benevolent but meant to maintain the enslaved in steady supply. The play achieves this by creating a shock effect (the rupture accompanied by an apparently random and purely grotesque reframing mentioned above) followed by new contextual anchoring effects (the clarification, through Vladimir and Estragon's encounters with Pozzo and Lucky, that the reframing was not random but meant to illustrate the exploitative nature and sheer inhumanity of some social injunctions to "preserve life"). "The rope," "the knot," and "the chafing" (*CDW* 25) are thus meant to further foreground the truth behind the suicide interdiction (deceitfully buried under manipulative disjunctions that broadcast assurances of infinite benevolence and coming nourishment) and to make it manifest in even starker terms: that the very structures of power responsible for some individuals' development of suicide ideation wish us to forego killing ourselves not in order to engage us in reasonable forms of exchange but so they can work us to death (or consume us in some other fashion).[2]

As I show here and in Chap. 6, despite their intense mobilization of anxiety and challenging sophistication, Beckett's shock effects *increase* the attractiveness of his works, largely due to their connection to empowering forms of paradox-based humour. Vladimir and Estragon's serially botched suicide—within patriarchal morality-based schemata, a clownish act symbolic of a tragic lack of meaning, courage, and responsibility—is an example. If so many interpreters perceive it as solidarity and hope-inducing rather than depressing, it is because it aptly shocks them into reassessing and expunging deleterious cognitive frames/ scripts/ schemata wired into their notions of social cohesion, prompting them to seek cohesion modes more akin to Vladimir and Estragon's compassionate and generous interactions. (Let us recall that Vladimir and Estragon already have the carrot, that one gives it to the other without much ado or deliberation, and that nobody else gives them food. Godot will not help—should he ever come, he will likely use them to death, as Pozzo does Lucky.) The shock of this paradox-based "forcing open" of an otherwise staunchly resilient cognitive frame (capitalist, heteronormative, and exclusionary) reverberates throughout the play, effectively bolstered through a systematic use of repetition. Structural echoes, consistent deconstructive techniques, and repetitions and reiterations with a difference compel interpreters' productive engagement with increasingly complex aggregates of divergent frames/ scripts/ schemata. At the most basic narrative/ dramatic level, everything happens "twice"—but, as also discussed in previous chapters, there are many other forms of repetition with a difference in the play: the characters' repetitive linguistic patterns, the iterative mockery of social institu-

---

[2] Readers may recall the 2010 media revelations—eerily resonant with Beckett's enactments of the functioning of repression—that followed a string of Chinese workers' suicides in a Foxconn factory connected to several North-American tech companies. A report by Moore for *The Telegraph*, based on information obtained by a team of seven undercover Chinese reporters who infiltrated the Foxconn Longhua plant, mentions the following measures taken by the company to avoid further incidents: "stringing nets between dormitory buildings to try to catch any further jumpers" and "blocking windows and locking doors to roofs and balconies." Apparently, overtime had been, on average, 120 hours per worker per month in 2009 and was reduced to 80 hours per month in the wake of the suicides. Zhu Guangbing, who organized the investigation, reports having been told by workers that the long shifts caused their hands to "twitch at night" and to "mimic the [assembly line] motion" while "walking down the street" (see Moore for additional details). Exploitation and repression take a wide variety of forms, but their *logic* is always the same.

tions like the family, the school, or organized religion, or the increasingly grotesque depictions of the effects of using and abusing others. For interpreters as for the characters themselves, such repetitions function as effective *cognitive rehearsals* of frame-level interventions—all the more necessary given the resilient character of the structures in question. A central point of my argumentation developed later in this section is that, as Beckett's later works intensify both the production of anxiety and instability and that of cues meant to facilitate effective paradox-based responses, interpreters are enticed to operate at ever-increasing levels of connectivity and speed while becoming increasingly at ease during the execution of such operations—a process apt to foster interpreters' development of higher cognitive functions of arguable evolutionary utility in the information and globalization age.

In this chapter, I further explicate my theoretical approach and illustrate it through a discussion of some of Beckett's best-known postwar works. In Chap. 6, I examine several other plays and fiction works, emphasizing, for each, two main aspects. One is Beckett's encoding of increasingly complex liberatory procedures that corrode constricting frames/ scripts/ schemata, stimulating enrichment and expansion, into texts that are increasingly complex and challenging in their intensity and condensation. The other is Beckett's ever-expanding attempt to dramatize and narrativize not just "people's stories" but also literary, art, or conceptual histories, foregrounding the narrative foundations of all "origins" and "fixed" categories alongside the mind's uncanny ability to use categories against themselves while still processing, ordering, and storing information.

5.2   From Resonance to Editing and Actualization

Building on experimental and theoretical findings by Evan Thompson, Vittorio Gallese, Giacomo Rizzolatti, and others, Popova proposes that Beckett's late dramas prompt readers/ audience members to connect to the suffering of others through what neuroscience defines as "empathic projection" (458). Gallese notes that "mirror neurons," situated in the premotor cortex, appear to activate when we *observe* someone's goal-oriented actions in the same way they do when we *perform* those actions ourselves—suggesting that "action observation implies action simulation" (qtd. in Popova 458). Such "resonance mechanisms" characterize the functioning of emotions, too—the same cortical network activates when we *perceive others' emotional states* and when we *experience* the same emotions ourselves, as Rizzolatti and Gallese, in collaboration with Luciano Fadiga and Leonardo Fogassi, show (qtd. in Popova 458). According to Thompson, such processes as simulation and empathy constitute involuntary and prereflective couplings of the self and the other at the level of the lived body (qtd. in Popova 458). Popova uses these theoretical concepts to emphasize that, while comprehending narratives, insofar as it is a form of thinking, implicitly constitutes a form of "simulated acting" understood as "effecting actions," theatrical performances are uniquely apt to *enact* or *actualize* the simulation, "with the possible consequence that our empathic imagination is excited more than in the purely verbal arts" (459). In Popova's view, theatrical performance offers a more intense enactment/ actualization of the situation than the act of reading a dramatic or narrative text. While I do not wish to negate the power or the specificity of the performance in terms of the cognitive experiences it mediates, I would suggest that Beckett's dramas can, in fact, mobilize the phenomena discussed by Popova, to a large extent, even when they are read rather than experienced in performance, and that Beckett's fiction can also achieve those effects. This is because both Beckett's drama and his fiction contain easily discernible textual markers meant to reproduce, at least in part, the effects of a theatrical performance for the reader, so that, whenever these texts are staged, this dimension is *enhanced* rather than created entirely anew through performance-related acts.

In Chap. 3, I argued that Beckett's texts aptly prompt readers/ spectators to resonate with characters' expressions of anger, often manifested in the under-the-radar form of feigned ineptitude and inability. While "resonance mechanisms" like action simulation and empathy may be generally wired into the human brain, Beckett's texts appear to be particularly loaded with features apt to trigger and amplify such effects. For instance, Vladimir and Estragon's supposedly unproductive fretting (removing and putting on boots, discussing carrots and turnips, debating the Apostles' stories, "playing at Pozzo and Lucky"—all, of course, while waiting for Godot) reveals itself as serving significant cognitive functions in this perspective, as it likely triggers readers/ spectators' simulation-based resonance with the characters' state of disenfranchisement and amplifies their empathic response. While unrealistic both in its specific details and in its overall exhaustiveness, this fretting constitutes an iterative enactment of dispossession and pain that is intensely, unquestioningly, and overwhelmingly human, as well as empowering and humorous in its under-the-radar rejection of subjectification-as-subjection. With each iteration, Vladimir and

Estragon's gestures amplify interpreters' resonant solidarity. In anti-parallel fashion, the Pozzo-Lucky couple likely intensifies interpreters' revulsion towards the act of exercising mastery over others, by equating it with physical consumption and abuse (Lucky's body literally bears the appalling marks of Pozzo's mastery, and Pozzo's frequent jerking of the rope repeatedly points to those marks, stressing the hideousness of this hierarchy-based form of empowerment).

Such effects are enhanced through stage performance, but they are already embedded in the text of the play (through both stage directions and the characters' lines)—and the overwhelming presence of features apt to trigger and amplify such resonance effects equally characterizes Beckett's fiction. Sam and Watt's "walk" within the barbed wire enclosure during their stay in the mental health institution, also discussed in Chap. 4, is an example. The description of the characters' movements is repetitive, ostentatiously meticulous, and flat—"instructions manual"-like and unrelenting in a way that is deeply corrosive in relation to productivity-based social injunctions. These qualities can arguably trigger and amplify cognitive resonance. Let us recall that the "walk" is undertaken after a number of explicitly "recuperative" actions on Sam's part—he pulls Watt into the barbed wire enclosure in between their fenced pavilions through a hole in the fence, and he wipes the sweat, blood, and dust off Watt's skin and clothing through gestures and props contextually anchored, in corrosive "inclusive disjunction," to religious rituals and economic servitude. The description of the "walk" builds on the shock effects generated by that corrosive contextual anchoring, through its pronounced anti-heteronormative and anti-integrative (in a productivity and exploitation-based logic) features. For instance, Sam mentions, supposedly in passing, that they "walked pubis to pubis" but subsequently inserts the idiom "so much balls" into the sentence (163)—ensuring that, despite the meaning of the idiom not being sexual, its composition would stress the sexual implications of the previous phrase. Relentlessly repetitive, the description extends over three quarters of a page. Since I quoted a longer portion in Chap. 4, I will provide only a few lines here: "And so we paced together between the fences, I forwards, he backwards, until we came to where the fences diverged again. And then turning, I turning, and he turning, we paced back the way we had come, I forwards, and he of course backwards, with our hands on our shoulders, as before" (161). The repetitive sentence/ sequence structure arguably works to stimulate interpreters' *visualization* of the scene, likely leading to a cognitive resonance loop that may trigger interpreters' first painful, then progressively angry, and finally empowering observation/ simulation-based experience of Sam and Watt's conditions of existence and subsequent engendering of an empathy-based "walking machine." (This "product" of their anti-heteronormative and anti-integrative coupling can be described, in Deleuze and Guattari's terms, as an element of "anti-production," *AO* 31.) The text thus uses conspicuous forms of repetition to secure the activation of cognitive resonance mechanisms and to keep them running until the hideousness of productivity and exploitation-based forms of (socio-economic) coupling such as those promoted by Knott and his ilk has been made manifest in clear enough terms to elicit interpreters' anger and rejection. Concurrently, the empowering dimension of Sam and Watt's "walk" works to entice interpreters to accommodate increasingly compassionate and inclusive forms of cognitive resonance potentially leading to inclusivity-based frame enrichment and multiplication.

Herman reads the stronger focus on characters' perception of events in modernist fiction not as a shift from external to inner reality but as a conceptualization of a new "geography of mind" that rejects "Cartesian mappings of the mental as a bracketed-off interior space," imagining the mind as a "distributional flow interwoven with rather than separated from situations, events, and processes in the world" ("Re-minding" 255). He relates this model to Francisco Varela, Evan Thompson, and Eleanor Rosch's "enactivist approach" to cognition (cognition as *enactment* or *embodied action* rather than a matter of representations/ projections), noting that "modernists put characters' mental states and dispositions into circulation with the possibilities for action and interaction that, from a postcognitivist perspective, help constitute the mind in the first place" (258). Herman briefly discusses Beckett's *Murphy* as an enactment of such a model of the mind, but the approach can be productively extended to Beckett's use of first-person or focalized narration throughout his prose and in some monologues in his dramas, as well as to his subversion of the subject as a consistent, localizable entity throughout his works. Beckett's fragmented, elusive "people" obsessively engage in what Andy Clark designates as "action loops" that "criss-cross the organism and its environment" (qtd. in Herman, "Re-minding" 260). In narrating, they assess opportunities for action, trying to escape victimization and capture—or, conversely, attempting to create socially sanctioned contexts for their acts and safeguard their abusive/ exploitative pleasures against potentially adverse reactions from an assumed audience. (As discussed in previous chapters, this awareness of being watched and propensity to act for an audience characterizes both Beckett's drama and his fiction.) Beckett thus exposes, in an enactivist framework, repressive Oedipal, socio-cultural, and economic structures as sensorimotor assemblages whose sole functions are exploitation and self-perpetuation, prompting readers/ audience members to pursue any opportunity for positive change identifiable in their environment.

Vladimir and Estragon's enactment of ineptitude and inability, their repetitive and ceaseless fretting, and their waiting act constitute powerful illustrations of *cognition as enactment or embodied action* aimed at assessing opportunities to escape victimization and capture while promoting relational patterns disconnected from patriarchal socio-economic frame injunctions. Throughout the play, Vladimir and Estragon ceaselessly put on display their ailing bodies, claim feebleness of memory and mind, and insist they are waiting for Godot—the arch-master and employer. However, while their physical discomfort and lack of basic resources (shelter, food, or clothing) are indisputable, at least Vladimir's memory is better than generally advertised: he does recognize Pozzo and Lucky the second time, as he confesses after their departure, and repeatedly expresses frustration with Estragon (and, briefly, with the boy and Pozzo) when he appears to be the only one to possess some sense of a timeline. Moreover, as discussed in detail in previous chapters, Vladimir and Estragon's falsely inept and pointless conversations damningly enact the emptiness and deceitfulness of patriarchal promises and of the deleterious effects of patriarchal socio-economic integration. Finally, their very act of waiting—ultimate proof of their "genuine" wish for patriarchal immersion—is assiduously vitiated through under-the-radar contestations ("desperate" thoughts of suicide, mocking debates on fundamental tenets of religious doctrine, and even a supposedly conscientious "rehearsal" of patriarchal integration— their "playing at Pozzo and Lucky"). Thus, Vladimir and Estragon "try out" whatever their environment has to offer, including—or rather, especially—the psychosomatic *cost* of integration. Concomitantly, their trials and rehearsals unrelentingly explore strategies meant to block integration processes while keeping their resistance undetected. They settle on constant enactments of inability for good reason: patriarchal socio-economic assemblages would *punish* resistance but might tolerate and merely *marginalize* inability, since it can be used as a prop for their pretend-compassion. (Godot *promises* employment/ meaning/ salvation, but these many blessings are forever meant to come *tomorrow*. Each "today" sees Vladimir and

Estragon still sharing their meagre resources, having only each other, and still impervious to patriarchal frame injunctions—while Lucky is psychosomatically collapsing under the weight of all the benefits of integration.) The positive, solidarity-based, and action-oriented audience reactions to this play, as discussed in Chap. 1, are arguably mobilized, to some extent, by Vladimir and Estragon's empowering enactment of *cognition as embodied action*—a recipe for cautious, solidarity-based engagement with the environment. Exposure to this play thus has a powerful *reframing* effect—it disconnects patriarchal frame injunctions from their advertised benefits, prompting interpreters to question and reject any analogous frames/ scripts/ schemata governing their interactions and seek modes of cognitive processing free of hierarchical and exclusionary features.

A more disquieting representation of cognition as embodied action begins to emerge in Beckett's writing starting with *Molloy*. While Vladimir and Estragon "try out" and reject the benefits of abusing others, Molloy routinely alludes to patriarchal frames to justify his violent and exploitative relational patterns. While describing his encounter with a policeman early in the novel, Molloy explicitly connects his articulation of a response within *any* verbal exchange to a fear of physical abuse based in prior experiences, while subversively pretending to consider his inability to "get used to blows" peculiar: "I hasten to answer blindly, fearing perhaps lest my silence fan their anger to fury. I am full of fear, I have gone in fear all my life, in fear of blows. Insults, abuse, these I can easily bear, but I could never get used to blows" (22). As obvious from this, as from several fragments discussed in Part I, Molloy's fear and pain are authentic and undoubtedly apt to mobilize resonant cognitive responses in interpreters. But what is more striking about Molloy's manifestation of cognition as embodied action is his ceaseless enactment of the frame-based wiring of pain and fear into every aspect of social dynamics. Jeffers sees in Molloy's comments on his relationships a peculiar *indifference* to heteronormativity (78) that threatens to "upend the very logic on which the system operates" (79). While I agree that Molloy's display of indifference is corrosive, I would suggest it is doubly so because it is *feigned*. Molloy's supposed failure to perceive the relevance of heteronormative injunctions absolves him of the duty to internalize them fully. However, his consistent framing of abuse and exploitation as "organic," "natural" developments in the contexts in which he is "caught" reveals a *mockingly selective* internalization process that makes manifest all the analogous frames/ scripts/ schemata into which heteronormative injunctions may be wired. The comic hideousness of Molloy's meditation on love (*M* 55–56), of his beating of the coal burner (85–86), or of his abuse of his mother (14–15) originates from an enactment of patriarchal relational patterns devoid of typical pretenses at fulfilment and benevolence and stripped to their disjunctive/ oppositional/ exploitative/ hierarchy-based frame. Noting our cultural conditioning to predict character behaviour and development based on gender, Jeffers stresses that, insofar as Molloy's performance "disrupts our ability to read gender and sexual conduct in predictable ways," it also "challenges our ability to read *at all*" (79). Indeed, in enactivist terms, Molloy's horrific-comic pursuit of frame-based allowances for his acts troubles interpreters' reading of gendered relations, forcing them to question the naturalization—in fiction as in life—of hierarchical patterns to the point of concealing that they are predicated on adversarial, oppositional, exclusionary cognitive frames/ scripts/ schemata.

As Van Hulle aptly notes, despite the prominent presence of "skulls-capes" in Beckett's works, Beckett "anticipated the untenability" of other modernist writers and critics' model of the mind as an interior space and "never stopped searching for alternative models" (277). In Van Hulle's view, texts like *The Unnamable* and *Worstward Ho* reject "internalist" and ordered models positing the mind as the origin of all thought and action and implying a clear division between conscious and unconscious content, and prefigure "a model of consciousness that anticipates Daniel C. Dennett's so-called Multiple-Drafts Model and the models suggested by enactivism" (281). Dennett's model posits that mental activities of various types (conscious/ unconscious acts, perceptions/ evaluations, etc.) happen in parallel and undergo "editorial processes" whereby "various additions, incorporations, emendations, and overwritings of content can occur, in various orders" (qtd. in Van Hulle 282). Molloy's resourceful identification of allowances and theatrical attempts to demonstrate their legitimacy within patriarchal socio-economic frameworks can be said to anticipate the "multiple drafts" model more obviously present in *The Unnamable*—and the model can be effectively mapped on the "repetitions with a difference" from Beckett's plays, too. Vladimir and Estragon's repetitive actions—meaningless in a functional/ productivity-based logic and from the point of view of the frames/ scripts/ schemata that sustain it—demonstrate indomitable effectiveness in a "multiple drafts" perspective. Each "repetitive" act can be defined, in Dennett's terms, as a step in an "editorial process" that mobilizes conscious/ unconscious content wired into perceptions, evaluations, projections, etc. Both this process and the resulting "additions, incorporations, emendations, and overwritings of content" obtain throughout the play—for Vladimir and Estragon as for any interpreters exposed to it. When, in the end, Vladimir and Estragon utter, "Let's go," but "do not move" (*CDW* 51), they are not as much trapped as successful at "overwriting" productivity-based action enough to reveal its emptiness, in terms of individual benefits, within a patriarchal social framework. (Spectators would likely leave the theatre in a state of depression if they perceived the ending, at a conscious or unconscious level, in another key.) This radical "overwriting," which stays under the radar by proceeding through multiple small-scale edits and countless successive drafts, is not an invitation to self-abandonment and inaction—the play does not function on any level in an oppositional, disjunctive mode. What it offers, instead, is an effective deactivation of injunctions to maintain adherence to oppositional, disjunctive schemata, so that new modes of relating to other living bodies can begin to form through subsequent drafts.

Later plays incrementally extend this process in engaging more explicitly with institutional forms of repression, including imprisonment and torture. In *Happy Days*, Winnie is literally sinking into the ground while voicing conscious and unconscious content. Act II conspicuously "edits" multiple elements of Act I (through additions and emendations)—but, in fact, each sequence of words corrodes and delegitimates the environmental elements it supposedly attempts to recall. In the later *What Where*, Beckett's recursive character reduction sequence offers even starker "overwritings," explicitly linking the everyday maintenance of hierarchy-based systems to torture and mass murder. These "anti-realistic" types of repetition, through their shock effects, are likely to quicken and intensify cognitive processes that generally occur at a slower and steadier pace. Interpreters may experience increasing levels of anxiety in the process, but the positivity of reader/ audience reactions suggests that the increasing speed and intensity of the "editing" sequence must also generate an exhilarating effect that encourages rather than blocking engagement. The discovery of yet unexplored overwriting possibilities must be part of this process. Moreover, *awareness of the process* must come into play, as the increasing speed, intensity, and compression of Beckett's late plays *make noticeable*—through a kind of forced exposure—mental processes interpreters may have previously undergone automatically and unconsciously. Exposure to Beckett's texts is thus likely to result in an eerie kind of cognitive "high"—nourishing, alluring, and entirely devoid of damaging effects. (More on this shortly.)

Both the "multiple drafts" and the enactivist models promote an understanding of the mind as a dynamic, mutable aggregate constantly engaging with stimuli and "updating" both itself and its assessments and projections—radically different from the unified, coherent, ordered model corresponding to more traditional theorizations of the mind/ the subject. The Unnamable is perhaps the quintessential example of this embodied mind/subject-in-process, but his "avatar" Molloy is already busily engaged in such enactments. Molloy's recounting of his acts is "historical" in a remarkably consistent way. In discussing his abuse of his mother, experimentations with "love," or beating of the coal burner, he continually injects experiences of past abuse into his accounts of more recent actions, as though keen to posit himself as a late "draft" having undergone "editing" and "formatting" processes that have incorporated the recourse to violence into his cognitive constitution assiduously and inescapably, to the point of "writing it in" as a compulsion. He is persuasive enough to ensure interpreters' empathy. Concomitantly, he is dismissive enough in discussing the truth value of his claims and theatrical enough in his enactment of self-indulgence to invite interpreters' multiple-draft realization—at their "end" of the storyworld and of the "editing" process—that the subjection of others to violence is always, ultimately, not a matter of compulsion but profitable complicity. "Overwritings" that accommodate one's infliction of violence on others support systemic maintenance and are mobilized through allowances of enjoyment that are supposed to remain secret—always disguised as undesirable but necessary practices safeguarding order and the common good. However, Molloy's supposed attempts to support this script—like his account of his "communication" with his deaf mother—are too grotesquely implausible, fixated on physicality, and self-satisfied not to compromise any systemic claims to necessity and order. Here is a sample:

> I got into communication with her by knocking on her skull. One knock meant yes, two no, three I don't know, four money, five goodbye. ... During the period of training ... as I administered the four knocks on her skull, I stuck a bank-note under her nose or in her mouth. In the innocence of my heart! For she seemed to have lost, if not absolutely all notion of mensuration, at least the faculty of counting beyond two. ... By the time she came to the fourth knock she imagines she was only at the second ... . She must have thought I was saying no to her all the time, whereas nothing was further from my purpose. Enlightened by these considerations I looked for and

finally found a more effective means of putting the idea of money into her head. This consisted in replacing the four knocks of my index-knuckle by one of more (according to my needs) thumps of the fist, on her skull. That she understood. (*M* 14–15)

Here and elsewhere, Molloy's ostentatiously *transactional* infliction of harm frames the very notion of "necessary violence" as a repulsive systemic grotesquery that needs to be "edited out" of any processes of social aggregation. Interpreters' decoding of this process is supported by the fact that, similarly to Beckett's other "creatures," everything about Molloy and his environment is physical, enacted rather than explained, painful, smelly, and grotesque, with any attempts at abstraction used solely to enhance slapstick or scatological comedic effects, as in Molloy's mathematical breakdown of his farting habits (*M* 28). There is no interiority because the inner/outer disjunction has been compromised as a convenient systemic frame injunction (as a way to localize, capture, and load the subject with guilt). Despite seemingly generating a state of unnerving indeterminacy in interpreters, this process of decoding in fact carries exhilarating promises of freedom from constricting frames/ scripts/ schemata and of renewed and enhanced capabilities for cognitive enrichment.

5.3   Shock and Anchoring Through Style, Intertextuality, and Dramatization

Abbott notes that "grammatical references of subject and object are at once inter-identified and set in conflict" in Beckett's texts ("Immersions" 136), to the effect of creating "a sustained sentence-by-sentence vertigo" (137). Abbott analyses this "crisis of 'person deixis'" (137) in a fragment from *The Unnamable*, but his observations apply to most of Beckett's works. He contrasts Beckett's procedure to what Ann Banfield has termed an "empty deictic center" (qtd. in Abbott, "Immersions" 137). Thus, modernist writers like Katherine Mansfield or Virginia Woolf generated a "subjective center" within the storyworld unaccompanied by sufficient contextual clues to clarify whose voice is being heard—an initially "disturbing" narrative condition that most readers have eventually learnt to "'naturalize' and thus accept without much strain" (137). In contrast, "Beckett has crammed the subjective center of *The Unnamable* with a superabundance of personal deictics, a conflict of grammatical schemata that cannot be naturalized and thus never loses its power to disturb the reader" (137). Consequently, readers are forced to "let go of the explanatory impulse" and its correlate, a perception of the self as unitary, coherent, and "well within the grasp of language," and assimilate the "experiential knowledge of our ignorance about who we are" imparted by the text (138). Abbott sees such textual transactions as "not only useful but urgent" in the context of today's overreliance on science as a means to control the world (139). While I agree with Abbott on most points, I would suggest that Beckett's "crisis of 'person deixis'" points to "our ignorance about who we are" as a typical result of our adherence to disjunctive frames/ scripts/ schemata rather than as a general human trait. I would further argue that the peculiar textual transactions generated by Beckett's texts dissolve our dependency on unified concepts of selfhood by revealing to what extent a unified self runs an increased risk of repressive capture; increase our resistance to anxiety-based forms of social control by revealing that coherence and stability do not always equate with happiness or comfort; and, finally, serve an evolutive function in their insistence on operating with increasingly complex and open experiential frameworks.

If Molloy maintained his identity in a state of flux mostly by enacting its "historical" and transactional nature, starting with Malone, the ostentatious use of "avatars" (no longer fully recognized as "former selves" through the use of "I") becomes the primary means to resist systemic localization and capture in the form of repressive impositions of an internalized sense of a unified self. Malone deviously refers to Sapo as "that other who is my little one" (*TN* 52), ambiguously suggests that he might be a son he engendered, then one he would like to engender, to finally conclude, "Yes, a little creature, I shall try and make a little creature, to hold in my arms, a little creature in my image, no matter what I say. And seeing what a poor thing I have made, or how like myself, I shall eat it" (53). He promptly "finds" the "child" on a bench (53), refers to him as Sapo and then switches to Macmann, while claiming to dislike both names (56). Connections between avatars are thus ostentatiously forged and disassembled within the space of a sentence/ a few lines/ a few pages, and the process extends, at multiple levels, over the entire novel. Malone's main concern is not to hide factual evidence (that the boy/ youth he calls Sapo grew up to become the man he calls Macmann, who advanced in age to become Malone, the name he now associates with the "I"—"that is what I am called now," 49). His meandering narrative and disorienting use of "person deixis" do require alertness on the part of readers, but the information is clearly there—and it can be used, if needed, to prove that

Malone is hard at work to produce the unified life story (of a unified self) presumably demanded by the "powers that be" (6) that detain him. Malone's main concern and corresponding strategy is, then, to flaunt his inability to connect his "scattered" thoughts/ identities while imparting to readers this very procedure of keeping oneself too fragmented for full immersion into repressive social aggregates.

From Malone's perspective, identifying with more or less coagulated former selves runs an increased risk of repressive capture, and the advertised benefit of "finding peace with oneself" (or any variation on the theme) is predicated on the false premise that coherence and stability equate with happiness and comfort. Malone uses his avatars Macmann and Sapo to compromise that equivalence. Sapo's witnessing of the viciousness of the family unit (through the Lamberts' interactions) and Macmann's experiencing of the violence and confinement of the religious charity machine (through his stay in the House of Saint John of God) expose the punitive framework underlying societal structures entrusted to secure coherence and stability. In addition, identifying with former selves would minimize the role of environmental conditioning in shaping successive versions of the subject and misrepresent the process as organic individual development/ growth. In Malone's view, we are not our former avatars or selves, however defined, and they are not naturally or organically consistent. A more accurate representation of the process is to say that we "make" them in our image and "eat" them, as Malone says about his "little creature" (53)—that is, we continually reimagine them in a teleological perspective and then reabsorb them *as successively reimagined former states or "drafts."* Any coagulation or coherence would be nothing but an imposition derived from the current frames/ scripts/ schemata we operate under—and failing to question this process would allow those cognitive structures to become increasingly resistant to enrichment or multiplication.

The textual transactions prompted by Malone's narrative may additionally increase interpreters' resistance to anxiety-based forms of social control. As also discussed in Part I, through elements such as Mr. Lambert's aggressions or Lemuel's abuses and killing spree, the text foregrounds the fact that individuals' demands for personal space, intimacy, and self-determination are typically perceived as systemic threats within repressive social assemblages and punished with extreme severity in order to discourage future iterations. From a cognitive perspective, this punitive response associates, within the cognitive scripts/ frames/ schemata individuals live by, the enactment of those demands with fear and anxiety. This pattern's reoccurrence within contexts involving any number of societal institutions in Malone's narrative acts, again, as a kind of forced exposure, likely prompting interpreters to assess to what extent societal manifestations of anxiety they may have previously perceived as objective/ reality-based might be sheer effects of frame-based injunctions. This realization may trigger interpreters' dissociation of anxiety from the individual demand for self-determination, as well as their subsequent *rejection* of any cognitive frameworks that associate punishments with that demand (and of any societal structures that reinforce/ are reinforced by such frameworks). This radical reshaping of associated cognitive frames/ scripts/ schemata may prompt interpreters' increased interest in achieving self-determination alongside their increased tolerance towards others' attempts to assert their own.

Finally, textual transactions like those triggered by Malone's narrative may serve an evolutive function in their insistence on operating with increasingly complex and open experiential frameworks. Abbott suggests that the value of Beckett's works is best discussed *outside of* evolutionary views ("Immersions" 138; "Garden Paths" 206, 214, and 217). However, his comments on this value engage the current socio-historical context in ways that may in fact lend support to evolutionary claims. For instance, in "Garden Paths," Abbott suggests that Beckett's textual transactions are effective largely due to his use of humour and to the increased tolerance for uncertainty and instability elicited by his texts. He uses Mitchell Marcus's notion of "garden-path sentences"—challenging and initially ambiguous/ misleading syntactical constructions used by Marcus to prove that we interpret sentences incrementally—to suggest that the pleasure typically experienced in disambiguating a challenging sentence is enhanced by the way it "tempts linguistic chaos in the split second before we parse [it] correctly and restore linguistic order" (208). In the cognitive process of disambiguation, "chaos is brought under control by your own acuity. It is a way to achieve the excitement of living on the edge" (208). Abbott analyses fragments from *Ill Seen Ill Said* and *Worstward Ho*, showing that they continually elicit intense adaptive moves from interpreters through acts of grammatical "discourtesy" (212) such as missing punctuation, missing words, and syntactic displacements, and that the resulting "garden path" sentences are not meant to converge into *one* meaning at the end of the disambiguation process but to concurrently obstruct *and* maintain all possible meanings (214). Consequently, "the struggle for meaning and the release from it are experienced simultaneously" (215), prompting readers to develop an increased tolerance for uncertainty and instability, states of mind whose importance alone should counter critical objections that works such as Beckett's engage in isolationist forms of aestheticism (216–17). Building on Abbott's observations and based on my analysis of individual works by Beckett in previous chapters, I would suggest that readers' increased tolerance for uncertainty and instability is stimulated by the fact that the expected stress and strain of any adaptive process repeatedly dissolves into laughter, and that the disambiguating sensation Abbott mentions ("living on edge") renders the experience addictive.

As also shown in Part I, satisfying and empowering interpretive experiences seem to occur even when Beckett extracts his humour from the darkest human experiences—emotional/ physical pain, exploitation, and repression, which may appear to fit more squarely within the domain of the tragic or the horrific. While Beckett's humour consistently courts the intensity of insanity and terror, it always maintains an edge of sanity through its cognitive (embodied, enactivist, emotively-inflected) appeal. One way in which Beckett achieves this is by ensuring that all instances of discourse always register as *also quoted and/or dramatized* discourse.

Beckett's extensive use of quotations and allusions should be afforded its due credit for the intensity and attractiveness of his texts, as it grounds interpreters into the safe "outside" of the text while also facilitating more sophisticated cognitive operations for interpreters qualified to process them. Many critics have anthologized Beckett's rich literary and philosophical references in *Waiting for Godot* and elsewhere. While much of this dimension remains inaccessible to non-specialists, as Worton notes, interpreters would likely notice at least Beckett's frequent references to canonical texts of Western culture like the Bible and "metatheatrical" references such as Vladimir and Estragon's comments that their evening is "worse than being at the theatre," the circus, or the music-hall (*CDW* 33). According to Worton, these references "fragment the surface message of the text by sending the reader off on a series of speculations" that "[open up] the text and ... counterbalanc[e] the progressive closure of entropy experienced by the characters" (74). Far from proposing such references as "creeds" or "models of existence" (85), Beckett uses them to prompt readers to "think and speculate" and thus "participate in his anxious oscillation between certainty about what is untrue and uncertainty about what may be true" (89). Worton concludes, "Our strongest defence against the absurdity and the entropy of existence is the necessity—and the joy—of co-creating the text by continually changing its shape as we connect different ideas and images, as we perceive it to be unauthoritative precisely because it is a *cento*, a patchwork of manipulated quotations" (89). Taking Worton's argument one step further, I propose that Beckett's obsessive use of intertextual references (to works by others or to his earlier texts) engages readers and audience members in a type of *work* with the text that is bound to expand their perception of specific frames of reference and the connections between them, creating new cognitive pathways for future evaluations and judgements. In addition, intertextuality increases the dramatic quality of Beckett's literary discourse—in Beckett's plays *and* in his fiction—and the likelihood of empathic projections on interpreters' part by inviting interpreters to process intertextual connections alongside Beckett's characters (as "inside jokes") and thus participate in a liberating and empowering process of fragmentation, re-anchoring, and reframing.

The last lines of *The Unnamable* and the first from *Texts for Nothing* offer a good example of Beckett's unruly use of intertextual connections to his previous works to corrode narrative conventions of major effect on cognitive frames/ scripts/ schemata such as the incipit and the closing:

> You must go on, I can't go on, you must go on, I'll go on, you must say words, as long as there are any, until they find me, until they say me, strange pain, strange sin, you must go on, perhaps it's done already, perhaps they have said me already, perhaps they have carried me to the threshold of my story, before the door that opens on my story, that would surprise me, if it opens, it will be I, it will be the silence, where I am, I don't know, I'll never know, in the silence you don't know, you must go on, I can't go on, I'll go on. (*U* 134)
>
> Suddenly, no, at last, long last, I couldn't any more, I couldn't go on.
> Someone said, You can't stay here. I couldn't stay there and I couldn't go on. I'll describe the place, that's unimportant. The top, very flat, of a mountain, no, a hill, but so wild, so wild, enough. ... How can I go on, I shouldn't have begun, no, I had to begin. Someone said, perhaps the same, What possessed you to come? I could have stayed in my den, snug and dry, I couldn't. (*CSP* 100)

The first sentence of *Texts for Nothing* ostentatiously preserves the tentative tone of the ending of *The Unnamable* while corroding its claim to exhaustion (*Texts for Nothing* obviously "goes on" for dozens of pages amounting to thirteen short texts). The following sentences translate the phrase "go on" specifically into physical/ spatial *motion*—but, rather than significantly altering the connective and corrosive effect created by the first sentence, the "clarification" would likely be perceived as a horrific-comic "step back" typical of Beckett's angry but apprehensive speakers. In addition, the "clarification" provides an enactment of oppositional/ contradictory claims much blunter than what we typically experienced with the Unnamable. The latter often "walked back" on his claims, too, but in so doing, always feigned inability (to recall or express). In contrast, the speakers from *Texts for Nothing* anchor such contradictions explicitly to adversarial environmental interactions, cuing interpreters, in a recognizably dramatic mode, to their different status and to the potentially different nature of their storyworld.

In ostentatiously connecting and inviting a comparison between the closing of *The Unnamable* and the opening of *Texts for Nothing*, Beckett does not simply link his works but makes problematic narrative notions of incipit/ closure and their wiring into cognitive frames/ scripts/ schemata resulting from and supportive of our perception of events within our lived environment. The cognitive processes triggered are likely open-ended—they may extend from speculations on the nature of the storyworlds defined in the two novels to reassessments of textual and real-world features interpreters associate with beginnings/ ends to further reassessments of the manageable and reassuring but inaccurate encapsulation of experience resulting from such "logical segmentations." Such forms of cognitive processing—always supported by Beckett's trademark horrific-comic mode—may, then, gradually enhance interpreters' ability to decode the potential meanings of complex sets of allusions without retracting into familiar territory through reductive simplifications, as well as to perform such cognitive operations without experiencing overload. Significantly, as also discussed in previous chapters, Beckett's texts do not appease readers/ audience members' anxieties—they do not allow for basic, univocal readings, and, as Critchley notes, never provide reassurance in the form of "redeeming" narratives (*Very Little* 211–12). On the contrary, they use any available methods (narrative, stylistic, performative, referential, metatextual, etc.) to generate increasing levels of anxiety, to the point of denouncing and corroding both the social *mechanisms* of producing anxiety and its *systemic function* (its role in maintaining the status quo). The liberatory procedures offered in Beckett's texts thus bypass traditional (patriarchal, parochial, and patronizing) forms of reassurance and operate instead through a kind of forced exposure whereby repression mechanisms that might have been embedded in the frames and scripts we process mentally and live by become grotesquely, unbearably present—as rattling chains rather than safety nets. As we become aware of their modes of articulation and come to perceive their parasitic nature, our minds proceed to expunge them and generate, in the process, more satisfying frames and scripts. Beckett's use of literary and cultural allusions offers us, from this perspective, countless opportunities to exercise and develop our cognitive functions of evaluation, expulsion, enrichment or expansion, and reframing. One major literary/ cultural convention systematically compromised in this way is the comedy/ tragedy disjunction—"naturalized" and continually reinforced at the level of cognitive frames/ scripts/ schemata through a variety of conceptual formations, from categories of the dramatic genre to categories of intellectual and empathic responses predefined as appropriate for specific human experiences.

5.4 Staging a Raw Experience of the Grotesque, or, Against Tragedy/ Comedy as Cognitive Frames/ Scripts/ Schemata

Uhlmann insightfully defines Beckett's notorious attempts to control all performances of his plays as "an attempt to organize or stage an expression rather than offering an interpretation" ("Staging Plays" 180). He quotes one of Beckett's favourite directors, Donald McWhinnie, who describes Beckett as open on interpretive matters such as whether or not Hamm was mad but "rigid" concerning the rhythm of speech and general structure of the performance (177). As Uhlmann notes, Beckett's stage directions include "diagrams explaining movements of the characters and giving detailed instructions on the level of pitch and voice desirable" (174), and in his work with actors and directors, he consistently stressed the importance of using voice and movement both to delineate contrasts and to emphasize repetitions (179). Repetitions "at once establish a sense of order and unease," since "[t]he status of a phrase or action is immediately altered once we realize it is being repeated," which can activate spectators' awareness of "patterning" and of a "limiting structure": "The characters inhabit a world in which habit establishes not only a sense of order, but also limitation, and such limitation, if necessary to their survival, is also necessarily oppressive" (180). What Beckett has consistently tried to control, then—through written dialogue, stage directions, as well as direct staging interventions—are the verbal and visual markers that guide under-standing, which "at once enable and limit meaning" (180). Uhlmann's assessment easily lends itself to translation into (post)cognitivist interpre-tive terms. The elements of his plays Beckett adamantly wanted to pre-serve are those likely to activate audiences' reassessment of the frames/ scripts/ schemata they process mentally and live by.

In Chap. 2, I discussed several letters in which Beckett defended his use of elements of language disapproved by censors, like the phrase "The bas-tard! He doesn't exist" from *Endgame* (*CDW* 119). I suggested there that Beckett consistently rejected changes that would flatten his paradox-based textual constructs into mere oppositions and disjunctions inapt to mobilize audiences' solidarity-based anger and promote anti-hierarchical relational patterns. In cognitive terms, Beckett's refusal to tone down the violence of his language reflects a need to preserve textual shock effects that would trigger interpreters' reassessment of cognitive frames/ scripts/ schemata. Hamm's offensive reference to God, alongside other iconoclastic and/or obscene elements, forcibly disconnects the play's scenario from predeter-mined cognitive formations rooted into traditional conceptualizations of the apocalypse. As the tragic tenor of eschatology is violently and unscru-pulously supplanted by scatological humour, elements of cognitive anchor-ing that may have seemed reasonable and rational to interpreters before now appear to be nothing but rattling chains fastening them to fear-based frames/ scripts/ schemata of no obvious benefit and preventing their engagement in more satisfying environmental exchanges. Significantly toned-down versions of Beckett's consistently corrosive language would be less likely to activate those cognitive reassessment processes.

There is also ample evidence, in Beckett's letters, that he considered specific *staging* elements essential for the transmission of meaning, as Uhlmann and others noted. Some of this evidence gains added relevance in a cognitive reading. In a 3 January 1951 letter to Georges Duthuit, Beckett explains that *Waiting for Godot* would need a minimalist set "with-out painting, without music, without embellishments," which "come[s] out of the text" without adding to the "speech and acting"—"sordidly abstract as nature is," and implicitly allowing for a raw experience of the play (*L2* 218). "As for the visual convenience of the audience, you can guess where I put that" (218), he adds—an acid comment indicating, in cognitive terms, a conviction that an "embellished" set would activate, in audience members, preformed and predetermined frames/ scripts/ sche-mata detrimental to their experience of the play. Beckett's rejection of conventional forms of mediation between text and audience is not limited to the dismissal of "embellished" sets. He also steadfastly refused to provide explanatory "companion texts" for any production. In a text sent after 23 January 1952 to Michel Polac and meant to be used as an introduction to a reading of the play on the radio, Beckett systematically demolishes the notion that the characters and action should be "framed" for easier (i.e., preordained) cognitive processing:

> I know no more about this play than anyone who manages to read it attentively.
> I do not know in what spirit I wrote it.
> I know no more about the characters than what they say, what they do and what happens to them. ...
> I do not know who Godot is. I do not even know if he exists. And I do not know if they believe he does, these two who are waiting for him. (316)

In several other letters, like the one dated 25 July 1953 to Carlheinz Caspari (392), he also rejects the idea of including an introductory text signed by him in the printed programme for any performance.

In addition to rejecting such consecrated forms of mediation, Beckett was, as Uhlmann (cited earlier) noted, strict on matters of voice, rhythm, and gestures. In a 9 January 1953 letter to Roger Blin, Beckett insists that the actor playing Estragon must allow his trousers to "fall right down, round the ankles" instead of holding on to them half-way down—"as it is in the text, and as we had always planned in rehearsals"—stressing the "vital" importance of that visual element as follows: "The spirit of the play, in so far as it has one, is that nothing is more grotesque than the tragic, and that must be put across right to the end, and particularly at the end" (350–51). The word "grotesque" appears again in the 25 July 1953 letter to Caspari, in a related context:

> The farce side seems indispensable to me as much from the technical point of view (comic relief) as for reasons to do with the spirit of the play. Therefore neither to be hurried through nor to be overdone. Here unhappiness is the height of the grotesque and every act is a piece of clowning. Laugh at them then and get them laughed at, at unhappiness and at the act, but not all the time, that would be too good, and always a little reluctantly. (392)

What consistently transpires from these letters is that directors, in the incipient phase of their work with Beckett's *Godot*, instinctively sought to return the play to old, recognizable, cohesive, and unchallenging patterns—tragedy, comedy, tragicomedy, etc. That did not coincide with Beckett's vision. He wanted to transform the very notions of the tragic or of comedy into an experience of the grotesque (a recurrent word in his letters concerning the play). As the quotations provided above indicate, he wanted verbal and visual elements ugly, repulsive, and shocking enough to immediately direct laughter at *unhappiness* and at *the act* rather than at the characters at their origin—in other words, at the *mechanisms* setting those acts and affects into motion. Moreover, in cognitive terms, he seemingly pursued shock effects that would expose *comedy* and *tragedy* (and the disjunction-based composite *tragicomedy*) as cognitive frames resulting from and supportive of placating notions of coherence that prevent the mind from rejecting large numbers of damaging scenarios. "Nothing is more grotesque than the tragic" because the tragic lulls the mind into accepting pain as a prerequisite for greatness/ value. In Part I, I explained Beckett's rejection of the tragic in an affect-based framework. In cognitive terms, the shock effects that bolster this rejection bar the activation of cognitive frames/ scripts/ schemata ossified through millennia of cultural reinforcement and use, and thus trigger and intensify cognitive processes of reassessment and reframing.

The four main characters of *Waiting for Godot* bear clown names, and many of their gestures evoke the vaudeville—the play even includes a sequence of exchanging hats (*CDW* 66). However, such "light" comedic elements are ostentatiously embedded into scripts evocative of poverty, exploitation, and repression—Vladimir and Estragon's near-absolute lack of resources and Pozzo's unrestrained consumption of Lucky's diminishing psychosomatic energy, as obvious from the master-slave pair's first minutes on stage:

Pozzo: [*He jerks the rope.*] Up pig! [*Pause.*] Every time he drops he falls asleep. [*Jerks the rope.*] Up hog! [*Noise of Lucky getting up and picking up his baggage. Pozzo jerks the rope.*] Back! [*Enter Lucky backwards.*] Stop! [*Lucky stops.*] Turn! [*Lucky turns. To Vladimir and Estragon, affably.*] Gentlemen, I am happy to have met you. ... [*To Lucky.*] Coat! [*Lucky pulls down the bag, advances, gives the coat, goes back to his place, takes up the bag.*] Hold that! [*Pozzo holds out the whip. Lucky advances and, both his hands being occupied, takes the whip in his mouth, then goes back to his place. Pozzo begins to put on his coat, stops.*] Coat! [*Lucky puts down the bag, basket and stool, helps Pozzo on with his coat, goes back to his place and takes up bag, basket and stool.*] Touch of autumn in the air this evening. [*Pozzo finishes buttoning up his coat, stoops, inspects himself, straightens up.*] Whip! [*Lucky advances, stoops, Pozzo snatches the whip from his mouth, Lucky goes back to his place.*] (23–24)

The passage continues for another half a page, as Pozzo requests his stool and then the basket with the food and wine, forcing several more repeats of Lucky's walking and bending motions. While Pozzo's barking commands and Lucky's mechanical movements may evoke a clown act, this particular form of encroachment of the mechanical on the living in no way aligns with Bergson's famous definition of the comic. Bergson's association of laughter with the presence of a "living and thinking being that gives the impression of being a thing" (*Laughter* 133) has often been linked in criticism to the use of puppet-like characters lacking psychological depth in avant-garde drama and to Beckett's use of slapstick elements and characters incapable of change. However, Bergson's turn-of-the-century theorization, relevant for earlier comedic forms, is of limited relevance in this context, as it failed to anticipate the radical mutations of the comic in avant-garde works or in the works of Beckett. Bergson sees the encroachment of the mechanical on the organic as comical insofar as it seems unintentional (133) and the performer does not connect emotionally with the spectator (131)—so that laughter can serve a corrective function (the spectator's consciousness laughing at its own imperfections in the guise of the character and returning the spectator to a community-/ norm-oriented state, 121, 158, 175, etc.). Avant-garde artists' and Beckett's use of slapstick elements is more complex and of a different orientation.

Slapstick elements are consistently used, in avant-garde works as in Beckett's drama and fiction, to render grotesque (and denounce as forces against life) various categories of socio-historical conditioning. Characters' inability to escape conditioning and behave "organically" (vs. mechanically) is consistently enacted as the horrific-comic result of the *weight of repression* rather than as an inherently human inability to adapt. Consequently, the "corrective" function of previous comedic forms is denounced, in such works, as a normative cognitive frame supporting repression and exploitation—and the resulting category of the horrific-comic rejects "corrective" communitarian concerns as ossified cognitive formations meant to reinforce existing hierarchies. The scene from *Waiting for Godot* quoted above activates, on multiple levels, readers' reassessment of cognitive frames/ scripts/ schemata related to communitarian notions of duty and reward. Perhaps, if it were shorter, it would seem simply comical, but it is painfully long and repetitive, fully exposing Pozzo's colossal self-absorption and monstrous dehumanization of his servant, as well as the cognitive limitations of basic comedic forms. If

Lucky seems to act like a "thing," it is because Pozzo has effectively made him into one through unremitting exploitation and abuse.[3] Spectators' laughter is likely not directed at Lucky but at Pozzo's postulation that, between the two of them, he is the one still recognizable as human, as well as at the notion that there are benefits to being "tied." Thus, the scene integrates elements that anchor it to more traditional comedic modes specifically in order to denounce those modes as feeding into cognitive frames/ scripts/ schemata that legitimate and reinforce exploitation and repression.

Similarly, Vladimir and Estragon's act of "waiting" seemingly courts tragedy, but—since Godot's supposedly munificent nature is arguably of the same order as Pozzo's—in fact dismantles tragedy as a legitimate cognitive frame. In Act II, Vladimir and Estragon's waiting act consists of a long series of enactments of adherence to various cognitive frames/ scripts/ schemata—each enactment paired with an act of *naming* ("being happy," "playing at Pozzo and Lucky," etc.) that, in effect, annihilates the coagulating power of the cognitive structure in question. Significantly, at the start of Act II, after Vladimir and Estragon convince themselves that companionship equals happiness, Estragon asks, "What do we do now, now that we're happy?" and Vladimir replies, "Wait for Godot" (55). The exchange points to the framing of economic exploitation as a natural development within any human cluster. The conversation that follows loops through several interpersonal practices traditionally framed as apt to intensify intimacy and social connectivity, alongside cultural practices codified as contributors to the advancement of civilization: "That's the idea,

---

[3] Besides, Lucky is not entirely dead inside, as his subsequent speech demonstrates. Moreover, once "stirred" through the speech, Lucky falls to the ground and Pozzo has to enlist Vladimir and Estragon's help to return him to his automaton state: "Raise him up! [*Vladimir and Estragon hoist Lucky to his feet, support him an instant, then let him go. He falls.*] ... Don't let him go! [*Vladimir and Estragon totter.*] Don't move! [*Pozzo fetches bag and basket and brings them towards Lucky.*] Hold him tight! [*He puts the bag in Lucky's hand. Lucky drops it immediately.*] Don't let him go! [*He puts back the bag in Lucky's hand. Gradually, at the feel of the bag, Lucky recovers his senses and his fingers finally close round the handle.*] Hold him tight! [*As before with basket.*] Now! You can let him go. [*Vladimir and Estragon move away from Lucky who totters, reels, sags, but succeeds in remaining on his feet, bag and basket in his hands. Pozzo steps back, cracks his whip.*] Forward! [*Lucky totters forward.*] Back! [*Lucky totters back.*] Turn! [*Lucky turns.*] Done it! He can walk" (43). This is another scene apt to trigger interpreters' intense processes of reassessment of cognitive frames/ scripts/ schemata that reinforce subordination as a "natural" and mutually beneficial social arrangement.

let's contradict each other" (58), "That's the idea, let's ask each other questions" (58), "We should turn resolutely towards Nature" (59), "That wasn't such a bad little canter" (59), "We could play at Pozzo and Lucky" (66), "That's the idea, let's abuse each other" (69), "Now let's make it up" (69), "We could do our exercises" (70), etc. When Pozzo appears, Vladimir and Estragon—at the end of these seemingly silly but terrifyingly effective "training" sessions—deliberate at length whether or not they should help Pozzo without financial compensation (72–77). Finally, the effects of their rehearsal of "proper" socialization wear off: Estragon asks, "What are we waiting for?" (78), and they help blind Pozzo to his feet without requesting payment. However, as they return to this benevolent attitude, Pozzo (who had previously been crying for help and promising increasingly more money in return) no longer mentions compensation, gradually reasserts control over the conversation, regains control over Lucky, and returns to jerking the rope and barking commands (81–82). By the end of Act II, as Vladimir and Estragon resolve to continue to wait for Godot and to try to improve on their hanging act "tomorrow," they have successfully facilitated, for interpreters, increasingly intense series of reassessments of cognitive frames that support models of social integration based in exploitation and repression. From a cognitive perspective, intense frame reassessment work dominates the conclusion of the play rather than feelings of tragic emptiness. Various means of converting conservative elements of cognitive framing into elements of shock and of using elements traditionally associated with the comedic/ tragic modes to dissolve such placating notions of coherence and order emerge from all of Beckett's dramatic and fictional works, stimulating interpreters' cognitive reassessment work and enticing them to develop more genuinely nourishing and satisfying cognitive frames/ scripts/ schemata.

CHAPTER 6

Evaluation, Expulsion, Expansion, and Reframing: Building Processing Speed and Tolerance to Cognitive Strain

6.1 FROM FEIGNING INABILITY TO PLEASURE AND EMPOWERMENT: GOD, LABOUR, AND FAMILY TIES REASSESSED AND REFRAMED

For Bryden ("Bestiary"), Weller ("Forms"), and Maude, the recurring dehumanization or degeneration of Beckett's characters blurs the cognitive divide between humans and animals, questioning the "major premises—consciousness, intentional subjectivity, and language—that have served to privilege the category of human" (Maude 92). In Bernini's view, Beckett explores the "creaturely level" of "undeveloped human cognisers" (40) of limited speech, locomotive, and teleological abilities, whose perpetual "crawling away from the ontological prison of becoming creating created creatures" (52) enacts a rejection of being. My analysis contributes to the exploration of the cognitive dimension of Beckett's works by focusing on a number of characters/ speakers difficult to relegate to *one* spectrum of identity (animal/ human, or lower/ higher-order cognitive ability), whose inability and impotence are, at least in part, *feigned* as a means to resist the formation/ break the consistency of constricting cognitive frames/ scripts/ schemata. In the process, such characters/ speakers share increasingly complex means to sabotage such cognitive formations with readers and audience members—and, most importantly, they encourage interpreters to appreciate and enjoy frame multiplication and enrichment processes and to

© The Author(s) 2020   211
C. Ionica, *The Affects, Cognition, and Politics of Samuel Beckett's Postwar Drama and Fiction*, New Interpretations of Beckett in the Twenty-First Century, https://doi.org/10.1007/978-3-030-34902-8_6

break with the limiting, damaging habit of withdrawing into familiar cognitive terrain at the slightest sign of uncertainty or discomfort.

The Act I fragment from *Waiting for Godot* juxtaposing Vladimir and Estragon's apparently clueless discussion of the Crucifixion story and memory-impaired exchange concerning Godot is an example. The first sequence mocks Christian rituals as nagging attempts to legitimate unfounded claims through sheer repetition. Vladimir relentlessly insists on telling the story despite Estragon's lack of interest. He mimics consecrated theological rhetoric in raising doubts concerning inconsistencies in the scriptures only to find means to overcome them, but Estragon violently sabotages the game from his first interventions:

> V: Gogo.
> E: What?
> V: Suppose we repented.
> E: Repented what?
> V: Oh... [*He reflects.*] We wouldn't have to go into the details.
> E: Our being born?

Estragon's replies reveal sarcastic anger rather than confusion. As Vladimir repeatedly recasts his statements on "the thieves" and "our saviour," Estragon's curt questions accumulate: "Our what?"—"Saved from what?"—"Who?"—"What's all this about? [*Pause.*] Abused who?"— "Why?"—"From hell?"—"Well, what about it?"—"And why not?"— "Who believes him?" (*CDW* 13–14). He is neither unable to process the story nor an embodiment of a cooperative "chorus" whose questions/ comments are meant to invite additional details. He is a reluctant listener whose replies challenge Christian doctrine through shock effects of increasing intensity. This hijacking of a consecrated rhetorical procedure aimed at mitigating doubt is likely to activate interpreters' reassessment of cognitive frames/ scripts/ schemata supported by/ supportive of religious doctrine. The subsequent discussion concerning Godot craftily aligns Christian promises of salvation to Godot's promises of employment, potentially intensifying interpreters' reassessment processes. The conversation moves from the first mentioning of "waiting for Godot" (14) to speculations on the passing of time (15–16) and the first iteration of the idea of hanging themselves (17–18) to an exchange on what Godot may have promised them and what factors might determine his final offer (18–21, with the conspicuous carrot interlude towards the end). Elements of anchoring such as divine benevolence and economic rewards are placed in destabilizing alignment. Vladimir and Estragon define their request of Godot as "[a] kind of prayer" and "[a] vague supplication" met with promises "[t]hat he'd see" and "think it over" (18). These ostentatious redundancies, as everywhere in Beckett, do not serve purposes of clarification but *contestation*. They pose as innocuous elements of contextual anchoring but function primarily as elements of shock, triggering further cognitive reassessments of religious and class-based frames/ scripts/ schemata. By no coincidence, both the eating of the carrot and the first discussion of the possibility of getting an erection while hanging themselves appear as "asides" in Vladimir and Estragon's discussion of Godot. Given their reactions, these appear to be the only authentically satisfying experiences within their universe. Everything else would happen "[o]n our hands and knees," in Vladimir's assessment, their rights "waived" in the process (19)—and it is, again, by no coincidence that, at the end of this conversation, Lucky, the long rope, and Pozzo appear, in grotesque succession, on stage (21). An iterative reactivation/ intensification of interpreters' reassessment of religious and class-based frames/ scripts/ schemata runs, through such destabilizing redundancies, alignments, and asides, throughout the play, being undoubtedly at least in part responsible for its hope and solidarity-inducing quality.

Endgame makes the employer-employee couple central to the narrative and dramatic development and aligns class-based exploitation and repression more explicitly to the family and religion as exploitative sociohistorical machines, as discussed in Part I. In (post)cognitive terms, this alignment—established, as in *Waiting for Godot*, through repetitions with a difference, analogous dramatic setup and dialogue constructions, and violent linguistic choices that pose as elements of contextual anchoring ("clarifications") but function as elements of shock—triggers interpreters' reassessment of previously unquestioned cognitive frames/ scripts/ schemata precisely by foregrounding their perceived legitimacy as a mere matter of *repetitive reinforcement*. In a 21 June 1956 letter to Alan Schneider, Beckett describes *Endgame* as "[r]ather difficult and elliptic, mostly depending on the power of the text to claw, more inhuman than Godot" (628). Indeed, this text "claws" more violently at preestablished cognitive frames/ scripts/ schemata, given its more explicitly apocalyptic setup. Since the outside of Hamm's house is a lifeless expanse, the character in control of resources (Hamm) may seem more powerful, yet he is limited in what he can afford to do to others, given the unavailability of "help" with the exception of Clov. Additionally, the setup enacts the *consequences* of the alignment discussed above in a more damning manner: "[s]omething is taking its course" (*CDW* 98) in this play, as Clov notes—and that turns out to be the patriarchal socio-economic exploitation project. Finally, the diction is more violent here—characters are less preoccupied with feigning acquiescence to rules, and their sarcasm and anger become more explicit. However, as Beckett's description suggests, these features do not make this play more accessible than *Waiting for Godot*. The latter's more under-the-radar expressions of non-compliance and anger are likely closer to individuals' everyday assessments of possibilities of action within their environments and related reassessments of the cognitive frames/ scripts/ schemata they live by. The more confrontational tone and tenor of *Endgame* results in a more explicit text that is, counterintuitively as this may sound, more difficult to process. While successful for a play of its nature, *Endgame* was never as successful as *Godot*—likely because it required more intense cognitive adjustments and more radical frame/ script/ schemata reassessment, multiplication, and enrichment work. Still, it could also be argued that exposure to *Godot* aptly prepares the way, for interpreters, for the enhanced processing required by *Endgame*. I will return to this point later, as one of my arguments concerning the cognitive effects of exposure to Beckett's texts is that successive works trigger and sustain increasingly sophisticated and intense cognitive processing of significant evolutionary import.

The opening scene shows Clov performing mechanical movements somewhat reminiscent of Lucky's, but his recurrent "[b]rief laugh[s]" (93) reveal an autonomy Lucky lacked. Rehearsals of consecrated modes of social connectivity are more ostentatiously angry in *Endgame* and more explicitly reduced to cognitive frame injunctions:

> HAMM: I'll give you nothing more to eat.
> CLOV: Then we'll die.
> H: I'll give you just enough to keep you from dying. You'll be hungry all the time.
> C: Then we won't die. [*Pause.*] I'll go and get the sheet. [*He goes towards the door.*]
> H: No! [*Clov halts.*] I'll give you one biscuit per day. [*Pause.*] One and a half. [*Pause.*] Why do you stay with me?
> C: Why do you keep me?
> H: There's no one else.
> C: There's nowhere else. [*Pause.*]
> H: You're leaving me all the same.

C: I'm trying.
H: You don't love me.
C: No.
H: You loved me once
C: Once!
H: I've made you suffer too much. [*Pause.*] Haven't I?
C: It's not that.
H: [*Shocked.*] I haven't made you suffer too much?
C: Yes!
H: [*Relieved.*] Ah, you gave me a fright! [*Pause. Coldly.*] Forgive me. [*Pause. Louder.*] I said, Forgive me.
C: I heard you. [*Pause.*] (*CDW* 94–95)

The characters' attitudes indicate not an inability to perform "proper" socialization but an angry *unwillingness to pretend* that there is positive meaning and substance to any such acts. This fragment explicitly denounces language as a vehicle for endless reinforcements of conservative frames/ scripts/ schemata:

H: Do you remember when you came here?
C: No. Too small, you told me.
H: Do you remember your father?
C: [*Wearily.*] Same answer. [*Pause.*] You've asked me these questions millions of times.
H: I love the old questions. [*With fervour.*] Ah the old questions, the old answers, there' s nothing like them! [*Pause.*] It was I was a father to you.
C: Yes. [*He looks at Hamm fixedly.*] You were that to me.
H: My house a home for you.
C: Yes. [*He looks about him.*] This was that for me.

Clov's linguistic interventions—consistently sarcastic and corrosive— explicitly link language to the site of authority ("you told me," "same answer"). His final replacement of differentiating nouns with demonstrative pronouns (this/ that) markedly moves from weary sarcasm to anger, as it denounces the family and the home as too devoted to the reinforcement of predetermined and constricting cognitive formations to accommodate any other meanings.

The shock effect of this alignment of class and family-based injunctions is further enhanced by adding divine authority to the list. At some point, Hamm wants to tell a story and promises his father a "sugar-plum" if he listens (116). The story is followed by the famous prayer scene whose line "The bastard! He doesn't exist!" attracted censorship—but the scene is more corrosive and of larger cognitive import than that line might suggest:

> HAMM: [*Pause. He whistles. Enter Clov.*] Let us pray to God.
> NAGG: Me sugar-plum!
> CLOV: There's a rat in the kitchen!
> H: A rat! Are there still rats?
> C: In the kitchen there's one.
> H: And you haven't exterminated him?
> C: Half. You disturbed us.
> H: He can't get away?
> C: No.
> H: You'll finish him later. Let us pray to God.
> C: Again!
> N: Me sugar-plum!
> H: God first! [*Pause.*] Are you right?
> C: [*Resigned.*] Off we go.
> H: [*To Nagg.*] And you?
> N: [*Clasping his hands, closing his eyes, in a gabble.*] Our Father which art—
> H: Silence! In silence! Where are your manners? [*Pause.*] Off we go.
> [*Attitudes of prayer. Silence. Abandoning his attitude, discouraged.*] Well?
> C: [*Abandoning his attitude.*] What a hope! And you?
> H: Sweet damn all! [*To Nagg.*] And you?
> N: Wait! [*Pause. Abandoning his attitude.*] Nothing doing!
> H: The bastard! He doesn't exist.
> C: Not yet.
> N: Me sugar-plum!
> H: There are no more sugar plums! [*Pause.*] (118–19)

The passage aligns cognitive frames/ scripts/ schemata supported by and supportive of family/ class/ religious injunctions based on their *transactional* nature while denouncing any *actual* transaction within related social processes as a scam. Divine munificence is just as immaterial as Hamm's kindness and "honour" (116) or the promised sugar-plum—and the three participants know it even before their prayer exercise. Clov first responds to Hamm's request to pray by mentioning the rat in the kitchen, then protests having to do it ("Again!"), and finally cooperates only to conclude, sardonically, that God does not exist "yet." Nagg laughs "heartily" when Hamm swears on his "honour" to give him the sugar-plum (116), seemingly repeating his request strictly to undermine Hamm's control of the prayer proceedings. Finally, for Hamm himself the scene functions mostly as an exercise in authority over the others (one he must have practiced frequently, considering Clov's comments).

This alignment of cognitive frames/ scripts/ schemata supported by and supportive of family/ class/ religious injunctions is less gradual and more violent than similar alignments in *Waiting for Godot*, and the cognitive reassessment processes it may elicit, themselves likely more violent and intense. However, the trigger meant to break resistances and start the process is, as always, Beckett's trademark humour. There is something addictively humorous and empowering to the iconoclastic sequence "Let us pray to God"—"Me sugar-plum!"—"There's a rat in the kitchen!"—and knowing what those phrases refer to and why, in the narrative logic of the play, they occur in that sequence does not reduce that effect. The cognitive processing intensity and speed required by the prayer sequence is supported through such horrific-comic power boosts, which associate violating inherited frames/ scripts/ schemata and engaging in intense processes of reassessment/ multiplication/ enrichment with *pleasure and empowerment* rather than effort—with an energy increase/ investment rather than an energy decrease/ loss. Interpreters are, thus, likely to *seek* cognitive work of this nature rather than retreat from it in fear of discomfort. This effect of Beckett's earlier plays effectively prepares interpreters for the increased condensation of the later ones. It also likely prompts them to seek increasingly flexible and inclusive frames/ scripts/ schemata that may accommodate this type of cognitive work with more ease.

6.2   Staging Systemic Confinement, or, Dissolving Clusters of Repressive Frames/ Scripts/ Schemata

Disquieting images like Winnie's sinking body in *Happy Days* may function for interpreters—especially, but not exclusively if they have been exposed to the earlier works—as cognitive shortcuts. Winnie's sinking body could be described as a frame-forcing device—so alien, yet so ostentatiously obvious that it may forcibly trigger interpreters' immediate reassessment of frames/ scripts/ schemata connected to heteronormative and religious socialization-as-conditioning. She is a middle-aged woman ostentatiously codified as sexually attractive ("well-preserved, blonde for preference, plump, arms and shoulders bare, low bodice, big bosom," *CDW* 138), and the supposedly prone-to-temptation *lower half* of her body is immobilized in the peculiar form of being *buried*. Still, in case the frame alignment was insufficiently obvious in strictly visual terms, her first lines and gestures enhance the effect:

> [*Gazing at zenith.*] Another heavenly day. [*Pause. Head back level, eyes front, pause. She clasps hands to breast, closes eyes. Lips move in inaudible prayer, say ten seconds. Lips still. Hands remain clasped. Low.*] For Jesus Christ sake Amen. [*Eyes open, hands unclasp, return to mound. Pause. She clasps hands to breast again, closes eyes, lips move again in inaudible addendum, say five seconds. Low.*] World without end Amen. (138)

The activation of interpreters' cognitive framework reassessment processes is likely stimulated by Winnie's repetitive gestures and by the sharp disparity between her words and her conditions of existence—she has about as much reason to be thankful as Vladimir and Estragon to repent. For readers of the play, Beckett's ostentatious repetitions with a difference in the stage directions—especially the "inaudible prayer"/ "inaudible addendum" and "say, ten seconds"/ "say, five seconds"—may additionally read as sarcasm. The primary purpose of the repetition is not clarification but derision and disdain. As some quotations from Beckett's letters included in this and the previous chapter show, Beckett rejected traditional forms of clarification and mediation between his texts and their interpreters—yet, in forcibly triggering frame/ script/ schemata reassessments, his trademark category of the horrific-comic appears to have heuristic qualities.

Throughout the play, the alignment of frames/ scripts/ schemata responsible for heteronormative-religious forms of socialization-as-conditioning is enacted and contested through manifold means, from Winnie's constant references to "blessings" and "mercies" and attempts to excuse her husband's disengagement to Willie's minimal interventions. Willie's most cogent contribution is his reading of the irreverent and ostentatiously redundant newspaper headline "His Grace and Most Reverend Father in God Dr Carolus Hunter dead in tub" (142). Two lines he utters repeatedly (based on newspaper ads) are "Opening for smart youth" (142, 159) and "Wanted bright boy" (143, 159). Otherwise, he seemingly passes his time examining pornographic photographs (144) and offers some brief comments on insect and swine sexuality (150, 159). In short, Willie enjoys all the advantages of the system, meagre as they may be (he still thinks highly of himself, is irreverent without incurring punishment, and, at the end of the play, still crawls around freely—

Beckett's slapstick rendering of masculinist privilege in a system of crushing repression), while buried Winnie does all the thanking.

Winnie's rummaging through her bag full of vestiges of civilization and concomitant verbal rummaging through purportedly vague memories support the play's outing of repressive scaffoldings of cognitive frames/ scripts/ schemata. Winnie's performance resembles Vladimir and Estragon's rather than Clov's. Her seemingly subdued, forgetful, and corny discourse mounts a tenacious under-the-radar attack on the heteronormative-religious cognitive frameworks responsible for her (and women's, and humanity's) confinement to deleterious relational patterns. In Part I, I discussed her rendering of lines from famous poems—typically read in Beckett studies as a symptom of her failing memory but too consistent in deflating pretenses of gravity and substance not to attract interpreters' laughter and not to suggest covert sarcasm and anger. I also showed that Act II, which shows Winnie buried deeper into the ground and supposedly stages her *further diminishing* memory and cognitive control, in fact offers *more violent and corrosive* "repetitions with a difference" of episodes/ ideas from Act I. From the perspective of cognitive shock and anchoring effects, the monotony, redundancy, and slow pace of Winnie's rehearsal of her personal history alongside that of human civilization and culture is a construct meant to safely broadcast—under the cover of so much supposed debris—her attacks on constrictive cognitive formations. (We should not forget—Winnie certainly doesn't—the bell that "rings piercingly" at the start of the play, and again later, indicating a censoring and perhaps fearsome presence.)

Thus, the first time she removes the revolver from her bag in Act I, supposedly acquiescent and happy Winnie "kisses it rapidly" before putting it back (141). Later, as she handles it again, her reaction is more complex and revealing:

[*Disgusted.*] You again! [*She opens eyes, brings revolver front and contemplates it. She weighs it in her palm.*] You'd think the weight of this thing would bring it down among the… last rounds. But no. It doesn't. Ever uppermost, like Browning. [*Pause.*] Brownie… [*Turning a little towards Willie.*] Remember Brownie, Willie? [*Pause.*] Remember how you used to keep on at me to take it away from you? Take it away, Winnie, take it away, before I put myself out of my misery. [*Back front. Derisive.*] *Your* misery! [*To revolver.*] Oh I suppose it's a comfort to know you're here, but I'm tired of you. [*Pause.*] I'll leave you out, that's what I'll do. [*She lays revolver on ground to her right.*] There, that's your home from this day out. [*Smile.*] The old style! [*Smile off.*] (151)

Her mockery of high culture is obvious here ("Ever uppermost, like Browning"), alongside that of Willie's self-absorbed dramatism ("*Your* misery!"). More importantly, her deceivingly nonsensical comments on the *weight* of the revolver denounce the functioning of socio-cultural determinations—always on top ("uppermost"), weighing us down. She enacts disgust and weariness at seeing the revolver, yet she does not to push it to the bottom of the bag but places it on the ground, *within reach*. Her smiles and reference to the "old style" are perhaps not enough to mask the corrosiveness of her enactment. In Act II, while the revolver is still there, her arms are below ground.

As Winnie craftily moves from the weight of the revolver to *gravity*, her seemingly absurd claims further denounce the crushing effects of patriarchal rule:

> WINNIE: Is gravity what it was, Willie, I fancy not. [*Pause.*] Yes, the feeling more and more that if I were not held—[*gesture*]—in this way, I would simply float up into the blue. [*Pause.*] And that perhaps some day the earth will yield and let me go, the pull is so great, yes, crack all round and let me out. [*Pause.*] Don't you ever have that feeling, Willie, of being sucked up? [*Pause.*] Don't you have to cling on sometimes, Willie? [*Pause. She turns a little towards him.*] Willie. [*Pause.*]
> WILLIE: *Sucked* up?
> WINNIE: Yes love, up into the blue, like gossamer. ... Ah well, natural laws, I suppose it's like everything else, it depends on the creature you happen to be. (151–52)

Patriarchal socio-cultural determinations have always legitimated their hold by posing as organic social developments inherent in the nature of the universe—as natural laws as unquestionable and life-preserving as gravity. Winnie's intervention makes this cognitive frame alignment obvious, likely triggering reassessment processes in interpreters, as her paradoxical imagery emphasizes the substantial ways in which patriarchal determinations are *not* natural laws like gravity and are neither objectively valid nor beneficial. She asks Willie if he ever had to "cling on," pretending to worry about being "sucked up," but her phrasing in describing that potential occurrence is conspicuously positive, suggesting an *escape* rather than a deadly dissipation into the void ("yield," "let me go," "let me out," "up into the blue, like gossamer"). Her biting conclusion that "it depends on the creature you happen to be," delivered in her usual tentative tone, is immediately followed by another covertly poisonous comment: "All I can say is for my part is that for me they are not what they were when I was young and... foolish and... [*faltering, head down*]... beautiful... possibly... lovely... in a way... to look at" (152). Winnie's melancholy tone and redundant syntax and diction camouflage an irreversible process of reassessment of cognitive frames/ scripts/ schemata—by this perilous point in her existence, such structures still have repressive power but have lost their ability to deceive.

The setup of *Play* uses the same visual means of triggering processes of frame/ script/ schemata reassessment as *Happy Days*: a haunting image of confinement. This time, the characters are in urns, with only their heads showing—two women and a man formerly involved in a love triangle and currently in an unexplained "afterlife" state. A major difference from earlier dramas is the end indication "Repeat play" (317), requiring a word-for-word repetition of the text in performance, followed by a closing segment suggesting that the repetition would extend beyond the time of the performance. However, this word-for-word repetition is yet another version of Beckett's repetition with a difference—as Kenner notes, the second time, spectators see "a new work" as they gradually process previously registered clues and realize that the characters may be forced to enact their ritual forever (*Reader's Guide* 157). This repetition and the setup of the play likely have radical cognitive effects on interpreters.

The stage setup strongly suggests claustrophobia and total, inhuman external control. The actors' necks are "held fast in the urn's mouth" (307). The urns are identical and "one yard high" (319), with the actors standing below stage level if traps are available or with the urns open at the back and the actors kneeling. An alternative offered to avoid the kneeling posture is enlarging the urns to full length and moving them to mid-stage (319). "The sitting posture results in urns of unacceptable bulk and is not to be considered" (319), Beckett insists. In short, the visual setup is meant to forcefully indicate total captivity and deep discomfort. Interpreters' visual shock would immediately trigger attempts at contextual anchoring, and the setup offers cultural notions of the "afterlife" as immediate options (funerary urns, enclosure in coffins, hell as a space of captivity and physical torture, etc.). The faint, intermingled, and "largely unintelligible" (*CDW* 307) mix of voices that opens the first iteration of the text would enhance the anxiety and shock produced by the visual setup, accelerating interpreters' search for means of anchoring their cognitive experience. As the voices then separate and the story begins to coagulate, interpreters are offered an abrupt clarification (that the characters are members of a love triangle) of radical cognitive impact in the established context.

Since the "love triangle" is a frame commonly and cross-culturally wired into notions of sin, merging the characters' lines into a coherent narrative would require minimal cognitive work regardless of interpreters' familiarity with literary phenomena. Consequently, what would likely emerge most forcefully within interpreters' cognitive processing as the character dynamic is revealed is a sadistic discrepancy between acts and consequences, further enhanced by the comedic elements of the play. The man's self-serving comments, his hiccups, and the women's vitriolic insults, reminiscent of the vaudeville, define their "crimes" as petty domestic betrayals (the man) and empty threats (the women)—yet their punishment has the gravity of an Ancient Greek tragedy. Thus, Beckett's deceivingly simple love triangle story is likely to trigger, fairy early during the reading/ viewing experience, interpreters' reassessment of the cognitive frames/ scripts/ schemata making it possible for them to "anchor" and interpret the setup and character dynamic of this play—that is, interpreters' reassessment of any aspects of cognitive processing connected to religious and heteronormative environmental injunctions.

The second moment in the first iteration of the text when the spotlight forces the characters to speak in unison marks an abrupt shift. Going forward, the characters no longer voice recollections but meditate on their current condition and try to engage the presence behind the spotlight. As discussed in Part I, their interventions in this section are gender-inflected in conspicuous and disturbing ways. The man speaks mostly of being at peace, speculates that the women, united in their grief, likely became friends after his disappearance, and worries mostly that there might be no one behind the spotlight to witness his self-important blabber. Conversely, the women fear that there is a physical presence behind the spotlight and that their current state is a prelude for more vicious forms of physical torture—including, perhaps, sexual violence. This disturbing sequence offers a forceful enactment of women's exploitation and mistreatment within religious-patriarchal frameworks. Even if interpreters do not register the women's fear of torture fully in the first iteration, they would still likely register their intense anxiety, as manifested in most of their lines. Since I discussed this section extensively in Part I, I will offer brief highlights here:

W1: "Mercy, mercy, tongue still hanging out for mercy" (312)—"Hellish half-light" (312, 316)—"Get off me!" (313, 317)—"Is it something I should do with my face, either than utter? Weep?" (314)—"Bite off my tongue and swallow it? Would that placate you? How the mind works to be sure!" (314)

W2: "things might disimprove, there is that danger" (313)—"You might get angry and blaze me clean out of my wits. Mightn't you?" (313)—"I say, am I not perhaps a little unhinged already? [*Hopefully.*] Just a little? [*Pause.*] I doubt it." (316)—"A shade gone. In the head. Just a shade. I doubt it." (317)

As the third sequence with the characters speaking in unison starts, transitioning to the second iteration of the text, interpreters' processes of reassessment of the cognitive frames/ scripts/ schemata activated and contested by the play plausibly increase in intensity. The effect would be stronger in performance, but readers of the text would probably read the play at least twice, too, to ensure they have grasped more of its implications. (As Beckett's later texts—drama and fiction—exhibit ever-increasing forms of linguistic condensation, the likelihood that they would elicit immediate re-reading increases.)

During the second iteration, interpreters' cognitive processing would likely consist, in part, of clarification, but also incrementally involve elements of *contestation*. The excessiveness and inhumanity of the characters' fate, likely to have already transpired during the first iteration, would register more forcefully in the second—but what the latter would additionally activate is interpreters' reading of the frames/ scripts/ schemata involved as *illegitimate*. In other words, during the second iteration, interpreters would be more likely to perceive the cognitive formations that allowed them to make sense of the play the first time—which they may have accepted as meaningful and reasonable before—as placing irrational and crushing burdens on human relations. Moreover, the second iteration would likely trigger interpreters' anchoring of the play to religious-heteronormative forms of control they themselves may have experienced within their lived environments, causing them to perceive that control (and their acquiescence to it) as deleterious and repulsive.

Beckett's corrosive engagement with religious and patriarchal injunctions alongside the frames/ scripts/ schemata that sustain them, more violent and sneering in *Play* than in *Happy Days*, intensifies with *Not I*, where the only visible element of the female speaker's body is her mouth. The speaker shares a number of disturbing recollections with the audience while consistently negating that she is their subject. The setup is likely to immediately activate disquieting notions of a forced confession. Given the strangeness of Mouth's presence, the looming figure of the Auditor might initially evoke a guard or an inquisitor. Religious imagery related to the notion of divine/ inquisitorial judgement may thus constitute the first series of anchoring elements interpreters use in decoding Mouth's situation. The activation of related frames/ scripts/ schemata would then be followed by processes of reassessment as Mouth's discourse and the Auditor's gestures proceed.

As discussed extensively in Part I, there are fragments of unquestionable sarcastic quality in Mouth's discourse, like her recurrent claim to have been "spared" love and pleasure or her consistent mockery of the notion of a "merciful God" (336, 337, and elsewhere). As I explained there, these are not mere reversals but paradox-based attacks on the social order. In cognitive terms, such fragments typically produce corrosive alignments of frames/ scripts/ schemata likely to trigger interpreters' reassessment of three major aspects of their lived environments they may have perceived as non-problematic before: family/ communitarian socialization, gender-based conditioning, and religious faith. Thus, Mouth's comments on love and pleasure denounce the transformation of these categories of experience, within most familial or communitarian frames/ scripts/ schemata, into *injunctions* meant to restrict mobility and render acceptable any requirements placed on the individual, however exploitative or repressive. The sequence "brought up as she had been to believe... with the other waifs... in a merciful... [*Brief laugh.*]... God... [*Good laugh*]" (377) appears twice in the first half of the play, specifically within the context of Mouth's reflections on punishment. Within the same fragment, she explicitly wonders if she will be punished later for having been intended to suffer *or* experience pleasure, at various points in her life, and not having complied (377). The fragment thus aligns religious belief with other forms of social conditioning (based on gender, on prevalent notions of appropriate socialization, etc.), countering the notion that they might offer any benefits and bolstering interpreters' reassessment of related frames/ scripts/ schemata.

One effect of this reassessment is likely to be interpreters' realization that Mouth is not *unable* to internalize the "I" but *unwilling* to engage in this act of social reinsertion for such meagre benefits as the Auditor's/ the social body's empty compassion. In perhaps the most disturbing sequence in the play, Mouth offers an enactment of *screaming in pain* likely to produce significant effects of shock and reassessment in interpreters. While reflecting on her condition, Mouth suddenly surmises that "she might do well to... groan... on and off... writhe she could not... as if in actual agony..." (378). Next, she claims she could not perform socially in that manner due to an inability to deceive she describes as a "flaw," designates herself as a dysfunctional machine, and, finally, screams twice while pretending to be unable to do it:

> but could not... could not bring herself... some flaw in her make-up... incapable of deceit... or the machine... more likely the machine... so disconnected... never got the message... or powerless to respond... like numbed... couldn't make the sound... not any sound... no sound of any kind... no screaming for help for example... should she feel so inclined... scream... [*Screams.*]... then listen... [*Silence.*]... scream again... [*Screams again.*]... then listen again... [*Silence.*]... no... spared that... all silent as the grave... (378)

Significantly, Mouth's disturbing expression and denial of pain attract no reaction from the Auditor, who seems strictly invested in her internalization of the "I"—that is, in an expression of full acquiescence to environmental injunctions. Towards the end of the play, Mouth twice utters the sequence, "God is love... tender mercies... new every morning..." (381–82, 383)—a more under-the-radar sarcastic comment reminiscent of Winnie's deceptive performance of subdued femininity in *Happy Hays*. Like Winnie's requests for Willie's help, Mouth's screams produce no reaction within the universe of the play—and, like Winnie's, the "new mercies" Mouth can expect every morning are likely to cause her further discomfort. She is fully aware of that, too: the phrase "so far... ha!... so far..." is uttered three times, always in relation to the possibility of feeling pain (378, 380, 382).

Interpreters' acknowledgement of Mouth's performance as *noncompliance* rather than inability would likely trigger further cognitive processing of the role of religious, family/ communitarian, and gender-based injunctions in interpreters' own interactions with their environment. Perceived in alignment, any frames/ scripts/ schemata that support such injunctions would no longer register as objectively meaningful ways of synthesizing data of experience but as repressive structures based, at their repulsive core, on torture threats and meant to prevent the formation of more flexible frames/ scripts/ schemata—nourishing for individual experiencers but restrictive of systemic control. Just as Mouth seemingly continues her unintelligible discourse of resistance beyond the time of the performance, interpreters are likely to continue to experience, beyond the space of the reading room/ theatre, the reassessment processes triggered and bolstered by the play.

Later plays like *What Where* enact the torture threat at the core of traditional socialization modes in even more disturbing terms. In *What Where*, a small universe of four players (Bam, Bem, Bim, Bom) undergoes a recursive process of elimination until only one individual is left alive. The four players are supposed to be "as alike as possible," with the "[s]ame long grey hair" and wearing the "[s]ame long grey gown" (469), and the means of elimination is torture to death, with each torturer subsequently becoming the victim at the hands of another. As discussed in Part I, while the pantomime at the beginning of the play and the repetitive character of the elimination sequences may suggest interchangeability and mechanical indifference, other elements emphasize that what we are witnessing is a hierarchy-based, goal-oriented, and carefully managed process of total consumption of the human "unit" by a system that always preserves its chief executioner alive and well for the next round.

Bam, the leader, is redoubled—in addition to the grey silhouette on stage, there is a "voice of Bam" consisting of "a small megaphone at head level" (469) outside the central playing area, "[d]ownstage left" (470). Both the playing area and that occupied by V are "dimly lit, surrounded by shadow" (470). As with other plays by Beckett, the opening is eerie and haunting enough to create cognitive shock and elicit adaptive contextual anchoring work. The players' physical characteristics and attire may evoke religious rituals or a detention system. The megaphone would likely evoke an authority of malignant intent, given the notorious twentieth-century uses of propaganda for genocidal/ totalitarian purposes. The lighting device would further anchor interpreters' reading of the setup to authoritarian-punitive socio-historical structures. Finally, the pantomime that previews the recursive elimination process—while not as explicit or accurate as V suggests (see his comments "First without words" and "Now with words," 471–72)—additionally stimulates interpreters' anchoring of the stage enactment to frameworks related to subjection, abuse, and repression. (In Part I, I listed the Christian hell, sadistic/ paranoid social interactions, or totalitarian/ police state practices as examples.)

The pantomime deceivingly suggests an endless cycle of interchangeable roles and elides what happens to the players who enter the stage "head bowed" once they exit the stage followed by players holding their "head haught" (471). Still, from the beginning, both the characters' lines and the stage directions elicit intense reassessments of cognitive frames/ scripts/ schemata connected to notions of social connectivity, hierarchy, subjection, and repression. Bam's special status is immediately apparent: V is introduced, in the initial list of characters, as "the voice of Bam" (469), and spectators are made aware of that connection a few lines into the play, when the phrase "I am alone" can be heard from the megaphone and the light is on Bam, alone in the playing space (471). Since, as discussed above, interpreters are likely to respond to the megaphone and the lighting device with anxiety and suspicion, associating them with abusive control, they are also likely to notice fairly quickly that, while torturers do become victims in subsequent sequences, Bam remains the one who gives orders through-out (he never exits the stage until the final sequence, when he becomes Bem's torturer and everyone else is dead). They are also more than likely to notice the callousness and maliciousness of Bam's dehumanizing refer-ences to the victims. The revelation that victims are tortured to death comes in a gradual build-up of cruelty and horror (the following quota-tion is from the first sequence, but the second is nearly identical, and the third is interrupted soon after it starts by V's dismissive "So on," 476):

> BAM: He wept?
> BOM: Yes.
> BAM: Screamed?
> BOM: Yes.
> BAM: Begged for mercy?
> BOM: Yes.
> BAM: But didn't say it?
> BOM: No.
> BAM: Then why stop?
> BOM: He passed out.
> BAM: And you didn't revive him?
> BOM: I tried.
> BAM: Well?
> BOM: I couldn't.
> [*Pause.*]
> BAM: It's a lie. [*Pause.*] He said it to you. [*Pause.*] Confess he said it to you. [*Pause.*] You'll be given the works until you confess. (473)

The repetition likely intensifies interpreters' empathic projection/action simulation-based cognitive resonance with the suffering bodies elided from the stage space and referenced so dismissively by Bam. It is also likely to activate interpreters' reassessment of situations, in their lived environment, when individuals' subjection to unwanted treatment may have been justified through processes of contextual anchoring to frames/

scripts/ schemata similar to those activated by the play. Most importantly, however, the *ending* of the play may have a radical cognitive impact on interpreters.

As also discussed in Part I, a character dynamic based in *interchangeability* might have functioned in a tragic key, rendering the play an allegory of the meaninglessness and randomness of the human condition. However, interchangeability is not the core organizational principle here—it is merely a ruse. Bam/V is and remains at the top of the hierarchy. At the end of a line of dead bodies, he pontificates briefly on the meaninglessness of existence, feigns weariness, and disappears ("I am alone. ...Time passes. ... Make sense who may. I switch off," 476)—but interpreters are likely to register his attempt to use tragedy as a framing device for atrocious and unrepentant acts of torture as an affront. This intense reaction would further mobilize their reassessment of frames/ scripts/ schemata of remarkable tenaciousness in their deceptive casting of constricting and abusive social acts as legitimate components of fully logical and objective, "scientific" social maintenance operations. The genocidal fascist or Stalinist state machines would be the most obvious large-scale examples, but Deleuze and Guattari's notion of "microfascisms just waiting to crystallize" (*TP* 9), present in any hierarchical interaction, is worth recalling here. The resulting reassessment process may trigger interpreters' increased resistance to manipulative framings of the infliction of harm as a necessary social maintenance mechanism or as an inevitable *datum* of the state of being human. Interpreters are likely to *reframe* any socially sanctioned infliction of harm, instead, as a repugnant act of power meant to discourage resistance while reinforcing systemic notions of functionality.

6.3   Eliciting Advanced Decoding and Accelerated Reassessment, or, Reaching a Cognitive "High"

Beckett's fiction offers an equally intense enactment of the generally exploitative and abusive nature and, on occasion, genocidal effects of traditional notions of social functionality. Beckett's repetitions with a difference and his elements of intertextuality, of significant import in his dramas, gain even more textual space and cognitive prominence in his fiction—which, as a consequence, becomes additionally charged with markers meant to stimulate readers' rapid reprocessing of high volumes of complex information, as well as their ability to differentiate between reliable and unreliable data and rehearse appropriate reactions accordingly. Such textual features are of vital relevance today: two major adaptive challenges typically discussed in relation to the "information age" are the ever-increasing *volume* of information interpreters are forced to navigate and the ever-increasing *difficulty in differentiating* between valuable and substantial information and countless varieties of "noise" (false or distracting, pointless information).

The processing of large volumes of information and the ability to discern on matters of relevance are core concerns in *Watt*. Watt's experiences in Knott's house and his interactions with Sam are examples. As also discussed in Part I, Watt invests tremendous energy into decoding the logic of Knott's household and person, rigorously registering everything, from the elaborate idiosyncrasy of Knott's rules for menial tasks to some uncanny aspects such as Knott's seeming ability to change his physical appearance. However, instead of progressing towards clarification, the novel ostentatiously enacts the notion of absent/ deferred information ("mysterious" or "elusive") as a systemic ruse—a way to maintain the exploited (Erskine, Watt, Arsene for a time, and others) too busily engaged with their state of unknowing to notice their state of exploitation, for as long as they can be of use. For example, the parasitic rather than nourishing nature of Knott, suggested first in Arsene's monologue, transpires more forcefully through Watt's later recollections and is denounced most definitively through Sam's "recuperative" acts in Part 3. Interpreters' witnessing of this structural repetition of shock effects of similar intent but increasingly stronger tenor is likely to have *cumulative* effects. By the end of the demonstration, interpreters laugh, as Abbott suggests, "in the face of an absence of meaning" (*Form and Effect* 73), but do so in a liberated state of disenchantment rather than in a mode of heroic disdain. There is no lost meaning to recover and no existentialist perseverance in the face of universal emptiness to experience—in fact, such notions are themselves denounced as restrictive elements of anchoring that can severely delay interpreters' enrichment and multiplication of the frames/ scripts/ schemata they process mentally and live by.

Kenner notes that "[t]here are sentences in *Watt* that cry out for flow-charting, so orderly is their display of branching options" (*Mechanic Muse* 93). In his view, Beckett's uncanny anticipation of programming language, with its reduction of communicative modes to the description of possibilities and the issuing of orders, does not articulate a simplistic claim that technology has dehumanizing effects but a larger-scope commentary on the socio-historical articulation between exploitation and freedom:

> For centuries, routines of trivial order-giving were preparing Western society for computerization: a list-comparing, paper-copying, bill-collecting society which had already turned vast numbers of people into machines when real machines began being invented to set them more or less free. ... All rolls on wheels towards certain liberations. (101–2)

Franklin further identifies in Beckett's use of characters exhibiting automaton behaviours a commentary on the late capitalist reconceptualization of social systems as information-processing systems. In Franklin's view, this reconceptualization recasts computational practices such as "self-regulation, distribution, and statistical forecasting" (xi) as grounding *social* principles—to some utterly damaging effects. Individuals' increased access to information and the easier and faster circulation of information in general implicitly facilitate the institution of a control society whose operating principles of continually increased efficiency can be supported only by "exploiting and dispossessing human life" (xviii). As I also noted in Chap. 2, in Franklin's assessment, Watt illustrates the full transformation of the individual into an information-processing unit: he is institutionalized because he "internalize[s] machinic logic too fully," becoming "purely analytical and recursive" in capturing, processing, and communicating data—a "pathological" development within the logic of machinic control, as it is "antithetical to value-productive work" (124). Kenner similarly notes that Watt's obsessive and exhaustive analyses of possibilities, even if formalized into a programming language, "don't give the computer anything to do" (*Mechanic Muse* 95).

What allows *Watt*'s enactment of social structures as information-processing structures to remain relevant for contemporary concerns with digitalization and control is its paradoxical alignment between information-processing functions, the physical consumption of the individual's body through hard labour, and religious conditioning. As discussed at length in Chap. 4, Arsene's "short statement" continually juxtaposes thinking processes focused on self-discovery and the nature of things with minute descriptions of menial work often involving varieties of refuse, as do Watt's recollections of his time in Knott's house (mediated through Sam's voice). While Watt appears to revere Knott as quasi-divine, Sam perceives Knott as parasitic, as his under-the-radar expressions of anger in relaying Watt's recollections and his corrosive "recuperative" actions show. In fact, Sam's actions and comments denounce, perhaps more forcefully than Arsene's, the parasitic nature and analogous enforcement mechanisms of *any* hierarchical socio-cultural patterns, from those safeguarding economic servitude to those (more general) that enforce social integration to those (illusively immaterial) that implement religious conditioning (see Sam and Watt's walk within the barbed wire enclosure in between their pavilions, as discussed in cognitive terms in Chap. 5).

At the end of Part 2—when Erskine leaves the house, Watt takes over Erskine's obligations on the upper floor, and Arthur is hired to take over Watt's on the lower floor—Watt's state is described as follows:

> A friend, sex uncertain, of Mr. Knott telephoned to know how he was.
>   Cracks soon appeared in this formulation.
>   But Watt was too tired to repair it. Watt dared not tire himself further.
>   How often he had pooh-poohed it, this danger of tiring himself further. Pooh-pooh, he had said, pooh-pooh, and set to, to repair the cracks. But not now.
>   Watt was now tired of the ground-floor, the ground-floor had tired Watt out.
>   What had he learnt? Nothing.
>   What did he know of Mr. Knott? Nothing.
>   Of his anxiety to improve, of his anxiety to understand, of his anxiety to get well, what remained? Nothing.
>   But was not that something?
>   He saw himself then, so little, so poor. And now, littler, poorer. Was not that something?
>   So sick, so alone.
>   And now.
>   Sicker, aloner.
>   Was not that something?
>   As the comparative is something. Whether more than its positive or less. Whether less than its superlative or more. (147)

The depiction of Watt's state of exhaustion conspicuously overlaps mind and (bodily) matter. His work is described as "repairing cracks"—an ostentatiously concrete image, though it initially refers to a "formulation" (a matter of discourse). We are told that Watt had routinely dismissed his feelings of exhaustion, and the diction is, again, corrosive ("pooh-pooh" is used three times in two relatively short sentences). The questions enacting his (lack of) progress conspicuously move from the somewhat redundant pair of verbs "learn" and "know" to *anxiety* (a noun used three times in one line), as the recurrent pronominal forms "he" and "his" betray an attitude of self-condemnation. Finally, he immerses himself further in guilt and self-loathing, embracing his diminution and decay as positive markers of his dedication. The last comment in the sequence above—unlikely to belong to Watt and more plausibly an under-the-radar sarcastic aside from Sam, or a reminder of the intrusive presence of the implied author— "translates" the issue from a matter of hierarchy (and sacrifice for a higher meaning or power) into one of grammar, stressing the role of language in the articulation and reinforcement of restrictive and self-sacrificial frames/ scripts/ schemata. "[T]he comparative is something" in that it creates the illusion of significant difference and offers the false comfort of a form of "progress" that merely immerses us further into exploitation and exhaustion.

Watt's syntactically contorted accounts of his final experiences in Knott's house align in even stronger terms information-gathering and processing acts with menial tasks as types of activities undertaken, in an attitude of self-denial, to exhaustion:

> Say he'd, No, waistcoat the, vest the, trousers the, socks the, shoes the, shirt the, drawers the, coat the, dress to ready things got had when. Say he'd, Dress. Say he'd, No, water the, towel the, sponge the, soap the, salts the, glove the, brush the, basin the, wash to ready things got had when. Say he'd, Wash. Say he'd, No, water the, towel the, sponge the, soap the, razor the, powder the, brush the, bowl the, shave to ready things got had when. Say he'd, Shave. (165)

Such passages are apt to trigger interpreters' cognitive shock in several ways. First, they may sharpen interpreters' perception of the *magnitude* of Watt's disorientation and pain. Furthermore, they may enhance interpreters' perception of frames/ scripts/ schemata supportive of hierarchical structures of supposedly different orders (religious vs. domestic servitude) as *repressively analogous*. Finally, they may boost interpreters' perception of artificially detached notions such as mental and physical strain *in conjunction*, as mere varieties of exploitation facilitated by the frames/ scripts/ schemata previously mentioned. This multilayered experience of shock is likely to activate, in interpreters, adaptive moves resulting in processes of cognitive reassessment and enrichment, as exploitation-based structures they may not have previously perceived as such are made unbearable—and unbearably obvious—by the text.

For contemporary interpreters, the novel's enactment of information-processing in conjunction with menial tasks and its framing of both types of work as leading to psychosomatic deterioration may activate additional reassessment processes. Specifically, it may prompt interpreters to acknowledge that, while today's prevalence of technical and digital machines has eliminated or eased countless forms of exploitation of the human body, it has not abandoned the *logic of exploitation* situated at the root of profit-based transactional relations and hierarchical structures in general. In other words, if older socio-economic structures treated the human *body* as a machine to be used to exhaustion, in the age of digitalization, the human *mind* runs that risk. Corporate capitalist structures' increasing addition of "knowledge management" tasks—information-gathering, processing, dissemination, and instrumentalization for profit—to employees' workloads is an example.

In *Molloy, Malone Dies,* and *The Unnamable,* Beckett continues to use both logic and other elements of presumably coagulating cognitive effect to destabilize interpreters' reliance on long-reinforced frames/ scripts/ schemata, triggering intense processes of reassessment. Abbott notes that, in *Molloy,* the use of the report format creates "expectations of fact" and foregrounds notions of value, purpose, and closure only to ultimately "augment anxiety about issues of epistemology" and "issues of evaluation if not metaphysics" (*Form and Effect* 104–5). Indeed, Molloy and Moran's accounts proceed through obsessive affirmations/ identifications immediately followed by denials, deconstructions, and revisions—eerie and corrosive re-enactments likely to create intense shock and anchoring effects in interpreters through their obsessive alignment of frames/ scripts/ schemata that support religious, psychoanalytic, and bureaucratic-capitalist processes of meaning-making *and repression.* The intensity of these interpretive and adaptive processes is compounded by the contrasting rhetorical, emotive, and ethical nature of Molloy and Moran's discourses.

As discussed in detail in Part I and more briefly in the previous chapter, Molloy's discourse is angry and self-deprecating and his pain appears authentic—which makes his acts of violence and abuse and his general vision on life horrific-comic rather than simply repulsive. Conversely, Moran's discourse exudes conceit and self-pity, and his claims to pain and victimization sound hollow—which denounces him as a sadistic actor in a system of repression that seldom demands the levels of abuse he happily inflicts. I discussed several examples of Moran's interactions, focusing on his abuse of his son, in Part I. I will additionally analyse here the episode in which Moran, unable to fully bend one of his knees and fearing worse pain and stiffness, instructs his son to walk to the closest town and buy a bicycle, "second-hand for preference," with "a very strong carrier" (*M* 147). The conversation extends over more than three pages. Moran dismisses his son's apparent illness: "Finally he told me he did not feel well. My son's replies were often beside the point" (147). He repeatedly suggests that his son is too stupid to understand basic requests, let alone decide anything for himself—yet he accuses him of stealing from the money he had just been given and makes him empty his pockets to check (148–49). Though it is clear that the closest town is hours away and that Moran plans to be carried on the bicycle, he repeatedly presses his son to express pleasure in the purchase: "I asked him if he was pleased. He did not look pleased. I repeated these instructions and asked him again if he was pleased" (147); "Are you not pleased, I said, to have a nice brand-new bicycle, all your own? I was decidedly set on hearing him say he was pleased" (150). Pleasure in mistreating others and a superior dismissal of others' concerns are constant components of Moran's discourse and actions. The stiffness in his leg miraculously disappears after he beats an unknown man to death (158–59). In an earlier episode, he is left with the "painful impression" of a "lack of nobility" in his confessor's character after hearing him express deep concern for his parishioners' everyday problems (105).

This contrast does not cast Moran as a negative and Molloy as a positive character but prompts interpreters' further reassessment of cognitive frames/ scripts/ schemata that may favour problematically simplistic categorizations and responses. It also draws attention to the destructive and ugly cognitive work compelled by experiences of repression and pain. Far from bringing Molloy (or anyone else, for that matter) to higher states of enlightenment, such experiences force him to internalize, in part, notions and practices he obviously considers grotesque (given his constant use of sarcasm) and enacts as such. As for Moran, a systemic tool sadistic enough to enjoy his work but also vain enough to insist on projecting respectability, inflicting such experiences on others automatically triggers verbose and bombastic attempts at justification foregrounding a repugnant dismissal of reality. *Malone* and *The Unnamable* continue this process by enacting in increasingly conspicuous (and more sophisticatedly camouflaged) ways the deleterious effects of frames/ scripts/ schemata that codify hierarchical impositions (often abusive/ violent) as necessary guarantors of social functionality, and the slightest resistance to such impositions as a grievous offence. Malone and the Unnamable's deep (and horrific-comically expressed) self-loathing is the outcome of countless acts of acquiescence that required grotesque cognitive adjustments. Both enact the existence of avatars (Sapo and Macmann for Malone; Mahood and Worm for the Unnamable; any number of earlier Beckettian protagonists for both—all of them neither consistent nor stable) and otherwise find countless means to resist full acquiescence to the frames/ scripts/ schemata they live by (a failing memory, failing senses, an inability to express, etc.).

After several sequences describing Sapo's experiences, Malone articulates and deconstructs connections to his avatar(s) as follows:

> A minimum of memory is indispensable, if one is to live really. Take his family, for example, I really know practically nothing about his family any more. But that does not worry me, there is a record of it somewhere. It is the only way to keep an eye on him. But as far as I myself am concerned the same necessity does not arise, or does it? And yet I write about myself with the same pencil and in the same exercise-book as about him. It is because it is no longer I, I must have said so long ago, but another whose life is just beginning. It is right that he too should have his little chronicle, his memories, his reason, and be able to recognize the good in the bad, the bad in the worst, and so grow gently old all down the unchanging days and die one day like any other day, only shorter. That is my excuse. But there must be others, no less excellent. (*MD* 33–34)

Malone continually advertises his failing memory as a source of confusion and inability. The first sentences in this passage dutifully maintain this illusion, but the last three—tightly controlled and powerfully corrosive—scream deliberation. The longer sentence starting with "It is right" ends with what Kenner designates as a "guillotine phrase": the modifier "only shorter" forces interpreters to read the earlier "growing gently old" and, with it, the entire passage as cynical rather than sentimental, even if they had missed the prior clue in the phrase "recognize the good in the bad, the bad in the worst" (*Mechanic Muse* 104–5). Beckett's texts consistently produce shock and anchoring effects through such repetitions with a difference apt to trigger powerful cognitive reassessments. "[R]ecognize the good in the bad" anchors the sentence to structures of contemplative acquiescence, whereas "the bad in the worse" uses the syntactic structure of the previous phrase only to angrily explode its semantic and pragmatic anchoring, transforming the entire construction into a paradox-based contestation. One can "grow gently old" only by acquiescing to social injunctions for positivation, beautification, and closure without a reminder, but the price is a grotesque falsification of experience that renders all days virtually indistinct—the last one "only shorter." Interpreters are thus repeatedly cued, first, to the repressive nature of cognitive formations that equate comfort with acquiescence to social injunctions for positivation/ beautification/ closure, and second, to the wiring of such formations into linguistic structures—even *before* the last two sentences, which suggest that any of Malone's claims about his writing exercise could be *deliberately* inaccurate ("my excuse," "there must be others"). These cues repeatedly articulate shock effects likely to destabilize frames/ scripts/ schemata interpreters may have perceived as settled and unquestionable before, triggering interpreters' engagement in processes of reassessment that are never brought to a stop during the reading process: sentences like the ones discussed above appear on every page, continually enacting Beckett's characters' struggle to remain slightly out of phase with socially enforced and long-accepted frames/ scripts/ schemata governing hierarchical living and hierarchy-based assignations of identity.

Based on recent medical studies, Barry identifies several major elements of schizophrenic language in *Malone Dies* and *The Unnamable*: ipseity disturbance (difficulty and uncertainty in applying the pronoun "I"), hyperreflexivity (a perception of oneself/ a feature of oneself as foreign), and distortions of perception concerning time and space, including a blurred internal/ external divide. Building on Barry's analysis, I would emphasize, first, that Beckett integrates such elements of schizophrenic language into patterns of paradox-based humour—which allows interpreters to associate them to frames/ scripts/ schemata denoting intentionality and disdain rather than impotence or compulsion; and second, that he consistently couples such elements with literary, cultural, or socio-political allusions of obvious anchoring effect—which, again, suggests intentionality, control, and purpose rather than a cognitive impasse of failure. These aspects speak to Beckett's *political* deployment of schizophrenic language as a camouflaged denunciation of any aspects of embodied cognition "customized," in time, to better accommodate and preserve exploitation and repression. As my analyses included in Part I and here show, Malone and the Unnamable are not confused concerning their identity but anxious to prevent its conscription to repressive schemata. They are not confused concerning internal/ external distinctions but keen to denounce and sabotage their repressive and exploitative social uses.

Both Malone and the Unnamable *feign* confusion, weakness, and inability in a mode that is equal parts terror and disdain—an eerie mix of disturbing yet empowering implications. Projecting weakness is meant to limit their further subjection to discomfort and pain, as they more or less explicitly admit on occasion—as in the ending of *Malone Dies* analysed in Part I or in this deeply distressed confession from *The Unnamable*: "And sometimes I say to myself I am in a head, it's terror makes me say it, and the longing to be in safety, surrounded on all sides by massive bone" (*U* 65). However, their loathing for the injunctions they are expected to follow is so intense that they find themselves unable to submit without protest—sometimes veiled, as in the fragment from *Malone Dies* analysed earlier, and other times sharper, as in Malone's comments on his "benefactors" from the House of Saint John of God or in the Unnamable's rants against "masters," as discussed in Part I. Exposure to these speakers' intense vacillation between terror and disdain is likely to activate interpreters' perception of cognition as an embodied act and bolster its anchoring (through action-simulation and emotional resonance mechanisms) to an extended number of everyday experiences, to the effect of rendering it into a dominant cognitive frame for interpreters' future interpretive and interactive acts. This process is likely to lead to the formation of frame-encoded counter-responses, in interpreters, to the activation of frames/ scripts/ schemata that codify abusive/ violent hierarchical impositions as necessary guarantors of social functionality and acts of resistance to such impositions as offences deserving harsh punishment.

As my analyses in Part I and here show, *Molloy*, *Malone Dies*, and *The Unnamable* mark a progression towards more radical and better camouflaged paradox-based attacks on societal injunctions to preserve hierarchical relational patterns and modes of thinking and action. From a cognitive perspective, the heuristic quality of this progression is readily apparent. Beckett's protagonists become increasingly apprehensive of increasing levels of abuse from increasingly ubiquitous "agents," "powers," or "masters"—and it's not all in their heads: while Molloy mostly feigns physical inability, Malone is confined to a bed, and the Unnamable is in a grotesque state of dismemberment. The same protagonists become increasingly adept at concealing their resistance to indoctrination and exploitative integration. If Molloy's sarcasm is often cheerfully conspicuous, Malone tends to be both more resentfully angry and more carefully under-the-radar in venting that anger, and the Unnamable, even more so. Concomitantly, the three narratives elicit anxiety concerning the effects of hierarchy-based frames/ scripts/ schemata with growing intensity, as they create shock and anchoring effects of increasing violence and sophistication. Interpreters are thus immersed in progressively more intense cognitive work through processes of reassessment of progressively wider scope and reach. The repetitive and incremental nature of these processes is of major heuristic import, as it permits interpreters to adjust and re-anchor in between shock effects while gradually building pathways likely to facilitate faster and more efficient information processing.

I suggested, in Chap. 5, that Beckett's horrific-comic humour can transform experiences of cognitive effort into experiences of relief likely to stimulate interpreters' engagement with his texts. I also suggested, especially concerning the late plays, that Beckett's repetitions with a difference may trigger interpreters' *awareness* of mental processes they may have previously undergone automatically and unconsciously, which may further trigger an empowering experience of a "cognitive high." The *increasing processing speed* elicited and nourished by Beckett's texts can now be added to the list. As interpreters engage in processes of reassessment, multiplication, and enrichment of the cognitive frames/ scripts/schemata they live by, they likely build and strengthen pathways allowing faster and more efficient cognitive processing, which would intensify the exhilarating effects previously described and thus further encourage textual engagement and cognitive work. While the narrative situations in *Molloy*, *Malone Dies*, and *The Unnamable* may be the stuff of tragedy in their objective narrative features, the cognitive processing work they elicit likely induces interpreters to experience, alongside Beckett's angrily resilient characters, not the tragedy but the *cognitive high* of being human. This *nourishing and energizing* (rather than exhausting) form of intense and constantly accelerated cognitive processing is no doubt also supported by the "singular-universal solidarity" (Nail's phrase) effects discussed in Part I, which further validate the experience through ethical grounding.

6.4   Deactivating Covert Hierarchy-Based Frames/ Scripts/ Schemata: Survival and Companionship as Threat-Based Impositions

This cognitively satisfying effect does not weaken with the later fiction, where the speakers' engagement with language and the world becomes even more adversarial. As already discussed, *Texts for Nothing* ostentatiously connects to *The Unnamable* in opening with a passage that recalls and emends the latter's last lines, first maintaining its tentative tone but soon evoking, in straightforwardly angry language, adversarial environmental interactions. Given this explicit connection, interpreters may wonder at the apparently less torturous conditions of existence of the speakers from *Texts for Nothing* (none is dismembered or kept in a jar) and at their seemingly more daring attitude. However, as it soon becomes apparent, these details mark a progression to conditions of existence that come with their own threats and traps.

The new regime invests massively into devising a sense of *choice* for its subjects, so as to more convincingly frame acts of acquiescence as exercises of personal will. The voices interacting with the main speaker from Text 1 stress choices he supposedly made—"What possessed you to come?" "All you had to do was stay at home," etc. (100–1)—but he bluntly rejects any notion of inner motivation: "To change, to see, no, there's no more to see, I've seen it all, till my eyes are blear, nor to get away from harm, the harm is done, one day the harm was done, the day my feet dragged me out that must go their ways, that I let go their ways and drag me here, that's what possessed me to come" (102). He repeatedly draws oppositions between "I" and "They," stressing his lack of options: "I am down in the hole the centuries have dug, centuries of filthy water, flat on my face on the dark earth ... . They are up above, all around me, as in a graveyard" (101). He sarcastically defines the many places he had supposedly been free to roam as *spaces of death*, and any death threats or dangers as masked *injunctions to live*:

> Sometimes it's the sea, other times the mountains, often it was the forest, the city, the plain too, I've flirted with the plain too, I've given myself up for dead all over the place, of hunger, of old age, murdered, drowned, and then for no reason, of tedium, nothing like breathing your last to put new life in you, and then the rooms, natural death, tucked up in bed, smothered in household gods, and always muttering ... the same old stories, the same old questions and answers. (103)

Finally, he negates the nourishing character of human interactions, locating any form of solace ever experienced on the inside:

> I was my father and I was my son, I asked myself questions and answered as best I could, I had it told to me evening after evening, the same old story I knew by heart and couldn't believe, or we walked together, hand in hand, silent, sunk in our worlds, each in his worlds, the hands forgotten in each

other. That's how I've held out till now. And this evening again it seems to be working, I'm in my arms, I'm holding myself in my arms, without much tenderness, but faithfully, faithfully. (103–4)

The first text, then, frames movement and interaction—major tenets of cognition as an embodied, enactivist, and emotively-inflected process—as forced and empty insofar as they occur within an adversarial, opposition-/ hierarchy-based environment. Interpreters' first impulse may be to anchor this framing to storyworld aspects like the speaker's loneliness, disappointment, and failing body, but the text repeatedly cues them against that move by systematically injecting sarcasm into any seemingly meditative passage. Some sequences are ostentatiously rhythmic and composite: "I'll never try to understand any more, *that's what you think*, for the moment I'm here, *always have been, always shall be*, I won't be afraid of the big words any more, *they are not big*" (103, my emphasis). In other passages, the sarcasm builds insidiously towards "guillotine phrases," as in the last sentence of Text 1: "Sleep now, as under that ancient lamp, all twined together, tired out with so much talking so much listening, so much toil and play" (104). While the "toil" is apparent in the text's enactment of being human, the "play" is entirely absent—unless we count the manifestations of sarcasm as play. "Toil and play" is, then, a paradox-based phrase—while seemingly defining the human condition in a traditionalist mode of positivation, contemplatively stressing harmony and balance, it in fact denounces this perspective as deceitful and empty. The only source of positivity in this text is its angry sarcasm, which repeatedly cues interpreters to register the *constraining* functions of frames/ scripts/ schemata they may have previously deemed common-sensical and beneficial. The process continues in the following texts, again through sarcastic derailments of settled cognitive structures.

The purportedly meditative opening of Text 2 is repeatedly punctured by shock effects conducive to cognitive reassessments:

Above is the light, the elements, a kind of light, sufficient to see by, *the living find their ways*, without too much trouble, *avoid one another*, without too much trouble, unite, avoid the obstacles, without too much trouble, seek with their eyes, close their eyes, halting, without halting, among the elements, the living. ... *Here you are under a different glass*, not long habitable either, it's time to leave it. ... Go then, no, better stay, for where would you go, now that you know? Back above? *There are limits. Back in that kind of light*. (105, my emphasis)

The first highlighted phrase abruptly defines the narrator as an *external observer* of human experience. The second horrific-comically defines routine communal living as "avoiding each other"—and, as with other sequences in Becket that use this technique, later additions or "clarifications" (supposedly meant to recast "avoid each other" as "not collide with") draw attention to the corrosiveness of the initial iteration rather than cancelling it. Cognitive shock effects cannot be undone: once interpreters' reassessment of frames/ scripts/ schemata related to communal living has been triggered, the other examples likely register as a mockery of frame-encoded injunctions. The third highlighted phrase augments the previous shock effects and further supports interpreters' reassessment processes by evoking surveillance ("under a different glass") and redefining the references to light and seeing from the previous lines (which may have initially suggested nostalgia on the speaker's part) in the same key. The fourth highlighted phrase pushes the effect even further—"[t]here are limits" seems to suggest that the speaker is barred from returning "above," but the next sentence implies, instead, that there are limits to his acquiescence (he is *unwilling* to return to that state of exposure).

The speaker's frequent attempts to define his state and environment are meant as sarcastic jabs rather than clarifications: "something is changing, it must be in the head, slowly in the head the ragdoll rotting, perhaps we're in a head, it's dark as in a head before the worms get at it, ivory dungeon" (106); "To need to groan and not be able, Jesus, better ration yourself, watch out for the genuine death-pangs, some are deceptive, you think you're home, start howling and revive, health-giving howls, better be silent, it's the only method, if you want to end, not a word but smiles … burst with speechlessness" (107). The former fragment recalls the Unnamable's feigned inability to express his conditions of existence and puts another twist on "being in a head"—here, it is the head of a rotting cadaver. The latter fragment connects to Text 1 (and various earlier texts) in mocking the notion that survival is always a desirable outcome.

This concerted horrific-comic attack on the injunction to live (on the socio-culturally enforced cognitive framing of survival as an unconditional obligation of unquestionable benefit rather than as an individual decision depending on one's circumstances) continues throughout the thirteen texts. Text 3 eerily enacts frame-based injunctions to "stir" (maintain oneself physically functional) through ostentatious vacillations between the second and the first person: "Start by stirring, there must be a body, as of old, I don't deny it, no more denials, I'll say I'm a body, stirring back and forth, up and down, as required" (109); "There you are now on your feet, I give you my word, I swear they're yours, I swear it's mine" (110). Next, it caustically connects physical functionality to social integration, both construed as traps rather than comforts: "I'll have a crony, my own vintage, my own bog, a fellow warrior, we'll relive our campaigns and compare our scratches" (111). The speaker in Text 4 parades through the entire range of grammatical persons and uses intertextuality to spread himself even thinner: "His life, what a mine, what a life, he can't have that, you can't fool him, ergo it's not his, it's not him, what a thought, treat him like that, like a vulgar Molloy, a common Malone, those mere morals, happy mortals, have a heart, land him in that shit, who never stirred, who is none but me" (115). All express distaste for physicality and stories, though perhaps none as intensely as the speaker from Text 10, wary and resentful of "our committal to flesh, as the dead are committed to the ground, in the hour of their death at last, and at the place where they die, to keep the expenses down, or for our reassignment, souls of the stillborn, or dead before the body, or still young in the midst of the ruins" (142). The list continues, dismissed in the end as "junk ... dead with words, with excess of words" (142). The speaker from text 12 has fun with personal pronouns—"There's a pretty three in one, and what a one, what a no one" (150)—and derides the notion of divinity as an effect of high numbers: "at the end of the billions you'd need a god, unwitnessed witness of witnesses, what a blessing it's all down the drain" (151). The Unnamable's code-scrambling strategies appear here in mutated but recognizable forms. Interpreters are continually cued to acknowledge—through short texts ostentatiously repetitive both thematically and in their relentless search for new syntactic and semantic means to evade frame-based injunctions—to what extent their notions of identity may have relied on frames/ scripts/ schemata that deceivingly tout survival as an unconditionally desirable outcome and death as the worst of all fates. In the *Texts for Nothing* speakers' relentless denunciation, this notion of survival at all costs is a frame-encoded injunction meant to safeguard an environment of acquiescence to exploitation and pain.

The shock effect of this denunciation is compounded by the speakers' generally even or angry (rather than depressed) tone: they seem to have decided that there are fates worse than death and that exclusion is preferable to certain forms of belonging—and, in communicating their convictions, they appear lucid and mildly positive rather than desperate or mournful. In Franklin's view, any elements that "escape the world picture of control" in Beckett's works merely *gesture towards the possibility* to "evade or impede this world model without foreclosing one's prospects for survival" (133). While this may be true of Beckett's *speakers* in *Texts for Nothing* and elsewhere, for *interpreters* the margin of positivity is much wider. Their perception of survival and companionship as frame-encoded injunctions is likely to trigger processes of cognitive reassessment of major impact on their environments but free of life-threatening consequences. Systemic control can remain effective only insofar as enough of its human units acquiesce to its injunctions fully and only relatively small numbers rebel. If enough individuals subject themselves to those injunctions *pro forma* rather than working to perpetuate them, systemic maintenance and the enforcement of punishments may become prohibitively expensive in terms of systemic energy consumption, and the maintenance of the system may be threatened. Interpreters' reassessment-based *withdrawal of support* for frames/ scripts/ schemata that codify survival and social integration as absolute obligations (not decisions at least partly under one's control) is thus likely to weaken the dominance of such structures within interpreters' environment, if only minimally and locally. In time, such incremental environmental changes may result in a paradigm shift, given the likelihood of interpreters' *increasing preference* for frames/ scripts/ schemata free from such injunctions.

The later *How It Is, Company, Ill Seen Ill Said,* and *Worstward Ho* continue to combat such constrictive and repressive cognitive structures. However, compared to Beckett's representations in his first postwar works, the argument is posed in terms increasingly evocative of the late capitalist structures and modified versions of militarism and imperialism Beckett witnessed in the last decades of his life. In addition, these patterns of universal exploitation and consumption are even more explicitly and grotesquely linked to masculinist privilege.

Bom, the speaker from *How It Is*, explains at some length that his living conditions (he has canned food and is crawling in mud) preclude dying of hunger or thirst—but his supposed expressions of relief, full of repugnant details and references to endless time, suggest instead exasperation and veiled sarcasm: "no appetite a crumb of tunny then mouldy eat mouldy no need to worry I won't die I'll never die of hunger" (8); "the mouth opens the tongue comes out lolls in the mud and no question of thirst either no question of dying of thirst either all this time vast stretch of time" (9). Similar suggestions that Bom would prefer his journey to end occur throughout Part 1, typically camouflaged through self-imprecations, excuses, or corrections: "abject abject ages each heroic seen from the next when will the last come when was my golden each rat has its heyday I say it as I hear it" (10). References to bodily excretions abound, insistently posited as essential data of experience: "when the great needs fail the need to move or the need to shit and vomit and the other great needs all my great categories of being" (15). References to God are creatively and elaborately dismissive: "curse God no sound make mental note of the hour and wait midday midnight curse God or bless him and wait watch in hand" (44). References to Pim are frequent enough to suggest frantic anticipation and to seem ominous. In short, Part 1 offers interpreters an "underworld" of darkness, mud, and barely hidden anger in line with what they had encountered in the earlier *Texts for Nothing* but more consistently grotesque—likely apt to elicit more frequent and intense reassessments of cognitive frames/ scripts/ schemata. This cognitive work effectively prepares the way for the major shock effects of Part 2.

Bom describes Pim as "perhaps a foreigner" or "an oriental," basing his assumption on half-muttered words heard while pressing Pim's face to the mud (62). He subsequently muses, "a human voice there within an inch or two my dream perhaps even a human mind if I have to learn Italian obviously it will be less amusing" (63). These comments cue interpreters to Bom's fabrication of Pim's otherness as a first step in dehumanizing him, followed by all the "logical" steps of subjection, exploitation, and abuse masquerading as positive and nourishing developments: "problem of training and concurrently little by little solution and application of same and concurrently moral plane bud and bloom of relations proper" (63). The specifics of the training are soon clarified: "first lesson theme song I dig my nails into his armpit right hand right pit he cries I withdraw them thump with fist on skull his face sinks in the mud his cries cease end of first lesson" (69). The text enacts for interpreters, in a form much too brutal and repugnant to ignore, the socio-cultural integration of physical abuse and torture into a wide range of cognitive frames/ scripts/ schemata of everyday use—its encoding as *necessary* for the sake of progress. Bom self-servingly construes Pim's mental processing of pain as a means of acquiring knowledge:

> but this man is no fool he must say to himself I would if I were he what does he require of me or better still what is required of me that I am tormented thus and the answer sparsim little by little vast tracts of time
> not that I should cry that is evident since when I do I am punished instanter
> sadism pure and simple no since I may not cry

something perhaps beyond my powers assuredly not this creature is no
fool one senses that
what is not beyond my powers known not to be beyond them song it is
required therefore that I sing. (69–70)

It is, of course, mainly the knowledge of *subjection* Pim is expected to
acquire—not just to develop specific responses to specific painful stimuli
but, most importantly, to *revere authority*. Bom is so crassly self-indulgent
in imagining this process that interpreters are bound to acknowledge its
malignity and deceit. Significantly, later, one of the questions Bom carves
in "Roman capitals" into Pim's back "from left to right and top to bottom
as in our civilization" (77) is, "DO YOU LOVE ME" (83), with the subsequent variation, "DO YOU LOVE ME CUNT" (98, 105). Pim likely
never comes to revere Bom but simply—deeply—fears him, yet the fiction
of the victim's reverential acquiescence to authority is a fundamental component of the torturer's conceit. Interpreters aware of the historical context
of the writing of *How It Is* might identify here anchoring contexts like the
French actions in Algeria—but Bom's treatment of Pim would likely evoke,
for interpreters of various socio-cultural backgrounds, cognitive frames/
scripts/ schemata resulting from and supportive of any number of exploit-
ative/ repressive/ totalitarian societal or state practices, from the mistreatment of women to colonialism to the violent repression of opponents of
totalitarian regimes. Discerning the necessity of *torture* as such practices'
shared foundational principle would likely trigger interpreters' widening-
scope reassessment of a large number of previously unquestioned cognitive
frames/ scripts/ schemata and corresponding practices.

The speaker's compulsive engagement in repetition consistently transpires not as an inherently human behavioural pattern but as the result of
his internalization of patriarchal-militaristic injunctions to consume,
exploit, and abuse. The text thus takes aim, with increasing intensity, at
socio-historical mechanisms involved in the coagulation of frames/
scripts/ schemata wherein abuse and exploitation are inscribed as necessary components of companionship, reciprocity, and justice. By the end of
Part 2—after a "vast stretch of time" (70, 72, 73, 74, etc.)—Pim's "training" is complete and this "table of basic stimuli" is provided:

one sing nails in armpit two speak blade in arse three stop thump on skull
four louder pestle on kidney
five softer index in anus six bravo clap athwart arse seven lousy same as
three eight encore same as one or two as may be. (76)

Bom claims, "I say it as I hear it that with someone to keep me company I would have been a different man more universal," but soon amends that as, "saying to myself too late a companion too late" (74). However, in truth, Pim's company does make Bom "universal"—as an embodiment of the frames/ scripts/ schemata built through and grounding the perpetuation of exploitative, repressive, and abusive socio-economic systems (patriarchal, colonialist, capitalist, fascistic, communist, etc.).

The move towards "universality" continues in Part 3 through Bom's meticulous mathematical and logical formalizations meant to define his world's organization and structure. The preclusion of death and the injunction to be thankful are clearly and grotesquely reasserted as this storyworld's defining traits: the speaker, "half in mud half out," describes his condition as "no more head in any case hardly any no more heart just enough to be thankful for it" (112). Pim is said to have escaped, and a certain Bem, to have "come to cleave to me … [as] I had come to cleave to Pim" (118). The verb "cleave," used three times within a few lines, further cues interpreters to the foundational hypocrisy of the social aggregate described—to its positing of exploitation and torture as logical and agreeable means of social cohesion. Bom's formalization of his conditions of existence horrific-comically offers interpreters countless cues that his utterly grotesque environment is not as far removed from theirs as they might have assumed. Bom insistently describes the dynamic of this social aggregate as a matter of *companionship*, as well as *logic, functionality*, and *justice*: "the instant I reach Pim another reaches Bem we are regulated thus our justice wills it thus fifty thousand couples again at the same instant the same everywhere with the same space between them it's mathematical it's our justice" (121). The population number varies with Bom's mood or focus—"millions" (123), "a million strong" (124), and so on—but the description of the "coupling" processes involved continues, horrific-comically repetitive, over several pages. As with previous repetitive descriptions, this is not a clarification but a *demonstration* and the effect of environmental injunctions:

> as for example our course a closed curve and let us be numbered 1 to 1000000 then number 1000000 on leaving his tormentor number 999999 instead of launching forth into the wilderness towards an inexistent victim proceeds towards number 1
>
> and number 1 forsaken by his victim number 2 does not remain eternally bereft of tormentor since this latter as we have seen in the person of number 1000000 is approaching with all the speed he can muster right leg right arm push pull ten yards fifteen yards (127)

Throughout his explanations, Bom continually employs semantic reversals, using positive words to describe processes of capture and torture and negative words to describe victims' escape. These systematic reversals, like other types of repetition with a difference in Beckett's texts, insistently cue interpreters to the repressive and deceitful nature of frames/ scripts/ schemata resulting from and supportive of various social processes of positivation supposedly oriented towards the "common good."

Another means to trigger interpreters' reassessment of cognitive formations wired to notions of social cohesion in hierarchy-based environments is the use of grotesquely comical phrases to define horrific arrangements: companionship becomes "two strangers united in the interest of torment" (131); individuals' inability to recall past experiences becomes "when on the unpredictable arse for the millionth time the groping hand descends ... for the hand it is the first arse for the arse the first hand" (132); and the social aggregate's movements are described slapstick-style: "when we crawl in an amble right leg right arm push pull flat on face mute maledictions left leg left arm push pull flat on face mute maledictions ten yards fifteen yards halt" (137). Finally, an effect of the same order but of added intensity obtains from more brazenly sarcastic or angry statements: "I am always was with Pim Bom and another and 999997 others journeying alone rotting alone martyring and being martyred oh moderately listlessly a little blood a few cries life above in the light a little blue little scenes for the thirst for the sake of peace" (138); "the fuck who suffers who makes to suffer who cries who to be left in peace in the dark the mud ... who drinks that drop of piss of being and who with his last gasp pisses it to drink the moment it's someone each in turn as our justice wills and never any end it wills that too" (144). As they even more openly belie the speaker's supposed satisfaction with the order of things, such statements are bound to trigger extended reassessments of cognitive frames/ scripts/ schemata generated through and supportive of hierarchy-based regulations. Perhaps more importantly, they might also stimulate interpreters' development of an automatic anger and rejection response at the activation of such frames/ scripts/ schemata, supporting interpreters' resistance to hierarchy-based injunctions favouring the abuse and exploitation of designated "others."

The speaker from *Company*—also lying in a dark expanse, though on his back—is spared the torturous forms of companionship and movement seen in *How It Is* but must work to rebuff the phantom of the universally beneficial character of socio-economic productivity-oriented and hierarchy-based acts. Similarly to other characters in Beckett, one main strategy he uses to evade identity convergence and full capture is a destabilizing shift between grammatical persons: "Use of the second person marks the voice. That of the third that cankerous other. Could he speak to and of whom the voice speaks there would be a first. But he cannot. He shall not. You cannot. You shall not" (6). The comedic verve of this passage derives from its ostentatiously adversarial distribution of grammatical persons (the second and the third against the first) and from its predication from a perspective ostentatiously posited as impossible (that of the "I"—see especially "there would be a first" and the subsequent negations). This indexical comedy may activate, in interpreters, a taste for intense decoding and reassessment loops. We are dealing, once again, with a text that technically elicits cognitive strain but repeatedly dissolves it into energizing laughter, so that the interpretive experience remains nourishing and pleasurable rather than approaching overload.

The baseline tone is sarcastically pedantic throughout, with frequent bursts of more intensely angry or eerily cheerful mockery in the first half, especially in formulating "clarifying" examples:

> Your mind never active at any time is now even less than ever so. This is the type of assertion he does not question. ... Yet a certain activity of mind however slight is a necessary complement of company. That is why the voice does not say, You are on your back in the dark and have no mental activity of any kind (7);
>
> Another trait [of the voice he hears—*my note*] the flat tone. No life. Same flat tone at all times. For its affirmations. For its negations. For its interrogations. For its exclamations. For its imperations. ... You were once. You were never. Were you ever? Oh never to have been! Be again. Same flat tone (15–16);
>
> Crawling on all fours. Another in another dark or in the same crawling on all fours devising it all for company. Or some other form of motion. The possible encounters. A dead rat. What an addition to company that would be! A rat long dead (21–22).
>
> Some movement of the hands? ... raised to brush a fly away. But there are no flies. Then why not let there be? The temptation is great. Let there be a fly. ... A live fly mistaking him for dead. Made aware of its error and renewing it incontinent. What an addition to company that would be! (22)

This combination of pedantry and sarcasm likely engages interpreters in a cognitive processing spiral: while the pedantic explanations may initially decelerate the interpretive process, the sarcasm accelerates and intensifies it by requiring continual reassessments of previously processed statements. As similar combinations reoccur, the horrific-comic effects render the cognitive load manageable despite any added intensity.

In the second half, the tone seemingly becomes more meditative, but the anger is better camouflaged rather than extinguished. The speaker imagines that the body lying in the dark could, instead, move: "Devised deviser devising it all for company. ... let him move. Within reason. On all fours. ... let him crawl. Crawl and fall. Crawl again and fall again" (37–38). Next, it is suggested that this crawling act might serve to "chart the area" (39), but—given the body position and the comment that the activity should continue "till he drops" (40)—it becomes clear that the exercise is meant primarily to preserve servitude as a pattern of cognitive functioning. Moreover, the suggested purpose itself can be seen as a sarcastic allusion to colonialism: no sooner is the body imagined to move that the notion of mapping, historically the first step in asserting colonial rule, activates. More or less veiled expressions of anger continue to appear throughout the description of the crawling act. In this passage, the notion of a divine presence is associated with carrion smells and flatly disassociated from love:

> Smell? ... Such as might have once emitted a rat long dead. Or some other carrion. ... Might the crawling creator be reasonably imagined to smell? Even fouler than his creature. ... How much more companionable could his creator but smell. Could he but smell his creator. Some sixth sense? Inexplicable premonition of impending ill? Yes or no? No. Pure reason? Beyond experience. God is love. Yes or no? No. (42)

Here, the notion that the effort involved might not necessarily include both physical and mental overexertion is dismissed in a pedantic tone that betrays anger: "Can the crawling creator crawling in the same create dark as his creature create while crawling? ... Come what might the answer he hazarded in the end was no he could not. Crawling in the dark in the way described was too serious a matter and too all-engrossing to permit of any other business were it only the conjuring of something out of nothing." (43). Following other pedantic considerations, the "most endearing" body position is proclaimed to be lying "prone"—the position of maximum voluntary acquiescence to authority—with the questions remaining, "Prone how? How disposed the legs? The Arms? The head?" (46). The closing lines of the text include, "Till finally you hear how words are coming to an end. With every inane word a little nearer to the last" (51). These constant undertones of anger, allusions to colonialism and exhausting labour, and sarcastic avowals of companionship for companionship's sake cue interpreters to read this text as a rejection of a large range of seemingly innocuous normative injunctions wired into the cognitive frames/ scripts/ schemata we live by. The same textual markers are likely to trigger interpreters' reassessment of prevalent socio-economic notions of reciprocity or fair compensation and of the interpersonal and economic frames/ scripts/ schemata that sustain them.

In *Ill Seen Ill Said*, the notion of reciprocity/ fair exchange is explored with a significant shift of focus. Here, the character under observation is a woman, and the speaking voice is clearly gendered male. To no surprise, the regime of visibility returns to the day-and-night cycle, facilitating voyeurism, and the environment is more contained (the woman can reach its limits, walking from her cabin, in "five to ten minutes," *NO* 58). Through countless elements of style and structure, the text enacts the psychosocial functioning of gender-based injunctions and masculinist privilege, cuing interpreters to react not just to their most egregious manifestations but also to their more insidious and seemingly innocuous remnants still active at the level of the cognitive frames/ scripts/ schemata we process mentally and live by.

The speaking voice tendentiously introduces the woman as someone who hates the life-giving light of the sun (see the emphasized phrases): "From where she lies when the skies are clear she sees Venus rise followed by the sun. Then *she rails at the source of all life*. On. At evening when skies are clear *she savours its star's revenge*" (*NO* 57, my emphasis). However, the subsequent extended comments on her physical traits and movements indicate, first, that she is under surveillance and might dislike daylight for that reason, and second, that her observer(s) might be unreliable. The voice claims that she moves with difficulty and often takes long pauses but offers the following unlikely example: "Down on her knees especially she finds it hard not to remain so forever" (57). The choice is suspicious—a body position quick to become uncomfortable, cross-culturally associated with acquiescence and subjection, and additionally suggestive of *sexual* domination within heteronormative frameworks. This is not a random detail. Later, the voice questionably implies that she spends significant stretches of time on her knees: "All in black she comes and goes. The hem of her long black skirt brushes the floor. But most often she is still. Standing or sitting. Lying or on her knees" (68). Later yet, in a longer sequence, the voice speculates that she would be less visible from the window if she were to "grovel deeper" or "grovel elsewhere" while praying—with the list of potential locations conspicuously ending in one of maximum exposure: "at the edge of the pastures with her head on the stones" (81).

After describing the cabin's surroundings, the voice slyly wonders at the presence of "man" (59), commenting, as if at random, "How many? A figure come what may. Twelve. Wherewith to furnish the horizon's narrow round. She raises her eyes and sees one. Turns away and sees another. So on. Always afar. Still or receding" (60). Next, the voice pictures an "imaginary stranger" attempting contact and uses surveillance language and masculine third-person pronominal forms to describe his potential actions: "To the imaginary stranger the dwelling appears deserted. *Under constant watch* it betrays no sign of life. *The eye glued to one or the other window* has nothing but black drapes for its pains. *Motionless against the door he listens long.* No sound. Knocks. No answer. *Watches all night* in vain for the least glimmer" (61, my emphasis). The description, presumably aimed to stress the woman's motionlessness, betrays a stalking quality in the speaking voice—a trait later reinforced through additional cues.

As the woman is walking in the better-lit area of the stones, the voice interjects, "quick seize her where she is best to be seized" (63). The subsequent passage dismisses her distaste for being observed as an effect of old age, posits the act of surveillance as a mutually beneficial act of intimacy, and masks the speaker's resentment as an expression of existential uncertainty: "What is it defends her? Even from her own. Averts the intent gaze. Incriminates the dearly won. Forbids divining her. What but life ending. Hers. The other's. But so otherwise. She needs nothing. Nothing utterable. Whereas the other. How need in the end?" (64). As discussed at length in Chap. 4, the woman's unwillingness to co-operate in her voyeuristic exploitation is met with increasingly aggressive remarks—obsessive descriptions of her "flesh" abound, replete with both dismissive claims that she is unattractive and resentful comments on her minimal exposure and preferred motionlessness. The speaker obsesses over her boots and stockings (65–66), constantly watches her window (66), and resents her *not* being a figment of his imagination (67) while describing her as "old so dying" (67). He dismisses her as an "ancient mask" even while noting that she has no wrinkles and her eyebrows are "jet black" (70–71). He obsesses over the placement of her hands close to her pubis while lying down (75) and resents the lack of action ("Still as stones they defy as stones do the eye," 76). He obsesses over the "pulp" of her lips while dismissively describing her mouth as an "[u]nlikely site of olden kisses" (89). He repeatedly refers to lambs or "ovines" that might or might not be part of her environment (59, 60, 79)—animals symbolically associated with docility and feeble-mindedness. Interpreters are thus repeatedly cued to note the entitlement bubbling under the speaker's supposedly meditative tone—including in its more insidious forms of articulation as an organic component of presumably acceptable patterns of interaction. In cognitive terms, the speaker's diction betrays his cunning use of preestablished frames/ scripts/ schemata supposedly supporting non-restrictive and mutually beneficial forms of human interaction only in order to reinstitute the legitimacy of consecrated patriarchal forms of consumption, exploitation, and abuse.

The closing lines confirm the predatory nature of patriarchal cognitive patterns by allowing their associated entitlement to reach full expression: "First last moment. Grant only enough remain to devour all. Moment by glutton moment. Sky earth the whole kit and boodle. Not another crumb of carrion left. Lick chops and basta. No. One moment more. One last. Grace to breathe that void. Know happiness" (97). The horrific-comic spectacle of this entitlement of megalomanic proportions (which equates "happiness" with the full consumption of the universe—the matter and the "void" alike) likely intensifies and extends the scope of interpreters' reassessment of cognitive frames/ scripts/ schemata generated through and supportive of patriarchal and hierarchy-based social injunctions.

Worstward Ho offers interpreters a substantially more intense decoding and reassessment experience. Sentence fragments—also used in previous texts, typically triggering a switch from a more linear interpretive mode to a recursive interpretive "loop" apt to produce radical reassessments of the meaning-generating work of cognitive frames/ scripts/ schemata—take over the writing to an unprecedented degree. This textual feature likely decelerates the reading process while significantly accelerating the processing speed, as interpreters are continually prompted by the text's elisions and "corrections" to engage in new processes of reassessment. There is, then, a heuristic dimension to this text, too—through multiple features, it simultaneously and repeatedly cues interpreters both to the substance of its statements and to the most effective means to decode them, progressively creating and enforcing pathways that can allow for faster and larger-scope cognitive processing. Concurrently, the text continues to support the conversion of interpreters' cognitive efforts into nourishing experiences of empowerment and elation through Beckett's trademark category of the horrific-comic, which may be more difficult to decode but does not disappear here.

The text begins, "On. Say on. Somehow on. Till nohow on. Said nohow on" (*NO* 101). These short sentences/ sentence fragments reinstitute the typical intertextuality of Beckett's texts ("on" as a reference to previous narrators' difficulty to begin and slow advancement towards the trademark "nearly there" ending), as well as the equally characteristic adversarial relation between grammatical persons (note especially the imperatives and the switch from the active to the passive voice). These aspects, familiar to interpreters already exposed to some of Beckett's late fiction, emerge in more compressed form here. However, interpreters are soon offered additional (and perhaps more accessible) means of decoding this text's attack on ossified cognitive frames/ scripts/ schemata and associated environmental actions through the mediation of basic narrative conventions. The third short sequence reads, "Say a body. Where none. No mind. Where none. That at least. A place. Where none. For the body. To be in. Move in. Out of. Back into. No. No out. No back. Only in. Stay in. On in. Still" (101). The sequence uses the basic narrative conventions of character and setting (a "body" and a "place") to facilitate the activation of interpreters' cognitive anchoring processes. Simultaneously, it begins to cue interpreters to the risks of ossification and capture involved in allowing cognitive framing and anchoring processes to proceed unchecked. As soon as the voice acquiesces to the positing of a place, restrictions predefine the body's range of movement. The sequence rejects the positing of a *mind* to inhabit the body, but the admission of a body and a place calls pain into existence, coercing the activation of the mind: "Say bones. No bones but say bones. Say ground. No ground but say ground. So as to say pain. … Say remains of mind where none to permit pain. … Other examples if needs must. Of pain. Relief from. Change of" (102). Alongside this insidious reassertion of physicality and consciousness into a supposedly abstracted and ever-diminishing medium, the text offers—in the form of repetitions with a difference—a series of comments on failure that feign support for that reassertion but cue interpreters to a different decoding: "All of old. Nothing else ever. Ever tried. Ever failed. No matter. Try again. Fail again. Fail better" (101); "Throw up and back. The body again. Where none. The place again. Where none. Try again. Fail again. Better again. Or better worse. Fail worse again. Till sick for good. Throw up for good. Go for good. Where neither for good. Good and all" (102). In case interpreters failed to decode the first "fail better" as a potential reference to previous Beckettian speakers' feigning of inability in order to evade repression and capture, the recurrent references to vomit and the variation "fail worse" might remind them of strategies of resistance continually reshaped and refined by Beckett's speakers since Molloy.

Rather than expressing acquiescence to injunctions to accept physicality and intellection as "necessary" and to toil at social integration with an attitude of abnegation (in a variation on the redeeming theme of the "tragedy of being human"), the phrasing in question generates subversive shock effects meant to trigger interpreters' reassessment of the exploitative and abusive social uses of physicality and intellection. Subsequent iterations even provide a more pronouncedly horrific-comic sense of progression, complete with ostentatious suggestions of intentionality (see "with care"): "All of old. Nothing else ever. But never so failed. Worse failed. With care never worse failed" (102). Again, these are not mere reversals of socially sanctioned values but paradox-based attacks on cognitive frames/ scripts/ schemata resulting from and further supporting repression and exploitation-based modes of social engagement. The process involved is not negation but reframing. The text does not simply reject physicality and intellection but *repurposes* them—uses them to trigger reassessments of consecrated frames/ scripts/ schemata that may facilitate exploitation and repression and to prompt processes of frame multiplication and enrichment. For instance, the sabotage of processes of acquiring practicality and productivity-based knowledge is explained as follows: "Dim light source unknown. Know minimum. Know nothing no. Too much to hope. At most mere minimum. Meremost minimum" (103). The key suggestion ("Know minimum") is followed by the blunt assertion of an impossibility ("Know nothing no") otherwise sarcastically proclaimed as deeply desirable ("Too much to hope") and by an expanded redefinition of the initial suggestion. The concentration of expression in this sequence becomes itself horrific-comic—the impossible ideal is expressed with ostentatious crustiness, yet the advanced condensation still accommodates repetition.

Horrific-comic turns of phrase appear on every page, making the textual condensation easier to process and more gratifying. The pensive head ("sunk on crippled hands") is craftily described as "Seat of all. Germ of all" (103). In a later version, this sarcastic "equivalence" is coupled with an even more corrosive repetition with a difference, involving falsely inept questions and horrific-comic nested-doll imagery: "the head said seat of all. Germ of all. All? If of all of it too. Where if not there it too? There in the sunken head the sunken head" (109). The supposed progress towards dissolution (already compromised through the depiction of insertions of physicality and intellection) is described, in paradox-based terms, as "No future in this. Alas yes" (103)—or, in a more linguistically focused mode, "The words too whosesoever. What room for worse! How almost true they sometimes almost ring! How wanting in inanity!" (110). An even more exuberantly acerbic version emerges later: "Least best worse. Least never to be naught. Never to naught be brought. Never by naught be nulled. Unnullable least. Say that best worst. With leastening words say least best worse. For want of worser worst. Unlessenable least best worse" (118). In a mockery of basic oppositions and disjunctions, the setting is described as "How small. How vast. How if not boundless bounded" and thoroughly denounced as restrictive, in a spectacle of sarcastic pedantry: "Whence never once in. Somehow in. Beyondless. Thenceless there. Thitherless there. Thenceless thitherless there" (104). Varieties of Beckett's "walking back" of definitive statements abound, though now they tend to further qualify formulations that are already paradox-based: "One old man and child. At rest plodding on. Any others would do as ill. Almost any. Almost as ill" (105); "Worsening stare. For the nothing to be seen. At the nothing to be seen. Dimly seen" (115); "Better worse what? The say? The said? Same thing. Same nothing. Same all but nothing" (122). Depersonalization is offered as yet another means to evade capture: "No words for him whose words. Him? One. No words for one whose words. One? It. No words for it whose words. Better worse so" (110). The recurrent "Something wrong there" from *How It Is* becomes "Something there badly not wrong" (*NO* 111). Finally, a meditation on the state of the void ends with an apparently exhausted, truly definitive statement still compromised through the presence of "almost" at the end: "Enough. A pox on void. Unmoreable unlessable unworseable evermost almost void" (125). There is an eerie verve to this supposed advancement towards dissolution—not cheerfully suicidal but joyfully lucid. While production-oriented knowledge is obstinately rejected in the name of finally "ending," forms of cognitive processing of no immediate production-oriented purpose are accelerated and enhanced. Once adaptation to the processing method required by the text has started, the text reveals itself as a cognitive enhancer of maximal efficiency and exhilaration.

Some passages are explicitly phrased as cyphers: "Said is missaid. Whenever said said said missaid. From now said alone. No more from now now said and now missaid. From now said alone. Said for missaid. For be missaid" (121)—but in fact all passages are cyphers of varying orders. Longer or shorter sequences explore, in virulently sarcastic fashion, the notion of an ending while *screaming* intertextuality. For instance, even the very last lines play the black comedy of simulating definitiveness and cessation ("Enough. Sudden enough. ... In dimmost dim. Vasts apart. All bounds of boundless void. Whence no farther. Best worse no farther. Nohow less. Nohow worse. Nohow naught. Nohow on," 128) only to add the solitary line "Said nohow on" (128) at the end—the phrase that ends the first short sequence of the text (101) and otherwise recalls various other false endings/ "impossible" beginnings in Beckett's fiction (the end of *The Unnamable*/ beginning of *Texts for Nothing*, the end of *Texts for Nothing*/ beginning of *How It Is*, etc.). The text thus uses repetitions with a difference to mobilize all the strategies of instigating reassessments of cognitive frames/ scripts/ schemata wired into traditional conceptualizations and practices of socialization and intellection ever explored by Beckett's character-narrators. The move is both reassuring and apt to intensify the processing experience for interpreters familiar with Beckett's previous texts.

Beckett's treatment of frames/ scripts/ schemata derived from and supportive of coercive and exploitative hierarchy-based socio-economic structures remains both deeply corrosive and eerily positive throughout his drama and fiction. While it delegitimates and effectively kills the appeal of hierarchy-based injunctions to survive and keep company, it consistently affirms our cognitive ability to develop relational/ interactional means to block the input of such traditional injunctions and produce, in the process, more inclusive and mutually satisfying cognitive frames/ scripts/ schemata of major environmental reshaping import. The idea is not to avoid companionship but to radically reassess traditional predications of companionship on principles and practices that are restrictive/ repressive, exploitative, and abusive rather than mutually beneficial and satisfying; not to exalt suicide but to radically reassess traditional predications of being alive and having value on unilaterally performing service ("self-sacrifice" and related notions). Perhaps the abiding power of *Waiting for Godot* derives first and foremost from the fact that it offers a model of resistance, reassessment, *and redefinition* of traditional companionship (through Vladimir and Estragon) that other texts approximate diagrammatically but do not actually *embody* into characters. However, even a play as horrific as *What Where* or a fictional text as ostentatiously preoccupied with "emptying out" space, mind, and meaning as *Worstward Ho* does more than merely stimulate interpreters' anger and shock-based reassessment of frames/ scripts/ schemata that justify the infliction of harm as a necessary systemic maintenance function. Such texts continue to show a preoccupation with training interpreters to process high volumes of cognitive stimuli faster and more effectively while blocking wide varieties of attempts at manipulation. Beckett's sophisticated discursive means of triggering such processes are of major import today, when the frames/ scripts/ schemata that preserve hierarchy-based coercive, repressive, exploitative, and punitive patterns have progressively been endowed with features meant to downplay the violence and destructiveness of their injunctions, so that at least some of them can survive attempts to regulate social environments in the direction of *excluding* interpersonal and systemic violence.

6.5   Evolution

As I suggested so far in relation to several texts, as Beckett's later works intensify both the production of anxiety and instability and that of cues meant to facilitate fitting and effective interpretive responses, interpreters are enticed to operate at ever-increasing levels of connectivity and speed while becoming increasingly at ease during the execution of such operations—a process apt to foster interpreters' development of higher cognitive functions. This is a development of arguable evolutionary utility in the information and globalization age. Literary scholars have always claimed, in some form or another, that exposure to literary texts is likely to enhance higher cognitive functions such as critical/ "lateral"/ creative thinking, emotional intelligence, and perhaps also one's ability for ethical thinking and action. As discussed here and in the previous chapter, recent (post) cognitive narrative studies have persuasively demonstrated the validity of those claims—at least in part and in relation to *some* literary texts—by grounding their argumentation in scientific studies in artificial intelligence, neuroscience, cognitive science, and so on. My own claims, in this and the previous chapter, focus specifically on texts by Beckett whose *paradox-based* mode of expression is maximally loaded with features apt to stimulate interpreters' *reassessment* of the frames/ scripts/ schemata they process mentally and live by, and unlikely (given their sophisticated shock effects) to allow interpreters to simply "consume" texts in a preformed and uncritical cognitive mode. As I explained, the processes of reassessment triggered by Beckett's texts are likely open-ended and highly consequential for interpreters' further manifestations of intellection and empathy. At the most basic level, these processes are particularly apt to trigger and amplify "resonance mechanisms" like action simulation and empathy. Given

Beckett's emphasis on the grotesque accumulation of repressive injunctions within all the frames/ scripts/ schemata resulting from and supportive of hierarchy-based socio-economic structures, his texts' activation of "resonance mechanisms" is also likely to trigger interpreters' radical reassessment of their own conditions of existence alongside those of Beckett's "creatures." Finally, prolonged/ repeated exposure to Beckett's paradox-based texts is likely to intensify and advance higher-level cognitive functions: increasing abilities to process complex information effectively, at higher speeds, and with more ease.

What drives this cognitive processing spiral is, again, Beckett's paradox-based discursive mode, with its compelling rejection of the basic oppositions and disjunctions that legitimate hierarchy-based socio-economic structures (from the family, the school, and the church to labour relations and governmental policies and actions) and its constant generation of black humour. Beckett's horrific-comic enactment of the life-consuming nature of hierarchical structures that claim to nourish and protect us is energizing and addictive—and "negative" only in relation to/ within the framework of the hierarchy-based conceptualizations of human interactions it has set out to attack. What consistently transpires from that enactment is the predication of our subjection, within contemporary hierarchical structures, on ludicrous and contemptible forms of "doubletalk" whose "persuasiveness" rests, at the core, on the same threats with physical violence used by power structures since the beginnings of civilization. This enactment of the *sheer brutality* of a system self-proclaimed as the guarantor of human progress (and quick to demand sacrifices in the name of that principle) is likely to prompt interpreters' empowering disengagement from cognitive frames/ scripts/ schemata suffused with repressive features they may have perceived as strictly functional before. The same enactment further supports interpreters' subsequent search for more equitable and inclusive patterns of interaction by pre-emptively countering and compromising any relational/ environmental features likely to permit the reinsertion of hierarchical principles. One such feature is the traditional framing of uncertainty and fragmentation as negative categories—as sources of anxiety apt to propel us into an abyss of unknowing, impotence, and pain. Conversely, Beckett's texts frame uncertainty and fragmentation as positive categories enabling us to evade total systemic capture and to continually pursue processes of multiplication and enrichment of the frames/ scripts/ schemata we live by.

There is no potential (linear) "final result" of these processes: in their rejection of traditional conceptualizations of social integration and the value of life, they do not "edge" interpreters ever-closer to isolationism or suicide. They are non-linear and open-ended, and—as previously shown— they allow interpreters to experience a nourishing form of "cognitive high" that has energizing, empowering, and solidarity-building qualities. I would suggest that exposure to Beckett's texts has evolutionary value for several reasons. First, in repeatedly enacting the parasitic nature of hierarchical structures and their insidious wiring into a wide variety of cognitive frames/ scripts/ schemata seemingly strictly functional in nature, Beckett's texts train interpreters to recognize such malignant features. Second, in featuring a variety of characters' obstinate attempts to evade full systemic capture, Beckett's texts allow interpreters to assimilate effective means to block hierarchical injunctions from restricting them to acquiescent cognitive frames/ scripts/ schemata. Third, since the previously mentioned features aptly trigger and amplify "resonance mechanisms" like action simulation and empathy, they additionally elicit the formation of solidarity/inclusivity-based cognitive pathways. Fourth, in exposing interpreters to paradox-based texts of increasing complexity and to sophisticated forms of encoding, Beckett's texts train interpreters to process high volumes of complex information at increasing efficiency and speed while avoiding overload. Fifth, in making this cognitive processing pleasurable and empowering rather than strenuous, Beckett's texts offer a form of respite of nourishing and insulating qualities in a contemporary economic environment dominated, on the contrary, by exhausting demands and diminishing rewards. Sixth, in rehearsing a wide variety of rhetorical modes of encoding and manipulating information, Beckett's texts may additionally elicit interpreters' realization of the value and weight of "knowledge management" functions—common requirements in any field today. The first three points relate closely to contemporary societal trends towards increasing distrust in corporate capitalism and increasing inclusivity—in opposition to a reactionary push towards total corporate control of the world economy and extreme-right state policies. (It is, by now, a truism that younger generations situate themselves more to the left of the political spectrum than the generations before them, in Western countries and elsewhere, and that individuals with such views are becoming a progressively larger portion of the electorate everywhere in the world.[1]) The last three relate to specific challenges pertaining to the

---

[1] See, for example, two recent *Pew Research Center* studies by Cilluffo and Cohn and by Parker, Graf, and Igielnik.

digitalization age—the demand to engage with increasing volumes of information at increasing speeds and preferably without pause.

Thus, Beckett's texts are likely to accelerate interpreters' transition towards more equitable and inclusive relational patterns, as well as enhance their ability to cope with today's information-processing demands without experiencing overload and without remaining unaware of the value of their information-processing work. These can be described as adaptive moves of major evolutionary value in today's political and cultural context.

CHAPTER 7

Conclusion

Textual Excess: Revolutionary Potential and Evolutionary Utility

In 2011, to prove that Super PACs[1] enjoy unethical privileges under US laws and engage in unethical political activities, comedian Stephen Colbert pretended he would run for the US presidency, created his own Super PAC, and reported on its activities on his comedy show, *The Colbert Report*. In 2012, he received a Peabody Award for his innovative means of educating American viewers on the specifics of highly consequential recent

[1] "PACs" are US Political Action Committees that raise funds from individual donors and use them to support/ oppose political campaigns, ballot initiatives, or legislation. PACs are allowed to donate relatively *small* sums directly to political campaigns, but there is no federal limitation on what they can spend "independently" of a candidate/ political party. Prior to the 2010 *Citizens United v. FEC* Supreme Court decision, PACs could not receive contributions from corporations or labour unions but were allowed to receive sponsorship for their administration and fundraising costs from such organizations. So-called Super PACs are Independent-Expenditure Only Committees made possible by two 2010 decisions: the US Supreme Court decision *Citizens United v. FEC* and the Court of Appeals for the District of Columbia Circuit decision *SpeechNow.org v. FEC*. Super PACs are allowed to receive unlimited donations from individuals/ corporations/ labour unions as well as spend unlimited amounts of money "independently" of political campaigns. They are not allowed to coordinate directly with political campaigns/ candidates but can discuss campaign strategy points through the media. Unsurprisingly, countless media commentators have argued that the notion of "independent" expenditures is ludicrous—and, especially since 2010, when it became even easier for major donors to influence the political campaigning process, many comedians have been attacking the *Citizens United* decision as a most egregious manifestation of today's increasing corporate control over the democratic process.

© The Author(s) 2020
C. Ionica, *The Affects, Cognition, and Politics of Samuel Beckett's Postwar Drama and Fiction*, New Interpretations of Beckett in the Twenty-First Century, https://doi.org/10.1007/978-3-030-34902-8_7

court decisions. Colbert named his Super PAC "Americans for a Better Tomorrow—Tomorrow." This phrase qualifies, in Deleuzean terms, as a paradox of "subdivision ad infinitum (always past-future and never present)" (*LS* 75), and it is eerily akin to Beckett's use of "tomorrow" in *Waiting for Godot*. The point, in both cases, is to undermine the present/future disjunction typically employed as an exploitative ruse in hierarchical socio-economic frameworks. As discussed in Chap. 2, in *Waiting for Godot*, Vladimir and Estragon are promised socio-economic integration "tomorrow," but they hijack the word in a process of *feigning* eagerness for social integration and acquiescence to any associated demands. Colbert's "tomorrow" similarly hijacks a deceitful continual deferral of benefits—the repetition of "tomorrow" transforms the promise into an ostentatious proclamation of an intention to deceive. This was, in fact, the premise of Colbert's since-discontinued *The Colbert Report*: to demonstrate the hypocrisy and inhumanity of ultraconservative socio-economic principles, he played an ultraconservative pundit on his show, building each segment of each episode as a *reductio ad absurdum* (a procedure often used by early twentieth-century avant-garde artists as well as by Beckett to emphasize the deceit and destructiveness of traditional models of social coherence and sabotage their claims to constructiveness and benevolence).

In Chap. 1, I presented extensive evidence that Beckett's *Waiting for Godot* has been consistently successful with general (non-academic) audiences despite its intellectual sophistication, and that some of the specifics of its reception indicate that it can mobilize action-oriented and solidarity-based affects and cognitive processes in interpreters *even in the most unpropitious conditions* (prisons, disaster areas, conflict-torn regions, etc.). In Part I and Part II, I discussed the appeal of this play in interpretive frameworks based on affect theory and (post)cognitive narrative theory, respectively, while also analysing several other works by Beckett from those perspectives. In Part I, I explored Beckett's paradox-based discursive operations as compelling means of translating, for interpreters, class/ gender/ other forms of subordination and repression into *processes* rather than *data* of experience—processes that can be sustained or, conversely, suspended. As I explained in Chap. 2, Beckett's paradox-based discourse aptly mobilizes action-oriented and solidarity-based affects in interpreters through forms of linguistic excess leading to a positive mobilization of anger largely unacknowledged so far in criticism. This is achieved through corrosive forms of repetition with a difference that meticulously decompose the advertised benefits of any opposition and disjunction-based mode of human interaction, from definitions of "love" within patriarchal frameworks to definitions of equitable exchanges within late capitalist socio-economic structures. In Chap. 3, I examined *Waiting for Godot* and a number of Beckett's later dramas' articulation of a model of empowerment based in intersectional solidarity and apt to short-circuit hierarchical distribution on multiple levels. I further defined Beckett's positive mobilization of interpreters' anger as a solidarity-based appeal to reject all forms of socially enforced "closure" for our unresolved pain—one of the main ruses used by repressive structures to convincingly pose as social cohesion structures before potential victims, so as to co-opt their support. In Chap. 4, I examined Beckett's trademark angry humour as articulated in his fiction, further defining his use of the "horrific-comic"—a category of humour directed, unlike earlier, opposition and disjunction-based forms, not as much at human foibles as at the self-perpetuating and self-serving *logics of repression* (religious, economic, Oedipal, or socio-political) that typically govern communal living. Finally, I related Beckett's radically disruptive comedic mode to Nail's recent theorization of revolution, which abandons the traditional anchoring of this concept to aspects like the central role of the proletariat or the capture of the state. Within that framework, I argued that Beckett's texts galvanize a form of solidarity free of the dangers of corporate/ authoritarian/ fascistic containment because it is based in a state of mutability facilitating immediate and continual transformation at the contact with others' struggle and pain.

In Part II, I explored the work of the paradox in (post)cognitive terms, as a means to trigger interpreters' reassessment of the frames/ scripts/ schemata they process mentally and live by (cognitive structures generated through their successive processing of lived experiences alongside their exposure to a wide range of cultural products/ phenomena). I used Herman's notions of shock and anchoring effects and several other (post) cognitive narrative concepts to define the cognitive effects of exposure to Beckett's texts as likely to trigger and nourish, in interpreters, a preference for more sophisticated, inclusive, and open frames/ scripts/ schemata, as well as the formation of automatic rejection responses to oversimplification and manipulation. In Chap. 5, I translated into (post)cognitive terms Beckett's corrosive denunciation of the suicide interdiction in *Waiting for Godot,* showing how Vladimir and Estragon's enactments remove the suicide interdiction from its morality-based cognitive framing, revealing its core socio-economic purpose as an injunction to remain alive in order to be worked to death. I then used this and other examples of radical cognitive reframing from Beckett's works to show that Beckett's texts are replete with elements apt to trigger and amplify, in interpreters, the activation of resonance mechanisms such as action simulation and empathic projection—phenomena of major relevance in terms of learning, as well as social connectivity. Finally, I suggested that prolonged and/or repeated exposure to Beckett's texts is likely to generate, in interpreters, an eerie, exclusively nourishing form of "cognitive high" and an increased tolerance to cognitive strain, due to Beckett's consistent conversion of shock and anchoring effects into laughter. In Chap. 6, I traced these effects through a larger number of Beckett's works, showing how, first, as these effects progressively gain in intensity, interpreters are likely to adapt by developing increased abilities for the processing of complex information at increasing speed; and, second, how such operations are likely to be of evolutionary relevance in the current digitalization and globalization context.

While I am not suggesting that *all* of Beckett's texts are easy to decode by interpreters regardless of their training in literary analysis, I showed that *Waiting for Godot* creates an accessible framework that engages interpreters in a decoding mode based on *contagion* rather than traditional modes of "understanding," and that the increasing sophistication of Beckett's later dramatic and fictional works is paralleled by a development of textual features likely to support interpreters' adaptive abilities—an unobtrusive but substantial heuristic dimension. Thus, *Waiting for Godot* uses several thematic elements—the suicide interdiction, the Crucifixion story, the notion of servitude, and stark images of poverty—highly likely to mobilize powerful affects as well as intense cognitive frame reassessment processes. Its allusions to other literary and philosophical works enrich the interpretive experience but do not block it if unnoticed, and the diction and syntax are relatively tame. The later plays and the postwar works of fiction become increasingly sophisticated and challenging on all these levels but offer, as discussed throughout this study, countless cues (typically embedded into sequences of repetition with a difference of various orders—sentence-level or structural) to guide readers/ spectators' interpretive experience in the direction of establishing impactful connections to their own conditions of existence.

In Part I, I aligned my reading with claims by theorists like Adorno, Deleuze and Guattari, Badiou, and Critchley in arguing that Beckett's writing does not articulate a diagnostic-based mode of representation (a critique) but a *practice*. I supported that argument, throughout the section, through analyses of individual works that emphasized the solidarity-building and action-oriented character of Beckett's discourse even in his latest texts, typically discussed in criticism in terms of tragic weakness, diminution, and failure. At the end of the section, I connected my argument to Nail's theorization of revolution, and specifically to his notions of "future anterior" (85), "revolutionary consistency" (116), and "singular-universal solidarity" (159). As explained there, as Beckett's works enact countless forms of repression and pain inflicted by socio-historical machinic structures with the full, partial, or reluctant participation of human components and sabotage machinic claims to constructiveness and benevolence, they foster interpreters' conceptualization of a positive future not in terms of gradual reform but radical change. Even while still not fully formed, interpreters' projection of a future of increased self-determination, non-exploitative exchange, and nourishing connectivity may begin to influence their perception of their current conditions of existence and of their interactions. It is at this level of composite consistency and perpetual mutability that I locate the revolutionary value of Beckett's works and their continued relevance in today's political context of sharpened polarization between more solidarity and equity-based socio-economic orientations and ultraconservative/extreme right views.

In Part II, I proposed that Beckett's texts also have evolutionary value today—an argument perhaps more daring than the former because, so far, Beckett scholars have either never attempted to explore it or have resisted it. I believe, however, that recent developments in neuroscience and cognitive science and their integration into narrative theory have provided the interpretive tools needed to support an argument of this nature. I would also suggest that the reason this argument has not emerged sooner may relate to the widespread critical relegation of Beckett to the category of a critical observer of human nature—an interpretive framework likely to undervalue the action-oriented features of his discourse: its angry humour and eerie energy, its relishing moments of cognitive "high," its constructive articulation of cognitive pathways resistant to exploitative manipulation and prone to inclusivity, its repetitions with a difference apt to increase interpreters' tolerance for high-volume cognitive processing and intensify their processing speed, and so on. In emphasizing these features through an analysis of several of Beckett's postwar works, I built a case for his continued relevance in the context of today's globalization and digitalization challenges.

My reference to *The Colbert Report* at the start of this section was not random. One final argument I would offer in support of my thesis is that Beckett's revolutionary and evolutionary value is additionally confirmed, albeit indirectly, by the presence of paradox-based strategies similar to his in contemporary comedy shows of major impact on matters from public discourse, generally speaking, to public support for changes in policy/ legislation and voting decisions. Some such media products are the discontinued *The Daily Show, The Colbert Report*, and *Key and Peele* and more recent productions such as *Full Frontal with Samantha Bee* or *Last Week Tonight with John Oliver*. These shows' uncanny combination of sophistication and accessibility in their assault on inequality, discrimination, and exploitation has baffled and charmed audiences and critics alike, similarly to *Waiting for Godot*.

Let us recall that Deleuze and Guattari define paradox-based constructions as apt to force open, through various forms of excess, any attempt to use language as an enforcement tool for exploitation and discrimination projects. This is achieved through concerted attacks on the ideologically based disjunctions that structure our understanding of the world, and through an obstinate unveiling of connections between the different "machinic structures" of exploitation and repression to which we are "coupled," such as the family, the education system, the church, the state, the media, and so on. The previously mentioned comedy shows' attacks on corporate and political hypocrisy, unpacking of the process of formation and propagation of racist assumptions, and mockery of heteronormative frameworks are constructs of this category—and, although presumably requiring some intellectual sophistication to be understood, they have proved to be eerily attractive and clear. Let us briefly discuss some examples.

In 2010, in response to what he perceived as a worrisome increase in the level of negativity of public discourse throughout the political spectrum, Stewart announced a "Rally to Restore Sanity." Colbert immediately announced a competing "Rally to Restore Fear," and soon after that, the two decided to consolidate their forces as the "Rally to Restore Sanity and/or Fear." "Sanity and/or Fear" qualifies, in Deleuze's definition, as a paradox of the "*abnormal set* (which is included as a member or which includes members of different types)" (*LS* 75), since one cannot restore *sanity and fear* at the same time or restore *either sanity or fear* through the same means. (The set would not become functional no matter which of the two logical operators we use.) In creating this impossible juxtaposition, Stewart and Colbert denounced contemporary public/ political discourse as a barely disguised attempt to manipulate large numbers of individuals by scaring them *and/or* making them believe that they are bastions of sanity in a world gone insane.

A memorable use of the *reductio ad absurdum* during Colbert's campaign against the *Citizens United* decision is his response to presidential Candidate Mitt Romney's off-hand remark to an audience member at one of his rallies, "Corporations are people, my friend." In a TV advertisement funded by his Super PAC, Colbert proclaims, "As head of Bain Capital he [Romney] bought companies, carved them up, and got rid of what he couldn't use. If Mitt Romney really believes 'Corporations are people, my friend,' then Mitt Romney is a serial killer." This is technically a false analogy, but within the legal context generated by the most recent court decisions on "corporate personhood," that element of erroneous reasoning merely takes corporate legal claims to their ultimate logical consequences. Colbert thus employs a *reductio ad absurdum* to denounce the disjunction between corporations' pursuit of personal rights and their eschewal of personal responsibility. In refusing to recognize the logical validity of that disjunction, Colbert's advertisement creates a space of political contestation that exposes corporate actions as fundamentally inhuman and legislative/ governing bodies as deeply complicit in processes of corporate exploitation.

Oliver's show consistently focuses on the practical implications of major US policies and pieces of legislation, too. A prominent example of his attack on insufficiently publicized racial/ gender/ economic inequities is his creation of a church in August 2015. Oliver called it "Our Lady of Perpetual Exemption" and appointed himself "Megareverend and CEO," in a mockery of televangelism and "prosperity gospels." Over the course of several weeks, he created and broadcast several segments focused on this church on his show, emphasizing the lack of government oversight concerning the tax-exempt status of religious and charitable organizations in the US. The name of the church—a paradox-based construct—mocks religious organizations' claims to spirituality by stressing their "perpetual" association, throughout history, with material advantages. The word "exemption" references current taxation law but can additionally be seen as an allusion to the various "indulgences" dispensed by the church to the wealthy and "allowances" offered by governing bodies to the church throughout history. The phrase "Our Lady of" stresses the historical instrumentalization of the church for purposes of economic domination. Oliver's viewers responded to his *reductio ad absurdum* in kind—by sending him envelopes of money with sarcastic messages, bags of seeds, a large statue of a penis, vials of sperm, and so on.

Key and Peele's series of sketches in which Peele imitates President Barack Obama's controlled and reasoned public speaking style and Key plays "Luther, the anger translator" can be described as a paradox-based, corrosive enactment of racial stereotypes. The sketches denounce several oppositions and disjunctions supportive of hierarchical and exclusionary thinking: intellectual vs. physical, controlled vs. angry, rational vs. emotional, formal vs. colloquial—which have consistently been aligned with the white vs. black racial distinction in the history of the US and have been used to justify racist practices from slavery to the still-current voter suppression, employment discrimination, police brutality, and so on. Enacting the presence of an agitated, "angry black man" behind a public figure internationally recognized as one of the most "presidential" leaders the US has ever had forcibly foregrounds that history, implicitly countering claims that the Obama presidential win marked the disappearance of racial discrimination in the US. The two comedians focused many of the sketches included in their show on racial assumptions and race relations, consistently creating paradox-based scenarios and often using other disruptive techniques reminiscent of avant-garde contestations, as well. Significantly, in an interview with Gross, Key used the phrase "code switching" to refer to his and Peele's enactments of racial identity as they were growing up (both comedians are biracial), and suggested a connection between that practice and their acting careers. Indeed, the foregrounding of historically aggregated social encoding appears to be a core concept of Key and Peele's comedic acts.

Finally, Bee's blunt enactments of the absurdity and hideousness of heteronormative injunctions are consistently paradox-based and often use comedic elements with a pronounced "absurdist" feel. The 8 February 2016 premiere of *Full Frontal with Samantha Bee* (the first late-night show featuring a female host) starts with a mock-press conference in which various journalists ask her questions such as "How does it feel to be a female woman" and whether she has had issues with her "ovaries falling out or anything" since having been signed on the show. Bee explains her success as "hard work, a great team, maybe just a little bit of magic" only to switch to a witchcraft sequence replete with horror movie effects and to then confirm, back in the press conference room, "It's true, we're all witches—what? Any other questions?" The sequence places in alignment several disjunction-based frameworks defining women's discrimination and exclusion throughout history, from their demonization as "temptresses" and "witches" to their still-ongoing exclusion from some areas of labour and public life, including from comedic forms of entertainment. Like Key and Peele's political enactment of race-related issues, Bee's attacks on heteronormativity consistently make use of exaggeration, arguments to absurdity, and non-realistic setups to derail heteronormative hierarchical and exclusionary alignments of oppositions/ disjunctions.

Rather than perpetuating social constructs based on oppositional or hierarchical logic, such contemporary comedy shows force audiences to acknowledge the artifice and the imposition of power that form the basis of the oppositions they live by and, implicitly, of the anxiety that consumes them. Thus, similarly to Dadaist and surrealist works and to Becket's texts, they use forms of humour that are multilayered, "historical," and often horrific as they consistently denounce the past as influencing the present in the particular form of *preying on it*, and traditional forms of socialization as profoundly exploitative and repressive. Implicitly, they foreground the role of oppositional and hierarchical logic in fabricating and magnifying the various social anxieties governing the "nostalgia" for an idealized past still driving political action on the ultraconservative/ far-right side of the political spectrum today. Ultimately, through their consistent attacks on socio-historical structures that aim to maintain us in states of stark division so as to prevent us from engaging in concerted solidarity-based action, such contestations prompt viewers to develop a more empathetic view of the other and to act to achieve social justice.

I suggested, in Chap. 1, that such comedy shows, like many avant-garde texts and like Beckett's works before them, encode threat and comfort, or anxiety and exhilaration not as opposing states but values in a range, and most importantly, outputs regulated by the same socio-historical switches, allowing audiences to realize that they are socio-linguistically conditioned to fear chaos and seek the safety of machinic structures in a world controlled to the point of dehumanization and ordered to death. This realization is of revolutionary and evolutionary import, as it is likely to stimulate solidarity-based political choices while increasing individuals' ability to meet the digital and globalization challenges of the current context. This affectively and cognitively adaptive development already registers in the progressively left-wing values of the so-called generations X, Y, and Z, respectively, as confirmed, among others, by the Pew Research Center studies I mentioned in Chap. 6.

Placing Beckett's works in dialogue with contemporary media forms that appear to relate to audiences through similar means and to prompt similar affective and cognitive responses allows for the articulation of an even stronger case for Beckett's relevance in a contemporary context. Far from speaking to the ethical concerns and aesthetic tastes of another era, Beckett's *diagrammatic* textual constructs continue to nourish contemporary audiences through their solidarity-based and cognition-enhancing traits. As paradox-based discourses continue to gain prominence in contemporary forms of entertainment, interpreters may in fact become *better adapted to* (rather than increasingly disconnected from) the ethical and aesthetic configuration of Beckett's texts, continually interacting with them in a solidarity, mutability, and cognitive enhancement-focused mode.

BIBLIOGRAPHY

Abbott, H. Porter. *Beckett Writing Beckett: The Author in the Autograph.* Cornell UP, 1996.

———. *The Fiction of Samuel Beckett: Form and Effect.* U of California P, 1973.

———. "Garden Paths and Ineffable Effects: Abandoning Representation in Literature and Film." *Toward a Cognitive Theory of Narrative Acts,* edited by Frederick Luis Aldama, U of Texas P, 2010, pp. 205–26.

———. "Immersions in the Cognitive Sublime: The Textual Experience of the Extratextual Unknown in García Márques and Beckett." *Narrative,* vol. 17, no. 2, 2009, pp. 131–42.

Ackerley, Chris. "*Lassata Sed*: Samuel Beckett's Portraits of His Fair to Middling Women." *Samuel Beckett Today/ Aujourd'hui,* vol. 12, 2002, pp. 55–70.

———. *Obscure Locks, Simple Keys: The Annotated* Watt. Edinburgh UP, 2010.

Adams, Jacob, director. *The Impossible Itself.* Herbert Blau, Rick Cluchey, Alan Mandell, Hans Freitag, Joe Miksak, Eugene Roche, Robert Symonds, performers. Produced by Jacob Adams and Podunc Pictures, 2010.

Adelman, Gary. *Naming Beckett's Unnamable.* Bucknell UP, 2004.

Adorno, Theodor W. *Aesthetic Theory.* Edited by Gretel Adorno and Rolf Tiedemann, translated by Robert Hullot-Kentor, Continuum, 2002.

———. *Notes to Literature.* Edited by Rolf Tiedemann, translated by Shierry Weber Nicholsen, Columbia UP, 1991, 1992. 2 vols.

Apollinaire, Guillaume. *Les Mamelles de Tirésias.* Gallimard, 1972.

Artaud, Antonin. "Ci-gît." *Oeuvres completes,* vol. 12, Gallimard, 1961, pp. 75–100.

———. *The Theatre and Its Double.* Translated by Mary Caroline Richard, Grove, 1958.

© The Author(s) 2020

C. Ionica, *The Affects, Cognition, and Politics of Samuel Beckett's Postwar Drama and Fiction,* New Interpretations of Beckett in the Twenty-First Century, https://doi.org/10.1007/978-3-030-34902-8

Astbury, Helen. "How to Do Things with Syntax: Beckett's Binary-Turned Sentences and Their Translation into English." *Samuel Beckett Today/ Aujourd'hui*, vol. 11, 2001, pp. 446–53.

Badiou, Alain. *In Praise of Love*. Written with Nicolas Truong, translated by P. Bush, Serpent's Tail, 2012.

———. *On Beckett*. Edited by Nina Power and Alberto Toscano, Clinamen, 2003.

Balzac, Honoré de. *Le Père Goriot*. Gallimard, 1999.

Barry, Elizabeth. "All in My Head: Beckett, Schizophrenia, and the Self." *Journal of Medical Humanities*, vol. 37, no. 2, 2016, pp. 183–92, https://doi. org/10.1007/s10912-016-9384-6

Beckett, Samuel. *The Complete Dramatic Works*. Faber and Faber, 1986.

———. *The Complete Short Prose, 1929–1989*. Edited by S.E. Gontarski, Grove, 1995.

———. *Dream of Fair to Middling Women*. Calder Publications and Riverrun Press, 1992.

———. *How It Is*. John Calder, 1996.

———. *The Letters of Samuel Beckett*. Edited by George Craig, Martha Dow Fehsenfeld, Daniel Gunn, and Lois More Overbeck. Cambridge UP, 2009–16. 4 vols.

———. *Malone Dies*. Edited by Peter Boxall. London: Faber and Faber, 2010.

———. *Molloy*. Edited by Shane Weller. London: Faber and Faber, 2009.

———. *More Pricks Than Kicks*. Pan Books, 1974.

———. *Murphy*. Grove, 1957.

———. *Nohow On: Company. Ill Seen Ill Said. Wostward Ho*. John Calder, 1989.

———. *Proust; Three Dialogues [between] Samuel Beckett and Georges Duthuit*. Calder & Boyars, 1999.

———. *The Unnamable*. Edited by Steven Connor. London: Faber and Faber, 2010.

———. *Watt*. John Calder, 1963.

Bee, Samantha, host. *Full Frontal with Samantha Bee*. TBS, 2016–present.

Ben-Zvi, Linda. "Beckett and Disgust: The Body as 'Laughing Matter.'" *Modernism/Modernity*, vol. 18, no. 4, 2011, pp. 681–98.

———, editor. *Women in Beckett: Performance and Critical Perspectives*. U of Illinois P, 1990.

Bennett, Michael Y. *Reassessing the Theatre of the Absurd: Camus, Beckett, Ionesco, Genet, and Pinter*. Palgrave Macmillan, 2011.

Bergson, Henri. *Creative Evolution*. Translated by Arthur Mitchell, Modern Library/Random House, 1944.

———. *The Creative Mind*. Translated by Mabelle L. Andison. Philosophical Library, 1946.

———. *Laughter: An Essay on the Meaning of the Comic*. Translated by Cloudesley Brereton and Fred Rothwell, Green Integer, 1999.

Bernini, Marco. "Crawling Creating Creatures: On Beckett's Liminal Minds." *European Journal of English Studies*, vol. 19, no. 1, 2015, pp. 39–54, https://doi.org/10.1080/13825577.2015.1004916

Bersani, Leo and Ulysse Dutoit. *Acts of Empoverishment: Beckett, Rothko, Resnais.* Harvard UP, 1993.

Blocker, H. Gene. *The Metaphysics of Absurdity.* UP of America, 1979.

Bloom, Harold. *The Anxiety of Influence: A Theory of Poetry.* Oxford UP, 1973.

Boulter, Jonathan. *Beckett: A Guide for the Perplexed.* Continuum, 2008.

Boxall, Peter. "Beckett and Homoeroticism." *Palgrave Advances in Samuel Beckett Studies*, edited by Lois Oppenheim, Palgrave Macmillan, 2004, pp. 110–32.

Bradby, David. *Beckett: Waiting for Godot.* Cambridge UP, 2001.

Bryden, Mary. "The Beckettian Bestiary." Bryden (editor), pp. 40–58.

———. "'That or Groan': Pain and De-paining in Beckett." *Samuel Beckett and Pain*, edited by Mariko Hori Tanaka, Yoshiki Tajiri, and Michiko Tsushima, Rodopi, 2012, pp. 201–15.

———. *Women in Samuel Beckett's Prose and Drama: Her Own Other.* Barnes & Noble, 1993.

———, editor. *Beckett and Animals.* Cambridge UP, 2013.

Camus, Albert. *The Myth of Sisyphus and Other Essays*, translated by Justin O'Brien, Alfred A. Knopf, 1969.

———. *The Stranger.* Translated by Kate Griffith, UP of America, 1982.

Caravaggio, Michelangelo Merisi da. *Beheading of St. John the Baptist.* 1608, St. John's Co-Cathedral, Valletta.

Caselli, Daniela. "Insufferable Beckett." *Samuel Beckett and the Discourse of Psychoanalysis.* Modern Languages Association Convention, New York, 6 Jan. 2018.

———. "Insufferable: Gender and Sexuality in the Work of Samuel Beckett." The London Beckett Seminar 2017–2018, 9 Mar. 2018.

Cavaliero, Glen. *The Alchemy of Laughter: Comedy in English Fiction.* Macmillan, 2000.

Cavell, Stanley. *Must We Mean What We Say? A Book of Essays.* Cambridge UP, 1976.

Chang, Darren. "Correcting False Information in Memory: Manipulating the Strength of Misinformation Encoding and Its Retraction." *Psychonomic Bulletin & Review*, vol. 18, no. 3, June 2011, pp. 570–78.

Chomsky, Noam. *Aspects of the Theory of Syntax.* MIT Press, 1965.

———. *Syntactic Structures.* Mouton de Gruyter, 2002.

Cilluffo, Anthony and D'Vera Cohn. "6 Demographic Trends Shaping the U.S. and the World in 2019." *The PEW Research Center*, 11 Apr. 2019. https://www.pewresearch.org/fact-tank/2019/04/11/6-demographic-trends-shaping-the-u-s-and-the-world-in-2019/

Citizens United v. FEC. 558 U.S. 310 (2010).

Cohn, Ruby. *Samuel Beckett: The Comic Gamut.* Rutgers UP, 1962.

Colbert, Stephen. "*Americans for a Better Tomorrow, Tomorrow* Mitt Romney Attack Ad." *The Colbert Report*, season 8, episode 4, 2011, Comedy Central. http://www.cc.com/video-clips/buf78z/the-colbert-report-colbert-super-pac%2D%2D-mitt-romney-attack-ad

———, host. *The Colbert Report*. Comedy Central, 2005–2014. Talk Show. http://www.cc.com/shows/the-colbert-report

Connor, Steven. *Beckett, Modernism, and the Material Imagination.* Cambridge UP, 2014.

———. *Samuel Beckett: Repetition, Theory, and Text.* Blackwell, 1996.

Critchley, Simon. *Infinitely Demanding: Ethics of Commitment, Politics of Resistance.* Verso, 2007.

———. *Very Little, Almost Nothing: Death, Philosophy, Literature.* Routledge, 2004.

De Keersmaecker, Jonas and Arne Roets. "'Fake News': Incorrect, but Hard to Correct. The Role of Cognitive Ability on the Impact of False Information on Social Impressions." *Intelligence*, vol. 65, Nov. 2017, pp. 107–10, https://doi.org/10.1016/j.intell.2017.10.005

Deleuze, Gilles. *Difference and Repetition.* Translated by Paul Patton, Columbia UP, 1994.

———. "The Exhausted." *Essays Critical and Clinical*, translated by Daniel W. Smith and Michael A. Greco, Verso, 1998, pp. 152–74.

———. *The Logic of Sense.* Translated by Mark Lester with Charles Stivale, edited by Constantin V. Boundas. The Athlone Press, 1990.

———. "Postscript on Control Societies." *October*, vol. 59, Winter 1992, pp. 3–7.

Deleuze, Gilles and Félix Guattari. *Anti-Oedipus: Capitalism and Schizophrenia.* Translated by Robert Hurley, Mark Seem, and Helen R. Lane, U of Minnesota P, 1983.

———. *A Thousand Plateaux: Capitalism and Schizophrenia.* Translated by Brian Massumi, U of Minnesota P, 1987.

———. *Kafka: Toward a Minor Literature.* Translated by Dana Polan, U of Minnesota P, 1986.

Descartes, René. "The Description of the Human Body." *The World and Other Writings*, translated by Stephen Gaukroger, Cambridge UP, 1998, pp. 170–205.

Diamond, Elin. "Blau, Butler, Beckett, and the Politics of Seeming." *The Drama Review*, vol. 44, no. 4, 2000, pp. 31–43.

———. "Speaking Parisian: Beckett and French Feminism." Ben-Zvi (editor), pp. 208–16.

Dennis, Amanda M. "Glitches in Logic in Beckett's *Watt*: Toward a Sensory Poetics." *Journal of Modern Literature*, vol. 38, no. 2, 2015, pp. 103–16.

Dow, Suzanne. "Beckett's Humour, from an Ethics of Finitude to an Ethics of the Real." *Paragraph*, vol. 34, no. 1, 2011, pp. 121–36.

Dowd, Garin. *Abstract Machines: Samuel Beckett and Philosophy after Deleuze and Guattari.* Rodopi, 2007.

———. "Beckettian Pain, in the Flesh: Singularity, Community and 'the Work'." *Samuel Beckett and Pain*, edited by Mariko Hori Tanaka, Yoshiki Tajiri, and Michiko Tsushima, Rodopi, 2012, pp. 67–91.

Ecker, Ullrich K.H., Stephan Lewandowsky, Briony Swire, and Dan M. Kahan. "Ideology, Motivated Reasoning, and Cognitive Reflection." *Judgment and Decision Making*, vol. 8, 2013, pp. 407–24, journal.sjdm.org/13/13313/jdm13313.pdf

Eliot, T.S. *Collected Poems, 1900–1962*. Faber, 1963.

Erickson, Jon. "Is Nothing to Be Done?" *Modern Drama*, vol. 50, no. 2, 2007, pp. 258–75.

Esslin, Martin. *The Theatre of the Absurd*. Doubleday, 1961.

Federman, Raymond. "Beckett [f]or Nothing." *Engagement and Indifference: Beckett and the Political*, edited by Henry Sussman and Christopher Devenney, State U of New York P, 2001, pp. 161–72.

Feldman, Matthew. *Beckett's Books: A Cultural History of Samuel Beckett's "Interwar Notes."* Continuum, 2006.

Fifield, Peter. *Late Modernist Style in Samuel Beckett and Emanuel Levinas*. Palgrave Macmillan, 2013.

Fisher, Philip. *The Vehement Passions*. Princeton UP, 2002.

Fletcher, John. *The Novels of Samuel Beckett*. Barnes and Noble, 1970.

Franklin, Seb. *Control: Digitality as Cultural Logic*. MIT Press, 2015.

Freud, Sigmund. *Civilization and Its Discontents. Standard Edition*, vol. 21, pp. 59–246.

———. "Humour." *Standard Edition*, vol. 21, pp. 159–66.

———. "Jokes and their Relation with the Unconscious." *Standard Edition*, vol. 8.

———. *The Standard Edition of the Complete Psychological Works of Sigmund Freud*. Edited and translated by James Strachey, Hogarth Press and the Institute of Psychoanalysis, 1955–1974.

Gaensbauer, Deborah B. *The French Theater of the Absurd*. Twayne Publishers, 1991.

Garrison, Alysia E. "'Faintly Struggling Things': Trauma, Testimony, and Inscrutable Life in Beckett's *The Unnamable*." *Samuel Beckett: History, Memory, Archive*, edited by Seán Kennedy and Katherine Weiss, Palgrave Macmillan, 2009, pp. 89–109.

Genet, Jean. *Théâtre complet*. Gallimard, 2002.

Genette, Gérard. *Narrative Discourse: An Essay in Method*. Translated by Jane E. Lewin, Blackwell, 1980.

Geulincx, Arnold. *Ethics, with Samuel Beckett's Notes*. Translated by Martin Wilson, edited by Han van Ruler, Anthony Uhlmann, and Martin Wilson, Brill, 2006.

Gibson, Andrew. *Beckett and Badiou: The Pathos of Intermittency*. Oxford UP, 2006.

Gidal, Peter. *Understanding Beckett: A Study of Monologue and Gesture in the Works of Samuel Beckett*. St. Martin's Press, 1986.

Gontarski, S.E. "From Unabandoned Works: Samuel Beckett's Short Prose." Introduction to *Samuel Beckett: The Complete Short Prose, 1929–1989*, by Samuel Beckett, edited by S.E. Gontarski, Grove, 1995, pp. xi–xxxii.

———. *The Intent of Undoing in Samuel Beckett's Dramatic Prose*. Indiana UP, 1985.

Gordon, Lois. "France: World War Two." Uhlmann (editor), pp. 109–25.

Gray, Thomas. "Ode on a Distant Prospect of Eton College." *Poetryfoundation.org*. https://www.poetryfoundation.org/poems/44301/ode-on-a-distant-prospect-of-eton-college

Gross, Terry. "For Key and Peele, Biracial Roots Bestow Special Comedic 'Power.'" Interview, broadcast on 20 Nov. 2013, transcript provided 31 Dec. 2013. https://www.npr.org/2013/12/31/256605611/for-key-and-peele-biracial-roots-bestow-special-comedic-power

Hardt, Michael and Antonio Negri. *Commonwealth*. Harvard UP, 2009.

———. *Empire*. Harvard UP, 2000.

———. *Multitude*. Penguin, 2004.

Harvey, Lawrence E. *Samuel Beckett: Poet and Critic*. Princeton UP, 1970.

Hayasaki, Erika. "The Pathology of Prejudice: What Neuroscience Tells Us about the Persistence of Hatred." *The New Republic*, 27 Nov. 2018. https://newrepublic.com/article/152299/white-supremacists-learn-hate

Herman, David. "Re-minding Modernism." *The Emergence of the Mind: Representations of Consciousness in Narrative Discourse in English*, edited by David Herman, U of Nebraska P, 2011, pp. 243–72.

———. *Story Logic: Problems and Possibilities of Narrative*. U of Nebraska P, 2002.

Hill, Leslie. *Beckett's Fiction: In Different Worlds*. Cambridge UP, 1996.

Hoefer, Jacqueline. "Watt." *Samuel Beckett: A Collection of Critical Essays*, edited by Martin Esslin, Prentice Hall, 1965, pp. 62–76.

Horkheimer, Marx and Theodor W. Adorno. *Dialectic of Enlightenment*. Translated by John Cumming, Herder and Herder, 1972.

Ionesco, Eugène. *The Killer, and Other Plays*. Translated by Donald Watson, Grove, 1960.

Ionica, Cristina. "Halting the Production of Repression: Paradox-Based Humour, or, Deleuze, Guattari, Beckett, and the Schizo's Stick." *Angelaki: Journal of the Theoretical Humanities*, vol. 21, no. 2, June 2016, pp. 99–118.

Jarry, Alfred. *Tout Ubu: Ubu roi; Ubu cocu; Ubu enchaîné; Almanachs du père Ubu; Ubu sur la butte; Avec leurs prolégomènes et paralipoménes*. Edited by Maurice Saillet, Le Livre de Poche, 1975.

Jeffers, Jennifer. *Beckett's Masculinity*. Palgrave Macmillan, 2009.

Johnson, Nicholas E. "Language, Multiplicity, Void: Politics of the Beckettian Subject." *Theatre Research International*, vol. 37, no. 3, 2012, pp. 38–48.

Jones, David Houston. "Néomorts et faux vivants: Communautés dépeuplées chez Beckett et Agamben." *Samuel Beckett Today/ Aujourd'hui*, vol. 17, 2006, pp. 247–63.

———. "From Contumancy to Shame." *Beckett at 100: Revolving It All*, edited by Linda Ben-Zvi and Angela Moorjani, Oxford UP, 2008, pp. 54–67

Juliet, Charles. *Conversations with Samuel Beckett and Bram van Velde*. Translated by Janey Tucker. Leiden Academic Press, 1995.

Kafka, Franz. *Metamorphosis and Other Writings*. Translated by Helmuth Kiesel. Continuum, 2002.

———. *The Castle*. Translated by Willa and Edwin Muir. Schocken Books, 1974.

———. *The Trial*. Translated by Willa and Edwin Muir. Schocken Books, 1995.

Kant, Immanuel. *Critique of Pure Reason*. Translated by Paul Guyer and Allen W. Wood, Cambridge UP, 1998.

Katz, Daniel. *Saying "I" No More: Subjectivity and Consciousness in the Prose of Samuel Beckett*. Northwestern UP, 1999.

———. "What Remains of Beckett: Evasion and History." *Beckett and Phenomenology*, edited by Ulrika Maude and Matthew Feldman, Continuum, 2009, pp. 145–57.

Kennedy, Séan. "'Humanity in Ruins': Beckett and History." *The New Cambridge Companion to Samuel Beckett*, edited by Dirk Van Hulle, Cambridge UP, 2015, pp. 185–99.

Kenner, Hugh. *A Reader's Guide to Samuel Beckett*. Thames and Hudson, 1973.

———. *The Mechanic Muse*. Oxford UP, 1987.

Key, Keegan-Michael and Jordan Peele, writers and performers. *Key and Peele*. Comedy Central, 2012–2015.

———. *Obama's Anger Translator: The Complete Collection*. Comedy Central, Jan. 2013. http://www.comedycentral.com.au/key-and-peele/videos/obamas-anger-translator-the-complete-collection

Knowlson, James. *Damned to Fame: The Life of Samuel Beckett*. Bloomsbury, 1996.

Kraft, Patrick W., Milton Lodge, and Charles S. Taber. "Why People 'Don't Trust the Evidence': Motivated Reasoning and Scientific Beliefs." *Annals of the American Academy of Political and Social Science*, vol. 658, no. 1, 2015, pp. 121–33, https://doi.org/10.1177/0002716214554758

Kreiswirth, Martin. "Trusting the Tale: The Narrativist Turn in the Human Sciences." *New Literary History*, vol. 23, no. 3, 1992, pp. 629–57.

Kristeva, Julia. "The Father, Love, and Banishment." *Desire in Language: A Semiotic Approach to Literature and Art*, by Julia Kristeva, edited by Leon S. Roudiez, translated by Thomas Gora, Alice Jardine, and Leon Roudiez, Columbia UP, 1980, pp. 148–58.

Krugman, Paul R. *The Conscience of a Liberal*. Norton, 2007.

———. *The Return of Depression Economics and the Crisis of 2008*. Norton, 2009.

Lacan, Jacques. "Kant avec Sade." *Ecrits*, Seuil, 1966, pp. 765–90.

Langlois, Christopher. *Samuel Beckett and the Terror of Literature*. Edinburgh UP, 2017.

Lecercle, Jean-Jacques. *Deleuze and Language*. Palgrave Macmillan, 2002.

Levi, Primo. *If This Is a Man*, and *The Truce*. Translated by Stuart Woolf, Sphere Books, 1987.

Locatelli, Carla. *Unwording the Word: Samuel Beckett's Prose after the Nobel Prize*. U of Pennsylvania P, 1990.

Martinot, Steve. "On the Epidemic of Police Killings." *Social Justice*, vol. 39, no. 4, 2014, pp. 52–75. http://www.socialjusticejournal.org/product/steve-martinot/

Marx, Karl. *Capital*. Translated by Eden and Cedar Paul, Dent, 1962. 2 vols.

Maude, Ulrika. "Pavlov's Dogs and Other Animals in Samuel Beckett." Bryden (editor), pp. 82–93.

McNaughton, James. "Beckett, German Fascism, and History: The Futility of Protest." *Samuel Beckett Today/ Aujourd'hui*, vol. 15, 2005, pp. 101–16.

———. *On the 'Utopian Scrap-heap': Samuel Beckett, Irish Modernism, and European Politics*. 2006. U of Michigan, PhD Dissertation. *ProQuest Dissertations and Theses*.

Mercier, Vivian. "The Uneventful Event." *Critical Thought Series 4: Critical Essays on Samuel Beckett*, edited by Lance St. John Butler, Scolar Press, 1993, pp. 29–30. First published in 1956.

Milton, John. *Paradise Lost*. Duquesne UP, 2007.

Montague, Richard Merritt. *Formal Philosophy: Selected Papers of Richard Montague*. Edited by Richmond H. Thomason. Yale UP, 1974.

Mood, John. "'The Personal System' – Samuel Beckett's *Watt*." *PMLA*, vol. 86, no. 2, 1971, pp. 259–62.

Moore, Malcom. "Inside Foxconn's Suicide Factory." *The Telegraph*, 27 May 2010. https://www.telegraph.co.uk/finance/china-business/7773011/A-look-inside-the-Foxconn-suicide-factory.html

Morin, Emilie. *Beckett's Political Imagination*. Cambridge UP, 2017.

Nail, Thomas. *Returning to Revolution: Deleuze, Guattari, and Zapatismo*. Edinburgh UP, 2012.

New York Civil Liberties Union. "Stop-and-Frisk Data." www.nyclu.org, 2018. https://www.nyclu.org/en/stop-and-frisk-data

Ngai, Sianne. *Ugly Feelings*. Harvard UP, 2005.

Nietzsche, Friedrich Wilhelm. *The Gay Science*. Translated by Josefine Nauckhoff, Cambridge UP, 2001.

———. *On the Genealogy of Morals: A Polemic*. Translated by Douglas Smith, Oxford UP, 1996.

O'Neill, Patrick. "The Comedy of Entropy: The Contexts of Black Humour." *Bloom's Literary Themes: Dark Humour*, edited by Harold Bloom and Blake Hobby, Infobase Publishing, 2010, pp. 79–103.

Oliver, John, host. *Last Week Tonight with John Oliver*. HBO, 2014–present.

Parker, Kim, Nikki Graf, and Ruth Igielnik. "Generation Z Looks a Lot Like Millennials on Key Social and Political Issues." *The PEW Research Centre*, 17 Jan. 2019. https://www.pewsocialtrends.org/2019/01/17/generation-z-looks-a-lot-like-millennials-on-key-social-and-political-issues/

Perloff, Marjorie. "'In Love with Hiding': Samuel Beckett's War." *The Iowa Review*, vol. 35, no. 1, 2005, pp. 76–103.

———. *Wittgenstein's Ladder: Poetic Language and the Strangeness of the Ordinary*. U of Chicago P, 1996.

Piketty, Thomas. *Capital in the Twenty-First Century*. Translated by Arthur Goldhammer, Belknap, 2014.

Popova, Yanna. "'Little is Left to Tell': Beckett's Theater of Mind, *Ohio Impromptu*, and the New Cognitive Turn in Analyzing Drama." *Style*, vol. 38, no. 4, 2004, pp. 452–67.

Prigent, Christian. "A Descent from Clowns." *Engagement and Indifference: Beckett and the Political*, edited by Henry Sussman and Christopher Devenney. State U of New York P, 2001, pp. 58–82.

Rabaté, Jean-Michel. "Beckett et la poésie de la zone: (Dante... Apollinaire. Celine ... Lévi)." *Samuel Beckett Today/ Aujourd'hui*, vol. 9, 1999, pp. 75–90.

———. "Love and Lobsters: Beckett's Meta-Ethics." *The New Cambridge Companion to Samuel Beckett*, edited by Dirk Van Hulle, Cambridge UP, 2015, pp. 158–69.

Rada, Michelle. "The Illusionless: Adorno and the Afterlife of Laughter in *How It Is*." *Journal of Modern Literature*, vol. 38, no. 4, 2015, pp. 149–67.

Ronquillo, Jaclyn, Thomas F. Denson, Brian Lickel, Zhong-Lin Lu, Anirvan Nandy, and Keith B. Maddox. "The Effects of Skin Tone on Race-Related Amygdala Activity: An fMRI Investigation." *Social Cognitive and Affective Neuroscience*, vol. 2, no. 1, Mar. 2007, pp. 39–44, https://doi.org/10.1093/scan/nsl043

Sade, Marquis de. *Juliette*. Translated by Austryn Wainhouse, Grove, 1968.

Saiu, Octavian. "Samuel Beckett behind the Iron Courtain: The Reception in Eastern Europe." *The International Reception of Samuel Beckett*, edited by Mark Nixon and Matthew Feldman, Continuum, 2009, pp. 251–71.

Salisbury, Laura. *Samuel Beckett: Laughing Matters, Comic Timing*. Edinburgh UP, 2012.

———. "Gloria SMH and Beckett's Linguistic Encryptions." *The Edinburgh Companion to Samuel Beckett and the Arts*, edited by S.E. Gontarski, Edinburgh UP, 2014, pp. 153–69.

Saussure, Ferdinand de. *Cours de linguistique générale*. Edited by Charles Bally, Albert Sechehaye, and Albert Riedlinger, Payot, 1969.

Scarry, Elaine. *The Body in Pain: The Making and Unmaking of the World*. Oxford UP, 1985.

Sartre, Jean-Paul. *Being and Nothingness: An Essay on Phenomenological Ontology*. Translated by Hazel E. Barnes, Methuen, 1957.

———. *Nausea*. Translated by Lloyd Alexander, New Directions, 1969.

———. *No Exit and Three Other Plays*. Translated by S. Gilbert and I. Abel, Vintage International, 1989.

Sherzer, Dina. "Portrait of a Woman: The Experience of Marginality in *Not I*." Ben-Zvi (editor), pp. 201–7.

SpeechNow.org v. FEC. 599 F.3d 686 (D.C. Cir. 2010).

Sloterdijk, Peter. *Rage and Time: A Psychopolitical Investigation*. Translated by Mario Wenning, Columbia UP, 2010.

Smith, David, Imogen Carter, and Ally Carnwath. "In Godot We Trust." *The Observer*, 8 Mar. 2009. https://www.theguardian.com/culture/2009/mar/08/samuel-beckett-waiting-for-godot

Smith, Russell. "'Uproar, bulk, rage, suffocation, effort unceasing, frenzied and vain': Beckett's Transports of Rage." *Journal of Medical Humanities*, vol. 37, 2016, pp. 137–47.

Stewart, Jon, host. *The Daily Show with Jon Stewart*. Comedy Central, 1999–2015. Talk Show.

Stewart, Paul. "Queer Relations or the 'Incoercible Absence of Relation' in Beckett's Watt and the Post-War Prose." *Samuel Beckett Today/ Aujourd'hui*, vol. 27, 2015, pp. 103–14.

Stevens, Andrea. "A Playwright Who Likes to Bang Words Together." *New York Times*, 6 Mar. 1994. https://www.nytimes.com/1994/03/06/theater/theater-a-playwright-who-likes-to-bang-words-together.html?mtrref=www.google.ca&gwh=6172899A4CACF2CE24492D44B260822D&gwt=pay

Tanaka, Mariko Hori. "Ontological Fear and Anxiety in the Theater of Beckett, Betsuyaku, and Pinter." *Beckett at 100: Revolving It All*, edited by Linda Ben-Zvi and Angela Moorjani, Oxford UP, 2008, pp. 246–58.

Trezise, Thomas. *Into the Breach: Samuel Beckett and the Ends of Literature*. Princeton UP, 1990.

Tucker, David. *Samuel Beckett and Arnold Geulincx: Tracing a "Literary Fantasia."* Continuum, 2012.

Tzara, Tristan. *Oeuvres complètes*. Edited by Henri Béhar. Flammarion, 1975.

Uhlmann, Anthony. *Beckett and Poststructuralism*. Cambridge UP, 1999.

———. "Introduction to Beckett's Notes to the *Ethics*." Geulincx, pp. 301–9.

———. *Samuel Beckett and the Philosophical Image*. Cambridge UP, 2006.

———. "Staging Plays." Uhlmann (editor), pp. 173–91.

———, editor. *Samuel Beckett in Context*, edited by Anthony Uhlmann, Cambridge UP, 2013.

Van Hulle, Dirk. "The Extended Mind and Multiple Drafts: Beckett's Models of the Mind and the Postcognitivist Paradigm." *Samuel Beckett Today/Aujourd'hui*, vol. 24, 2012, pp. 277–89.

Weber-Caflisch, Antoinette. *Chacun son dépeupleur: Sur Samuel Beckett*. Minuit, 1994.

Welchman, Alastair. "Machinic Thinking." *Deleuze and Philosophy: The Difference Engineer*, edited by Keith Ansell Pearson, Routledge, 1998, pp. 211–29.

Weller, Shane. *Beckett, Literature, and the Ethics of Alterity.* Palgrave Macmillan, 2006.

———. "Forms of Weakness: Animalization in Kafka and Beckett." Bryden (editor), pp. 4–26.

———. "Post-World War Two Paris." Uhlmann (editor), pp. 160–73.

Williamson, Peter J. *Varieties of Corporatism: A Conceptual Discussion.* Cambridge UP, 2010.

Wolfe, Charles. "Go Foget Me – Why Should Sorrow." *The Burial of Sir John Moore, and Other Poems*, Sidgwick & Jackson, 1909, pp. 5–6.

Worton, Michael. "*Waiting for Godot* and *Endgame*: Theatre as Text." *Samuel Beckett's* Waiting for Godot: *New Edition*, edited by Harold Bloom, Yale UP, 2008, pp. 71–92.

Index[1]

A

Absurd/absurdist/absurdism/
nonsense, 1–35, 41, 43, 52–54,
56, 105, 106, 220, 268
Action(s)/active, 7, 10, 14, 27,
30–32, 53, 59, 62, 64, 73, 78,
79, 81, 85, 103, 104, 106, 108,
111, 114, 115, 129, 130, 136,
141, 142, 147, 149, 151, 175,
176, 178, 181, 182, 184,
187–190, 192–195, 214, 230,
234, 237, 245, 251, 253, 257,
258, 264, 267, 269
Affect(s)/affective, 8, 17–22, 27–29,
33, 35, 43–45, 50, 52, 53, 55,
58, 60–62, 64, 71, 72, 74, 84,
90, 102, 104–108, 112, 113,
120, 124, 136, 141, 142, 150,
151, 157, 158, 163, 165, 170,
172, 176–178, 183, 206, 262,
264, 270

Anxiety, 25, 27, 41, 50, 51, 108, 141,
186, 187, 194, 199, 202, 221,
222, 227, 231, 233, 237, 257,
258, 269
Assemblage(s), 7, 18, 21, 42–45, 47,
51, 52, 54n5, 58, 62, 72, 74, 76,
77, 81, 90, 101, 116, 118, 121,
123, 125, 129, 132, 136,
138–141, 143, 145, 146, 148,
150, 151, 163, 176, 177, 191, 198

C

Cognitive/cognition, 2, 8, 17, 22, 23,
25–29, 31, 52, 178, 181–196,
198–209, 211–260
Comedy/comedic, 15, 22, 25, 30, 32,
42, 54n5, 69n11, 94, 95, 98, 100,
101, 103, 125–127, 138, 145, 147,
158, 170, 172, 196, 203–209, 222,
248, 256, 263, 266, 268, 269

---

[1] Note: Page numbers followed by 'n' refer to notes.

© The Author(s) 2020
C. Ionica, *The Affects, Cognition, and Politics of Samuel Beckett's Postwar
Drama and Fiction*, New Interpretations of Beckett in the Twenty-First
Century, https://doi.org/10.1007/978-3-030-34902-8